D1083027

THE PROFESSOR'S UMBRELLA

THE PROFESSOR'S

UMBRELLA

A NOVEL

MARY JANE WARD

 RANDOM HOUSE · NEW YORK

THE PROFESSOR'S UMBRELLA

1

"But it *is* a true story," said the girl. "It happened and I can prove it. You said to report something we witnessed during the summer and I did. I didn't invent a single thing, and look what he says." She leaned over to slap at the paper she had hurled on the desk.

Gregory didn't have to look at the paper to know which of his assistant's marginal notes had infuriated Miss Keane. Her gasp of dismay, when papers were returned after this morning's nine-o'clock, hadn't surprised him. "Come to my office this afternoon," he had said, to stop the protest which would have made him late for his next class. "I can give you a few minutes between appointments." He'd sounded like his dentist who, if you swore the tooth was murderous, sandwiched you between patients who had made appointments weeks in advance.

How he loathed having to parcel out his minutes as if they were droplets of rare vintage; but now that the university was bursting at the seams with students, a teacher's life was dominated by a schedule. "We have accepted this great challenge," said President Norton, "and we are proud to be able to announce that we are in complete control of what less optimistic persons may have considered a desperate or even a hopeless situation." By this the president meant that the tin huts and Quonsets had been erected in time for the opening of the fall quarter. "And to those of you who may have had doubts about Tamarack University being able to marshal a teaching staff equal to the severe demands of this inflated load, may I say that the teachers of America have risen nobly to this, Education's clearest call in all history." By this he meant that the old-time faculty members had been persuaded to forget that

3

their salaries had not kept pace with the rising cost of living, and had therefore enabled the university to add new teachers without seriously dislocating the budget. "And despite all of this I am happy to inform you that Tamarack insistently and sensibly refuses to relinquish its plan for the New Campus. However, my fellow-Americans, this doesn't mean that the great dream can become reality without your generous support. We welcome your young men and women. We shall never cease in our relentless determination . . ."

. . . to grab every student who comes our way, provided we can bed him, provided we can continue to make these noble teachers see that classrooms built for thirty students can be made to seat a hundred and thirty. These days if you had a class of thirty you felt as if you were giving private lessons. How many centuries ago was it that the fledgling Dr. Kitner stated he would always grade his own papers? "*I* certainly never intend to use readers," that young man had said. Well, even though he had long since been forced to give up grading without assistance, Gregory Kitner doggedly held to his resolution at least to glance through the themes corrected by his readers. When he had recorded the surprisingly low mark for Miss Keane, a girl who had been maintaining a very good average, he'd wondered if Jefferson's sadism would be cured by time. You could have endured the young man's infallibility if he hadn't persisted in rubbing your nose in it. "Me! You think I'd take a job at some cow college I never heard of?" Jeff had said when Gregory told him about the opening in the English department at Halter. "You must think I'm nuts. Don't you see I've got the drop on these birds who haven't even started on their doctorates? Maybe you think I don't know you've got to have a Ph.D. if you're going to get anywhere. Kit, you sure

4

have me figured wrong if you think I'd interrupt my graduate work for a small-time instructorship. . . ." Jefferson couldn't confine himself to no-thanks. He couldn't just underline the passage where Miss Keane had slipped into fiction; he had to make a snide comment and give her a low enough grade to remind her that she was, after all, only a sophomore.

The girl's tapping finger required Gregory to glance at his assistant's ornate handwriting: "Consult your catalogue for a description of B2." Leave it to Jeff to think of the snottiest way to put it. Gregory wished he could tell Miss Keane that her exasperation with Jefferson was mild in comparison to the emotion the assistant continually roused in him. Damn this obligation to keep a united front, even with the sub-faculty. "But didn't you bring a little fiction in at this point?" he asked. Oh, Jefferson knew his stuff, and unlike many readers who leaned on the curve as they skimmed, he was conscientious. "Here you say the old man never confided in anyone and yet in the same paragraph you tell us what went on in his mind."

She sat down in the chair at the side of his desk. "That's splitting hairs," she said, but her eyes revealed that she was beginning to understand why Jefferson advised her to study the catalogue. "Can't a reporter deduce what a person's thinking?"

"You don't say it's a deduction. I agree it's a matter of splitting hairs." He spoke gently because she was blushing now, with embarrassment rather than with anger. You could see she felt she had made a fool of herself. That was Jefferson's great crime against the students; he put them into indefensible positions and then goaded them into attempts to defend themselves. A good deal of Gregory's time went to combating his reader's determination to undermine the students' sense of

5

maturity. "However, isn't it splitting the hair that lies between fiction and nonfiction? We have to limit the course. Your instructor has a hard enough job trying to deal with one thing at a time."

"But it seems so artificial," said Miss Keane. She removed the modish glasses that made her look like a well-groomed raccoon. "I mean, it's obvious the old man's mind worked the way I said."

Gregory nodded. "Then why not put it that way? Or better, leave the deduction to the reader. That's the beauty of the story, Miss Keane. To have acted as he did, the man must have had the thoughts you attribute to him. By telling his actions you indicate his thoughts, don't you?" He looked at his watch. He was behind in his appointments and now it was past time for Pug Sanderson. Pug couldn't wait around forever; when he consented to the appointment he said, "Jeez, Doc, I'll try and work it in, but I gotta get out to the field. Hoffman don't like it when we're late for practice."

"I suppose it might be more subtle that way." Miss Keane chewed upon her glasses.

"I'm sure it would be. Rewrite the story and get it back to me by the end of the week. . . ."

She sighed. "Couldn't you just cross out his thoughts and give it a decent grade? I never got a D before in my whole life."

She was an attractive girl and a naturally endowed student, a delightful combination, so delightful that Gregory suspected she hadn't had to do much work in this whole life that weighed upon her. He enjoyed looking at pretty girls, but the enjoyment was avocational. She was mistaken if she thought he would rewrite her paper for her. Because I am a tough cookie, remember.

6

Several years ago he had overheard two students discussing a faculty member who, one of them insisted, was a tough cookie. At first Gregory marked the conversation only because he was fascinated by the use of the word cookie, but in a moment he'd listened with some avidity for, it transpired, he was the cookie whose toughness was under argument. "I imagine you'll want to make a few other changes, Miss Keane." Jefferson would have liked this. See, he would have said, you just waste a lot of time, palavering around. Jeff was always telling him how to teach school . . . and the devil of it is that the boy's not nearly the ape I'd like to think him. "Without the excursion into fiction the paper probably would have rated a B. I think you can do better."

"I should hope!" she said. "I certainly never got anything but A's in Freshman Comp. And I was editor of the paper in high school."

"It's likely that the farther you go in composition, the more rewriting you'll have to do. But when you reach the point of never being satisfied with your work, writing will no longer seem a chore." Yes, that's what we say to indicate it's time for you to clear out. It's about as meaningful as glad-to-have-met-you.

"But it doesn't seem like a chore now," she said. "I just adore writing. I've always known I'd be a writer, but I just don't have time right now. I'm one of the candidates for Woman of the Year, you know."

"No, I didn't."

"Why, Dr. Kitner! I bet you haven't voted yet." She whipped out a packet of what looked like raffle tickets. "We're letting the faculty in on it this year. You *will* vote for me, won't you?"

"I've never been able to understand these contests," he said

7

as he took the ballot. "Why select the Man and Woman of the Year before the year's more than a few weeks under way? How can anyone possibly tell now whether you'll turn out to be the Woman of the Year?"

She giggled and said he knew that had nothing to do with it. "It's just which side can get the most votes. My goodness, I'd think you'd know that."

She was laughing at him a little in the way that Jefferson laughed at him, but then Jeff wasn't pretty. After he had signed his name Gregory said he hoped she would win. "Gee, so do I," she said. "The winner gets lots of wonderful presents. Paris Modes is giving a fur coat. It's really only mouton, but it looks like beaver. And she gets her picture in the rotogravures and everything and maybe *Life*'s going to give her a picture-story. I might even get a screen test."

"But I thought you wanted to be a writer."

She picked up the theme and folded it so that Jefferson's insulting mark wouldn't show. "Oh, I do. But of course if I got a chance to go in the movies . . . It will be such a relief when it's over. I just haven't got a minute." Then, apparently deciding she had his sympathy, she asked if next week wouldn't be soon enough for the revised paper.

No, Jefferson was nobody's fool. "I'm sorry, but if I let you have extra time, I'd have to give it to everyone else, wouldn't I? Soon we'd be doing the first-quarter work in second quarter." He rose to steer her from the office. She went rather quickly, pausing only long enough to put on her glasses.

Another student was outside, but it wasn't the gridiron star. "Hi," said Miss Keane coldly to the waiting girl. "Hi," said Miss Spencer with equal frigidity.

Gregory, scanning the hall for Pug, thought what a shame

8

it was the girls were limited to so small a word to express a scorn which undoubtedly resulted from conflicting political ideologies on Man and Woman of the Year. "Have you seen Pug Sanderson?" he asked Miss Spencer.

"Yes," she said, "but he gave me his appointment. I just had to see you this afternoon and he said he really didn't have the time anyhow."

This was the girl who had been pestering Gregory since the beginning of the quarter. She always hung around after class, and somehow she had managed to wangle a second office consultation before he had made first appointments with more than a fifth of his students. And now here she was for a third session even though she hadn't displayed a flicker of interest in the course. Unlike Pug, who only wanted to repeat that his remaining eligible for the team was essential to the welfare of the university, Miss Spencer said nothing about desiring a passing grade. She took no notes in class, turned in carelessly written papers and after forcing Gregory's attention appeared not to listen to what he said. When he told the Dawsons about the strange girl, Mary said it sounded like love. The gazelle leaps of Mary Dawson's mind could be most amusing. "I wish you'd see the poor child," he'd said, and then Mary had asked if he thought interest in the opposite sex couldn't penetrate homely heads. "You're a gentle soul, Kit," she'd said. "I know you want to think that the only girls who dream on love are those who stand a chance. And then too, darling, even though you always resist, it's more interesting when they're cute. . . ."

That's what Mary calls good-natured kidding, he thought now as he tried to dismiss the revolting idea she had planted in his mind. "I have your last paper here," he said, drawing Miss Spencer's theme from the stack he had graded last night. "You

9

might as well take it now and have more time for the rewrite. There are fourteen misspellings and in several cases you've given me two or three versions of what I assume you mean to be the same word." If I sound like Jefferson, it's the girl's fault. Doesn't she have a home to go to? Friends to talk to? Why doesn't she go out and campaign for whatever candidate her club is pushing for Woman of the Year? Good God, if she's got more time than she can use, she could take up archery or hockey or baby-sitting.

She had removed the fringed rag that had been knotted under her chin and now she was stroking her hair as if she found pleasure in touching it. This fall quite a few of the girls were wearing their long bobs uncurled. The coiffure wasn't so appalling as the expression that accompanied it, a look Mary called chartreuse sophistication. "Misspellings?" said Miss Spencer, looking very chartreuse and sophisticated. "Oh, that's my typist." She took a pack of cigarettes from her satiny black raincoat. "I'm stuck with the most impossible sorority daughter this year. It's too hysterical. I don't follow these things, but I suppose she's somebody's relative."

If Gregory hadn't been tired he would have told himself Miss Spencer was eating her heart out because she hadn't been nominated for Woman of the Year. Tom Dawson was always saying Kitner excused any action, however deplorable, if the person responsible for that action were still an undergraduate. "Kit, won't you ever learn that you've got to wield that hickory stick?" Tom would ask.

There was something about Miss Spencer that made Gregory wish to flourish the stick to the extent of telling her to go haunt someone else. Maybe I'm getting a cold. I wonder if there's anything in these new shots Mary was talking about

. . . wouldn't hurt to try them, I suppose. "But, Miss Spencer," he said, "you could go over your papers and make corrections before turning them in."

She settled back in the visitor's chair as if she meant to stay there the rest of the afternoon. "I'm really quite bored with B2."

"Yes, I know you are. How would you like to transfer to Dr. Letting's section that meets at the same hour? I'm sure I could arrange it." This was a dirty trick to play on Ted Letting, but Ted had contrived to unload a few undesirables on the Kitner B2. "Although Dr. Letting and I cover the same general subject, it's possible you would find his approach more . . ."

"How could you say that?" She was looking at him in horror. "I know you don't really mean it. You can't. It just isn't possible that you don't know . . . not after all these weeks."

Damn Mary and her intuition. It was too bad Tom hadn't drawn this girl. "It happens to me all the time," Tom had said. "It just wants experience, Kit. You'll get onto it in time." Inasmuch as Gregory and Tom had been teaching the same number of years the assumption was that Dawson had had far more teacher-smitten students than Kitner had had, an assumption Gregory was happy to sponsor but one Mary Dawson wasn't kind enough to let pass. "Tom," she had said, "some day you're going to wake up and see that Kit's the perennial passion of the campus. I'm sure they *like* you, darling, but they *love* Kit. I've been hearing it for years."

Thinking about how Mary continually baited Tom, Gregory reminded himself that he must, once and for all, do something about moving from the Dawson house. This time he wouldn't repeat his former mistake; this time he would line up another place before saying anything to them. Several years ago, for their sake as well as his own, he had announced that he was going to look for another apartment. Tom had raged and Mary had wept. "See here, Kit," Tom had said, "when we bought this house it was with the understanding that . . ."

Gregory Kitner, it seemed, had inveigled the Dawsons into buying the house. Sometimes he wondered if his memory could be trusted. "We wouldn't have dreamed of taking such a large house," Mary told people who expressed surprise at the plunge, "but Kit talked us into it. The first time he saw it he said it had enormous possibilities."

I said it was enormous and when Mary asked if I didn't think it had possibilities I said yes. . . . Gregory hadn't even said that until after the contract was signed. He gave the Dawsons his promise and the deal was made before he knew which of the old houses on Clayton Place was the mansion of Mary's dreams, next, of course, to the Presidential Manse which always held first place. "All my life I've wanted that house," she said when she told Gregory that she and Tom had been out with a real-estate man the day before. "There was a Clayton girl who used to invite me to parties. I used to pretend I lived there."

"I think you'd better just keep on pretending," said Tom. "It's so big and so damned expensive. I believe the fellow when he says it's not out of line with other places in that neighborhood, but it's prohibitive for us. We'd have to fill it with roomers."

"I hate the way so many of Tower City's old show places are being turned into rooming houses," said Mary. "Especially those near the campus. It makes it look as if the whole school's going to seed. But I've been thinking if we had four students . . . We'd have to have at least four since they've made that ruling

12

about not charging them more than five dollars a week. I think it's mean of them because that way you just get the non-fraternity riffraff." This was before Tom's belated induction, which unfortunately had to be honorary, into a fraternity; but sometimes Mary forgot her husband's barbarian state. And why wouldn't she? Tom was the only nonfraternity man she had ever known. My goodness, when Mary Carr was in school if you'd told her she would end up married to a nonfraternity man. . . Of course Tom was different. He hadn't had the time or the money. And he'd made up for it later on when Sigma Gamma, on the brink of losing its Tamarack chapter, had shrewdly bestowed the clover pin on three faculty members who certainly wouldn't have joined if they had believed that ugly rumor about the Sigs having girls in the house overnight.

Mary looked around the crowded living room of the little apartment the Dawsons had when Gregory first knew them. She told him how different the Clayton Place house was from this apartment. "It has the most glorious drawing room, Kit. Parquet floors. I can't entertain in this two-by-four."

"Nonsense," he said. "You're my favorite hostess."

"Thank you, darling, but I mean on a big scale. Department heads and all. You can't ask the Peebles and big shots like that to come here."

When Gregory said he failed to see why not, Tom sided with Mary. "She's got something, Kit. When you start to branch out professionally, you've got to branch out socially. Maybe it goes the other way around. Anyhow you've got to have space."

That was when Mary asked Gregory how much his living expenses came to each month. "Rent and food, well, not lunch, but laundry. Yes, laundry because I'll have to have help and she can do the washing and that will save a little. Of course it won't

13

be clear profit, but it doesn't cost much more to feed three people, not a third more, on account of lowering the per capita. And since you'd be permanent I should think you'd buy your own furniture. You'd rather, wouldn't you? I know I would. I mean, have my own things. You'd have to promise to stay at least five years, unless you got married or something, because it will take that long to get the mortgage down to a safe amount."

"Wow!" said Tom. "If my figuring's the same as yours I don't call it a safe amount."

"You'll be making more," said Mary. "You always forget that you'll make more as time goes on. I'm sure five years would be safe. You aren't thinking of getting married, are you, Kit?"

"Well, not at the moment."

"Of course we'd want you to feel free to, if you really wanted to. But you aren't the marrying kind, darling, and so I wouldn't be afraid to take a chance. You *will* promise to stay five years, won't you? Except for getting married or some other act-of-God. It wouldn't be fair to get us involved and then walk out. You see that, don't you?"

We had fun that day. We got a little drunk, not so much on highballs as on the prospect of setting up a sort of perpetual open house in a fine mansion near the campus. A grand house where we could entertain big shots like the Peebles and so on. And with parquet floors. I remember I proposed a toast to those parquet floors.

That was how Gregory persuaded the Dawsons to buy the Clayton Place house. "None of us expected the arrangement to last more than five years," he said when he suggested it was time for him to move. "Don't think I haven't appreciated being with you. It's been swell. But you don't need me any more."

"As if it was ever a matter of finances," said Mary. "Kit, any

14

number of people would have jumped at the chance to come in with us, but you were the only one we wanted." Her eyes swam with reproach. "How can you talk about it as if it were nothing more than dollars and cents?"

"It isn't that at all."

"Then what is it? The girls don't bother you now that you're on the third floor, do they? If they do, it's your own fault. If you didn't always take their part they'd never dare go up there and you know it. I thought you liked your little retreat. You spent so much money on it. What's the matter, Kit? Aren't the meals good enough any more?"

"Mary, if he wants to be financial about it, let him," said Tom. "I don't think we ought to let friendship keep us from a frank discussion of finances. If he thinks he can buy more for his money elsewhere . . . Kit, I don't know what you're paying Mary these days, but I'll bet you a dollar to a doughnut you couldn't begin to match it. I don't want to pull a sob act, but if you don't know it would be tough sledding for Mary if you pulled out now, well, I think you should be told, that's all. Sure, we have more coming in, but we've got a hell of a lot going out. Our responsibilities are terrific."

"I just couldn't have strangers taking over the third floor," said Mary.

"Perhaps your mother . . ."

"My God, Kit, what did I ever do to you?" said Tom.

"You don't need to worry, Tom. Mother wouldn't dream of leaving the River Arms. . . . Kit, darling, you aren't a roomer, you're one of the family."

Even though he was giving most of his thought to wishing he weren't quite so much a member of the Dawson family,

15

Gregory was delivering a brisk lecture to Miss Spencer. If Mary's diagnosis were correct, the prescription should be effective. I'll talk the girl down, wear her out, ignore everything she says that doesn't pertain to B2. Presently Miss Spencer would be convinced that her boredom with the course wasn't a patch on her boredom with its mentor. He found himself starting to yawn, and to ease his straining muscles he looked down at the theme. By George! Last night I was so preoccupied with the spelling that I missed the point. "You're lucky I got this paper," he said. "I'm sure Mr. Jefferson would have given you an F, and properly so." Jeff's eyes wouldn't have been blinded by the sloppy presentation. Rather clever of the girl to make so messy a job of it, though. "This wasn't a bad story the first time we got it, but it hasn't stood the test of years. Why doesn't your sorority bring its files up to date?"

Miss Spencer waved her cigarette. "I am completely uninterested in the activities of my sorority. I've quite outgrown all that adolescent . . ."

"You've not outgrown copying papers in the house cache." Lord, I shouldn't have said that. Now she'll be weeping all over me.

But Miss Spencer smiled. "It was clever of you to spot it," she said, as if he had seen through a complicated card trick. "I changed it around quite a lot, but you are clever. I knew I couldn't keep it from you. Even in class I can feel your knowing. At first I didn't want you to. I don't know why, really. People shouldn't, should they? I mean that sort of thing leads to psychoses and all. I suppose I felt the way you did, or maybe you still do, but what's age after all but an illusion? It's what we are, Kit, not what some silly accident of birth did to us. I've always been old for my age anyway. I mean even before I

16

knew you I was utterly bored with all this petty little college act that one has to go through."

He was jerked back more than twenty years to another girl who had been utterly bored with all the petty little college act. Laura wanted me to help her shake off the fetters by going to some bohemia to practice free love. He would never forget his humorless panic when Laura said, "I don't care where we go, just so it isn't Chicago. I've got relatives there." Miss Spencer reminded him of Laura Grier, the Laura of State-University days, not the one who dazzled him in New York a few years ago. He was tempted to tell Miss Spencer that he'd once known a girl very like her, a girl who, believe it or not, had turned out quite well. "Why don't you try another of the schools?" he asked. "How about the School of Drama?"

There was an ashtray near her, but she had been flicking ashes on the floor. Now she dropped her cigarette and stamped on it with a dilapidated moccasin. "It's no use," she said. "We can't go on this way. One pretends just so long."

The Drama suggestion was inspired. She would be an A student in that flunkers' paradise. "You think about the School of Drama," he said. "Now I've several other appointments for this afternoon. . . ." He moved the appointment pad so that she couldn't see there was only one name after Pug's. "Get a new paper to me by the end of the week and I won't penalize you for this thing. Evidently I didn't make the requirement about original material strong enough. You won't be nearly so bored with the course if you do your own work, Miss Spencer. And I would do my own typing, if I were stuck with such an inferior secretary."

She pushed at her hair. "It's no go, Kit. You can't talk it out of existence. I'm in love with you. What are you going to do about it?"

Until rather recently Tamarack University had had so many more women than men students that its male faculty members naturally had come in for a good deal of attention from the girls. I can remember girls who intimated that they were fond of me, but none who ever had the gall . . . He sprang from his chair. "I must ask you to leave," he said. "I have to finish my appointments." It's the movies. More and more we become an imitation of education as interpreted by Goldwyn.

"I know the difference in our ages worries you. I know you think . . ."

"I'm not thinking about it at all. You won't be, either, the moment you're out of here. Now run along."

"You can't brush me off as if I were a child."

"Miss Spencer, you're fed up with the way I teach B2 and I'm fed up with the way you're trying to amuse yourself. I'd say we're quits." This was how Jefferson would have spoken to her. It isn't right to treat the wretched creature this way, Gregory told himself. She looks as if she might be running a fever, but what can I do about it? He went to the door and opened it. "Sorry to have kept you waiting, Robbins," he called to the sleepy-looking boy who was sitting on the top step of the stairs near the office.

"That's okay, Doc," said the boy. "Don't rush on my account."

"Come in. Miss Spencer is leaving."

Miss Spencer picked up her babushka and theme. "Yes," she said. "Yes, Miss Spencer is leaving. The matter she has to discuss with Dr. Kitner can't be settled in one afternoon anyway. It's more of a lifetime project."

There was a small but effective sound. In an effort to eradi-

18

cate the last trace of the old idea that Tamarack was virtually a girls' school, the modern Tama he-man had mastered the voluntary belch. Robbins slapped his face. "Why, Mr. Robbins," he said. "Miss Spencer will think you're crude. Maybe she won't even vote for you for Man of the Year."

"Don't tell me you're a candidate," said Gregory. "I'm beginning to think this office is a theatrical agency."

Robbins slumped into the side chair. "I'm running on the independent ticket," he said. "Unless Miss Spencer's machine would like to back me."

"Really!" said Miss Spencer. In spite of her dragging slippers she gave the illusion of flouncing out of the office.

"I think I'll vote for you, Robbins," said Gregory as he fished through his papers. "You'd be good in a remake of *The Dead End Kids*." He was feeling better. No need to monkey with cold shots. I might double my vitamin pills for a couple of days. . . ."I don't seem to find your paper. You are in Section 18, aren't you?"

"Sure," said Robbins, "but I didn't hand in a paper last week, if that's what you're looking for."

"See here, you can't hope to . . ."

"Well, Doc, that was what I wanted to see you about. Last week was sort of complicated. The Little Woman's having a baby took more of my time than I'd figured."

"My God, Robbins, how old are you?"

"Twenty-three, sir. It's a crazy world, isn't it, Doc? My wife's got her master's and here I'm just a sophomore."

"You're the last on the list for today," said Gregory. "Let's get out of here, that is, if you'll forget that crack about Dead End Kids."

"Jesus, Doc, the way I'm feeling now it's a compliment. The way I feel now I bet a small beer would just about throw me. But I'm willing to try, if you were thinking along those lines. . . ."

2   The Dawsons' back sitting room, inappropriately called the study, was far more comfortable than the drawing room. Mary's auction chasing had brought artistic groupings of furniture to the front room, but the brocaded chairs and sofas discouraged relaxation. Except in the heat of summer there was something about the great expanse of shining floor that reminded one of a skating rink. "But I thought you liked that parquet," said Tom when Mary made wistful remarks about more rugs or perhaps wall-to-wall carpeting. "I wasn't the one," Mary would protest. "It was Kit."

When Mary announced that they would take coffee in the drawing room, her mother, who had dined in Clayton Place tonight, asked the twins if they would throw one of Mummy's sweaters down to Grannie when they went upstairs. "Oh, all right," said Mary. "I suppose it's hopeless to get any of you to believe that the temperature in the drawing room is exactly the same."

"Such a cozy room," said Mrs. Carr when they were settled in the study. "I never sit here but what I remember how your father talked up to Lionel Bersbach. Mr. Bersbach was the most powerful of the trustees in those days." This last was for Tom and Gregory who hadn't been in Tower City in those days.

"Mother, you've told them that story a hundred times."

"I'm sure I never told them all of it," said Mrs. Carr. "I doubt if you know the whole story yourself."

"Do tell it," said Gregory.

"Pray do," said Tom. If he and his mother-in-law had never exchanged an uncivil word, they also could be said never to have exchanged an entirely civil one.

21

"Some persons might not appreciate the kind of courage my husband had," said Mrs. Carr.

"Darling, it's confusing when you change your stories around," said Mary. "I thought you always said it was a crazy thing to do."

"Of course it was. Crazy and courageous. Not an impossible combination, I believe."

Perhaps Gregory hadn't heard the story hundreds of times, just dozens. Mrs. Carr could make a rather long tale of it, but it boiled down to Professor Carr's informing Lionel Bersbach that the possession of millions of dollars did not necessarily equip a man for membership on a board of trustees of a university. Mary tells stories over and over—we all do. Why does she act so martyred when her mother starts on an old favorite? Maybe it wasn't boredom that made Mary resent the retelling of this particular story. Perhaps she saw, as Gregory saw, that Mrs. Carr's anecdotes about her husband illuminated more than the doubtful possibility that the old lady was getting into her dotage. In her brittle way Nettie Carr may have been trying to do more than preserve the memory of Wilfred Carr, she may have been trying to kindle interest in what had motivated Carr's crazy courage. Her father, Mary said, was a horrid example of what can happen to a man who doesn't look out for himself. "A world-known scholar," she would say, "and what did it get him? A stinking associate-professorship. Mother talks big now, but I wonder if she ever stops to think where she'd be if she hadn't inherited that money from her aunt." Whenever his wife said this, Tom would say he sure stopped to think about it. "I never saw Aunt Nancy," he'd say, "but she's my dream girl." Professor Carr's insurance had gone to educate his only child and so if it hadn't been for that aunt, Mrs. Carr

22

undoubtedly would now be living under Tom's roof. It was a wonder Tom hadn't insisted on naming both of his daughters Nancy.

". . . and to his face, big as you please," Mrs. Carr was saying now. She paused to sip at her coffee.

Save for the space given to the narrow windows and the small blue-green glazed fireplace with the portrait above it, the study walls were solid with books collected by the man who, big as you please, muffed his opportunity to become chairman of Classical Languages. Lester Gibbs, the artist, had said the Wilfred Carr portrait, a gift of the class of '12, was a perfect example of American barbarism; but Gregory had always liked the picture. Maybe just because when I look at it I think about the stories Nettie tells.

"You can't buy and sell education the way you buy and sell grain, Wilfred said to Bersbach. This was just after that terrible grain scandal that Bersbach was mixed up in. They say he'd have gone to prison sure as you're born if the governor hadn't been on his payroll. Why, for years most people hesitated to mention bread in Bersbach's presence. Of course he tried to make Billy Hathaway fire Wilfred, but Billy was about as bad as my husband. And was Wilfred ashamed of himself? Dear no, he wrote a poem about it and had it published in the *Classical Arts Quarterly*."

"Yes, Mother, we know. About the hog that tried to climb Olympus to cure his stomach-ache."

"Not a very accurate translation, my dear. The swine, having become quite ill on spoiled grain, commanded his slaves to carry him up the mountain because he'd heard that the clouds up there would cure all ailments. But although his slaves found plenty of health-giving clouds, wherever the swine went

23

there was nothing but vacuum. . . . If it hadn't been in Latin I'm sure Bersbach would have taken steps. I used to tell Wilfred it was a pity he didn't confine his speech to the language in which he apparently did all of his thinking."

"I wish he'd been in English," said Mary. At this point in the story about Daddy and Bersbach, Mary always said she wished her father had been in the English department. "All those damn books . . ."

"You don't find paper and bindings of that quality these days, my dear," said Mrs. Carr. "Take that set of your father's work . . ."

"She did," said Tom. "She took the whole damn outfit."

The library Mary had inherited consisted of books written in Latin or in Greek or, in the case of a few, in English rigidly dedicated to Latin and Greek literature. The ensemble made a respectable and even impressive wall covering for a room that was poorly lighted.

Tom's books were in the front room where visitors could see titles. His library wasn't large, but it included the heaviest of the cream of English literature up to the turn of the present century—Tom didn't go beyond 1900 professionally. If Mary caught a measuring look in a guest's eye she said something about how she had tried to persuade her husband to keep his entire library at home; presumably Dr. Dawson had a whale of a collection elsewhere, perhaps on tour.

"Mother and I were talking about that bare look," said Mary now. "Kit, if you'd bring your books down we could have shelves all the way around the drawing room and solve the problem."

"The room cries for large French paintings," said Mrs. Carr.

"But, Mother, books fit in with our kind of people."

24

"I am prepared only to argue that the drawing room would be more attractive if you had large paintings instead of those shabby little prints."

"Well, thanks for the compliment, Mother Carr," said Tom. "But I don't happen to have the kind of money one needs for large French paintings."

"Reproductions, Tom dear, and not of a very popular period."

"I'd rather have books," said Mary.

"And look like a public library." Tom reached for the sugar bowl. "I don't know why you're so infernally stingy with the sugar, Mary. I've told you I prefer not to have coffee if I can't have it the way I like it."

"I'm thinking of your figure, not the sugar. Darling, you forget how small these cups are."

"When people who live just a step from one of the finest libraries in the world," said Tom, quite as if it were a step he took regularly, "I consider that it looks very strange to spend a lot of money on books. Very strange. It would almost seem to smack of putting on a false front."

"Exactly my point, Tom dear," said Mrs. Carr.

"Oh, Mother, I meant to tell you, and the boys too," said Mary. "Speaking of false fronts. When I was in Paris Modes this afternoon I saw a suit exactly like the one Harriet Hough's been sporting and you'll never guess how much it cost. I priced it, just for fun."

"Not having seen the suit Miss Hough has been sporting, I couldn't possibly guess," said Mrs. Carr.

Mary set her cup down to free her hands for the surprise. "One of those dreadful plaids that a younger woman might get away with, but Harriet . . . Poor Harriet. One hundred and ten dollars!"

"Harriet hasn't got that kind of money," said Tom. "An instructor."

"Time has changed you, Tom," said Mrs. Carr. "I distinctly recall how you used to complain that the higher-ups acted as if instructors were mother's helpers."

"I was thinking only of Harriet's financial status," said Tom. "I don't question her academic ability, though of course one can't help deploring the situation that has forced us to put high-school teachers on the faculty. Not that I've any of this snobbery you find in some university people, but after all if you take all the teachers out of the high school and put them into the colleges and universities . . ."

"And take the grammar-school teachers for the high schools and the nursery-school teachers for the kindergartens when the kindergarten teachers move up into the grade schools," said Mrs. Carr. "Perhaps I can get a job in a nursery school?"

Mary's eyebrows were struggling to recapture the space from which they had been plucked. She frowns so much, thought Gregory. Maybe she should wear her glasses all the time. He realized that the donning of full-time glasses would be difficult for a woman who in her senior year was Queen of the May. And that, she often told them, was in the days when May Queen election wasn't simply a matter of campus politics. Today, with a strong political faction behind her, the homeliest girl in the world could win that crown of wilted spring flowers. Could, and usually did, said Mary, when she reminded them that it had been quite different in her day. Mary had been beautiful, or almost; at any rate as long as Gregory had known her she had had an expression of nervous concentration that

26

he didn't associate with complete beauty. "When you were talking about French paintings," he said, "I got to thinking about Lester. I wonder if we'll hear from him this Christmas."

"We didn't last year," said Mary. "I've taken him from our list. Really, if he can forget us that easily, not even a Christmas card, after all the meals he's had at our house . . ."

"I always told you he was a chiseler," said Tom.

"That charming young painter Gibbs?" said Mrs. Carr. "I'd forgotten about him. Where is he?"

"Starving in a loft in New York, the last we knew," said Tom. "Kit called on him last year."

"He seemed very happy," said Gregory.

"Kit, I must ask you to show me that painting he gave you. It's been so long since I saw it." Mrs. Carr looked at her watch. "There isn't time now, I'm afraid. Such an interesting painting, as I recall."

"Interesting for a psychologist," said Tom. "There was never any doubt in my mind about Gibbs being psychopathic."

"I never could understand why he gave it to Kit instead of to Tom and me," said Mary. "Not that I expected him to pay us back for all that food."

"I wouldn't give the thing house room," said Tom. "Thank God it's in the attic where I don't have to see it very often."

"Tom, I wish you wouldn't keep on referring to Kit's apartment as the attic," said Mary. "Oh, must you go, Mother?"

"Don't get up. I just want to be ready when Mrs. Woodburn stops by for me."

"Bridge as usual, I suppose," said Tom.

"I'm afraid not as usual. Mrs. Woodburn's cousin from Cleveland is here again. I can tolerate a poor player when it's plain she doesn't have any real interest in the game, but Mrs.

27

Woodburn's cousin has such zeal. The way she snaps her cards . . . Poor Mrs. Woodburn . . ."

"Thanks a lot for taking the girls off my hands this afternoon," said Mary. "I hate to pay a sitter when I'm just going shopping and the prices they're asking now, even if you can manage to get hold of someone . . ."

"*Merci, mon cher*," said Mrs. Carr when Gregory helped her into her coat. She moved toward the front door so that Tom and Mary couldn't see them from the study. "I was hoping I'd get a chance to have a word with you. It's getting worse at the hotel. Those of us who have been standing up for them are either going to have to shut up or get out. It's a wretched situation, Kit. If they weren't such disagreeable people . . . I know one shouldn't be idealistic only when it's comfortable, but . . ."

"Nettie, you hang onto your room for dear life."

"You really think I should?"

"Every drop of my French blood cries out against anyone you find disagreeable." Gregory's French origin was an old joke between him and Mrs. Carr. When Mary said she couldn't understand her mother's insistence upon calling him a Frenchman, Gregory reminded her that there had been French among his ancestors. "Mary dear," Mrs. Carr would say, "you forget that I've traveled far more extensively than you have. I know my France and I know a Frenchman when I see him." And then she and Gregory would laugh and laugh.

"I'm glad you're here with my children," she said now after she had renewed her lipstick. "They need you, Kit. It does my heart good to know there's some stabilizing influence . . . but there's Mrs. Woodburn tooting."

28

"I hope you have a hundred honors in every hand and fifth in partner's."

Mrs. Carr shuddered. "You're as bad as the woman from Cleveland. . . . *Bonne nuit, mon petit.*"

When he went back to the study Mary asked him what they had been whispering about in the hall. "It's been going on for years," he said. "How about some more coffee?"

"You drink entirely too much."

"Of your coffee? That would be impossible."

"Oh, you and my mother . . . Kit, do you think she's looking well?"

"Old battle-ax," said Tom. "She'll live to be a hundred."

"I wish you wouldn't be so rude to her, Tom. You go out of your way to . . ."

"Oh God," said Tom, "can't a man have a little peace in his own home?"

For a while the only sound in the study was the ticking of the clock. Then Mary, whose silent sulks were always brief, said of course Harriet Hough had got her parents' insurance money. "But I'll bet her brother and sisters are plenty burned up if they know how she's slinging it around. Of course she should have got it since she was the one who supported them and all, but even so . . . A suit like that's just the start. You get an expensive suit and then you have to have expensive things to go with it. I should think she'd rather have some decent furniture in that dinky apartment, but of course if she wants to put it all on her back it's none of my affair. I feel sorry for her, though. It's a shame a woman can't get anywhere." This was said with the complacency of a woman who is often asked to pour. "She can't hope for tenure."

"Lane got it," said Tom.

"It's not fair to count Lane. She's at least six feet tall." As a rule Mary gave her men time to savor her frivolous remarks, but now she rushed from Professor Lane. Tenure was a word tactful persons avoided in conversation with a teacher who in spite of long service was still on short-term contracts.

I've been around long enough to know that Tamarack's brand of tenure is a will-o'-the-wisp incapable of providing you with much warmth when you've finally imprisoned it on your own hearth, Gregory thought now while Mary hurried back to the subject of Harriet Hough's extravagance. No matter how often he reminded himself that a permanent contract didn't greatly limit the administration's power, his hope eventually to receive tenure was undiminished. He supposed he desired it as a sort of merit badge rather than as a guarantee of security. Certainly Professor Wilson's dismissal should have disabused the faculty of any illusions in regard to the sanctity of tenure. To be sure Wilson had got his guaranteed hearing; the Faculty Association, honoring its obligation to study the problems of any tenure holder, had handed down the opinion that Wilson hadn't taken undue advantage of academic freedom. There'd been no way to force the administration to accept the F.A. recommendation that Wilson be reinstated, but with that recommendation in back of him he'd been able to get a good job at another school. So the desirability of tenure, even of a form lacking enforcement teeth, wasn't negligible. . . . But what was Mary saying? That freedom had gone to Harriet's head?

". . . . if I were in her shoes I'd be careful. Her folks had her to fall back on, but who's going to take care of *her* in her old age?"

"Well, I doubt if Harriet will stay in teaching long enough to worry much about tenure," said Gregory. Unaccountably he had a vision of Harriet surrounded by children who strongly resembled Frank Teetor. From one standpoint the vision wasn't farfetched. Harriet and Teetor seemed to be inseparable these days. Give Teetor time to get a permanent contract and I suppose he and Harriet will get married, at any rate I trust she'll have sense enough to wait until he's established himself. Can't count on him for any sense. . . .

Mary shook her head. "I'm afraid poor Harriet will never marry. She's a grand person and I'm devoted to her, but she's not the type that appeals to men. No, I'm terribly afraid she should be planning ahead."

It would be nice to believe that Harriet wouldn't appeal to Frank Teetor, thought Gregory. Carefully he avoided asking himself just what he had against Teetor. The new man had his classes and office in Burnaby Annex and Gregory saw him infrequently. Harriet, though, with her office and classes in the annex . . . Gregory didn't consider it any of his business, but he did hate to see Harriet frittering her time away on a fellow who was such an unknown quantity.

". . . . and it's obvious that if she'd been going to marry she would have, long ago."

"The girl's still young," said Tom. "Give her time."

"Young! I know she's a bit younger than I, but you've got to admit that's rather old for an unmarried woman." Mary's conception of time was flexible. A woman ten years her senior was, in her opinion, old enough to be her mother; a woman ten years her junior was virtually a contemporary—perhaps a *bit* younger.

"Harriet was the sole support of two ailing . . ."

"Kit, you bring tears to my eyes. Women get married if they have a chance, ailing parents notwithstanding. Women aren't like men, darling. A woman never chooses not to marry." Mary gave him a look he'd got used to long ago. He didn't know if that look meant she thought she was his reason for not choosing to marry or if it meant she hoped that some day he'd tell her all his little secrets, but he had got used to that look. "I imagine she was quite attractive when she was young," Mary continued, "but the poor thing just doesn't know how to go about getting a man."

"How should a girl go about it? Slink into his office and declare herself?"

"Why, Gregory Kitner, you don't mean Harriet . . ."

"For God's sake! If there were anything of that sort between Harriet and me it would have to come from this direction."

Tom's eyebrows lifted. "Is this in the nature of a confession, old boy?"

Gregory struck another match and sucked at his pipe. "How old does a bachelor have to be before he can open his mouth without having a couple of wise guys jump into it?" He flipped the match into the fireplace. "I was just going to tell you, Mary, that you were right about that pesky student. Of course now I suppose you'll start trying to make something of it."

"What student?" asked Tom. "If I mentioned a pesky student it could be one of a thousand and twenty-nine."

"Why, darling, you mean you have some that aren't? But you remember the girl Kit was telling us about. . . . What a bore for you, Kit. Did you have trouble with her?"

Why had he started this? Gregory asked himself. Am I afraid of the girl? Am I trying to establish an alibi? Ever since Meade was kicked out we've been afraid to look at a woman student. "It's probably a sorority gag."

32

"Probably," said Tom. "They make them do the damnedest things. Last year one of my girls . . ."

"It's too early in the year," said Mary. "What's her name?"

"Spencer. Ruth, I think."

Mary's coffee cup clattered down on its saucer. "Dear God, not the Tower City Spencers! She would. That girl would."

"Ruth Spencer's a common name."

"Tallish scrawny girl with bad teeth?"

"I'm sure I didn't notice her teeth."

"She wore braces for years but they're still ghastly. Long, very hair-colored hair, Kit, and lipstick all over her face."

"You describe dozens."

"This is awful! Tom, you remember the trouble Marge Spencer made at the Woman's Club. If she gets the idea her Ruthie isn't having things exactly the way she wants them, all hell's going to break loose. I know for a fact that she caused a teacher at Ruth's boarding school to be fired. Absolutely. And just because Ruth had been expelled."

"Kit doesn't have to expel the girl, does he? It's probably just a gag, anyway." Tom looked at the clock on the mantel. "Good Lord, according to the Slightly Cuckoo Association, I've got to dash." He sighed as if the thought of pulling himself from the deep leather chair were unbearable, but Gregory had noticed that Tom couldn't endure the prospect of an entire evening in that chair. "But you better go easy, Kit, just in case the girl's the one Mary thinks. The Spencers are influential people. Money, you know . . ."

Often Mary and Gregory laughed after Tom had accomplished one of his dignified dashes, but Gregory sometimes wondered if they laughed in affection or in dismay. Tonight

33

when Professor Dawson used his habitual nickname for the Society of Classical Arts, the organization which had given Wilfred Carr the Greek-temple clock, neither Mary nor Gregory smiled; but Tom didn't bother to comment. Periodically he disposed of his friend and wife by telling them they had no sense of humor and that, for this, they had his great pity. Tonight when he finally got into his wraps he paused at the study door to say good-by. Touching his chin he cleared his throat slightly and said God only knew how late the affairs of the university would detain him this night.

When he was an instructor, Tom Dawson used to do a fairly recognizable take-off of President Norton, but now that he was no longer playing the role for laughs he gave a remarkable performance. He had Norton down pat. That gesture toward the chin created a diplomat's beard, that mannered clearing of the throat prepared you for a voice which had been schooled to sound far deeper than it actually was. A trick of phrasing, a trick of breathing, and the light voice became Norton's.

Mary poured herself another cup of coffee, but then shoved it away. "Kit," she said, "am I beginning to look like Myrtle? Sometimes when I look in the mirror I wonder if it's Myrtle Norton or me."

"Mrs. Norton's not a bad-looking woman. Older, of course. Nearly your mother's age, I imagine."

"You know what I mean. . . . Why does he have to act like Norton all the time? Does he think you have to look and act that way in order to be an administrator? It's a wonder he doesn't grow a beard. I suppose he would if he weren't afraid it would turn out red, the way his mustache did. Kit, do you remember the way he used to take Norton off? To be funny, I mean."

"Yes."

"I laughed like crazy. If I'd known I was going to have to live with it . . . Why pick Norton if you aren't going to be yourself?"

"Norton has been a very successful administrator."

"He's nothing but a stuffed shirt and you know it. Tom's getting that way and you know that, too. You've got ears and eyes."

"I know it's pretty certain that Tom will be our next president, if that's what you mean. I don't know what you're kicking about. It was what you wanted."

"Not this way. I wanted him to have ambition. God knows I didn't want him to be like Daddy and waste his life away in complete obscurity, but he didn't have to become a junior version of George Norton, did he?"

This wasn't the first time Mary had tried to drag Gregory into an intimate discussion of her husband's defects. Will she never learn that however much my opinion may coincide with hers I've no intention of ever saying so? "The reason they call women cats," his mother had said once, when she was sadly inspecting a violated roast chicken, "isn't because they spit at each other. It's because you can't trust them when your back's turned. I hate to say it, but it's true. Pussy is just like a woman. Butter won't melt in her mouth as long as I'm in the room. Oh, she sits in her corner and purrs like a lamb. But let me go out of the room for a minute and she's up on the table with the chicken. Never trust a cat or a woman, Gregory. I suppose there are exceptions, but you just remember that I thought Pussy was an exception. . . . What I was getting around to, son, is that I wouldn't tell Mary Dawson everything I knew if I were you. More than once she's put me in mind of Pussy here. . . ."

35

"I'd like to see a man get where Tom has, without emulating Norton to a certain extent," Gregory said to Mary now. Also I'd like to see a woman preserve a decent loyalty to her husband, or else divorce him and have done with it. You and your purring in the corner and expecting the roast chicken to be served to you on a golden platter. "It isn't sporting to criticize a man who's done exactly what you told him to do."

"You're crazy if you think I ever meant anything like this. His teaching's become a side issue. He isn't even remotely interested in it any more. He's right when he says he could deliver his lectures in his sleep. They don't mean enough to him to keep him awake. You know what he did? I wasn't going to tell you, but . . ."

"Then don't."

"But, Kit, yesterday when he went to the storeroom to look for his galoshes he came upon that box of notebooks, *The Outline* notebooks, and he burned them. Kit, he burned those notebooks as if they were so much trash. It was done before I knew anything about it."

"Oh, Mary!"

"I knew it would make you sick."

"I don't see how he could do it." But of course Tom could do it. Why not burn bridges you have no intention of crossing again? For several years after he stopped working on the notebooks Tom said he was saving them for his old age. What was in his mind when he destroyed that vast amount of research material? Does he plan to change the mandatory retirement rule after he becomes president and thereby insure himself an old-age occupation? Or is it possible that when Tom looked at those notebooks he saw they were written in a language lost to him? Gregory shied away from that last. You didn't like to think

36

that underneath Tom might sometimes suffer. Why was it you were so touched by the thought of Tom's highly problematical agony and so disgusted by Mary's obviously real suffering? "Mary, do you remember you used to say *The Outline* would have been written before, written exactly the way he planned to do it, if it had been very important?"

"Well, blame me! Next you'll be saying I told him to burn the notebooks."

"In a sense you did. Years ago."

"For heaven's sake, Kit, a woman naturally complains when her husband has his nose in research all the time. You don't seem to realize that Tom needed help. He didn't have much of a social background when I married him and he didn't know the first thing about faculty life. I only tried to make him see that a teacher has to use a little judgment. I don't know why you act as if I were a regular Svengali. My talking that you seem to remember so well certainly never made you turn a hair."

"Why should it? I'm not your husband." He had spoken carelessly and so was unprepared for the sudden catch in her breathing. Hustling into the bromide about all not glistering so brightly on approach, he knocked his pipe against the ash-tray. He tried to knock hard enough and long enough to cover the sounds she was making. If he meant to finish Section 20's papers in time to hand them back tomorrow he had better be going upstairs. "Haven't you got a handkerchief?" he asked, not looking up from his pipe.

There was a time when Mary, even a sniffling Mary, would have got a different response from Gregory Kitner; there was a time when he had sternly to remind himself that the sparkling dark-eyed woman was the wife of his dear friend. Sentimental yearning for Mary left him a little after he and the Dawsons

37

began living together. Something had to happen. Since she was his friend's wife, the normal and logical thing couldn't happen. He would have said the alternative was impossible, but it had turned out to be easy. He fell out of love with Mary even more easily than he had fallen in love with her. Perhaps, he decided, to stay in love with a woman living in the same house with you, you'd have to be married to her and therefore not so sharply conscious of her presence. He got tired of being hopelessly in love with Mary and so he stopped being in love with her. There had been times when her comments led him to think she believed that Amy Prentiss had cut her out, but this was not how it happened. Mary cut herself out, simply by continuing to be herself.

"Kit," she said after she had blown her nose, "what's happened to us?"

"Well," he said, "we aren't getting any younger." Then, ashamed of his peevishness, he added that his interview with Miss Spencer had made him age conscious. "She thinks we should ignore the accident of birth." He stuck his pipe in a pocket and got up. "If she corners me again I'll tell her I'm engaged to one of your daughters."

"You're in love with Harriet Hough, that's your trouble."

He leaned over to retrieve his tobacco pouch from the crack between the cushion and the chair. Her statement, her ridiculous statement, warranted no comment.

"I've known it for ages," she said. "There's no use in your denying it."

Remembering that the campaign against Harriet had started before he was aware of having met Dr. Hough, he wondered if Mary's habit of criticizing women, particularly younger women, were simply in the spirit of feminine fun or if she seriously desired Tom and him to dislike all women but one. Mary's saving grace was her over-emphasis. Almost always you had a feeling that she was giving you a burlesque of a catty woman; almost always you knew she not only was being ridiculous but that she was meaning to be that way. Almost always. Gregory had learned to enjoy Mary's acid conversation, but just now he saw nothing amusing in the memory that Mary had said Harriet Hough looked like a horse. "If you have such authentic information and have had it for ages, I should think you'd have the decency to stop sticking your knife into her."

"Sticking my knife! I don't know what you are talking about. After the way I slaved to launch that woman . . . If it hadn't been for me she never would have got anywhere in Tower City. And it wasn't easy, Kit. My God, nobody wants an extra woman. When I've gone out of my way . . . Kit, if I could *see* her I'd be delighted. I honestly would. I've tried. God knows I've tried, but I just can't see her."

"Frank Teetor can. So can I, but from a distance, Mary, from a distance."

"I wouldn't call the space between two theater seats such a distance. Sitting there with your heads together as if no one else were there. I watched you at the play. I'd suspected it before, but I knew it then."

"It's too bad you didn't hear what we were saying. We were discussing Sherlock Holmes. Harriet's amazingly uninformed on the subject." If you wanted me, he was thinking, why didn't you do something about it when the doing would have been comparatively simple? You stopped caring much for Tom long before the girls were born. . . . Why hadn't Mary done something about this undying devotion her eyes pledged Gregory Kitner? Undying enough to make him feel like a criminal

39

when he was interested in other women, but not undying enough to make her relinquish the possibility of getting to live in the presidential residence. I was never able to offer her a satisfactory substitute for the dream of the university presidency and that dream always meant a good deal more to her than anything else. "A person can't have everything," he said, as if she'd been reading his thoughts. "You knew that and you planned accordingly. To advance a bit in one direction you had to retreat a bit in another. It's only a matter of deciding what to hang on to and what to give up, isn't it? I'd say you made that decision about ten years ago."

"Is this an introduction to Freshman Philosophy?" She reached for her knitting bag. "Or do you presume to give advice to the lovelorn?"

"I drank beer with a student this afternoon," he said as he went into the hall. "Made me fuzzy, I guess."

3 The next day when he was turning to enter the Koffee Kup, Ruth Spencer leaped from a car that was parked in front of the restaurant. "What a coincidence!" she cried. "I was just going in here for a bite myself. How lucky to meet someone. If you're alone they always put you with such gruesome characters."

His hand fell from the door, but it was useless to pretend he hadn't planned to go in. Could I say I just now remembered an appointment somewhere on the other side of town? Why did my parents bring me up to hesitate about lying? "I'm in rather a hurry," he said. This was true enough. In these days you really had no business to take time out for eating. In fact the English department was working on a lunch-class program which would have been started this quarter if Commons had been more co-operative. He was about to enlarge on how little time he had for lunching, but Miss Spencer had darted into the Kup and already was speaking to the hostess.

No matter in what school or department you were enrolled, at Tama U. one of your majors was How to Get a Booth at the Kup. Fraternities assigned pledges to the chore of capturing booths and holding them for their superiors; independents formed strange alliances to combat monopolies. Booth holders with a little room to spare could pick and choose among the most luminous of campus stars.

"Name?" Shirley Vernon was asking Miss Spencer. "I'll call you when. . . ."

"Kitner," said Miss Spencer.

Shirley looked beyond the girl. "Oh, Doc, I didn't see you. Just a sec and I'll fix you up."

"Put us with someone, Shirley," said Gregory. "I haven't much time."

The hostess winked at him and then spoke in a loud voice that was directed to the persons who were waiting behind the frayed rope. "They've been expecting you, Dr. Kitner. Follow me, please."

"How super to have a drag," said Miss Spencer when they were installed in a booth that had been vacated a moment before. For once the girl sounded unrehearsed.

"It isn't fair," said Gregory. He was noticing that when she acted her age Miss Spencer was almost presentable. Now if she'd wipe some of that lipstick off her face . . .

"But is anything?" She took a lipstick from her bag and started to work on her mouth and the adjacent area. "I mean life is rather that way. And why not? Why shouldn't special people have special privileges? Isn't that so-called music utterly grim? Even when I was in high school I was quite nauseated by juke boxes."

The waitress, clearing the table, asked Gregory if he would have his usual.

"And what is your usual?" said Miss Spencer. "I should know these things."

"Kutlet Kake and Kuplets."

"How hysterical they are in this quaint place," said Miss Spencer, "but with a K. I'll have the same, and K-offee, of course."

The waitress, having given Miss Spencer one glance, wasn't looking again. "Milkshake, Doc?"

"No, Alice, I think I'll have coffee. I have a slight headache."

This appeared to amuse Alice. Grinning callously she said she would bring him an aspirin. "It's the pressure of modern

42

living, Doc. It's too bad you can't get away from it once in a while, but too hysterical."

"Now that the war is over," said Miss Spencer, "wouldn't one think restaurants would be able to get trained help?"

"And the money they make," said Alice as she stuffed crumpled paper napkins and doilies into the glasses on her tray. "But it can't last forever." She made the giddap clucks currently popular and picked up her burden.

"Of all the impertinent . . ."

"Careful, Miss Spencer, she's a Phi Bete and a graduate student who does a little paper-grading as well as table-waiting. But speaking of papers, have you done any work on the one you're to substitute for the theme we discussed yesterday?"

"Did we discuss a theme? Kit, can't you relax?"

It was a nightmare conversation. While Miss Spencer spoke of love, Dr. Kitner talked about English B2. When their food arrived he devoted himself to it as if he'd been famishing. Miss Spencer smeared lipstick on her hamburger bun, toyed with the French-fried potato strips and onion rings and orated about the danger of letting difference in age inhibit desire. Gregory said it was dangerous to let deep-fried foods go stone cold. "Allow Kuplets to cool and you inhibit appetite, Miss Spencer. If ever a dish deserved a rhapsodic name it's the Kup's potatoes and onions, but you've got to eat them hot. You know the poet John Trescott? He used to be a student of mine. My, the Kuplets John and I ate here . . . One of his finest bits of light verse . . ."

"Kit, you said to think about the School of Drama. Well, I did. I thought a lot about it, but I couldn't leave Liberal Arts."

"Flunk B2 and you'll have to," he said. "Oh, you can have a second crack at it, but don't count on sliding through under

43

Letting. He's good at ferretting out copied papers. . . . I wonder what's become of the girl who wrote that story. I haven't been able to think of her name yet, but it will come to me. Must be all of ten years ago. . . . It would be interesting to compile an anthology of themes used year after year. *Twenty Time-Tested Tales.* That's an idea. I'll present it at the next faculty meeting. We might even make some money on it. You know the one about the flowered hat that got mixed up with the funeral wreaths and was given a place of honor on the coffin? I get that one almost every quarter, always as a personal experience." Yesterday, he told himself, I thought she was running a fever. Today I bet I look it. Dizzy in the head and I've got chills running up and down my back—damn, I forgot my vitamins again. Might as well take those shots and be done with it for a while.

"Naturally I want to major in your subject," she said. "It works out better that way, but it's too hysterical of them to have composition a required course, I mean I loathe writing unless it's poetry. But if I can't make them let me major in English without getting a passing grade in B2, I mean if you keep on trying to resist this. . . . Kit, it's mean to flunk me just because you think you've got to prove you don't play favorites. After all, is it my fault this happened? You could at least help me, because you know very well it works out better."

What does? Don't tell me. But she was telling him that successful marriages must be based on mutual interest as well as on sex attraction and that therefore he should help her with her obligation to major in English. It sounded as if she'd been an A student in the special hygiene course all freshmen had to take, the course which divided the men and women into separate classes and didn't come within earshot of material such segrega-

44

tion would seem to insure. Many students had complained to Gregory that Hygiene just gave them the deep-frozen corn smothered in a sauce of the unimportance of sex. Miss Spencer was offering him Hygiene's unappetizing dish now. He had been mistaken when he'd thought she was like Laura Grier. Miss Spencer wasn't presenting a future that was free; and perhaps she'd decided that yesterday's line was a bit ardent for the old man. Now she was stressing compatibility based on mutual adoration of English literature, successful marriage built on appreciation of social values. By social values she meant her father and mother. Father, she said, had forty-three lines in *Who's Who*. She didn't mention her mother's fracas at the Woman's Club, but aside from that Gregory believed she omitted little of her family's public achievements. Well, if she wanted to use psychology he would play along with her. "Do you know anything about Dr. Inverly's work?" he asked.

For the first time since they had sat down he had her undivided attention. "That's a dirty trick," she said. "You surely don't think a psychologist could talk me out of the only real thing that's ever happened to me."

He was beginning to see she might not be so stupid as she looked. But she's not sane and I can outwit an insane person. . . . I hope. "I was thinking of his aptitude tests. He's done remarkable things in vocational guidance. When I made that Drama suggestion I was merely guessing. I'm no psychologist, but I do think I was on the right track when I advised you to consider another course or school. If you would go to Dr. Inverly and take one of his tests, he might discover hidden talents you've never dreamed of possessing."

"We had those things in grade school. Counting boxes and so forth. It always bored me to death."

45

"But this is quite different. It isn't an I.Q. He's one of the foremost men in this sort of thing. He's a very good friend of mine and I'm sure he'd give you a test."

She looked at him through narrowed eyes. "You wouldn't be trying to pull a fast one, would you, Kit?"

"I'm trying to help you, Miss Spencer." I am, he told himself. I honestly am. I'm sorry for her. "Think how fortunate your generation is, to be able to take such tests before it's too late. If you read Dr. Inverly's article in the last *Mercury*, I'm sure you . . ."

"All right, all right," she said. "I suppose I can take the silly test if it means so much to you. But I know what he'll find out." From older eyes that look would have been a leer. "But I can take it if you can. I mean I don't care who knows it. As I was telling my friend Patsy Hannegan, there's absolutely no reason to be ashamed of pure and honorable emotion. . . ."

"Splendid," he said, trying not to think what else she may have told Patsy Hannegan. "I'll make an appointment for you. Now if you'll excuse me . . ." Alice had carefully made out two checks, but he hadn't the courage to take only his. "No, you stay and finish your lunch."

"But I've finished. I have my car. I'll take you back to the campus, or anywhere you say. I haven't anything to do all afternoon."

"Thanks, but I have some business around town. After I've called Dr. Inverly, I'll leave word for you with Miss Chester at the Burnaby office. You can call her if you aren't in the building tomorrow."

"I'll be in the building tomorrow," she said. "Tomorrow and the day after that and the day after that." When she smiled he saw that Mary was right about her teeth. It was unfair to blame

46

the girl for those teeth, but she might have refrained from such a wide smile. "You'll have to get used to having me around, Kit, because that's where I'm going to be."

He called Inverly from a telephone in Mr. Martin's Attire for Gentlemen. "Dick," he said, "I've got a student who's batty as a loon. I've persuaded her to come to you for an aptitude test."

"That's big of you, Kit."

"You've got to steer her to a psychiatrist, Dick. It's something you can handle a lot better than I can. You see, she's obsessed with the idea that she's in love with me."

Dick chuckled and said that proved insanity, all right, but after he had had his little joke he was co-operative. "Shoot her to me tomorrow afternoon at three and I'll try to get her out of your hair. What's her name?"

"Spencer. Ruth."

"Okay, I've made a note of it. Aside from that how's the world treating you?"

"Fine, Dick. Couldn't ask for more."

"A decided symptom of abnormality. Come around to the house and I'll give you something to test your reflexes. . . ."

Near the telephone booth was a display of hand-painted neckties. Trying to decide if they were ugly or rather artistic, Gregory paused at the counter long enough to lay himself open to attack. "Something in a cravat, sir? Here is one that is especially suited to your type. . . ."

"You're the fellow who sold me this muffler."

"I shouldn't be surprised, sir," said the clerk. "Very inferior materials and dyes during the war period. If you would care to see some of our new imports after you've selected your cravat. . . ."

47

But Gregory was on his way out. *Was his depressed state due to his muffler's combination of synthetic and reclaimed wools? Am I yearning for my old muffler . . . or for Amy?*

But I stopped being in love with her long before the actual break. Now on the rare occasions when he saw Amy Prentiss he felt no desire for the former relationship, but at the same time he could feel her attraction and could understand why she had fascinated him so long. He considered this a very healthy attitude; he hoped she felt the same way about him.

Once or twice in the past three years when circumstances had required him and Amy to say more than how-do-you-do he had had a feeling, not entirely unpleasant, that Amy didn't regard him with complete detachment.

He pulled the scratchy muffler from his neck. The day was turning warm. After an early frost and many predictions that a hard winter was ahead there had been weeks of snappy mornings, balmy noons and dank nights. Influenza weather, said Mary, when she ordered the family to bundle up. When Gregory thrust the hated scarf in a pocket he wondered what Amy had done with his good plaid. *Did she save it, as I saved that lacy handkerchief? Did she put it away in a drawer? Does she come upon it sometimes and think that only very superficial persons could have let an old house stand between them and happiness?* But that old house symbolized all that was irreconcilable between him and Amy Prentiss. But their break had been inevitable, although he wished it hadn't been so childishly ill-humored. She should have taken into account the fact that it was examination week. *I didn't try to forget the damn concert. . . .*

"How could you forget? I've talked of nothing else for a solid month," she had said.

He couldn't tell her he had fallen in the habit of not listening to what she said. "I simply forgot that it was for tonight. Matter of fact I'd gone to bed. You see . . ."

"Gone to bed!" She shrieked so loudly that he had to hold the telephone away from his ear.

"I was up most of last night, grading term papers."

"Papers, papers. I'm sick and tired of hearing you talk about papers. When the world comes to its end you'll be sitting up in that attic grading papers."

"Not tonight. Tonight I'll be sleeping."

"I called to tell you to come at seven-thirty instead of eight. I want to check on the box-office people. I don't trust them."

"I can't do it, Amy. I'm bushed."

"I'll be tied up with photographers and so you'll have to keep an eye on the box office. I'll expect you at seven-thirty sharp, Kit. And we're dressing, in case you've forgotten that too."

He got away from the telephone and the first floor without having to explain to Mary, but when he came down again she was in the study, in the green velour chair of the carved walnut frame. The chair had belonged to somebody's grandmother, a grandmother Mary was gradually confusing with her own. Gregory thought this fair enough; people who wished to keep their grandmothers for themselves shouldn't sell heirloom chairs. It was all right with him when Mary waved an all-inclusive hand around the study and said the old things had been in the family for ages. So long as she said *the* family she was safe. If she said *my* family, Tom, always on the defensive about his humble parents, would snort, "How's that again department?"

From the green chair Mary commanded a slice of the hall,

49

and none but a ghost could have opened the closet door without being cross-examined by the brooding sentry. "Kit, you surely aren't going out?" she asked as she pulled her glasses down. "I thought you wanted to get to bed early."

He knew she hadn't missed a word of what he had said to Amy on the telephone and that she might have heard a good deal of what Amy had shouted. "I forgot Amy's concert."

"I don't know how you managed that. The papers have been full of it. They say she expects to clear ten thousand. I considered going until I heard that the cheapest seats were ten dollars. Tom said any time he'd pay ten dollars to sit in the gallery . . ."

"I'd be happy to give my seat away."

"Poor darling, you weren't cut out for high society, were you? I really don't see how you can keep it up."

Afterwards he saw that Mary had known his connection with high society was about over; skepticism on the subject of womanly intuition had been knocked out of him at an early age. Mary, not moving from her chair, could have told him he would go to sleep at the concert and thereby incur the wrath of the impresario. "I never was so embarrassed in my life," said Amy when they finally got back to her house. "After I slaved to get that orchestra to come to Tower City—one of the leading orchestras of the world . . . and you sat there and snored!"

"I may have closed my eyes. I usually shut my eyes when I listen to music. But I did not snore. Fat chance there was of sleeping through that caterwauling." He really hadn't followed the music closely enough to be sure that it was caterwauling, but her saying he had snored was intolerable. He snatched at the scarf thrown over the outstretched hand of the suit of armor he called Mac and used for a hall tree. Somehow he caught both ends of the scarf, and Mac's metal mitten came off. It rattled over the marble floor until it came to rest against the edge of a prayer rug. "If you didn't fill your house with such junk . . ."

"Junk!"

"Yes, junk." He looked down the long dim hall of armor, massive chairs, chests, tapestries and rugs. "All you lack is a mummy. Haven't you got one somewhere in storage? You ought to have a good mummy in this side show. No wonder you have to set up your own museum. No self-respecting outfit would take any of this as a gift. The Prentiss Museum of fake antiques, fake objets d'art . . . The whole place is falling to pieces and it was no good in the beginning. Artificial flowers sprayed with Chanel." He had sounded off on the subject before, but now with a feeling of dismay overlaid with relief he heard his voice demand finality.

She dropped her wrap on a chest that one of the Prentiss scouts had discovered in an Italian wash house and attributed to a Venetian doge. Gregory knew she was tired; the concert hadn't exactly flopped, but if the ten-thousand-dollar report were to be turned in the chairman was going to have to dig down into her own pocket. Amy's pocket digging was carefully controlled to assist her income-tax problem and she had not, she'd told Gregory on the way home, counted on subsidizing a concert. No gentleman would have picked a fight with Amy tonight, but when he looked at her drawn face Gregory was infuriated. "Amy, your whole life is artificial and none of your perfume spraying is going to make it come alive."

The woman who could burst into tears over losing a button which couldn't be replaced took her loss of a lover with magnified dignity. "I believe you know the way out," she said.

For a moment they stared at each other. It was one of those moments during which you have what seems a very long time to decide. He considered saying he was sorry; he even considered admitting that he may have breathed heavily during the concert; but he was tired and he knew a reconciliation would mean he wouldn't get to Clayton Place until dawn. He wished to get there immediately. "Good night," he said. As soon as the moment had passed it seemed unimportant.

He nearly smiled when he closed the door and heard the crash against it. She had thrown Mac's fist at him, an instant too late. Forgetting that she was First Lady of Tower City, she'd scooped up the mitten and slung it. Had the fist struck him he would have turned around and laughed and said that was more like her. Oh well, he told himself as he went down the steps that were guarded by badly chipped winged lions, it can wait. There was plenty of time later on, and none at all tonight.

The following week there was a heavy blizzard. During that bitter weather he wondered why in hell she didn't send his scarf to him or at least call up to remind him that it was at her house. Mary, assuming he had lost it at the concert, telephoned the hall and then told him he'd better get another muffler if he didn't want to die of pneumonia. A few days after that she said, "I suppose it's no news to you, but I was quite surprised when I read that Amy went to the Midwinter Ball with Jerry Steuben."

Gregory was astounded. He'd forgotten about the Midwinter Ball. The ticket was stuck into his bureau mirror. Amy might have been thoughtful enough to remind him that they had planned to go. She knew it was his heavy time and that he couldn't be bothered to keep track of the many social events she expected him to attend. Did she think her going anywhere with Jerry Steuben would bring him to heel? Whenever she had jabbed at him for speaking to another woman, for even smiling in the direction of some casual acquaintance like Harriet Hough, he had reminded her it was hard for him to see why she let the unspeakable Steuben hang around her house. "But Jerry's my lawyer," she said. "I've known him all my life. Of course he's loads older. He was a young man when I was still a child-in-arms."

"Whose arms? Slavering mangy old wolf . . ."

That had pleased her. She chortled that her Kitty-pie was jealous. . . . If she thought he would come crawling back simply because she went to the Midwinter Ball with that notorious . . . He bought a new scarf. It was an ugly scarf, but it had hidden beauty. It reminded him that at last he no longer had to answer to that nauseating name, Kitty-pie.

The next time Mrs. Carr was at the Dawson house for dinner she asked how *l'affaire aimée* was progressing. Mary often pretended to be shocked at her mother's indiscretion, but on this occasion there was no doubt about the daughter's genuine horror. "Mother!"

"*L'affaire aimée*," said Gregory, "*est finie.*"

Mrs. Carr nodded. "*Je suis heureuse.*"

"*Et moi.*" The odd part about it was that except for wishing he had his old muffler back, he was happy. It would have been more satisfying if he and Amy could have talked the matter over and reached the adult conclusion that it was time to bury something that had begun to smell a bit, but he and Amy had never acted very adult about each other. *L'affaire aimée* had been both adorned and disfigured by a youthful breathlessness that was exciting, embarrassing, and, after a while, tiring. If

Mary were to be believed, Amy Prentiss was several years older than Gregory Kitner, but he knew that in spirit Amy was too young for him. He felt a little sorry for the superannuated lecher who had taken his place.

If I had it to do over, and knew what the outcome would be, would I go ahead? Was his mother right when she said it was an unlucky day for him when he met That Woman? Mama had said this about several women, but *l'affaire aimée* lasted so long that she fell into the habit of blaming Amy for things that happened long before her son heard the name Prentiss. "You'd be married and settled in your own home, if it hadn't been for That Woman," Mama said. "Boarding out, at your age . . . It's a scandal. I can't understand it. Our people always married young."

"I was willing."

"Don't you talk to me about that girl at State. Charlie used to tell me how you never moved a muscle when she started running around with other boys."

"Boy," said Gregory. "There was only one."

"You made the match yourself," said Mama. "Charlie told me how you used to hire that boy to take her out. You can't make me think you ever wanted to marry her. Why can't you settle down and marry some nice girl like . . ."

When he was around thirty his mother had wearied of protecting him from grasping females. She made a complete about-face and began to present him with lists of suitable prospects. Her conception of suitable had no rational foundation. Directly after she met Harriet Hough she calmly asked why he didn't marry that sweet new teacher. "I scarcely know her, for one thing," he said, "and for another, she's nearly young enough to be my daughter."

54

Sometimes his mother would make a lightning recognition of his age. "I'd be ashamed to admit I was old enough to have a grown family and still not married," she said. "Excuses, excuses, that's all you ever give me. Excuses for sinful living."

"Why, Mama!"

"You forget I've seen Mrs. Prentiss. You forget I've had the privilege of listening for hours to that ridiculous, addle-pated old woman who pretends to be a girl. And to think I was pleased when you wrote that you'd been to Mrs. Prentiss' house to hear Rosa Trencantelli. I wish I'd never heard of either of them."

"Why, Mama, you always admired Trencantelli so much."

"I don't admire anyone who has to do with that Mrs. Prentiss. I sized that one up the first time I set eyes on her."

In a way Gregory supposed he had sized that one up the first time he set eyes on her. It had taken him a few years to admit to himself how accurately he had sized Amy up and how very artificial his thoughts of marrying her had been. Sop to the old Methodist conscience, that was all.

How thrilled Mary was when the invitations came. "We've arrived," she shouted when she opened the large square envelope. "You can't tell me a good address doesn't pay. Look, Kit, you got one too. We're asked to Mrs. Philip Prentiss' house to hear Rosa Trencantelli."

"She's dead," said Gregory. "Must be. My parents went to her farewell concert when I was still a boy."

"Maybe it's another one," said Mary, "but who cares? We've been asked to Mrs. Prentiss' house. Just you wait until I tell Mother."

"What's so wonderful about Mrs. Prentiss, aside from her ability to raise Trencantelli from the dead?"

"Kit, you can't have lived in Tower City almost six years without knowing about Mrs. Philip Prentiss. She's absolutely everything. Her picture's in the paper all the time."

"Very old packing family," said Tom. "You know the Prentiss Packers."

"They got skunked last Sunday."

"I mean the business, Kit. This woman inherited it from her husband."

"The football team too?"

"I suppose so," said Tom. "I don't follow professional football. It seems to me when you turn the game into a money-making . . ."

"What do you think it is at Tamarack? Money-*losing* enterprise?"

"The point is that this woman controls all the Prentiss holdings and at least half of the Leveright. You know the Leveright Drug people."

"I throw a little tobacco business their way now and then."

"And she's on the board of trustees," said Mary. "She's on every board in town. When her husband died . . . They say it was an accident, but everyone knew he'd been trying to kill himself for years. Well, after he finally did, they gave her his place on the board. Her brother Jimmy Leveright, you know, the drunk one, had got their father's place. Why, they're just everything, Kit. You know them."

"Not intimately, unless the redhead who calls me honey . . . Say, Tom, do you ever get tobacco at the store on the corner of Vine and River? Worth the walk, boy."

Mary said he wasn't funny and Tom agreed that a Prentiss invitation wasn't to be taken lightly. "Seriously, Kit, all the Leveright clan's bound to be there."

56

"Jimmy-the-drunk?"

"Mary's got no right to say that. Just because the one time she saw him he seemed to be a bit . . ."

"Bit! Everyone knows he's a drunk. He spends half his time in hospitals."

"All right, but during the other half he's a power around town, and don't you forget that he's on the board. You better be careful what you say. . . . And the Davises and Nortons and all the department heads will be there, I bet. For God's sake, Kit, don't breathe a word against the administration while you're in that house."

"Washington or Tamarack?"

"Three weeks," said Mary. "It doesn't give us a lot of time. I'll have to have a new dress and you boys will have to get tails."

"Well, that lets me out," said Gregory. "Much as I would like to hear Trencantelli and the owner of a football team . . ."

He changed his mind, though. Paul and Ruby Peebles made him change it. "Whether we like it or not," Paul said, "these *functions* are important. I'd like to think classroom performance still determined status, but I've seen too many promotions made in somebody's drawing room. There's no sense in going out of your way to avoid advancement, Kit."

"And you'll look so beautiful in full dress," said Ruby.

Feeling conspicuously if uncomfortably handsome in his new outfit Gregory beamed when Mary kissed him and said she wished polygamy were legal. He and Tom agreed that they wished so too, and she flirted her wide skirt at them and asked the mirror how she could endure living with two English teachers. And would they, for the sixth time, guess that she and her

57

mother had made this dress? "I don't mean that I have any hope of competing with Mrs. Prentiss. . . ."

Gregory laughed. He knew what Mrs. Prentiss would look like. Something large and chesty with a voice suitable for football fields and board meetings. He could forgive the woman for owning a football team, but never for owning a say-so in a university. He wasn't so naïve that he believed the Tamarack trustees had much to say about the university's policies; he knew the board didn't dare squeak against Norton. Fundamentally, though, he was opposed to any and all trustees. He believed that schools should be run co-operatively by the faculty and the student body; he believed that the students and faculty should elect short-term officers to carry out programs acceptable to the majority; he believed, in short, in the millennium in which a man like Norton would be used to make announcements when loud-speakers broke down.

Nevertheless, to please the Peebles and to be able to tell his mother that he'd heard her favorite singer of long ago, he went to the great railway station of a house that until tonight he'd assumed to be a public building. The Prentiss hallway delighted him when he first saw it. No wonder Philip Prentiss had devoted years of his life to trying to kill himself. The black-and-white checkered marble floor of the hall was spotted with oriental rugs; metal men guarded the tapestry-hung walls and the dark chairs and chests. All that was missing was a mummy. . . . oh, yes, and little glass-covered signs to explain the exhibits. He never got anywhere about the mummy, but Amy had put up small glass-covered plaques. Now anyone going into the Prentiss house could read just where and when the exhibited items were in more practical use. That's the one mark I made in that house. Thanks to Kitner, the tourist may now

58

read those little black-and-white lies invented by commission agents and perpetuated by the conservator. Oh, nobody appreciated a joke more than Amy did, provided she had been the one to tell it. "But I was just being funny," Gregory had protested when she showed him the new signs, but she paid no attention. She said it was a very good idea, so good that she didn't know why she hadn't thought of it. "It will save me so much time," she said. "People are always asking about this or that."

That first night when he dragged his feet up the wide staircase, he thought how fine the thick carpeting was for polishing shoes. "I'm glad I came," he said to Mary, and she said wasn't it wonderful.

Upstairs a maid directed the ladies; a footman with a face appropriate for the custodian of a morgue accompanied the gentlemen to a large bedroom hung with purplish velvet. Skulking in this chamber were men who spoke in funereal voices; they spoke as if the dead master were laid out on the dark counterpane that bore his initials. "This was *his* room," Gregory was told, very confidentially.

Mary's terror of arriving too early had made them among the last, but they had to wait a while before being received. The size of the crowd indicated that the party wasn't quite so exclusive as Mary had hoped and for some minutes there was something of a jam at the drawing-room door. During the wait Gregory studied the woman who was standing just inside the drawing room. It looked as if you had to shake hands with her before getting into the room. He assumed she was Mrs. Prentiss. She was large and chesty and she had a tremendous voice. The heavy accent surprised him, but he assumed she'd been educated abroad. He was wondering how many generations of

59

meat packers had worn that great fichu of lace when Paul Peebles whispered that Trencantelli was looking a bit long in the tooth. "Of course it's been about thirty years since I saw her last," Paul said, "but Ruby claims it's the same dress."

"I did not," said Ruby. "I merely said if it's the same one it hasn't been cleaned since. A singer of such prominence would have a very large wardrobe and I expect she has old lace on all of them. Priceless stuff, I suppose, but even so I'd take a chance on washing it. . . ."

Mrs. Prentiss wasn't revealed to Gregory until she was shaking hands with Paul. She was a tiny woman and she was beautiful. Her ash-blonde hair looked like the taffy carnival men used to throw over hooks and twist into glossy ropes. There was no old lace about Mrs. Prentiss. She was wearing something quite simple. Later, when Gregory commented that their hostess had had on a very plain dress, Mary hooted. "I suppose you think she ran it up herself," she said. "Kit, the person who made that dress is named Lanvin if I'm not sadly mistaken. . . ."

"And this is Gregory Kitner, one of my young men," said Paul when he turned to introduce Gregory.

"How do you do, Dr. Kitner," said Mrs. Prentiss. Her hand was very small but she had a firm handshake that was like a man's. Funny how long it took Gregory to realize that Amy gave herself away when she shook hands . . . well, gave away the businesslike aspect of her character. That wasn't all there was to Amy. No, there was the girlish voice that said how much she'd heard about Dr. Kitner and how she'd looked forward to meeting him. "I have your book, you know."

At that time he had had two books published. He not only wondered which one she was talking about, but why she would have either of them. As a trustee did she feel she had to keep

60

up on textbooks? He tried to make a suitable reply, but he was finding speech difficult. Had he ever felt this way? Although he had been interested in Sunny Tate, his college love, the first time he saw her, that interest hadn't swept through him like fire. Now it was as if his blood had been converted to oil and then ignited. I'm too old, he told himself. He told himself it must be indigestion and he tried to remember what they'd had for dinner. Because of the party it hadn't been much of a meal and it was possible that Mary had brought out a few scraps which should have gone into the garbage. Indigestion. At my age it can't be love. Anyhow this isn't the way I fall in love. I've never been what you could call precipitate.

Passed on to Madame Trencantelli he babbled about how his parents had made a special trip to Chicago for her farewell performance. She interrupted before he could say how much his grandparents had admired her. "Verr kine," she said. "I am moz heppy wiz you."

He joined the group that had formed around Ruby Peebles; the Dawsons had gone off to wiggle close to the Nortons and Trumballs. Sounds of stringed instruments emerged from a forest of palms and ferns. Two flunkies surrounded by crystal and silver dispensed iced water. The guests milled about sedately and talked of nonprofessional football and the weather. Both were unseasonable. After about an hour of this preliminary mixer the guests were invited to cross the hall to the music room.

That room, even larger than the drawing room, was set up for the business of the evening. Rows of heart-backed gilded chairs with rose-velvet seats faced a gigantic gilt piano. Near the piano, as if to mark the other boundary of the stage, was a large wicker basket of flowers and ferns. The basket was gilded and the roses matched the velvet trappings of the room. Where there weren't draperies there were large lighted paintings in heavy gold frames. Gregory tried to recognize a Great Master. This was the first time he'd ever been in a house grand enough to warrant thought of Great Masters, but all he was sure of was that the roses in the floor basket were artificial. This amused him very much. He thought he was in on a joke Mrs. Prentiss was playing on Tower City. Later, some months later, he learned that Amy used artificial flowers because although the original outlay was large, fabric flowers were cheaper in the long run. She said nobody could tell the difference when live fern was added and that she always sprayed the ensemble with perfume just before a party.

These people don't understand her, he thought when Mrs. Prentiss took her stand between the piano and the basket. Why, these people couldn't begin to see the aura of elfin mischief which was playing about her. Sometimes when he looked back on that night he reverted to his original diagnosis. He must have been suffering from ptomaine. Elfin mischief and Amy! Auras and Amy! If the iced water had been straight gin he couldn't have been more bemused.

Being no boy, he'd been able to maintain a decent facial immobility. One would have said there was nothing in Dr. Kitner's mind but weary determination to see the recital through. Knowing he was safe he made no effort to squelch the fairy fire of his infatuation; at his age it was necessary to treat so unique an experience with tenderness. Really, he hadn't felt this way since Louisa Carter had come to Seyno and into the eighth grade. . . . "And so, dear friends, it gives me even greater pleasure to present to you my good friend Rosa Trencantelli. Rosa dear, will you announce your own numbers?"

62

"I zing nuzzing you doan alread acquaint," said Madame Trencantelli.

The contrast between the two women was cruel. Rosa, ponderous in her dingy laces and soiled jewelry and old-fashioned posturing; Amy, dainty and simple and natural in rosy-grey chiffon and pearls—there was nothing artificial about the Prentiss pearls. . . . Eventually Gregory knew that poor Rosa had sung for no more than her supper. "I didn't know she'd got so old," Amy told him later. "Thank goodness she didn't try for any high notes. Before I saw her I thought she'd get some paying engagements out of my party, but when I *saw* her . . . Do you know she actually expected me to pay her traveling expenses? Why, darling, I told her, if I'd been going to pay expenses I would have had someone out from Chicago. I wouldn't have sent all the way to New York. I couldn't deduct it from my income taxes. I fail to see why. I certainly didn't give that party for fun. There's something so vindictive about those Washington people. I don't mind having the government against me when it's sincere and really trying to do good, but when it's so vindictive . . ."

Perched on a fragile chair and dreaming of a beautiful little princess shut in an ogre's castle, Gregory found Rosa Trencantelli's unambitious songs delightful. During supper he sat with the artist and talked of the large library of Trencantelli recordings owned by his parents. Madame Trencantelli had little English and he had no Italian, but they met on common ground in French; each spoke French so badly that there was no cause for embarrassment. All he regretted was that Nettie Carr wasn't here to add her aunt-and-pen French to the conversation. Nettie would have known at once that when Rosa

63

said she must go to take a bath she meant she wished to excuse herself only for a few moments.

It was too large a party for the guests to expect the hostess to shake hands a second time, but Gregory received a special farewell from Mrs. Prentiss. "It was so sweet of you to look after Madame Trencantelli," she said when she gave him that firm handshake again. "Old ladies adore having young men notice them. . . . You know, I've been wanting to call you to ask some questions about your book. Could we get together some time? Please?"

By then he was certain she had confused him with Kent. Kent was in the English department and although his recent biography of Byron hadn't exactly swept the country at least it was a trade book Mrs. Prentiss might have on her library table. Gregory wasn't going to set her right, though, not after that engaging request. He desired nothing more than getting together with her, even if it had to be over Kent's dull work. "I'd like that very much," he said.

"You'll think I've no education," she said. "I'm afraid I didn't have much. Convents and finishing school. But it wasn't my fault. I really want to know things. Could you come to tea to-morrow?"

Could he!

He and the Dawsons walked home. This was before Tom owned a car. They had gone to the party in a taxi, but there was no need to return home in style. In order to get out of being taken home by the Stewarts, who had asked first, Mary had had to decline several later, quite attractive invitations. "Why those Stewarts were invited is beyond me," she said. "Imagine going to a party like that in street clothes. She looked bad enough, but

64

he didn't even look clean. I can't imagine why under the sun they were invited."

"He's working on some crazy thing that the Science department is all excited about, something he claims will revolutionize society—a complete crackpot, if you ask me, but Norton seems to have fallen for some of the line." At the mention of Norton's name Tom's voice deepened. "He was telling me about it. I suppose he asked Mrs. Prentiss to include them. But, say, Kit, you made quite a hit with her. The way she nabbed you when we were leaving . . . Better watch your step, boy, I hear she's fireworks."

"I wouldn't get my hopes up," said Mary. "She's important socially, but she hasn't any say-so on the board. There's no use cultivating her for that."

"Women," said Tom. "What a drab life they have. Mary, I doubt if Kit was thinking about her influence on the board. Say, if you stood at the right angle you could see down to her stomach."

"Tom Dawson!"

"You never told me how beautiful she is," said Gregory.

"Are you referring to her stomach? I didn't happen to notice that. Even if I were a man I hardly think I'd be interested in an old woman's stomach. Oh, I remember that when I was a little girl I thought she was beautiful. It was a blow to see her tonight. I hadn't seen her close up in years. My God, but she's old. I should think she'd let her hair go . . . such an odd color. And didn't you notice that she's definitely cross eyed?"

That first winter with Amy was full of excitement; Gregory hadn't had such an active social life since his senior year in high school. Before Christmas Amy did a lot of entertaining and he

65

was invited to all of her parties and soon to the parties given by her friends. As Tom said, a bachelor could get around if he cared for that sort of thing.

As a rule Mrs. Prentiss went south shortly after New Years, but that year she decided to stay in Tower City. The society editors gushed about how gay the social scene would be with its Leader remaining in the center of the picture, but after the holidays Amy's Day wasn't for publication.

Gregory knew Amy Prentiss a long time before he gave even passing thought to what might be going on in her head, but when he began to be able to look at her and to listen to her at the same time he wasn't alarmed. He decided that she was stupid, but shallow or deep she was beautiful and she had not confused him with Kent. Dear no, she said that Professor Kent had such horrible eyebrows; the book on the tea table that afternoon was Kitner's *Basic Principles of English Composition*. He and she sat in the solarium where the string quartet had hidden the night before. The bulk of last night's forest had vanished; no more than a dozen indestructible-looking plants remained. These plants were in Chinese tubs meticulously spaced. From a panel in the center of the glazed semicircle a cement lion's head drooled into a small pool that was sunk into the tile floor. "The tropical kinds always die," said Mrs. Prentiss when she saw that her guest was looking at the fish. "The only ones that will survive are those from Woolworth's. I can't understand it. Do you think it's cold in here?"

He said he didn't. He was chattering, but he thought it must be from nervousness. Later he learned that the only way to bring the Prentiss mansion up to seventy degrees was to stuff it with people.

"But let's talk about you," she said when she gave him his

66

second cup of tepid tea. "I always think the person behind the book is even more interesting than the book itself." That was the end of Amy and the basic principles of English composition.

When he left the Prentiss house that afternoon he told himself he felt as if he had known her forever. At no time during the next eight years did he ever recapture that first afternoon's sense of being in complete rapport with Amy. The Little-Princess side of her character was pleasantly simple, but you couldn't continue indefinitely to ignore the small ogre who held that fair lady captive. However, in the beginning Gregory was interested only in the princess. He took her to concerts; he took her to plays put on by the University Theatre and by the Tower City Players, and to the two shows that came out from Chicago. He took her to the movies and then to the Koffee Kup. She had never been to the Kup before; she said she just loved its collegiate atmosphere. "You know," she said, "you can go along for months here in Tower City without thinking about it being a college town." It was weeks before Gregory thought that was an odd thing for a trustee to say. "I think we miss a great deal by not taking part in the university activities, I really do." But after a few visits to the Kup, Amy decided she wasn't the hamburger type. "My hair always smells so horrid after we've been there," she said. "Let's go to the Bersbach. And not walk, Kit. I definitely am not the athletic type. You've made me walk farther in the time I've known you than I used to walk in years and years. Darling, have pity on your little Amy. Your legs are so long, darling."

In her very own car, her very own as opposed to the three that presumably were the property of her chauffeur, they took rides. Her very own was an imported job that looked and sounded like a raffish insect, but they seldom had to drive far to find out-of-the-way places where they could have tea and talk. "Just suppose you hadn't come to my Trencantelli party," she said. "I shiver to think of it, Kit. We might never have met."

"But it was fated," he said. "It was in the stars." He was a complete fool. He rolled clichés around in his mouth and smacked his lips over ripe flavors he had never allowed himself to sample before. Such a dignified, scholarly man, he never before had had the fun of talking about pale-moonlight hair and lily-petal hands. Sometimes it did occur to him that this didn't necessarily prove that the present love was greater than any he had experienced before; perhaps all it proved was that it was different. Looking back on it he decided his mother's analysis may have been correct. "I suppose every man wants to go around with a chorus-girl type of woman some time in his life," Mama had said once. "That Prentiss woman's the first really common woman you've ever known. She's as common as dog meat."

During the first year of *l'affaire aimée,* Dr. Kitner treated his classes to an unusual amount of love poetry. Feeling a kinship for her he even revised his formerly somewhat carping opinion of Mrs. Browning. Amy told him he was a true poet and believing her he smiled benevolently upon students who wanted to become song writers. By spring he was being showered with invitations to be best man for students who swore that if it hadn't been for Doc Kitner . . . By spring he was thinking about his own wedding. He had no doubt that a proposal was in order and he chided himself for letting her money stand in the way. Amy didn't care about money, he told himself. Or, if she did, she cared more about saving it than spending it. Her piddling economies didn't annoy him, they encouraged him. As his wife she would have to pinch pennies. He hoped she would decide to give all of her money away, but he wouldn't be stuffy if she wanted to keep a little. If she wanted to keep something for an occasional luxury, he wouldn't be unreasonable. His salary was small, but his two textbooks were bringing in something and he had ideas for many more textbooks. Once he and she settled down he would write a textbook every year. He wouldn't be asking her to share a life of poverty.

The day she told him she had given her house to the university he thought she was paving the way for him. He said he had never heard better news. "All that bothers me is that I didn't think of it before," she said. "Sometimes I wonder if Jerry Steuben's entirely honest. Of course I keep an eye on him and I'm pretty sure he couldn't get away with anything, but why didn't he think of this? That's what I'd like to know. I wonder what he thinks I pay him for. You'd be amazed if you knew how many tax angles I've thought of that Jerry's overlooked."

It took a while for Gregory to get it through his head that the gift to the university was prompted by a determination to be relieved of monstrously unfair real-estate taxes. Under its charter from the state Tamarack was tax-exempt. "I wonder if there's any way of pre-dating the gift and recovering some of the back taxes," she said.

"I wouldn't know."

"No, darling, I know you wouldn't. I was just thinking out loud. I'll have to talk to Jerry."

"But what's the university going to do with the house?"

"No students," she said. "I insist on that. I'm not going to have my beautiful house wrecked by students even though I won't be here to see it. It will be a museum. We're working it out in my new will. Oh, it's very complicated, darling, and I'm sure you wouldn't understand it. George Norton tried to make me say a faculty club, but that's silly. I reminded him that the Town Club is practically that."

"The Town Club's much too expensive for most of the faculty."

"They could belong if they wanted to. That's the trouble with people these days, Kitty-pie. They're always wanting something for nothing. Do you think it should be the Prentiss Museum? I suppose Prentiss-Leveright would be awkward, and anyway we have the chapel. Just the same I don't know where the collection would be if I hadn't taken care of it. After Father Prentiss died Philip wouldn't do a thing about having the buyers stopped. Stuff kept coming in from all over the world and Philip wouldn't even have the boxes opened and checked. Poor Phil. Of course it stopped when I got the court order. He never was responsible, you know, but it took ages to prove. He had a lawyer friend who was completely unscrupulous and he kept fighting me long after Phil had agreed that I was far more logical . . . It's a wonder I was able to keep the Prentiss Packers from going into bankruptcy. No one will ever know what I've been through. My brother's not much more help than poor Phil was and so I've had all the Leveright responsibility too."

This was news to Gregory. His little princess had responsibilities? He had heard her talk about having to go to a directors' meeting and at times had gathered that she was speaking of organizations other than the educational and charitable ones she assisted, but he'd always assumed that her connection with Leveright Drugs and Prentiss Packers was limited to signing

70

papers. He thought Jerry Steuben was hired to read papers and to tell her where to sign. He had imagined charming scenes in which Amy dropped in to say hello to men high up in drugs and meat. "I lost track somewhere," he said. "Somewhere back there when you were talking about your will. I don't understand. I thought you'd already given the house."

"Darling, you really are a professor. You don't know a thing about business and that suits me. I get so tired of my business worries. You can't know what a relief it is to be with someone like you. Of course I've given them the house. So I won't have to pay taxes."

"But they aren't to have it yet?"

"Naturally not. Not until after I die. Silly boy, where would I live?"

It wasn't the most auspicious opening, but he was convinced she was waiting for him to say it. "I'd rather hoped with me . . . somewhere," he said. But he wasn't hoping so heartily as he had been hoping a few minutes back. It took him quite a while to adjust to the idea that he provided for Amy what Amy provided for him, a sort of relief that was almost comic.

4

"I had lunch with that Spencer girl today," he said after Mary had poured the coffee. "I gather that she is the one you had in mind."

Tom let the cover of the sugar bowl drop to the tray. "Good God, man. I would have given you credit for having more sense. Have you forgotten Meade?"

"What could I do? She collared me just as I was going into the Kup."

"Meade had lunch with a student," said Tom. "I suppose you've forgotten that."

"*I've a hunch it wasn't lunch*," said Mary, quoting from a jingle that had been popular at the time of Meade's dismissal from the university. "How did that go, Kit? I've been trying to remember the rest of it."

Gregory closed his eyes. "Let's see. . . . *It seems a very harmless clause, the one which says that naught but cause, can free us from this servitude. Means it sexy turpitude? Did Charlie Meade break moral laws, implicit in the phrase 'for cause'? I've a hunch it wasn't lunch, but talking pinko politics, not favored in the Tama sticks.*"

"Strange you can remember that so well," said Tom. He helped himself generously to the sugar. "I've always wondered who was responsible for that attempt to smear the administration."

"I may have got a line slightly mixed up here or there," said Gregory. There was no reason, at this late date, to claim or disclaim authorship of something Tom disliked so heartily, and anyway the creation had resulted from a collaboration. Kay Letting was as responsible for the verse as Gregory was, and certainly Kay was the one who had circulated it. During those tense days Kay would go around saying that she had heard the cutest little poem. Where had she picked it up? Oh, at a party somewhere.

"That misguided effort to whitewash Meade only proved how quickly some people lash out at any kind of authority. It certainly was well established that Meade had more than lunch with the girl."

"And it was never established that he didn't agree with Norton politically?" asked Mary.

"Norton's far too big a man to let political differences affect his interpretation of his position. As president of the university he's required to enforce its rules. When it became evident that Meade was carrying on with a student . . ."

"Well, I've no intention of carrying on with Miss Spencer," said Gregory. "I'll give my friend at the Kup a few instructions."

"I don't see why you eat in that dive," said Tom.

"It's close to the campus and the food isn't bad. Better than at Commons."

"Lord, I wouldn't expect a *dog* to eat at Commons."

"Then where would you suggest?" said Mary. "The Town Club?"

Tom set his coffee on the tray. "Mary, have you made a pact with yourself to be as disagreeable as possible? You're beginning to make me think the club's the only place I can have a moment's peace." He pulled himself out of the leather chair and stamped from the room.

The Town Club was known as Tower City's most exclusive organization for men. It was founded by Amy Prentiss' father, Old Jim Leveright, as a protest against the prices Lionel Bersbach was charging for meals at his hotel. This, of course, was before Old Jim's drugstores went into the food business. Toward the end of his life Old Jim used to make the rounds of his drugstore lunch counters and there were Tower City people still living who had heard him say, after finishing a Leveright Special, that he hoped it was clean, that certainly nothing else could be said for it. Poor Father, said Amy, really wasn't responsible for some years before he died. But in his bright period Old Jim set up the Town Club. At first the members met at the home of a widow who let them have a special table set a little apart from that of her regular boarders. There was no hoity-toity about membership; the group was limited only because the table space was limited.

When Leveright began to spend more time in Florida than in Tower City his club changed. A fine brick house was built and a staff of resident servants installed. The result was that the members had to pay a good deal more for their meals than the Bersbach Hotel had ever charged and so the matter of exclusiveness was brought in to take up the slack. It was said that Lionel Bersbach joined the Town Club only because he wanted to speak loudly in the dining room about the poor quality of the food; nevertheless he joined. For some years the club was a must for millionaires and a goal for all who aspired to become millionaires. The refined atmosphere became unbearable in 1930, though. Tower City was an industrial town, though the industrialists always referred to it as a college town and stressed its culture; but collegiate culture wasn't very satisfying when the Town Club's membership dropped to six. "Can you believe it, Kitty-pie?" said Amy. "It was heartbreaking. Six members! Naturally they couldn't carry on alone."

The six had two alternatives; they had either to sell the club house for a quarter of what it had cost or they had to let down the membership bars. "Jimmy was against both plans," said

Amy. "He wanted to carry on, but I couldn't see my way clear. He can't spend a nickel without my permission, you know. . . . " Nobody heeded the ineffectual Jimmy Leveright. The five who faced facts finally let down the membership bars; they let them way down—faculty men were admitted, even welcomed. One year the initiation fee was waived. That was the year Paul Peebles joined. His wife, he said, couldn't resist a bargain.

By the time Gregory and Tom were asked to join, the club had recovered enough to re-establish initiation fees. It took Mary a while to see that the attendant social prestige was worth the original cost and annual upkeep; Tom said she was the kind of person who would refuse an honorary degree if she had to pay for the hood. "The Town Club's a lot more Gown than it was in your father's time," he said. "A faculty man has to belong. Well, I don't blame Kit for not joining. It's a little steep for an assistant, but in my position I have obligations he doesn't have. Anyhow there's no sense in both of us joining. He can go as my guest whenever he wants to. I'll let you pay for your own food, old man, and so you must feel perfectly free . . ."

"You bet," said Gregory. He seldom went to the club with Tom, though. There was nothing strange about this. Men who had breakfast and dinner together naturally chose to lunch apart. Of course what seemed natural to you didn't always strike the other fellow as being free of hidden significance. Goldwater, also in the English department, told Gregory he lived in a dream world. Gregory considered Carl Goldwater's determination to seek out insults and rebuffs almost as wicked as the efforts of persons who tried to rouse public approval of such insults and rebuffs.

75

"Look, Carl, don't try any of your innuendoes about Tom on me. I live with Dawson, see. He's a friend of mine."

"In private, pal," said Goldwater. "Tell me, when were you last invited to join the club?"

"What's that got to do with it?"

"Tell me."

"Seems I used to get the card every year."

"Used to get." Goldwater smiled. "Did you get it this year?"

"I don't recall."

"Last year?"

"I may have. I don't remember. It never made any impression on me."

Goldwater nodded. "For the past two years Tom Dawson has been chairman of the admissions committee."

"You can cut that out, Carl. Tom knows I've no intention of joining. No sense in the club continuing to waste postage. . . ."

"Since you resent the specific, let's consider the general. I suppose you've noticed there have been fewer and fewer Jewish students in the past four or five years."

Gregory laughed. "Tom again?"

"Tom again—by which I mean persons of Tom's mentality. You've noticed the drop in the enrollment of Jewish students, haven't you?"

"Not particularly. You know, Carl, I've never been very good at spotting them unless they're named Cohen."

"It must be wonderful to have nothing on your mind but literature, beautiful literature. I envy you."

Everyone who came near Goldwater knew there was nothing very beautiful about the literature he had on his mind. Goldwater's position as a professional Jew was jeopardized by his resemblance to a Viking mother; only his surname assisted him in the matter of establishing himself as a Jew. Generally his claim was regarded as a sort of eccentricity to be compared with Paul Peebles' affection for the outlandish umbrella that had become his trademark. Most people laughed at Goldwater and said there was nothing wrong with him that a good dose of limelight wouldn't cure. Tom was among the few who were inclined to take Carl less lightly. Tom belonged to a minority of thinkers who said they took the realistic rather than the sentimental approach. "I never hesitate to speak frankly in Goldwater's presence," said Tom, but Gregory had noticed that whenever Tom started upon this frank speaking his face became somewhat rosy. But then so did Carl's. "Until Tom Dawson became chairman of admissions I received an invitation every year," Goldwater said to Gregory when they were speaking of the Town Club. "You received an invitation every year. But perhaps it's an economy program? Perhaps they need to save this six cents each year?"

Tom could always speak a little more frankly after Goldwater had left. "Trouble with that guy is that he's itching to wear a yellow arm-band," Tom said once after Goldwater had gone home and enabled the party to relax. "He's a born trouble maker."

"He looks like such an angel," said Mary. "He's really a very beautiful person. She's the one I'd take for the Jew in the family . . . such an unattractive woman. Oh, I'm sorry, Kit. I . . . of course I didn't mean anything. Heavens, you know me well enough to know I have no pattern ideas. Why, some of the most beautiful women in the world . . . your cousin, for instance."

This had been at the Lettings' house. Gregory saw that Kay

77

was looking at him, waiting for him to say something. "But they will wear high heels with slacks, won't they?" he said.

Tom slapped the arms of his chair. "*Touchée*, Mary. He's got you."

"I don't know what you mean," said Mary.

"He was quoting you, wasn't he, darling?" said Kay Letting.

"If Kit doesn't know that I'd be the last person in the world . . ."

"How depressing," said Gregory. "I often think about what a scramble there's going to be when all of you self-appointed last persons begin to jockey for the final position."

Tom frowned at him. Tom hated to see a party go sour. "That reminds me of a good one I heard at the club today," he said. He stopped frowning. Now he gave Gregory a friendly nod which meant that nobody appreciates a good Yiddish story as much as a Jew does. "It seems this Hebrew gentleman. . . ."

"Not in my house, if you please, Tom," said Kay.

That, said Mary on the way home, was the kind of attitude that was making life hard for Jews. "I simply can't bear Kay Letting," she said. "It seems to me that if you refuse to grant a people their right to be comical, you are denying them their right to equality. Don't you agree with me, Kit?"

"Of course, darling," he said. Life was so much simpler when you said of-course-darling to it.

He was a creature of habit, a victim of habit. As he grew up he formed the habit of thinking himself in no way different from his friends. After the disappointing discovery that being Jewish seemed not to alter his young life, he forgot about being a Jew. When he was older, when he went to larger communities he saw that many persons considered his Jewishness important. They didn't stress its undesirability; they merely stressed the

78

fact. It took him a long time to become accustomed to the inevitable reference and he never quite lost the feeling that something was expected of him, that he should perform a trick or tell a bright story to illustrate. When someone said maybe Kit, as a Jew, could throw some light on the subject, he felt as if he were in one of his recurring dreams. In those dreams he stood before a large class and couldn't think of anything to say. What did he think as a Jew? As a Jew what light could be shed? He was willing to co-operate, but his reaction to this as-a-Jew introduction was negative. He had the large dark eyes that he understood were considered typical, but was what he saw through those eyes different from what non-Jews saw? His friends had to tell him what he thought and saw and felt as a Jew.

He learned that the terse description carried a graphic picture in which his friends considered him an exceptional figure. If Kit didn't look it, they said, you'd never know he was a Jew. They appeared to think his face had played a foul trick on his character and that he was a regular in spite of his nose. He was glad not to be thought especially aggressive or greedy, but he wondered why he was supposed to be so grateful when assured he wasn't typical. It was a subject he gave little thought, though, so little that when he crossed the doorsill of the Town Club it never occurred to him that he was crossing a major social barrier.

It had happened last February. It was a fine day, the kind of day, said Ted Letting, that makes you forget that if spring comes, summer session's not far behind. "Now that it's safe to gripe, Kit," said Ted, "remember when we used to be afraid we wouldn't have a chance at the summer-school money?"

"I hear there is a move in the direction of a five-quarter year," said Paul Peebles. "Six, of course, in leap years."

Paul, Ted, and Gregory were on their way to the Town Club for lunch. Ted was to introduce a new course next quarter and Paul and Gregory were helping him with the outline. Today Paul had invited the younger men to have lunch with him to discuss possible textbooks.

The club house, three blocks from the campus, was set among careful plantings of evergreens which had recovered from wartime neglect. In the clean sunshine the Georgian house looked a perfect illustration of the Chamber of Commerce's motto: "Tower City, Where Hospitality Is More Than a Word."

When Gregory put his coat and hat on the counter the checkroom boy said it had been quite a while since he'd been around. "My most dependable host has been lunching at home," said Gregory.

Paul and Ted had started for the dining room. "Yes," said the boy. "He's not looking so good these days, is he? But you ought to come, Dr. Kitner. Close to school, and the finest cuisine in town, by which I mean the Kup, of course. But we've got more room, Doc. And no juke box. A great asset, they tell me. . . . Doc, do you think you could get me a job at the Kup? This place is driving me nuts. It's so damned quiet. If the Kup would just toss out one of those hostesses . . ."

"You're speaking of the girls I love."

"Well, if you hear of anything, Doc. I was thinking maybe a bowling alley, you know, somewhere I could study . . ."

Gregory and Ted and Paul stood for a moment at the top of the short flight of steps that led down into the dining room. Directly across the room, at a small table always reserved for him, was George Norton, president of Tamarack University. With him was John Trumball, vice-president and Dean of Faculties. The dean and a waiter were reading a menu to the president, but Norton seemed more interested in the new arrivals. Although the three newcomers nodded to him, the president made no response. It wasn't as if he were snubbing them; it was as if his thoughts were far away.

Peebles and his guests were nearing an empty table at the far end of the room when Trumball plucked at the host's sleeve. "Dr. Peebles, could I speak to you a moment?" Trumball's voice was quiet, respectful and solemn. Ted said that whenever he heard it he always expected to be told that his house had burned down.

"He sneaks up on you," said Ted when he took his place at the table, "but he never pounces. He just keeps sneaking. I wonder what he's biting Paul's ear about."

When Paul joined them he didn't say what Trumball had wanted. He picked up his glass, but before he got it to his lips he set it down again. Gregory and Ted studied their menus and pretended not to notice the splashed water or to hear the waiter who said he would get some more water directly and did the gentlemen wish him to change the cloth? "I'll spill more than water on it before we're finished," said Paul. "I am an old man with a tremor, sir. When you've been here longer you'll learn to avoid having to wait on me. Very messy."

"I'll have the liver," said Gregory.

"Omelet for me," said Ted, "but without the goo, please."

Paul said he would have the same. "Also without sauce, sir?" asked the waiter.

"Sauce? I see no mention of sauce. Broiled filet of sole."

"Oh, the sole, sir. Certainly, sir." The waiter gave Gregory

81

and Ted a look of commiseration. "And will the gentlemen have the soup du jour or . . ."

"Yes," said Paul. Then, raising his voice he added, "Go away."

It wasn't like Paul to speak that way to a waiter. Gregory looked up in surprise, but then he understood. Trumball had come up and now was standing just behind the confused waiter. As chairman of a department Paul may have had a perfect right to blat out at the Dean of Faculties, but it wasn't a very politic thing to do. The waiter, so new to the club that one doubted if he could find the way to the kitchen, appeared to think he was obliged to straighten out the tangle. "I believe he means you, sir," he said to Trumball.

Later on, when the furor about the serious aspect of that luncheon had died down, the humorous side was preserved. Among the rougher elements of the faculty "I believe he means you, sir" and the one about the soup being hot became popular tag lines.

"I wish to speak to Dr. Kitner," said Trumball.

Gregory rose. "Certainly."

"Dr. Kitner is my guest," said Paul as he got up. "Anything you have to say to him just now will be said in my presence."

"It's quite all right," Gregory told the waiter. "Just go along and get the soup. . . . Must be a new man. Very nervous. What was it you wanted to say, Dean Trumball?"

"You make it very awkward, Dr. Peebles," said the Dean.

"That was my intention," said Paul.

"Dr. Kitner, I deeply regret that Dr. Peebles has forced me to come directly to you. I'd hoped to avoid the embarrassment, the . . . er . . . mutual embarrassment, but I am forced to inform you that this is a private club."

82

Now Ted was on his feet. He slung his napkin down and forgot to use the library-voice considered suitable for these surroundings. "Anything you say goes for me too. I'm not a member."

"Please, Dr. Letting. I'm speaking to Dr. Kitner, if you please."

"I damned well don't please," shouted Ted.

"Dr. Kitner is my guest," said Paul. His voice was stern. "Now if you will excuse us, Dean Trumball."

Trumball's face was red but he didn't budge. "I must insist that Dr. Kitner leave," he said.

Thinking that in a perverted way Trumball had courage, Gregory raised a hand to keep Paul and Ted from taking over. "I have ordered a meal which will be charged to Dr. Peebles," he said, trying not to show the excruciating shame he felt for Norton and Trumball. "I intend to eat that lunch, you know."

"The charge will not be made," said Trumball. "Dr. Kitner, I regret this more than I can say, but I have no alternative."

"Neither you nor Norton is an official of this club," said Paul. "Gentlemen, I believe the waiter is coming with our soup. Kindly be seated."

"Of all the damned . . ."

"Please, Ted. No further reference to this unfortunate interruption." Paul spoke as if Trumball had vanished. "You were wondering about the advisability of using the Grimes text. In my opinion. . ."

Trumball leaned toward Gregory. "Dr. Kitner, I'm very sorry, but I must insist . . ."

The waiter gave him a slight push. "The soup, sir. Very hot, sir." The threat was obvious.

Trumball returned to Norton. The sudden rise of the sound

83

of talking made Gregory realize how quiet the dining room had been a moment before. It wasn't amazing that twenty-odd diners could be silent for several minutes, but it was startling to hear what a racket they could make when they put their backs to it. "I'm not sure I would use the Grimes. . . ."

A few days later Gregory confessed to Ted that he had spoken against a book he wasn't familiar with. "Never heard of it myself," said Ted. "I don't think Paul had either, but it was better than saying Smith. For a minute there I was afraid he'd have a stroke. Frankly, I wasn't sure of myself. You were cool enough. How could you take it, Kit? I would have gone over and punched Norton in the snoot."

"No, you wouldn't have."

"Well," said Ted, "I suppose if I'd been conditioned to that sort of thing since childhood . . ."

Gregory had few outstanding memories of his childhood. He recalled Prancing Beauty, a lazy fat pony, and generations of dogs, rabbits, turtles and snakes that he and Charlie raised and fought over. He and Charlie fished together in Indian Creek where, stringing worms for bluegills, you made great catches of crawdads; he and Charlie started to build innumerable tree houses and played at being cowboys and went swimming. . . . Incredibly Charlie, once champion swimmer of the gravel-pit gang, drowned during landing operations off the coast of France, not in the First World War, in the Second, the one you'd have said he was too old for. . . .

There were memories of school, of Sunday school, of playing at the store. Before his assistance was of any value Gregory was ardent about helping Papa. Marvelously conceited, he got in everyone's way and glowed righteously when patted on the head and told he was a born merchant. "Ham, I guess there's no doubt about who's going to fill your shoes," the head-patters said. But Ham Kitner was still filling his shoes, thank you, and he intended to keep on filling them another ten or fifteen years. There was no undercurrent of disappointment in his voice when he spoke of his son's failure to take a permanent job at the store. "I've no wish to end my days pitching horseshoes at some rest cure in Florida," he would say. "The store's not big enough for two bosses, and anyway I was never able to forget the time you sold Jed Clupp the best suit in the place. Ten dollars. I'd just stepped out a minute and when I came back you would have thought we'd struck oil, the way you were carrying on and waving that money around. Ten ones he gave you. He'd tried to make you take a ten-spot, but you were too foxy for that. Well, Jed let me squirm a couple of days before he came in and paid the difference. Ham, he said to me not long before he died, do you recollect the time your Greg sold me a suit for ten dollars? I figured to learn you and him both a good lesson, he said, but I don't reckon I done him any good. It's too dang bad about that boy, Ham, he said, off teaching school that way."

Papa liked that story. He was insufferably proud of Gregory's profession. Mama said his bragging bored her to death. When Mama said she was bored, she meant she was embarrassed beyond mortification. "He's got half of Seyno keeping your books on the parlor table," she said. "I tell him folks don't want to read textbooks, but he just says it will do them good."

When people asked Papa why his son hadn't come into the store he said that luckily his son had been able to choose his occupation. "Me," he would say, "I didn't have that chance. My father heard that this Seyno store was for sale for about all

85

he cared to invest in me, and since it was cheaper than setting me up on a farm . . . I was willing enough. I knew a good deal about plowing and milking and so I was willing to try keeping a store for a while. I got to liking it real well and the Mrs. liked living in town where she could crack her heels down on a sidewalk. . . . Gregory had plenty of opportunity to try his hand at the business, but somehow he never took to it. You should have asked Jed Clupp why."

Gregory had no real memory of having sold Jed Clupp a suit for ten dollars, but he had heard the story so often that it was almost the same as remembering. He did remember one thing that happened at the store way back and that memory was not jogged by reminiscing conversations. He couldn't say the memory had ever hung around his neck like a millstone; all he could say was that he remembered the day a drunken farmhand tried to get Papa to sell him a pair of pants at half price. . . . If I were an artist I could draw a picture of that farmhand. I remember exactly what he looked like. I remember that the stubble on his chin was grey and that after he went away, went away saying he would get Papa if it was the last thing he ever did, Papa said, "Poor old fellow. It's hard for a man to reach that age and still not have his own patch. But you don't dare give him anything or he just drinks that much more. . . ."

Seyno hadn't changed much over the years. Seynoites read out-of-town newspapers now and listened to the radio, but the more they learned of the outside the more they admired their own little village. We don't do things that way in Seyno, was the general conclusion Gregory heard every time he was at home. After the Town Club incident he said something to his parents about anti-Semitism. He had no intention of telling them about that day at the club, but he had a feeling he should prepare them for something he might not be able to keep from them. "There's no doubt about it," he said. "There's much more anti-Semitism in this country now than there was before the war."

"You've been listening to communistic propaganda," said his mother. "You don't need to think I'm going to listen to your wild talk."

"There are always some loud-mouths who like to blabber," said his father. "Just ignore them, I say. That's the one thing they can't bear. Pay no attention to them and they'll shut up soon enough."

"I wouldn't know about Tower City," said Mama. "But there's no one like that in Seyno. Gregory, if you'd go to church more, you wouldn't have so much time to listen to communistic talk."

"I go to church," he said.

"Well, then," she said, as if that settled the matter.

But was Seyno so well insulated? As a rule Gregory paid no attention to his mother's chatter about her church work, but that spring he found himself listening to her and he noticed that his father was listening. Mama had been browbeaten into accepting the presidency of the women's society at the church. No one in his right mind could have thought Mama a suitable executive. She had never been known to be able to make out a grocery list without bringing quite extraneous comments into it. Her letters were confusing mixtures of reminders to herself, quotations and gossip. She was a most likable woman, but even those who loved her couldn't deny that she was scatter-brained. It looked to Gregory as if the Methodist ladies of Seyno were in for a hectic year.

"Funny goings-on at the church here lately," his father said to him when they were going to the store. "Some new people here in town with big ideas, I guess. Kind of hard for our folks to cotton to them. Generally I wouldn't notice what the ladies were up to, but it got around to me that this new member doesn't think your mother ought to have a job in the society."

"Sound thinking," said Gregory.

"Well," said Papa, "it seems she thinks a Christian church ought to be run by gentiles, and I guess that made some of the ladies get up on their hind legs and decide to show her. Don't say anything to your mother about it. She hasn't caught on. The preacher was talking to me about it. . . ."

Gregory was six years old when he found out about being a Jew. He was in first grade, but if the teacher knew he was Jewish she didn't think it important enough to teach him along with the alphabet. He never learned anything in school about being Jewish.

Saturday mornings when the weather was unfavorable to activities with Charlie, Gregory would help at the store. One Saturday morning, when he was helping by making faces at himself in the large three-way mirror, he heard an argument; a man was shouting that the price was double what he would pay and Papa was saying he was sorry, but he couldn't lower it. Then the man called Papa an exciting new word. Charlie and Gregory were collecting swear words. Yesterday Charlie had contributed *Adam's off-ox* and crossed his heart to die if his father hadn't said his mother was as slow as that. Now Gregory had a good one to spring on Charlie. "Sheenie, sheenie," he whispered to the glass. The word had a snake-like charm missing in Adam's off-ox.

After dinner his mother overheard him trying the new word on the current puppy and she asked what on earth he was call-

88

ing that dog. "It's what the drunk man called Papa," he said

"It's a bad word," said Mama. "I don't want you saying it again. It isn't a word that is used in polite society."

No one could pretend that Charlie Riley's society was polite and so Gregory hadn't a qualm about promising and then running over to the Rileys' back yard. "Ya, sheenie," he hailed Charlie. "It's my word and you can't have it."

Presently both boys were crying sheenie as they wrestled in the wet grass. Everything was going splendidly until Jack Riley came to spoil the fun. Jack was in high school and he considered himself the whole cheese. "What's that you're calling Greg, you little snot-nose?" he said when he snatched Charlie up from the ground.

"It's my word," said Gregory. "He snitched it."

"Sheenie," squalled Charlie.

Jack smacked his brother hard on the mouth and the outraged Charlie kicked Jack's shins and yelled that Gregory had started it. "Why don't you hit him? He started it."

"It's all right for him because he is," said Jack, "but you leave me ketch you calling him that again and I'll whale the liver outa you."

When Gregory asked his mother to explain Jack's peculiar ruling she said she guessed it was time for Papa to have a little talk with him. Mr. Riley had already had a little talk with Charlie, a very dumb talk if you asked Charlie. "Zif I never seen that calf borned at your gramp's farm," he had said when reporting the lecture.

But Papa Kitner's little talk had nothing to do with birds and bees. Gregory learned he was a Jew, the polite-society way of saying sheenie. Papa apparently hadn't known about the far politer society way of always putting an ish on the end. Papa said the word Jew as if it didn't bother him to say it, but he said the explanation was difficult. "You see, Gregory, Jews aren't a race or a nationality. For centuries all they've had to hold them together is a religion and, you see, none of your people are religious."

"Why, Papa! Mama goes to church every Sunday."

He had been speaking of another church, explained Papa. He admitted he didn't go to church as regularly as Mama did, but even so he said he considered himself a Christian. Gregory would have liked to interrupt to ask why he didn't go to the Christian church, but he was stopped by the memory of how cross a similar question had made his Sunday-school teacher. That woman kept on calling them little Christians even though she surely must have known they were Methodists. "All Methodists are Christians, Gregory," she had said, "but all Christians aren't Methodists. Some of them go to the church that calls itself the Christian church, but of course we all know that that church across the street isn't any more Christian than ours. In fact we are Methodists because we think our church is more Christian than the others." When Gregory said that wasn't why he was a Methodist, that he was a Methodist because his Mama and Papa were Methodists, the teacher said that would be enough out of him for one day. He hadn't intended to annoy her, but when he saw that he had accomplished what was always the chief ambition of each boy in the class he was glad. However, as he had never had a special desire to irritate his father he let that about Christians go by.

"We are Christian Jews," said Papa, probably meaning Methodist Jews. "People with more education than I've had might say this is impossible, but for the time being I think it's the easiest way for you to understand it. It's something like the

90

Rileys being Protestants. Some people think all Irishmen are Catholics, but they aren't. When people say you're a Jew they mean it's something like Charlie being Irish, something that doesn't make any difference to an American boy. We talk about where our ancestors came from because, unless we're Indians, all of us came from some other country originally. Charlie's grandfather came from Ireland."

"Did Gramp come from Jew-land?"

"No, he was born right on his farm, in a log cabin that was torn down when I was a boy. Your grandfather's father and mother came from Germany. They were the ones who cleared the farm and built that cabin where Gramp was born. Your mother's people came from France and Switzerland."

"But you said I'm a Jew, Papa. Ain't I?"

"Don't say ain't. Yes, most people would call you a Jew even though you don't happen to belong to a Jewish religion, but it's nothing to get excited about, one way or another. If your great-grandparents had settled where there had been other Jews, I doubt if they would have taken up with a different religion. I never heard them say why they became Protestants, but you can be pretty sure it was just because their neighbors were Protestants. If they'd settled in a Catholic community you'd probably be a Catholic."

"Not me," said Gregory. "I wouldn't be no Cat-licker."

His father shook his head. "When you're older I hope you'll learn a little sense. You don't know anything about Catholicism and you don't know anything about Judaism. And precious little about Protestantism, I'd say."

"I'm a Jew, though," said Gregory. "You said so."

"You don't need to act so smarty about it. It's no more to your credit that your ancestors were Jews than it's to your credit that your folks are Methodists, nor is it to your discredit. From what I recall, my grandparents didn't stew around very much about any kind of religion. Your grandparents have had more time for churchifying. Sometimes I think you can run a thing like that into the ground, but if what I hear about the way you act in Sunday school's true you aren't in any danger of doing that. You learned your lesson for tomorrow?"

"But, Papa, why'd you tell Jack and not me? It wasn't fair."

"I didn't tell Jack anything."

"He knew it."

"Oh, that. Gregory, I didn't tell Jack. Everyone knows we're Jews. I certainly am sorry I didn't talk to you about it before. You quit thinking it's something special. It doesn't make any difference whether a boy goes to a Jewish Sunday school or a Catholic Sunday school or a Methodist or any kind or no kind."

"No kind?" That was an attractive possibility.

"Yes, no kind," said his father. He wasn't looking at Gregory now and his voice sounded more like the one he used when he was talking to Mama. "There are some people who prefer to keep their religion a private matter. Most people like to do things in groups, though. It's all right, so long as you don't get the idea your group's better than another group." He looked down at Gregory again. "All that counts is behaving yourself and living in peace with your neighbors. . . . Now you better learn your Bible verse before your mother gets after you."

Evidently if he didn't fight with Charlie, being a Jew would not change Gregory's life. It was like the first time you heard there was no Santa Claus. At the start of Papa's talk you had thought maybe you were heir to a throne, that maybe you would have to start right away for the Enchanted Forest. There was but one consolation; you didn't have to let Charlie know there was nothing special about being a Jew. On the way to Sunday school the next day Gregory bragged, but Charlie didn't rise to the bait. Charlie was very subdued. Nice people, he said, didn't talk about what Gregory was talking about.

"Well, my Papa does," said Gregory. He always itched to fight when he was wearing his best clothes.

Charlie wouldn't fight. He said it was different for Gregory's father to talk about it. "Jack told on me," he said. "Mama says I got to say I'm sorry because you can't help it. She says it's like niggers."

Gregory thought about the only Negro he had ever seen, a giant of a man who had come with the carnival. He sat over a tub of water and people threw balls at him and if they hit the right place the nigger fell in the water. Gregory had begged his father to let him try, but Papa said he didn't approve. Papa didn't care if the nigger did like it and smiled all the time, even when he was coming out of the water and crawling back on the plank. The nigger yelled at Papa, "What's the matter with you? Scared?" Naturally Gregory had been ashamed.

He looked down at his Sunday-clean hands and wondered what Charlie's mother had meant. "Papa said it's like you being a Methodist."

"Huh?"

"That's what he said."

Charlie laughed. "Gee, they don't know much, do they?"

Restored to common ground the two boys played chasey the rest of the way to the church. If Gregory's blood cried out for Jerusalem and Charlie's for Rome, neither boy recognized the call. In Sunday school they raised their shrill voices in a gay tune whose words confidently acknowledged the love of Jesus.

93

On the lapel of his best suit each wore the gold star awarded for attendance based solely on physical presence.

As time went on, sometimes remembering that he was a Jew Gregory reread lines he found here and there in books. He decided religious Jews were funny folks like Dunkards and that it was a good thing his people had dropped out of the religion. The Kitners were the only Jews living in Seyno, but that cut no ice with anyone. Oh, there was a Sunday-school teacher who embarrassed Gregory when he was around twelve years old. This teacher said that when Jesus went to the temple he looked just like Gregory Kitner. The class tittered and afterwards some of the boys teased him, but inasmuch as they were good little Methodists and fearful of taking the Name in vain or in any way at all they didn't do this loudly or long. Until his second year in college he would have said that being a Jew neither helped nor handicapped him. There were certain words he couldn't use because his use of them would have been uncomfortable for polite society, but they were words which had no appeal for him after he had progressed beyond the age of six.

5 Seyno was a great State-University town. When Gregory was a boy not many Seyno-ites went to college, but those who did go usually chose State. At State most of the Seyno boys joined the Sigma Gamma fraternity; Seyno was a great Sig town. All through high school Gregory and Charlie considered themselves Sig pledges and they jeered when Jack said maybe they wouldn't get their bids. That Jack, always trying to put on the dog. Why, the fall Gregory and Charlie entered State, Jack came back to the university and acted as if he had to guide them around, as if they couldn't have made Sig without his assistance. "The boob hasn't got a sense of humor," said Charlie. "Just because he made a couple of touch-downs he thinks the chapter's still eating out of his hand. My kid brother and my kid brother's best friend . . ." Charlie imitated his brother's loud voice. "Greg, I hope you appreciate being introduced as Jack Riley's kid brother's best friend."

"How could I miss? Seems like he's paying more attention to me than he is to you."

"I guess he figures I look enough like him to get by on my beauty. It's a doggone shame his boss was so big-hearted. He says he's going to stay until after pledging. He keeps saying that to the Sigs, do you notice? Like a threat or something."

During rushing Gregory and Charlie managed to elude Jack once or twice; they visited other fraternity houses, but really only to torment Jack. They had been sold on Sigma Gamma long before they ever saw a non-Seyno Sig. Why, they knew the grip when they were in seventh grade, though not from the saintly Jack, of course.

After he had been in college a few weeks Gregory found out that there were two Jewish fraternities on campus. It was the dumbest thing he'd ever heard of. He saw nothing dumb about boys becoming Sigs because they were from Sig strongholds, but he thought it was crazy for a bunch to get together simply because they were Jews. When he asked Charlie if he had heard about those two fraternities Charlie said yes. "Maybe they're all orthodox," said Gregory. "Maybe it's on account of the food. Must be. Otherwise there couldn't be any point to it."

When he learned what the Jewish pins looked like Gregory studied the wearers and discovered that Jews didn't necessarily resemble his relatives. The variations in coloring and feature and general build astounded him. He'd thought that Jews looked like Jews, in other words that they looked like the Kitners or the Ginsbergs. The conglomeration gathered together under the Jewish insignia convinced him there was even less foundation to the Jewish claim than his father had said. He grinned when he thought how surprised Papa would be if he saw some of these fellows that looked like Swedes and claimed to be Jews, or at any rate belonged to Jewish clubs. He didn't think about the Jewish fraternities long. Their houses were at the other end of the campus and he didn't become acquainted with any of the Jews. Nobody ever mentioned them to him and so he forgot about them.

The following year he learned that his pledging Sig had not been automatic; he learned that Jack Riley had had reason to come back to the fraternity house to throw his weight around, that the chapter had been very leery of pledging Kitner. Sig chapters, he learned, had been suspended for less. The boys treated Gregory fine. He never would have known about his pledging difficulty if it hadn't been for Alden King, plus the fact that Charlie couldn't keep his mouth shut. Charlie was developing into being a great talker. In addition to becoming

96

a great talker he was becoming a great radical and of course was always on the lookout for something to be radical about.

Alden King's name was read off at chapter meeting the fall of Charlie's and Gregory's sophomore year. The name was read, there was no comment, and then the next name on the list of rushees was discussed. Gregory saw nothing odd about the quick disposal of Alden King; he'd met King and hadn't craved him for a brother. But after the meeting Charlie fumed that he didn't like this keeping important matters from discussion. "I expected you to speak up for the guy, Gregory."

"What guy?"

"King. I felt it was your place to say we shouldn't drop him without even saying why."

"I don't see where I come in. It's obvious nobody thought much of him and so why talk about him?"

"We talked about a lot of others nobody thought much of. We should have talked about King on principle. I wish I'd said something to you before."

"But where do I come in?"

"Well, he's a Jew, Gregory."

Gregory didn't move away from Charlie physically or mentally, but something inside of him grew small and tight. Charlie went on talking. He was all for throwing his clover into the ash can. Alden King was a pain in the neck and so why didn't the fellows say so? Were they scared Gregory would try to cram him down their throats just because he was a Jew? "Jack told them last year. My God, didn't they believe him? He told them they didn't need to think you'd try to turn the chapter into a synagogue. Do they think you and King are twins or something, just because you both happen to be Jews?"

"I didn't know he was a Jew, Charlie."

"You didn't? Gee whiz, then I take it back. I thought it was funny you didn't say anything. I thought you'd say it was all right with you if they didn't want him."

"How'd you know? That he's a Jew, I mean."

"Why, I don't know. . . . Maybe someone told me. Must have. Of course you can't tell. . . . Greg, let's pull out of this bunch of snobs."

"And prove they were right to be afraid of me? No, thanks, not when we've got the best cook on campus." That was how you did it; you laughed it off. For the first time Gregory experienced the minority's sense of exclusiveness, the minority's sense of protection from general understanding; it was a feeling that masqueraded rather convincingly as one of security. He spent days feeling special and even after he got tired of feeling special he knew he was the only Sig who could sympathize with the lone Catholic in the chapter. That Catholic was bitter about the boys having blackballed a friend of his. Once at dinner he said he guessed the boys were afraid he and Kitner would take over the chapter. "It's an idea, Greg," he said. "What do you think?"

"Wouldn't have it as a gift," said Gregory. That was the right answer. The boys laughed. Well, Charlie didn't laugh. Charlie knew that Gregory's young cousin Bruce Ginsberg was coming to State next year. "We'll see," Gregory had said when he and Charlie talked about Bruce's chances. "If the boys don't take Brucie, well, they'll be relieved of their only Jew. Jack was wrong, Charlie. He was wrong when he guaranteed I wouldn't act like a human being. They've got to take Brucie or else. He's a decent, smart kid and if I'm good enough for Sig, so's he."

The war, however, prevented the young cousin from taking the Sig test. Brucie went to Europe and didn't come back.

98

Charlie and Gregory got no farther than Hoboken. Afterwards Gregory returned to State. Charlie, having had enough of formal education, went to New York City where he married a woman who, according to Seyno gossip, was as black as the ace of spades. There was no denying that Florence Riley had Negro blood, but her skin was a creamy coffee color that Gregory thought very beautiful. Sometimes when he visited Charlie and Florence he wondered if his friend's being reared to treat a Jewish boy as a brother was what started Charlie on the road to ruin. There was never any doubt in Seyno about Charlie's ruin. His mother said as far as she was concerned her Charles was dead, and there were few in Seyno who could blame her.

Tolerance wasn't the word for what Charlie had; Charlie had got so he just didn't see things the way most people saw them. Gregory thought Florence charming and lovely, but he was never able to forget that she was a Negro. He was under the impression that Florence herself was never able to forget it and that like his mother she felt that the mixed marriage was immoral. Florence's ancestors had played hopscotch on the color line, and she had a sister who had "passed." When Florence's children began to grow up she told Gregory her biggest worry was that some day they might try to pass. "It scares me," she said. "They look like white children, but they aren't. Charlie says it doesn't make any difference, but Charlie . . . well, he thinks different."

Like Florence, Mrs. Kitner thought the marriage was against God. Mama Kitner said Charlie wouldn't go against God on purpose, but that he had, just the same. She talked about the little birds in the yard and how they got along without mixing colors. "Suppose I decide to marry a non-Jewish girl," said

99

Gregory. "It looks as if I'll have to unless I marry a relative. I don't know any other Jewish girls. Angelina would suit me to a T, but . ."

"Gregory, she's your first cousin!"

"But I don't know any Jewish girls who aren't my cousins. I suppose if I marry a gentile you'll give me a sermon about the little birds."

"Don't be flippant," said Mama. "Jews are white and you know it. What Charlie did was against God. If the Lord hadn't wanted some of the people to be black he wouldn't have made them black, would he? I don't like the way you joke about poor Charlie and the mess he's in. His own mother making out that he's dead . . ."

After Charlie really was dead Gregory went to call on Mrs. Riley. "Gregory," the woman said, "my boy Charles has been dead over twenty years. I've grieved for him ever since."

"I just wanted to tell you that I went east as soon as I got the word. I thought you'd like to know that Jack's looking after Florence and the children. I thought he might not mention it to you."

"I'm sure he wouldn't. There's no reason for Jack to tell me about what he may be doing for strangers. Jack's charities are his own business."

"She's a strong character," Gregory told his mother afterwards. "I feel sorry for Mr. Riley."

"Land, yes," said Mama. "She's never once let him smoke his cigar in the house." She sniffed. "Lace-curtain Irish."

The daughter of the gentle failure who rotted away in Classical Languages was the one who most frequently reminded

Gregory he was Jewish. Mary adored having a Jewish friend; she was always careful to use the polite ending.

Almost the instant he sat down in the Dawsons' little apartment that Sunday evening fifteen years ago, his new friend's wife asked him if he were religious. Tom had prepared him for a poor cook, but not for a religious fanatic. "When I'm at home," said Gregory, "that is, in Seyno, I always go to church. I go here fairly regularly, but the service is a little fancy for a country boy."

"You mean your . . . church at home is the reformed?"

Why is it, he was thinking, that the unendurable hostesses are the ones who never give you a cocktail? Mind, I can get through an evening without liquor, but the ones who don't need to have the edges softened are the only ones you can count on. First glimpse of Mrs. Dawson had been reassuring, but now that she was craning her neck and looking like one of these crusading women . . . well, he wished he had had a drink before coming. "I don't know much about religious technicalities," he said, "but I suppose you could call the church at home low. I've never heard Methodists use the terms high and low, but I suppose . . ."

"Methodist!" said Mrs. Dawson. "You don't mean you're a Methodist! How in the world did that ever happen?"

"Mary, a man's religion is his own affair," said Tom.

"Why, Tom, it hardly ever is. It's almost always the way he grew up."

"Certainly I never had any choice in the matter," said Gregory. "It was different in the case of my parents."

Mrs. Dawson leaned forward. "Yes?"

He wondered if she were always so vivacious. If she could act this way about his church affiliation, what energy she might give something halfway interesting! "My mother's people were Baptists and my father's were Presbyterian. Both very hardshell. My mother said the only way to have harmony between the in-laws was for her and Papa to make everyone mad. There were only two churches functioning in Seyno at the time anyway, and since the Christian church was without a minister . . ." Somewhere during this speech he had caught on. Mrs. Dawson had expected him to be a religious Jew. He was reminded of the time a marriageable, oh, for ten years that poor girl had been marriageable, young woman ran to catch him on Main Street in Seyno. "Oh, Gregory," she said, "I hear you're just back from Europe." When he had said no, he was just back from Hoboken, she seemed unable to think of anything else to say. She had looked as if a whole plan of attack had been thwarted, just the way this Mrs. Dawson was looking.

"Well, being a Methodist," said Tom, "you won't refuse a drink, will you? I never knew one who would. Name your poison—anything you say, bourbon and water, bourbon and gingerale, bourbon and sparkling water, bourbon. . . ."

"My husband fancies himself a humorist, Dr. Kitner," said Mrs. Dawson. She smiled at Gregory, but it was plain that he had let her down badly.

When they became good friends she often laughed about what a blow it was when he turned out to be a Methodist. She thought his being a Methodist was terribly funny, after she got used to it. She never seemed to think his being a Sig was very funny, but perhaps she never got used to that. Not knowing Jack Riley she couldn't be expected to understand how that miracle had been effected, and somehow Gregory never felt obliged to explain. "Oh, Seyno's in Sig territory," he'd said.

Mary didn't discover the Sig affiliation that first Sunday. It

102

was some weeks later when he was at the Dawson apartment for another Sunday evening. Mary was playing the piano. She played by ear, not too badly. When she began "Mother of Men" Gregory sang along with her. He had a fair tenor voice and in spite of his tendency to change keys with each phrase he liked to sing. "How did you happen to know those words?" she asked when she turned from the piano after the ending which she had failed to give the reverence intended by the wretched composers.

"I'm afraid I wrote them."

"But why?"

"As I recall it had something to do with a licking. I think Skinny Taylor and I would have taken the licking if we'd known what a future was in store for our hymn. You see, each of us had to concoct some sort of offering and so Skinny and I. . . ."

"You mean you're a Sig! But you don't wear a pin."

"Of course he doesn't," said Tom. "Undergraduate stuff. These old grads who keep on with that rah-rah stuff give me a pain. Kit, you know that Johnson in the department? Did you read that about him? He's going to address a gang of Betas on 'Beta Theta Pi Looks Ahead.' Makes me want to throw up."

Professor Dawson's stomach was steadier later on; later on he addressed a gang of Sigs on "Sigma Gamma Looks Ahead." Of course, as any Sig could tell you, Sigma Gamma had something to look ahead to, once it took its chapter out of a school where it had deteriorated to the extent of trying to pledge a Negro.

But if Mary had little to say about his fraternal ties, she didn't neglect Gregory's religious originality. "I can't tell you what I went through, getting that first meal," she would say.

103

"I expected you to ask me if everything was kosher. I'd walked my feet off to find kosher corned beef, and then you turned out to be just another person."

"I know how you felt," said Gregory once. "When I was five my father took me to Chicago to see the Cubs play. I'll never forget my disappointment. I'd been looking forward to seeing those cubs. . . ."

"But I wasn't really disappointed in you, Kit. I mean, after we got to know you. But I'd never known a Jewish person and I thought it would be such an experience. But how funny! I just now got it. You mean you thought they would be little bears playing baseball? That's darling."

He gathered that after Mary forgave him for not providing her with more experience she considered him rather darling too. . . .

Once Goldwater shoved a newspaper at him and asked if he could be complacent about that photograph. It was a picture of wedding rings picked up at one of the concentration camps, the kind of picture that makes a far deeper impression than those which leave nothing to the imagination. "Yes, I saw it," Gregory said.

"How you can shrug it off beats me," said Goldwater.

"I can't shrug it off, Carl, but at the same time I can't separate it from the rest of the world. I can't feel that one particular group is the only one that matters."

"So you sit on your tail and do nothing."

"I teach school."

"I suppose you think you're saving civilization by teaching appreciation of English literature."

"Can you think of a more effective occupation for me?"

"By God, they get a lot more than English from me. They

think I'm teaching an introduction to Lit, do they? I'm intro-
ducing these smug young aristocrats to a hell of a lot more
than literature."

"And maybe a hell of a lot less."

"Oh, go bob your nose. There's nothing that gripes my guts
more than a Jew who's turned against his own. Why don't you
have your face worked on and be done with it? Your movie-
actress cousin did, didn't she?"

6 "It's from the *president's* office," said Miss
Chester after she handed Gregory the letter
Friday morning. She seemed to expect him
to take the letter from his pocket then and
to tear it open and perhaps read it aloud to her.

"Yes," he said. "I noticed."

He went to his ten-o'clock. After class he shut himself in
his office to work until lunch. He'd been grading papers for
about an hour when he broke his pencil. A search of the desk
produced a large supply of pencils, but none with an unbroken
point. He would take them all down to Paul's sharpener at
noon. In the meantime . . . surely there was a pencil in one
of his pockets. There was. Also there was the letter.

Rumblings of dissatisfaction among the faculty had stepped
up Trumball's production. Each week brought a new form
letter "from the President's office." The institutional promotion
program emphasized the fact that Education, a synonym for
Tamarack University, was facing her greatest challenge: Now
when it is our turn to prove to our returned heroes that we
too can make sacrifices . . . Now when our great University
stands like a beacon for a civilization hesitating at the crossroads,
it is most heartening to observe the sacrificial spirit of our
illustrious faculty. . . .

Today's chit, however, wasn't to My Dear Fellow Colleague.
It was a personal letter. The salutation hadn't been typed in a
space left by a mimeograph. Dictated by JHT to mp this direct
communication stated that in accordance with the agreement
between Dr. Kitner and the University, his contract was automatically terminated as of Section A, clause 1. To enable him
to bring his affairs to an orderly close, actual severance would
not take place until one week from today. . . . Stupidly

Gregory glanced at his calendar to see if the date given in the letter were correct. It was. He reread the letter.

Section A, clause 1? . . . *to free us from this servitude, only sexy turpitude* . . . "The devil!" he shouted.

He ran down the stairs, but when he reached Burnaby's first floor a student's "Where's the fire, Doc?" slowed him to a less conspicuous speed. He had no plan, no thought beyond that of wishing to take Trumball and Norton and knock their heads together. Of all the asinine, unwarranted . . .

Administration was a handsome building named in honor of Billy Hathaway. Old Administration, where Billy had had his office, had been moved to the north end of the campus where it now served as tool shed and catch-all for the Department of Grounds. Hathaway Hall was a gem which indicated the direction Tamarack would go when materials became abundant enough to permit realization of the wonderful painting that hung in Hathaway's entrance hall. New Campus would be Gothic Moderne, executed in Indiana limestone mellowed, at any rate in the picture, by English ivy in rich shades of Morocco leather. Leveright Chapel, Tama's only other building-of-the-future, wasn't nearly so chapelesque as Administration.

There was an elevator for this two-storied masterpiece, but Gregory didn't bother with that; he took the steps of the curving staircase two at a time. He'd been on the second floor of Hathaway once before. Twelve years ago . . .

As a rule, and a highly cherished rule, an instructor came to Tamarack on a three-year contract. The rule was that the man was either dropped or promoted at the end of his probationary period. At the close of their apprenticeship Tom and Gregory were summoned to Trumball's office where they were greeted with a confusing mixture of sorrow and joy. In a way, said the dean, he had splendid news for them; in another way perhaps not quite so splendid. But if it were a disappointment for them, think what it was for the university! They could stay on, bless them, but they couldn't have any more money. "We've had considerable discussion about this, pro and con," said Trumball. "Nothing personal in the con, I'm happy to say. It's just that we hesitate to break rules. Bad precedent, you know. The three-year rule is quite rigid and yet, when no funds are available and when the work is satisfactory . . . We've been placed in a predicament by you two gentlemen, you know, but we agree with Dr. Peebles that it would be foolhardy to drop you even though it does mean a certain relaxing of . . ."

Tom, who for more than a year had been extremely restive under the belittling title of instructor, interrupted to ask if they couldn't be given the titular advancement even if it were necessary to delay the salary increase. The dean was shocked. "That would never do, Dr. Dawson," he said. "Dear, no."

"What made me think of it," said Tom, "was . . . well, thinking about Lieutenant Forbes, in R.O.T.C., you know. Well, he draws Captain's pay, I understand, and so I was thinking that maybe something like that, only in reverse . . ."

"Dear me, Dr. Dawson, this isn't the Army." Trumball raised his eyes. "Thank heaven."

Afterwards Tom said he hoped Trumball wouldn't pass that remark of his along to Norton. "I blurted it out without thinking," he said. "I was so bowled over. God, it knocked the wind out of me. Three years and no increase. But of course he's dead right."

"About what?"

"They can't go breaking rules right and left. Keeping us on

is quite a concession, because of course they could pick up a couple of replacements easily enough."

"Yes, they can keep on working the three-year gag indefinitely. Think how much money they can save by not letting anyone hang around long enough to advance."

"I don't know why you have to be so bitter about it, Kit. They're doing what they can for us. You know I'm getting wise to something. Peebles doesn't count for much, outside of departmental matters in the academic line, I mean. Oh, he's a swell guy and I admire him a lot, but when you come down to hard facts, Peebles doesn't have much say. Trumball's the boy for promotions and salaries, no matter what department you're in. You know he practically runs the Faculty Association single-handed. I'd sure hate to make a bad impression on him. I sure wish I hadn't said that about Lieutenant Forbes. I understand he and Norton are just like that." Tom crossed his fingers.

"Forbes? You mean Norton would associate with a Lieutenant, even one drawing Captain's pay?"

"Trumball, you dope. He's Norton's right-hand man. I think I'll have Mary ask the Trumballs to dinner. Of course we've never been to their house, but what do you think?"

"Just count me out," said Gregory. "He turns my stomach. What's he always looking for in his handkerchief?"

Trumball and Norton shared an outer office, a large bleached-wood and oyster-mottled leather cell presided over by a sharp-faced young woman who became a trifle sharper looking when Gregory approached her desk. "President Norton, please," he said.

"Your name?"

"Kitner, of English." The girl undoubtedly was the mp of

109

the letter in his pocket and he suspected that she'd recognized him the instant he entered the office.

"I'm sorry, Dr. Kitner, but President Norton is in conference. I'll see if Dean Trumball. . . ."

"I don't care to see Dean Trumball. Tell President Norton I'll wait until he is at liberty."

"The president's appointments are made in advance, Dr. Kitner."

"This one was made in advance, and not by me. Tell him I'm here, please. Or shall I?"

The secretary hurried to Norton's door. When she opened it Gregory saw that the president was in conference with the Dean of Faculties. "I'm terribly sorry to interrupt," said the girl, "but . . ."

Gregory stepped in front of her, and Trumball jumped up from a chair drawn cozily near to the president's desk. "Dr. Kitner, if you'll just step into my office . . . Miss Peterson, kindly show Dr. Kitner to my office. I'll be with you in a moment, Dr. Kitner."

"I haven't come to see you, Dean Trumball. I've come to see President Norton, but you may stay if you like."

"That's gracious of you, Dr. Kitner," said Norton. "John, if you'll take these papers and attend to them I can give our friend here a few minutes."

"There's no need for you to . . . If Dr. Kitner will . . ."

"Do you propose to throw him out, John? That will be all, Miss Peterson. And now, John, if you don't mind . . ."

Reluctantly Trumball crossed the expanse of carpet that lay between the desk and the door. As he passed Gregory he assumed a reproachful look that said this wasn't the way we were in the habit of doing things at Tamarack. "Don't be nervous," said Gregory. "I'm not armed."

Trumball drew himself up haughtily, but Norton chuckled. The president was leaning way back in his swivel chair and looking as if he were prepared to enjoy a good floor-show.

Everyone said Norton was handsome. It would have been un-American, said Ruby Peebles, to say anything against the appearance of a man who sported such a neat little white beard. In his undergraduate days Norton had played on the Varsity and now when his coat spread you could see the golden football that dangled from his watch chain. He owned a Phi Bete Kappa key, but that emblem was seldom brought out for public view. Norton avoided anti-social swaggering. "The people he wants to get next to are the kind who think a lot more of a gold football than they do of the Phi Bete key and, besides, Norton didn't have to sweat for his key, and he did for the Varsity emblem. Well, maybe he didn't have to sweat so much for it as the rest of us did," Paul Peebles had told Gregory. "George couldn't kick a ball, he couldn't even catch a ball, but, my Lord, how he could get in the way. I'm telling you it took no less than four men to knock him down, and without seeming to move he spread all over. Once our side learned how to avoid him, he was a great asset."

The famous brick wall had changed shape over the years, but it was still tall enough and broad enough to carry a bay window as an architectural adornment, and a massive head as a suitable dome. Ruby said little children used to mistake George Norton for Andy Gump. "So he grew a beard," she said. "Even before he was chairman of Chemistry. It made him look like a born chairman, a born president. Poor Carr, bumbling about with his nose scraping his chest—he didn't have a glimmer of a chance after George got that beard. Paul kept saying the trustees couldn't ignore Wilfred's international reputation and the fact that Billy Hathaway had him in mind for the presidency, but Paul was just dreaming. The trustees were counting the hours until they could get rid of Billy and everything Billy represented. They put that retirement rule through just before Billy's sixty-fifth birthday, you know, and I'll bet you George Norton had plenty to do with it. I wonder if he's thinking of amending the rule to except the presidency —now that he's getting along in years."

If Norton was worrying about his age it wasn't wrinkling his brow. Above his well-clipped goatee his face was as rosy and unlined as a picture-card Santa Claus. Pig-shrewd eyes rather contradicted the Father-Christmas impression, but only an ill-disposed critic would dwell on the eyes. Generations of loyal Tamarackians had willingly and even joyously joined in great locomotives for P-R-E-X-Y, yea, bo, PREXY!

"And now, Dr. Kitner, if you'll be seated," said Norton when the door had closed.

"What's the meaning of this?" Gregory threw the letter on the gold-framed blotter.

Norton picked the letter up and smoothed it. "Yes," he said. "Most regrettable. Cigarette?"

"Especially when it's unfounded and libelous."

Norton put the letter down and studied his manicured fingernails. "Ugly word, libelous."

"For an ugly business."

"Indeed. I dislike this sort of thing most heartily. I'm a sensitive man, Dr. Kitner. It was unkind of you to refuse to discuss your little problem with the good dean." He sighed as if he'd discovered a hangnail. "However, since you insist on going

112

over his head . . . I've never made myself inaccessible, you know. Students and faculty alike must feel perfectly free to come to me at any time."

"I'm here."

"Yes, but you're wasting your time as well as my time. Mrs. Spencer is an old friend of mine. She came to my home last night. Most upset. Distraught. Her daughter's friend, a Miss Hannegan whom I gather you must know quite well . . ."

"I do not know any Miss Hannegan."

"No matter. She knows you, or of you . . . being a close friend of the Spencer girl. I see no need to go into the details of something you're quite familiar with. Suffice it to say that Mrs. Spencer was distressed."

"Exactly what about? I'm interested in hearing only what concerns me. If the woman said anything that has any connection with this letter, President Norton . . ."

"But, Dr. Kitner, isn't that what we're talking about? Do sit down. I haven't much time, but when I grant an interview I prefer my guest to sit down."

"Norton, I've been at Tamarack fifteen years. Like Meade, I don't have tenure. . . ."

"Don't compare yourself with Meade, Doctor. Most depraved man. Also I wouldn't get the idea that a permanent contract would be of any assistance just now. Just because a man has tenure it doesn't mean he can get away with flouting . . ."

"A man with tenure can expect the Faculty Association to review his case."

The president nodded. "Then let us be thankful you haven't been on a permanent contract. It would be quite embarrassing for the F.A. to have to examine so sordid a matter."

113

"Yes, wouldn't it? But I'm not going to take this lying down, Norton."

"Dear me, Doctor, I wasn't asking you to. Just to sit, please. You make me nervous."

"If I were deliberately conniving to defame an innocent man I'd be nervous too."

"Such explosive language!"

"What did that woman say?"

"You insist on hearing what you already know?"

"I know nothing that could give you any possible justification for ordering that letter."

"Then you've a strange conception of morality, Dr. Kitner. I'm not especially surprised. No, for some years I've known yours isn't the conventional mind. However, not sharing your unconventional ideas, poor Mrs. Spencer was most upset when her daughter's friend intimated what was going on. The frantic mother confronted the daughter and the daughter finally broke down." Norton transferred his inspection to his right hand. "You insisted on this, remember. The girl admitted that on three occasions you and she . . . well, Doctor, shall I continue?"

"Continue."

"I believe *intimate* is the usual way of expressing it."

"It isn't possible that the girl said any such thing."

"I don't blame you for denying it, Doctor. I would be a poor sort of administrator if I failed to take immediate steps, however. When a teacher forgets his sacred duty to the extent of . . ."

"My God, Norton, have you ever seen my office? It's the one Anderson had. It's about the size of your desk. That Spencer girl was in my office three times, I believe, and I had the misfortune to arrive at the Koffee Kup one day when she was going

114

in. We ate lunch together." Gregory laughed as he looked around at the walnut paneling and the luxurious furnishings of the president's office. "If I were going to seduce any of my students you may be sure it wouldn't be in my office or in a crowded restaurant. If that Spencer girl used the word intimacy in connection with me she just didn't know what meaning you and her mother would give the term. The girl's not entirely normal, but I doubt if she's that crazy."

"I've known Ruth since she was a baby, Dr. Kitner. I don't appreciate your attempt to discredit . . ."

"Then you know what she's like. Theatrical and spoiled . . ."

"I'd hardly expected you to be quite so ungallant. In fact I had an idea that your relations with the fair sex were quite the reverse. . . . You're familiar with the agreement between the university and the faculty members. You signed it. You understand we're taking no step that isn't fully authorized."

Norton sounded bored, so bored that Gregory began to wonder in what way the floor show had disappointed the President . . . *but talking pinko politics not favored in the Tama sticks* . . . Meade had shot his mouth off on politics and so the cynics believed his dismissal had nothing to do with a flirtatious student. But what have I done? The son of a bitch wouldn't be so bored if he believed that Spencer fabrication. It's something else. But what?

It was true that Gregory had defied Norton by eating the forbidden food that day at the Town Club, but he'd left shortly afterward and never returned. The incident had caused some ripple. Seven members of the club had joined Paul Peebles in handing in a bitter resignation; Clif Davis, a former student of Gregory's, had interviewed these seven men and got quite a story for his paper, a story which his editor said would lay

115

the *Journal* open to lawsuits. "He asked me if I was trying to be funny," Clif had told Gregory. "He wouldn't even run the story after I toned it down. And he wouldn't use the letters three of those fellows sent in, said he had a family to support, and that the least said the better. . . ." This had been Tom Dawson's view. Tom said he had heard many versions of the incident. "It's queer how different those versions are," he said, "even among those who claim to have been eyewitnesses. Well, I've told them you've never mentioned it at home and that as your closest friend I certainly wouldn't feel free to raise a stink about something you obviously prefer to forget. And believe me if there were anything of that nature, even the slightest hint of it, in the club's policy, I'd know about it, wouldn't I? As chairman of admissions I'd be bound to know. I must say I get tired of people blaming every move of John Trumball's on to President Norton. Trumball means well, I suppose, but nobody can pretend he's any heavyweight. Poor Norton, the way he keeps people on, people who must be far more of a trial to him than anything else. Why, it just isn't reasonable to believe that a man of President Norton's caliber would stoop to anything so dumb. I'll bet you he had no idea what Trumball was up to. Of course he didn't. My God, I sized Trumball up years ago and decided he wasn't worth second thought. . . ."

Perhaps Tom actually believed that for once in his life John Trumball had given himself an order. Gregory would have liked to believe that Norton hadn't sent Trumball over to Paul that day, but it was impossible to forget the expression on the dean's face. It had been the expression of a man who is sent forth to die for another's ideals, for ideals he himself does not hold, the expression of the mercenary on his way to war. Although Gregory knew that Norton, not Trumball, was his

116

enemy, he hadn't been able to personalize the enmity. To hate a man you had to know him, didn't you? Norton doesn't know me well enough to have any special animosity for me. He was in the mood that day at the club, that's all; it would have happened to Goldwater or to Stein or to any of the other half-dozen Jews of the faculty; it would have happened to any Jew unfortunate enough to accept an invitation to the club that day. Norton had been in a black frame of mind and had acted impulsively. Or so Gregory had decided.

Paul Peebles didn't agree with this interpretation. "Norton isn't a temperamental man," he had said. "I doubt if he ever made an unpremeditated move. I've a feeling he had been watching that door for weeks, maybe months, waiting for you to come in. He's gunning for you, Kit. Ruby's always said so."

"You must admit she dramatizes," Gregory had said. "You know how I figure it? Somebody had just told him a Yiddish story that had made him hopping mad. . . . or he'd just finished reading something about Palestine. It couldn't have been premeditated, Paul. It was too gauche."

"With a purpose," Paul had said. "If you insist on hanging around, you'll see. Damn it, Kit, don't you see it was a warning?"

Was it? Was it a warning that today would come? Now Gregory took the chair Norton had offered. Had he given himself time to think, he wouldn't have rushed over here to protest that Ruth Spencer or someone had lied. All Ruth Spencer and her girl friend and her mother had done was provide Norton with a quick, cheap way to terminate a contract. A teacher fired for "cause" rated no notice. The clause was very clear in the specification that its enforcement relieved the university of any obligation to make a financial settlement in lieu of notice. The short, powerful paragraph did not define "cause," but the next sentence took up reasons "other than moral turpitude" and so the word was defined by implication. The agreement between the university and the faculty made no provision for the dismissal of a teacher whose facial structure or name displeased the president; no such deduction could be made from the wording of the statement or from the wording of the letter received this morning. The deduction was forced by the look of boredom on Norton's face. "I get it," said Gregory. "Sorry to have been so slow, but it's a bad habit of mine. I keep forgetting I'm a Jew. . . . I wish you'd tell me something. Tell me, in your position as president of one of the largest universities in the country, what can you possibly fear from a handful of Jews?"

"My dear Dr. Kitner, what a fantastic conclusion! What possibly?" Norton sat up in his chair and had he rubbed his hands together he couldn't have looked more like a man who was thinking Now at last we're getting somewhere.

"Then I'm wrong in thinking you're firing me because I'm a Jew?"

"Not at all," said Norton. He gave Gregory the look of commendation that a teacher bestows upon a bright student. "Not at all. But you generalize, Doctor. There are Jews and Jews, you know. Heavens, man, I hope you don't think I'm starting a purge. This is a democracy, Dr. Kitner. Tamarack takes great pride in keeping its doors open to all colors and creeds."

"Within the quota."

Norton smiled. "I know I'm supposed to quail before that word, Doctor, but it doesn't terrify me in the least. Within bounds consistent with population percentages. When we commit ourselves to a democratic way of life we mustn't forget we

118

also bind ourselves to certain democratic principles and . . ."

"And suddenly I'm over the quota?"

"I wish you'd stop barking at me. You're a reasonable man, at any rate your writings have led me to believe that, even though your actions today are hardly consistent with reason. Can't we discuss this calmly? You wish to bring up the Jewish question. Very well, let's examine it. Let's take Dr. Stein, for example. Stein's been at Tamarack longer than you have and as far as I'm concerned he may continue indefinitely. He's an unobtrusive, adequate little fellow. . . ."

"And I'm obtrusive and inadequate?"

"Obtrusive? Yes. Inadequate? Unfortunately, no. Too adequate, shall we say? Hasn't it ever occurred to you that a man can err in that direction? But let me ask *you* a question. Why on earth haven't you taken the hint? Why did you force me to kick you out? I've put it off, God knows. I've tried to help you. For years I've tried to make it clear I had no intention of allowing you to advance here. So why haven't you accepted one of the many offers that have come your way? I know about them. But you've stubbornly clung to Tamarack. Why? As other-worldly as Peebles is, he must have finally got it through his pate. He must have advised you to clear out."

Gregory nodded.

"But you couldn't bring yourself to believe that Paul might be right about which way the wind's blowing? Of course there were several years when I understood your reluctance to leave Tower City. . . ." Norton moistened his lips. Yes, he would have liked to talk about the Spencer business if he'd been able to make himself believe it; now he was licking his chops over the memory of a business he had been able to believe. "But that attraction no longer exists, does it? When that particular tie was

119

broken, why didn't you take one of those interesting offers? There are a few schools that don't hesitate to place Jews in high positions."

"I've never been interested in high positions."

Norton shook his head. "You've tried to convince yourself that your cloth's small, but if you'd been as modest as you pretend you wouldn't have written those books. Those books gave you away, Doctor."

"I don't follow you."

"In your textbooks you assume a position of authority. I imagine you assume a similar position in the classroom. Very inconsistent with this humble creature you'd like to make me believe in. Oh, no, Dr. Kitner. You can't make me believe you don't know you're the logical man to succeed Paul. Paul's a bit older than I am and so even if he's able to carry on until he reaches sixty-five, I'll still be around. Confidentially I might tell you I may be around longer than you and some others may think. Rules which have no exceptions are very dull, don't you agree? But be that as it may, Doctor, I'd be quite embarrassed if you were still available to Tamarack when Paul leaves . . . quite embarrassed. Tom's a dear chap, but . . . You write too much, Dr. Kitner. You're too well known. I'm no fool. I'm not in the habit of placing an inferior man at the head of one of my departments when a far more talented man is right there in the department. It was short-sighted and unrealistic of you not to see this. Perhaps you hoped I'd suddenly change my mind and that when Paul left I would wake up to your obvious ability? My dear fellow, did you think I'd permit a Jew to head one of my departments? What might it not lead to?" Norton stroked the arms of the presidential chair. "What indeed might it not lead to!"

"I've never had the slightest interest in administrative work."

"Nonsense. Everyone's interested in it."

"No. You say that because you want to believe it, but you know it isn't true."

Norton shrugged. "Perhaps there are some men who are honestly without ambition. Billy Hathaway may not have wanted to be president of the university. . . . If you'd left in time, Doctor, you might have risen to great heights in another school. It's unfortunate that you waited until I was forced to act in a way that will jeopardize your future in teaching. Unfortunate."

"Well," said Gregory, "this has been interesting."

The President bowed as if to acknowledge a compliment. "I shouldn't bother to repeat any of this if I were you. It would be quite futile. I'm not alone in my feeling that a democratic society should be ever watchful to guard against domination by a minority, a tenacious and most talented minority. I hope you understand my point of view, Doctor. I'm no advocate of concentration camps. I simply believe that the majority should rule and that the minority should keep to its proper place in society."

"I take it you limit society to the portion of the world inhabited chiefly by white men. You wouldn't by any chance allow thought of the world population to intrude upon your calculations?"

"That's an interesting point, Doctor. Yes, I admit to certain inconsistencies. One has to make some compromise with life."

"I'm making no compromise with you, Norton."

"I admire spirit, Dr. Kitner, but I don't admire wasted effort. Evidently you've not thought this through. Naturally I weighed the possibilities before taking action. I am aware that there will be a certain amount of repercussion. I deplore the fact that Ruth Spencer is such an unattractive child. Dear me. But one uses what one has. I could have wished for a pretty girl, and I imagine you would have preferred that, eh, Doctor?"

"When the girl has nothing to do with . . ."

"Now you're being unrealistic again. If she'd been pretty, people would have believed the charge without question. Poor Ruth's lack of charm and her undeniable instability . . . I've advised her mother to take her away for a long rest. But you evade the nicest point, Dr. Kitner. People who hesitate to believe that you were guilty of misconduct with a student, particularly with so unattractive a student, will be reminded that they've heard similar talk about you before. Now of course Amy Prentiss is a beautiful . . ."

"You will leave Mrs. Prentiss out of this."

"Gladly. But will you? I warn you, Kitner. Any attempt to establish your innocence will of necessity drag Amy Prentiss into the picture. Do you think you could establish yourself as an innocent victim of slander? You? You who for years made no effort to conceal a most unconventional liaison . . . Why, you and Amy were the center of breathless attention for . . . how many years, Doctor? Seven or eight? I imagine enough people envied you then to form quite an impressive group of moralists, a group which won't be deterred by any charges of prejudice which you and your comrades might make. Be sensible, Doctor. You're licked. Can't you see that nine out of ten people will think the charge was made in spite of your being a Jew, rather than because of it? I've a reputation for being democratic, and so few people have any real understanding of democracy. I'm sorry. I honestly am. Last spring I tried to warn you. Why didn't you take that warning? Are you thick-skinned or do you live in a dream world? Well . . . sometimes it becomes necessary to wake up." Norton frowned at the telephone which had been clicking and then he picked it up. "Yes, Muriel, what is it? Well, tell him to hold on."

Gregory got up.

"Personally I've never had any but the most pleasant of contacts with Jews," said Norton as he rose. "It distresses me to have to separate my own personal feelings from those of the president of the university. When you've had time to think this through, I'm sure you'll see that it was a matter of business. The time has come when the threat of communism has made it imperative for education to free itself of any Jewish domination. I certainly am not among the stupid masses who confuse communists and Jews quite indiscriminately, but I am forced to recognize the very real threat of that confusion. I fully believe that the time will come when no Jew, however humble, will be permitted to remain in educational work. My advice to you is to get out of teaching."

"You've fixed it so I'll have to, haven't you?"

"The present shortage is in your favor. On the face of it, in your favor. But beware of it, Doctor. Wherever you go you'll come up against this sort of thing eventually. It's tough luck, but there it is."

"Thank you for speaking so frankly."

"I'm sorry we never became acquainted. I've a feeling that under other circumstances you and I could have become good friends, very good friends."

"I'm unable to imagine such circumstances."

"Don't be bitter, Doctor." Norton picked up the letter and held it out to him. "Bitterness has a way of turning inward. You may want to show this letter to Paul. I haven't had time to tell him about it. If you see him before I do, tell him to keep his shirt on. There's a limit to what we can put up with and Paul has stretched that limit almost to the breaking point. If you like you may tell him that his resignation would be accepted with regret and alacrity. If he wants his pension . . ."

Gregory stuffed the letter in his pocket. If Norton had planned how best to take the fight out of him he had planned well. "I see now that you realize, far more than anyone else can realize, that for years you've occupied a chair that rightfully belonged to another man." As soon as he had said this Gregory was disgusted with himself. Do you wish to sink to his level?

"You've been listening to a sentimental woman's loyalty to her departed father," said Norton. "I believe you never had the privilege of knowing Wilfred Carr."

Carr? Who said anything about Carr? "I wasn't thinking of him. I didn't know he was an important enough rival for you to have carried him on your conscience all these years. That's interesting, Norton, and illuminating. However, I was thinking of the man who didn't have the grace to die."

Norton's laugh sounded forced. "My dear chap! Do you actually mean poor old Paul?" The president sat down and leaned back in his chair, but his eyes continued to be alert. "It's amazing what affection Paul rouses in some people. Most admirable of you to stick up for him, Doctor. A broken man. I hope you'll bear his welfare in mind when you discuss this matter with him. I've no desire to have any part in Paul's losing a much-needed pension." He leaned forward and picked up his telephone. "You'll excuse me?"

The murderous rage that had brought Gregory over to Hathaway Hall was gone. Norton hadn't left him the clean satisfaction of unadulterated anger. Norton had given him what he was supposed to accept as man-to-man frankness, a curious combination of flattery and insult and threat.

"All right, Muriel, put him on," the president was saying when Gregory opened the door into the outer office.

"I'm sorry, President Norton," said the secretary, "but he got tired of waiting. He's rung off." The girl glared at Gregory as if he were to blame for this unprecedented action.

7 He stood as if in the recurring dream. As in the nightmare he didn't know which class this was or what today's lecture should cover. Where are my notes? My outline? While he felt in his pockets, an adroit and invisible ventriloquist entertained the class. On the rising steps facing him were dairy-lunch chairs occupied by young men and women; some of the students yearned toward the windows, some frowned over notebooks and some, tricked by the clever manipulator, stared at the dummy on the podium.

Suddenly, as if desperate to catch an illusive truth, pens and pencils sped upon paper. "It's in the textbook," commented a cynic who dared to interrupt, but there was no scratching out. Several students nodded wisely to indicate they had known this, several underscored what they had written in their notebooks, and others furtively made parenthetical notes. "It's all in the textbook, all but the only rule upon which there is general agreement. So far as I have been able to discover, no authority questions the rule that the comma's tail must hang down."

Pug Sanderson, dominating the first row, mouthed to his notebook and laboriously shoved his pen. Then, after the sound of laughter had nearly died down, the football star looked up. He leaned over to look at his neighbor's notebook and then squinted back at his own. Again his lips moved.

Get them off guard with a laugh and then stuff them with another quotation from the book, this time with a rule worthy of an examination paper. Remember when you had ideas about examinations, big ideas that scorned memory work? "I agree with you," Paul had said. "Yours is the ideal way, but how can you use it unless you're in a tutorial system? Perhaps with a few of your smaller classes, Kit, but you've got four hundred students in just one section of Survey. It would be impossible to grade the kind of examinations you want to give. . . ." Four hundred students in one section of Survey. My smallest Survey class now has twelve hundred and nine. . . . But where are the rules for them to memorize?

He didn't have to worry. The machine was operating smoothly. It quoted from *Fundamentals of Punctuation*. It gave the rule twice. Pug's face cleared. Well, it's nice to know Pug got that one. Oh, but that wasn't the one Pug had just now got. A great guffaw jarred the class. Pug had got that about the tail hanging down. A hand shot up. Dutifully the machine repeated the textbook rule. "Page twenty-three, third paragraph. It would be a good idea to memorize all of the italicized material on that page." Nobody failed to take this tip down; this was right from the horse's own mouth; this was telling what would be on the exam. Now with that understood, we can relax for a few moments before preparing our minds for the next body blow. "Unfortunately the use of punctuation for purely decorative purposes or for the purpose of conveying emotions beyond the writer's powers of vocabulary has been too fully exploited to have further interest." By which I mean I am no longer interested in that kind of experimental writing? By which I mean them to believe that all the fun is over? "Or at any rate it has struck me that this territory has been explored. You may not agree. It would be unwise of you to take my opinions on experimental writing as final, of course. Experimental writing of the kind that was done in the Twenties would seem to have died out, but of course this doesn't mean that there can be no further experimentation. The matter of punctuation seems to me to have lost its attraction as a literary frontier, but I may be quite mistaken. It is advisable to learn certain rules, however, if only to know how to break them."

Pug waved his hand in the air. "Would you repeat that, Doc?"

"This isn't for the notebook, Mr. Sanderson. It's for thought after the textbook has been studied. The serious painter learns the fundamentals of art before he undertakes to express his own personality in painting. The men and women who rebelled against the kind of rules that are still found in some of our handbooks may have produced some unintelligible results, but the rebellion was wholesome." He shook his head at Pug to indicate that he was still speaking of matters not worthy of the notebook. *Oh, it's not for knowledge that we came to college. . . .*

But to raise hell? What an obsolete song. The good old hell-raising days had vanished. Or had a nostalgic fragment been preserved by the faculty and the administration when they joined hands in an agreement to guard the student body from moral turpitude? Moral turpitude caused by wicked teachers who clung to the hell-raising tradition . . . What would I have thought if one of my State teachers had been fired on a morals charge? Those old men! Old when I was a boy. Yes, but on the rare occasions when he had gone back to State he had encountered some of those old men, miraculously no older than before. Who ever had a teacher young enough for moral turpitude?

Of course my generation was unsophisticated. Even Pug isn't so naïve as we were. Pug, shifting his weight in the cramping chair, had relaxed his grip on his pen. There was no use for Pug to listen to talk that had nothing to do with exams. Now and then he smiled at the joke that had become his private prop-

128

erty. . . . Time to get my affairs in order, a week . . . "The comma should be employed only when its omission would distort the meaning of the sentence." Pug jerked. A rule, Doc? "That is a personal interpretation, by the way. Learn the rules in the textbooks and use them until you discover your own rule. Just remember that your own will need as much foundation as those in the book." That's leaving it wide open. Fellow who wrote that book simply copied, copied from men who had copied from other men. . . .

The overcrowded room was becoming stuffy. Dust particles shimmered in the heat that rose from the radiators, and the odor indigenous to Burnaby was becoming more oppressive. Several years ago, at an annual department banquet, Gregory had made a speech on that stench. At the last minute Professor Lane had wrenched her ankle—she was the only female on the English faculty at the time, and so, encouraged by her absence, the diners had added considerable extemporaneous material to the program. Gregory had remarked that for years he had been baffled by a feeling that he had encountered the Burnaby smell elsewhere and that at last he had remembered. In his grandfather's barnyard, near a pile of rotting lumber, was an old privy used by the extra help during harvest. "Your grandfather was a farmer?" asked one of the faculty afterwards. "How unusual . . ."

Without interrupting the ventriloquist Gregory now went to the door of the classroom and opened it. By comparison the corridor air seemed quite fresh. Pug was making signs toward the windows, but Gregory shook his head. Let in the blast that was blowing outside and they would all catch cold. Nonsense, this about drafts not making you catch a cold. I always catch a cold when I'm in a draft. "If the paragraph is composed of a family unit of sentences, then the adjoining paragraphs may be said to be the next of kin. . . ." Carl said it would catch up with me some day. "Smooth transition, from sentence to sentence, from paragraph to paragraph . . ."

A boy near Pug took out a pack of cigarettes. He was the nervous type that does well in radio control rooms. He looked at his watch and then began to fiddle with a lighter. Because of his self-appointed timing duties he would never know how perfectly the professorial recordings fitted the class periods. Anyway mine do. I never run over the hour, but by God I take my full time and so stop looking so hopeful. Here is one for the notebook, an important comment on transitional phrases. . . . It was a pleasure to see the timer drop the miniature blow-torch and reach for his pencil. That's right, take it out on the kids.

The final word came with the bell and with the flaring of matches and lighters. The smoking ban had gone out with the war—Norton was clever about rescinding rules which couldn't be enforced. In swirls of smoke students came to the platform to scrabble among the returns of day-before-yesterday's quiz. "Jeez, Doc," said the massive cherub who always lingered to polish apples, "if they're going to have rules, I mean, if they break them all the time, why do they have them?"

"Don't worry about breaking rules, Pug. Worry about learning them."

"I don't get it, Doc."

"It's like Picasso," said another student. "When he wants to he can be a perfect draftsman."

"But Doc said that's out," said Pug. "That about for decoration, giving with the punctuation for art work, he said that's

130

out. I got it written down." He thumbed through his note-book.

In the college of my dreams there's a place for athletic boys snubbed and neglected by high-school teachers, but it's a special place. "Pug," said Gregory, "are you going to be able to give me some time this afternoon?" Only a week to get my affairs in order. . . .

"Jeez, Doc, I'd sure like to, but you know how it is. Hoffman's getting pretty nervous about the game."

"So long as *you* don't, boy," said the student who certainly hadn't been of much help when he dragged Picasso into Pug's troubles.

"They're a tough outfit," said Pug. "They got that guy Levinsky."

"Hell, the Swedes can lick the . . . those guys any day. We're all pulling for you, Pug. Aren't we, Doc?"

"You bet," said Gregory. "Well, try to make it next week, Pug."

The athlete groaned. "If I'm alive, Doc. I figure if Levinsky don't kill me, Hoffman will."

In the student-filled corridor Gregory saw Paul hazily through the smoke, but now was no time. There were several appointments and if you were to bring your affairs to an orderly close . . . He climbed up to his office. His? For another week, but already he felt like a trespasser. After the last of the day's consulations he stood at the windows and looked down at the bench where Anderson had spent many of his *emeritus* hours. Out on the plum-colored lake two boats moved slowly over the floating vegetation. *O, little Tama coed queen, come lily-dip with me; O, fairest of the college scene, come to our private sea.* . . . Hit of the *Tama Trials* of 1932,

131

lyrics by a young man now receiving money for his literary endeavors. A few years back that young man made a special trip from Hollywood to be told, before a large audience of applauding alumni, that his was a worthy achievement which had reflected credit upon his alma mater. "The only reason I didn't break up the ceremony," Paul Peebles had said, "was because I thought the young skunk might endow a chair of poetry in expiation." So far the young skunk had returned the university's compliment only by sending Peebles a stunning photograph of a handsome man without a necktie. The picture was inscribed, "For Pablo, Prince of Poetry—from his Studious Singer." Paul kept the photograph on his desk, as a character stiffener, he said.

Wondering how many students that photograph had lured into taking poetry courses, Gregory watched the sunset coloring of the lake. When the richness had nearly faded Harriet and Handsome Brute Teetor rounded the corner of Annex and walked slowly north along Lake Lionel. Had Harriet so little to do with her time? There was scant satisfaction in dwelling on the fact that Mary had been mistaken, but what else could you think about?

"I'll have to find a nice girl for that stunning new man in the department," Mary had said at the beginning of the quarter. "Heavens, he's a handsome brute."

"If you mean Teetor you're a little late," said Tom. "Didn't you notice the way he was hanging around Harriet at the tea?"

"Harriet? Harriet Hough! Don't be silly, Tom. She's much too old for him."

"Bet you anything she's younger."

"But he's a *man*, darling. It makes all the difference in the world."

"Viva la difference," said Tom. This was a phrase he brought in whenever possible. A really good joke, he often said, can't be overworked.

"Seriously, Tom . . . I'd like to find a girl for Mr. Teetor. He should get married, don't you think? I mean, such an attractive young man . . . well, he'll be a lot safer when he's married."

"I'm sure Harriet wouldn't wipe her feet on him," said Gregory, though an instant before he would have sworn he wasn't even listening to the conversation.

When Mary gave the opinion that it was highly unfair to judge a man you hardly knew, Tom laughed. "Mary, haven't you noticed what an interest Kit always takes in Harriet? A fatherly interest, of course. Ever since she first came to the house . . ."

Before that. Gregory had come in late on the subject of Harriet Hough, but not that late. They said, the Dawsons and even Harriet, that he'd met her at the annual faculty tea at the Nortons' four years ago, but he knew this wasn't so. Had he met Harriet at that party he wouldn't have joined Mary afterwards in making fun of Tom. When Tom said that at least English had got the only good-looking woman among the new faculty members, Gregory had agreed with Mary that Professor Dawson must need new glasses.

"Say, you two don't know what you're talking about," Tom had protested. "I told Paul he ought to give us a break and put Lane in the Annex and give us Hough."

"I admit Miss Hough doesn't take up as much room as Lane does, but aside from that . . ."

133

"New woman looks like a pig," Gregory had stated. The mystery was never solved. At the tea he had talked to a woman who looked exactly like a pig; he talked with her long enough to discover she was new to Tower City and that she took lemon in her tea, and then he never saw her again.

Mary had rewarded him with her loveliest smile when he'd said Miss Hough looked like a pig. "Aren't you a meanie, darling. I'd have said a horse."

"Horse!" Loving horses he had resented having them classed with the porcine woman.

"Well, pony then," Mary had said. "A plump pony. She'd better watch her diet. That woman's going to be definitely fat if she doesn't count calories. . . ." And when Tom had insisted that he still thought Miss Hough a beautiful girl, Mary had informed him that the new teacher was no chicken. "Why, she's been teaching in high school for perfect ages. She's just another old-maid schoolteacher."

In the weeks that followed, Gregory passed Harriet Hough on the campus almost every day. Without thinking of pigs, horses or ponies he spoke to this girl and tried to remember who she was. He decided she must have been in his Survey. He'd always taken great pride in his ability to remember former students. A couple of years ago when he was in Chicago for a few days he'd run into a bald-headed tub of a man who, slender and hirsute, had been in one of the Kitner classes at State; without a moment's hesitation Gregory had called that man by name. Let the genius who startled Addison Sims of Seattle try to beat Gregory Kitner. Not counting the Survey classes. No mortal could keep track of all those students.

Having decided that the attractive girl was a former Survey student, he found himself worrying about why she hadn't gone on with any Kitner courses. Evidently she was taking English, but from one of those Annex people. Why?

She would give him a type of greeting seldom heard in these surroundings. He would have been depressed if students hadn't yelled Hiya-Doc at him, but this girl's unconventional Good-morning-Dr.-Kitner was refreshing. And she was different from the mine run in other ways. She wore stockings and hats. Even in the days when such an attitude was unpatriotic, Gregory had hated seeing the bare legs that too often were chapped and reddened, nor had he ever worked up enthusiasm for the practical peasant headgear that had become so popular. Polly and Nan Dawson looked cute enough with their heads done up in bright cloths, but Gregory judged the style unsuitable for females of college age.

Hats and stockings and even shoes that could be called shoes. Sometimes he wished the girl were slowed up by the moccasin drag. He wanted to ask which of his Survey classes she'd been in. He wanted to get a line on why she hadn't continued to take courses under him. When Paul said his choice among the new teachers was Miss Harriet Hough, Gregory didn't stop to wonder why he hadn't seen Miss Pigpony since the tea; admirable though the woman might be, who would care to see her again? "Good," he said when Paul remarked upon Dr. Hough's excellence. "That's good."

Just before the Christmas holiday that year Mary threw one of her Unavoidables. Tom said it was crazy to entertain the small fry of the department, but he didn't say it with much conviction. Mary could point out that Norton Himself gave what might well have been classified as Unavoidables. How else had the Dawsons first got into The Manse?

"Unavoidables have been our family tradition for generations," said Mrs. Carr. "My side, of course. My husband and his people lacked social finesse."

"Never return a plate empty," said Gregory. "I was brought up properly."

"Yes. Even though the cookies that came on it were quite poisonous."

"*Noblesse oblige.*"

"*Mais en vérité.*"

"When you two have quite finished," said Mary, "maybe you'd give me some help. Kit, you've got to be on deck. I'm not asking Amy. I do hope you understand. If I start going outside of the department I'm sunk."

"My husband developed a great passion for Unavoidables," said Mrs. Carr. "There was no fooling him. Why Wilfred, I would say, it's just an Unavoidable, but I couldn't fool him. He'd check my list. What a row he would raise if it struck him as being made up of avoidable people. Mary, let me see your list."

"It's gruesome, but what can I do? The department is swarming with new people, and most of them from high schools, damn it . . . they're so different, I mean, they just haven't the university attitude. I'm having the Lettings and the Peebles to keep it from being too grim for us, though Ruby, my God . . ."

"Dear me, Mary, is Grace Lane still unavoidable, after all these years?"

"Oh, she's taken to saying extravagant things about Ruby's ghastly writing," said Mary. "Of course it's just another of her disgusting crushes, but Ruby's too stupid to catch on."

"My dear, Ruby's and my generation just didn't know about such things."

"Ruby thinks it's literary appreciation. So I'm counting on Lane to keep her out of circulation. One has to try to preserve a certain illusion about the chairman's wife, at least for the new people."

"Such an unsuitable woman," said Mrs. Carr. "Odd how well liked she's always been, isn't it?"

The first game was under way when Gregory arrived at the Unavoidable which quite a few of the guests would doubtless remember as an exceptional party. Gregory, however, had seen Ruby Peebles stand on her head before and so would cherish the evening for another reason. When he came down the stairs his admirable young woman, paper and pencil in hand, was exploring the hall. It was the first time he had seen her without a hat and so he paused on the landing to gaze upon the hair that was the color of the buckeyes he used to carry in his pockets for lucky-pieces. "Lose something?" he asked when he reached the bottom step.

"Good evening, Dr. Kitner," she said. As usual she had the advantage, not only of knowing his name but of seeming prepared for his appearance. "You're late for the game."

Before he had a chance to ask what game, Mary rushed into the hall and began to scold him for being late. She thrust a paper at him and said he was to locate the listed items and to record where he had discovered each article. Then, spotting what looked to be collusion in the study, she hurried away. She considered herself such an expert hostess and yet she hadn't bothered to say Of course you and Miss Blank know each other. If the girl had been homely you could be sure that Mary would have introduced them.

"I'm down to the bobby pin," said the girl.

"Have you looked on the floor?" asked Gregory.

"The things can't be in their logical places."

"Then I shall put you on my list. I was told this was to be a faculty party."

"Then you *don't* know me. I've wondered about that this fall, even though you've always spoken. I should have known that no Annexer . . ."

"Annexer?"

"How many years does it take to work your way into the main building? The annex is so drafty that papers and people blow about like autumn leaves. Oh, all right. I'm Harriet Hough, a new member of the department. I forgive you for being surprised to find me here. I was amazed when I got the invitation. Before I came to Tower City I was told it was next to impossible to get in with the old university crowd, the charmed circle."

No wonder Wilfred Carr had placed Unavoidables above all other kinds of entertainment. Gregory was barely able to stifle a comment that the circle had not been charmed until now; association with Amy had given him slovenly social habits. His perception had been dulled, but he could see that the florid compliments which enchanted Amy would nauseate this young woman. It was better to speak of bobby pins.

Never had one of Mary's mixers been so rewarding. Hough and Kitner, tying for first prize, were disqualified for cheating; the virtuous Lane, though she failed to find the elusive paper clip that only Hough and Kitner had located, was given the award.

"But where was the woman who looks like a pig?" asked Gregory when the party was over. "You know, the one who was at the tea, the one I thought was Miss Hough."

"Darling, I told you it was more like a horse or a pony. Of

course when you met her before she was wearing the most god-awful hat."

"Good Lord, a hat wouldn't do it. I've seen Miss Hough on the campus almost every day this fall. Why, she's a beautiful woman, with or without a hat."

"And on no liquor," said Mary. "But speaking of liquor, I was never so mortified in all my life. A woman of Ruby's age and not a drop for an excuse."

"It's not every woman who can stand on her head," said Gregory.

"It was Ted's fault," said Tom. "He kept egging her on. You know Ruby can't resist a dare."

"Don't blame Ted," said Mary. "Didn't you see her pants? A woman doesn't wear black pants unless she means to show them. Disgusting old fool. She's sixty if she's a day."

"Good legs, though," said Tom. "Kit, can you stand on your head?"

"Only on a galloping horse. . . . By the way, I asked Miss Hough to drop over New Year's afternoon."

Mary set down the ashtray she had just emptied. "Why in the world . . ." It was the same every year. Every year she reminded Gregory that the New Year open house was as much his party as their party and yet when he mentioned that he had invited someone she hadn't already asked she invariably said Why in the world. "You know we only ask our closest friends. Of course if you've already asked her it's too late, but I suppose she'll put a damper on the whole party. She's just the type."

"I don't see that she'll cramp anyone's style but Kit's," said Tom. "Or Amy's. Do you think Miss Hough is up to the professional competition? It will be very interesting. Hough

139

versus Prentiss, and the prize, ladies and gentlemen, is Dr. Gregory Kitner."

"Stop trying to be so damn funny. Amy's bad enough. I mean I've never felt that she quite fits in with our little crowd, but at least she's not a prude. Miss Hough certainly strikes me as being the Virtuous Virgin personified."

"Hell, it won't hurt us to have one virgin at the party. Kind of stimulating, I'd say," said Tom.

"I know a prude when I see one," said Mary. "And if Harriet Hough isn't the perfect example . . ."

For four years Gregory had defended Harriet against Mary's scathing charge, but now he wondered if perhaps Harriet were something of a prude. You wouldn't have to be a prude to be shocked by a colleague's dismissal for moral turpitude, though; you'd be a queer sort if you weren't shocked. . . . Why couldn't Norton have used a respectable charge? He could have got me on disloyalty—any sharp operator can pin a disloyalty charge on a teacher; but no, he had to brand me with something more elusive and ignoble, with something I couldn't fight. . . . What bothers me most is what Harriet will believe.

By the time Harriet Hough came to Tower City the Prentiss-Kitner story was stale, but Gregory imagined that the gossips perked up when Amy began to go around with Steuben. Harriet couldn't have missed all of the story. Knowing something about him and Amy, would Harriet believe his dismissal justified?

The jangling of the chapel bells reminded him he must go to Paul. As a favor to Paul or as a favor to Norton, or, conceivably, as a favor to himself, the culprit was to bear the tidings to his chairman. Rehearsing approaches that wouldn't endanger a weakened heart, Gregory knocked on Paul's office door, but Paul had left for the day. When he telephoned the Peebles' house to ask if he might come around that evening Ruby insisted he come to dinner. "Come right away," she said, "and we'll have a cocktail. Hurry. I've got something to show you."

He called home and told Polly to tell her mother he wouldn't be there for dinner. Polly hadn't developed feminine curiosity; she didn't ask where he was going. "Okay," she said. "I have to go now. They're going to find the murder only he's got the secret power and maybe they won't catch him yet."

If Mary Dawson were to be believed, the Peebles' living room contained the only mission furniture to be found in the whole of Tower City. Worse, in that cluttered room were several cherry pieces that never should have belonged to a woman who didn't appreciate fine antiques. "You know what Ruby Peebles does with those really museum pieces? She *uses* them!"

The walls of the Peebles' inartistic living room were splattered with photographs of the Peebles children and grandchildren, of former students, of cousins, and even of an incredibly dignified Ruby in ruffles beside a chunky, strangling bridegroom. Mary said it was queer that anyone who considered herself such a creative artist made no effort to translate her so-called artistry into terms of interior decorating. Except for the incongruously magnificent desk and tables and chairs that Mary coveted, the room was one you wouldn't have hesitated to turn over to the Boy Scouts for a jamboree. And the whole place, said Mary, smelled like a pet shop. But she exaggerated the abilities of two small animals.

Tonight the animal fragrance was overwhelmed by that of wood smoke. "I can't make it go up the chimney," said Ruby as she pushed at the smudge with her grandfather's cane which she kept handily by to discipline fires and pets and, if rumor were to be given credence, George Norton. Ruby swore she had never hit George; she had merely tapped him to get his attention.

Gregory, tripping slightly on one of the threadbare rugs that rumpled the scuffed floors, went to the fireplace and opened the damper. "Was the smoke what you wanted to show me?"

"Did I want to show you something, darling?"

"On the phone you said . . ."

"I remember. Maybe I can find it. Would you say I'm an existentialist?"

"I would if you wanted me to, but I've never felt you could be classified."

She went to the desk and began to rummage among the piles of books and magazines and papers. "I was rereading some of my *Ardentia* pieces, the first *Ardentia*. That was before your time. We sent copies all over the world. Bother, where did I put it? I'm thinking of starting the magazine up again, you know."

"There goes the vacation money," said Paul, coming into the room. "But look at what Susie's made for us."

"The way that girl spoils us," said Ruby. "I can't understand why Mary won't take a student helper. Of course Sue will leave us when she gets a place at her sorority house or in one of the dormitories. She says not, but I can't believe that a girl who's made her bow will keep on doing housework. Imagine having a debutante in the house! It's been so educational. I'd be quite nervous about it if she weren't such a lamb about putting us at our ease. Kit, you make the cocktails, won't you? Paul says I never get them right. You'll find everything there in the bookcase, I think. Paul says so too, about me being an existentialist. . . ."

Why spoil the cocktail hour with unpleasant news? Gregory pushed the cat from the shelf where the bottles and glasses were kept. "I'm afraid ice is indicated," he said. "Everything seems to be at cat temperature."

"She's taken such a liking for glass," said Ruby. "I wonder if it means she's pregnant again. Let's see, who hasn't had one of her kittens, Paul? The twins are old enough now, I think. If she had two exactly alike, wouldn't that be . . ."

"I'm afraid Mary wouldn't stand for it."

"Poor Mary takes life so hard," sighed Ruby. "Do you really have to have ice? Oh, here's Susie with some. I swear the child's a mind reader. Sue, do sit down and have a drink with us."

"Ruby," said Paul, "the child doesn't drink."

"She doesn't even sit," said Ruby. "I don't know what there is about that kitchen that fascinates her. I always found it a deadly place."

"At least let me wipe them off," Sue was whispering to Gregory. "I know she can't get in them but she rubs against them. She was in the punch bowl last night."

"Oh, the punch bowl," said Ruby. "Are you telling him about that? But you shouldn't be nervous when she's in the cupboards, Sue. That cat never broke a thing in her life. She's just shopping around for a nest, I imagine. No, you don't need to worry about that cat breaking anything, which is more than I can say for *some* people." She pointed her long cigarette holder at the dog. "Yes, you . . . Kit, please hurry. I want your rattling done with before time for Grantham."

"Oh, Lord," said Paul. "Kit, we'll take our drinks to the study."

"You shall not," said Ruby. "I'm perishing to know how it's going to come out and I should think you'd be too."

"How what's going to come out?"

"Mr. Wilde's trial. Grantham's covering it this week."

"On the radio!" said Sue as she took the tray from Gregory.

"With beautiful discretion, Sue. You should listen."

"I have to keep an eye on dinner, Mrs. Peebles."

"Lucky you," said Paul. "How a supposedly intelligent woman can listen to Grantham's drivel every night in the world . . ."

"Not every night, dear. He's only on five days a week. You'd be surprised how much I learn from Mr. Grantham." Ruby leaned over to switch on the radio. Under the lamp the hair that Mary called such an obvious dye job had the iridescence of butterfly wings. "Relax, Paul. For once you're not going to walk out on him."

". . . and now, my dear friends, permit me to lead you down the halls of literature." The rich voice of Francis Grantham, book editor of the *Tower City Journal* and literary commentator for station WTCJ paused to let his listeners prepare for the trip. "Tonight we continue the tragic story of Oscar Wilde who, as we said yesterday, did not adhere to the Queensberry rules. [Throat-clearing to mark joke.] Charging the Marquis with libel, Wilde, unworldly in the sense that he believed his self-fabricated world inviolate, deliberately challenged the moral foundations of society."

"Hear, hear," said Paul.

"Shut up," said Ruby.

". . . an attempt to avoid the realization that his genius fell

144

short of the mark he had set for it? Was this wretched man . . ."

In spite of the censoring that had cut away much of the sense and all of the continuity, Gregory quickly identified the source of Grantham's talk. The mutilation hadn't quite obliterated the forceful personality of the critic who had written the original essay. Phrases betrayed the radio script's source as definitely as portions of a print identify a thumb. As he listened Gregory recalled the first time he heard Peebles lecture. Paul had come to State on an exchange lectureship shortly before Gregory completed his graduate work. Young Kitner had been too shy to make any attempt to become personally acquainted with the visitor, but before the series of lectures was finished the student's greatest ambition was to teach at Tamarack University. He had taught at State several years before the Tamarack job was offered. He had enjoyed his work at State and had received an unexpected promotion, but his desire to be associated with Paul Peebles hadn't been forgotten, nor had the decision to accept the Tamarack position ever been regretted.

How solid, the radio was asking now, was the foundation on which Oscar Wilde's literary reputation was based? Ruby waggled the cigarette holder to warn Gregory to keep his peace. Paul had set his cocktail down and now with a hand cupped around his good ear he listened intently.

And could the breath of scandal blow out the lamp that had been blazing so brightly? He would, Grantham assured his audience, tell them at this same time on Monday, but now for a word from our sponsor. . . . Ruby flicked the radio off. "It's wonderful how he can leave us hanging on the side of a cliff almost every night. I can hardly wait until Monday. Poor Mr Wilde! Whatever do you suppose he's done? With quotations,

I should say quotations within quotations, Grantham may be able to make him last another week."

Absently Paul drank his cocktail as if it were water. "That boy . . . well, I suppose he's no longer a boy—it's been twenty-odd years since he was in school, but I remember him well. An exceptionally poor student. This is the first time I've ever listened to one of his broadcasts. Impressive voice, but shockingly poor delivery."

"Yes," said Ruby. "It's as if he didn't quite understand what he was reading."

"No wonder," said Paul. "The way that article had been butchered . . . it's unfair when you've no proof, but I couldn't help feeling I'd read parts of that somewhere, parts taken out and badly restrung. Of course I've no right . . ."

"Who better?" asked Ruby.

"Thank you, my dear, but I've never made a special study of Wilde. He's never interested me except in relation to his period. As a matter of fact it's been years since I've read much about him and so I must be mistaken in thinking some of Grantham's phrases . . ."

"No," said Gregory. "I recognized them too."

"It was before this recent rage for Wilde. My guess is that Grantham was lifting from a magazine article that came out in the Twenties. Give me a moment and I'll have the man's name. Begins with an S. Can you think of it, Kit?"

"Easily."

"Don't tell me. I hate the way my memory's going. No, you're wrong. Southward took exception to that paper. It was in the old *Literary Quarterly* and Southward, a great devotee of Wilde, was infuriated. I remember he and I exchanged several huffy letters. Dear me, I wonder if he's still living." During

146

these remarks Paul had begun to grin. "Grantham may have been a poor student, but you must grant him this much—he's wonderfully discriminating, and one might even say that his cutting was an attempt at originality. Do you read his newspaper stuff?"

"Wouldn't miss it," said Gregory. "He waits until all the big reviews are out and then makes a compilation. It's fun to try to spot the various reviewers. Of course it's rather confusing when there's been no basic agreement among the big boys. When that happens Grantham has to say that on the one hand, although the book stinks to high heaven, on the other hand it is undoubtedly the masterpiece of the year. You know, a trivial book composed of the most exciting writing these weary eyes have seen in many a moon. . . ."

"There ought to be a law against him swiping things and not giving credit," said Ruby.

"Well," said Paul, "reviewers undoubtedly see that they are like teachers, in the public domain. Certainly a teacher exists to be plagiarized. Grantham's paid me a pretty compliment. Kit, remember this before you decide a student is hopeless. Why, your friend Pug Sanderson may end up in radio and give your words a far wider audience than you'd ever dreamed of reaching."

"You boys are reaching a wider audience now than you ever dreamed of," said Ruby. "You know what I heard at Faculty Wives? I heard they're thinking of converting all of the larger offices into classrooms. But I think dinner's ready. Come on. You can be thankful you've got such a little office, Kit. They'll never want it for a classroom. . . ."

His eviction notice was heavy in his pocket. For once the silent battle for domination of the Peebles' dining table failed to amuse Gregory. Glaring at each other, each as haughty as if not a member of short-haired varieties considered worthless, the dog and cat jealously waited for tidbits. The dog, looking over the rim of Paul's plate, and the cat, no less comfortably ensconced on the lap at the other end of the table, scorned the intruder.

8 As he walked slowly east on Clayton Place Gregory pondered upon the Peebles' reaction to his news. Neither of them seemed to sense the depth of his humiliation. "A man of that sort," Paul had said, "can't hurt your kind. Norton knows you've got something he can't touch. He knows that no matter what he does he can't penetrate what he thinks is your armor. And why can't he? Because unlike him you don't have to cower in a suit of mail."

Paul was a romantic. It's not *you*, Gregory had wanted to cry out. It's *me*. I haven't the protection of age. You're an old man and I'm comparatively young. I'm still under fifty and I can be hurt, damnably hurt.

But Paul hadn't recognized the vulnerability. "In a way," he'd said, "Norton's done no more than I've been trying to do. It took me far too long to realize that you couldn't progress here, but in the past four or five years I've known."

"I should have listened to you," Gregory had admitted. "I should have listened when there was still time."

"It isn't too late. Don't let him scare you out, Kit. Why, if I were your age again . . ."

"But think of Meade, Paul. This isn't another Wilson case. You know what Meade's doing now? He goes around and asks people questions or else he sits in an office and counts answers scraped up by other questioners. A man who was a Rhodes Scholar . . ."

"He may be more suited to work in surveys of public opinion, Kit. Don't glamorize Meade. He really wasn't much of a teacher. Very little to offer. . . ."

Gregory paused to light his pipe. In the flare of the match he saw successful teachers sitting in a comfortable circle; he heard

149

them saying not to glamorize Kitner, an almost forgotten educator who'd had little to offer. . . . Oh, Paul wouldn't be among those smug self-protecting biddies. Paul's my friend. He wasn't Meade's friend and so he's taken this line of least resistance which states Meade wasn't much of a teacher and so why bother about him. For his friend, Paul was optimistic. "Don't get the idea Norton can close other doors," he had said. "Do you think other university administrators pay any attention to him? Why should they? He hasn't come forward with a new idea in his entire regime. He's all negative, reactionary. He's interesting as a throwback, but the modern educator isn't giving him a second thought. You're *known*, Kit. Eight out of ten people who hear about this are going to weigh your reputation against Norton's and believe me that weighing won't be to your disadvantage. There are at least a half-dozen schools that will leap at the chance to sign you up for next year. There's no rush. Finish this year in writing. By next spring you'll have enough offers to enable you to pick and choose. . . ."

Ruby had spoken with enough vehemence to satisfy Gregory, hadn't she? She wanted lawsuits and wholesale resignations. She'd said the hell with the pension. If her scheme for impeaching Norton failed, all right, Paul would get a job at a school that wouldn't retire him at sixty-five. "We can get along without his filthy money," she had said. "I could even write for the slicks."

Ruby's feet seldom touched the ground; when they did it was only to give her time to deliver a swift kick. For years this naturalistic writer, this imagist, this dadaist, this existentialist whose literary creations were rejected by little magazines not edited by herself, had threatened to accept money from the *Saturday Evening Post*. "I'll revive the magazine," she had said, speaking of her own magazine then rather than of the *Post.* "I'll devote the entire first issue to George Norton. I'll give him hell in poetry, prose, and art work. It will be a collector's item."

Paul had smiled at her and then had turned to Gregory. "I'm not playing into George's hands. He'd be delighted to get rid of me. Of course the saved pension wouldn't amount to much on his books, but a big spender always likes small economies. You didn't see him weeping when Mackenzie got sore and resigned, did you? Mac's department was going to lose him the next year anyway and so . . . a little tiff with a sixty-four-year-old man, a resignation, and the new man comes in a year earlier, that's all. And a pension is avoided."

"Our whole pension plan stinks," Ruby had said. "I'll expose it in *Ardentia.* I'll give it the lead editorial."

"We'll take this calmly and sensibly," Paul had said. "Raise a big fuss and what would come of it? Perhaps a permanent black eye for Kit. No, we won't provide Norton with a chance to make pious statements about morality. . . ."

Gregory picked up a stick and began to vibrate it against the sidewalk as he went along. To save Paul the embarrassment I reminded Ruby of My Past. I said I could hear Norton giving an inspirational talk on how a teacher's life must be above the slightest suspicion of scandal, and then I saw a flicker in Paul's eyes and I knew, for the first time, that somewhere during those years with Amy I'd lost a little of Paul's confidence and respect. He didn't say anything to justify this knowledge. He just said he doubted if intrinsic merit could survive the airing of a moral-turpitude case. "I'm not going to lend my hand to overturning a whole apple cart in an effort to get at one very rotten apple. In the melee that small apple might very well roll off into safe

151

cover," was what Paul had said. "I'm profoundly sorry for the university, but I'm not sorry for Kit, Ruby. To be fired by George Norton is to be selected for a hall of fame. Look back over the names of the men he's fired: Carrothers, Harris, Wilson . . ." He hadn't included Meade in his list.

The stick broke and flew away. There was a chance, of course, that you didn't understand Paul any more than he understood you. We're so eager to analyze the other fellow. Ruby and her saying Tom's at the bottom of this. "Tom Dawson's whole career has been built on jealousy," she'd said. "When he found out that he couldn't beat you at teaching or writing he turned to administration. Paul seems to think this letter is final, but I know who could do something about it. Tom Dawson could. Don't talk to me about him being your friend. You'll see what a fine fair-weather friend he is when you tell him about this. Not that I've the slightest doubt that he doesn't already know."

Gregory kicked at fallen leaves and wondered if Tom could do something. Dared the Crown Prince try to exert influence? But why should Tom risk his future for the sake of a friendship that no longer existed? No longer? It never existed. Oh, I shouted at Ruby in defense of the Dawson-Kitner friendship, but I know we were never friends. We speak of our friendship as if it were historic; we prove what never existed by saying how long the never-existing state has prevailed. My God, we say, we've endured each other for fifteen years—it must be love. But even at the start there was no real friendship. We used each other as testing ground. I used Tom to see what impression I could make on a closed mind. Same way with him, I suppose. From his viewpoint I suppose I represent the closed mind.

Tom, extremely sensitive to the smallest of inklings that concerned himself, might suspect there were limits to what

Norton would take from his princeling. It's one thing to select your successor and another thing to feel his breath on the back of your neck. Norton had made Dawson and he could break him. Tom had poured himself into Norton's mold, but the Dawson material wasn't indestructible. Poor Tom, if you could know him you might love him, but he's always so busy being somebody else. When I first knew him he was trying to be Daddy Carr. He'd never met Carr, but he tried to fit himself into the pattern Mary drew. That was what he was up to when he was working on his notebooks, but even then his acting was caricature. I'll bet Wilfred Carr never would have announced that his research would produce a definitive work. Tom didn't know where he was going; all he knew was that he had to end up somewhere important. He may have had that idea even before Mary began to work on him.

Tom Dawson's first years of teaching were spent at two small colleges where Mary was miserable. She used to tell Gregory how she had hated those one-horse towns where she couldn't wear her sorority pin because she was ashamed to be identified with the hicks who wore it as if they had a born right to it. And the faculty people! "You can imagine, Kit. No, you probably can't. You don't know what small colleges are like. The teachers were callow youngsters and broken-down old hacks. . . . I suppose Tom couldn't help sort of liking it—being head and shoulders above all of them. It took me a long time to make him see that being a big duck in one of those puddles would be a lot worse than being one of hundreds in a really good school. Not that I expected him to be just one of the masses very long." Even before Tom put his *Outline* away in a packing case Mary knew he would end up with more than a set of stuffy books and a marble clock and a dozen pens and pencils to show for his life.

Mary's bridelike enthusiasm on the subject of her husband enchanted Gregory when he first knew her. How pretty he had considered her. Now when he heard people comment on her beauty he wondered what they meant. She was still attractive, he supposed, but the old glow was gone. He'd watched her joyousness dribble away. Most persons would have assumed that Mary Dawson was supremely happy. Wasn't she getting everything she'd ever wanted? In addition to her husband's success was her own personal triumph; she had established a distinguished salon, she had given birth to the only twins ever born to the English department, and she was the youngest president the Tower City Woman's Club had ever had.

Mary said her club activities were all for Tom's sake. Gregory doubted the truth of this statement, but Tom accepted the sacrifice gratefully. "A faculty wife's crazy if she thinks campus activities are enough," was how Mary explained why she had gone in for a type of endeavor she'd formerly scorned. "Mother did what she could to help Daddy. Why, she'd have been president of the Club if it hadn't been for Daddy. I distinctly remember when they told her they'd decided not to ask her even though she was their first choice. They *had* to have someone whose husband could be counted on."

God knew Tom could be counted on for receptions and parties at which the Woman's Club dignitaries desired male backing. "I don't mind admitting that every time Mary's name gets in the papers it's a decided help to me," he would say.

The Dawsons were in business together and they respected that business too highly to let a small matter like love, rather the death of love, interfere. When Gregory, reading the club news that Tom had handed him, said that the creaking wheel does indeed get the grease, Tom told him he was impossible. "But I know it's just a pose."

"Were *you* posing when you were working on *The Outline?*" Gregory had asked.

We weren't polite to each other in those days. We were young and outspoken and almost friends.

"Fella, I wasn't dry behind the ears," Tom had said. "I just hadn't learned how to stop working on a thesis."

We were almost friends. I think I would have said we *were.* Tom Dawson hadn't ever begun to take Charlie Riley's place, though. From the start Gregory considered Tom too pedantic to be stimulating, too full of facts to give room for ideas. Tom had gone through school the hard way. He'd had to earn every nickel, every hour of credit; neither the money nor the scholarship had come to him easily, but he'd made the most of his financial and intellectual assets. Once he got something into his head he kept it there and he hadn't put out any money for frivolous courses. He never had to brush up on names or dates and year after year he gave the same sharply emphasized lectures which were so easy to outline. It was as if he'd made a study of what constitutes the ideal lecture and had never permitted himself to waver from the ideal. "When I give a lecture," he said, "I concentrate on the bones. As I speak I see the structure and my students see it. Of course off-campus talks are in a slightly different category, but even then I feel I'm not earning my fee unless my theme is crystal clear. I abhor speakers who generalize, who haul in a lot of personal opinion that's neither here nor there. I stick to facts."

Commendable loyalty. Facts certainly stuck to Tom. So long as you confined your questions to works produced before the present century you could trust Tom as implicitly as you could trust the finest encyclopedia.

When Mary's resentment of the research project that was absorbing so much of her husband's time first broke out it was in darting flames against which Tom had little insulation. Oh, he'd pretended, but how easy it had been to see he was pretending. Suppose *The Outline* didn't make much money, he'd said. He had asked who would be dumb enough to expect to make a fortune on a big research job. Who indeed, unless a young instructor who had had his fill of poverty? Mary didn't have much trouble with him. Before long he was saying they, Mary and Gregory, were all wet if they thought he'd finance the publication of his work. "You people seem to think that when I bury myself in a project I'm six feet under," he had said. "Not me. No, sir, not me. I know this is the sort of thing that ought to be done on a Guggenheim."

From then on it had been plain sailing to the packing case. Tom not only stopped working on *The Outline*, he stopped talking about the survey that was to have been the definitive of definitives.

Save for the few hours he devoted to delivering his lectures, Tom had abandoned Literature. He defended his neglect of contemporary writing. Defended it? He bragged about it. Whenever he came upon a well-phrased statement on the decline of literature he would read it aloud to Gregory. "There's your modern writing," he would say. Had anything worthy of Tom's attention been produced during Tom's lifetime? Of course he made a few social concessions. Before a dinner party he might devote a half hour to *Omnibook* to prepare himself for scintillating conversation with a woman who had equipped herself for this contingency by attending a book review. But although life forced him to make passing recognition of the questionable fact that literature was still in production, on the campus Tom was secure in his snugly restricted world. What he had learned in school was good enough for him. "You know what they called contemporary writing when I was in college?" he would say. "My contemporary course ended with *Uncle Tom's Cabin*. You think that's funny, don't you, Kit? All right, go ahead and try to teach this modern crap, go ahead and try to pass judgment on stuff you haven't had a chance to get any perpective on, stuff nobody's sure of and can't be for a hundred years to come. . . . If the kids don't like what I give them they damn well know what they can do."

To his wrath, an emotion he would in these instances call amusement, students had been known to transfer from Dawson classes. "I get a bang out of these grinds who have a masochistic urge to find a teacher who'll flunk them," he said when he lost an A student.

The average student was satisfied with Professor Dawson's way of teaching. I suppose I say average, thought Gregory, because I've lost a few students to him; but I swear I can't recall losing any to Tom that weren't nearly as hopeless as people can get and still breathe. It had been different with Ted. Ted Letting gave you real competition; when you lost a student to Ted you needed to start riding your fences. Funny, we gripe about having too many students but how we yelp if we lose one to someone we admire. Half of the transfers are probably caused by a strong desire to have a coke with so-and-so at a certain hour. . . . Be fair to Tom. He's got a reputation for being fair.

If in recent years Tom's been suspected of tipping the scales in favor of members of the Sigma Gamma fraternity, re-

157

member you've been accused of having an equally unfair bias. They say if you're on the verge of flunking a man and you find out he's a Sig it's quick curtains for him. I've heard them. "Don't let Doc Kitner know you're a Sig, for God's sake," they say. "He never passes a brother if he can help it." Sheer nonsense that was adopted as truth after you refused to pass boys who did nothing to earn a grade but flash the clover at you.

He stopped to refill his pipe and then, noticing he was nearly home, he turned at the next corner and started around the block. He knew his thinking was unproductive, but there were a few more things his mind insisted upon covering before it would submit to the beating it was going to get when Tom and Mary were handed Trumball's letter.

Tom's a brilliant speaker. The size of his fees for the off-campus lectures prove that. Amy used to say he was almost as good as Francis Grantham, the canary of WTCJ. "Grantham has a better voice," Amy had said, "but Tom's much easier to follow and his illustrations are better." Before deciding it might look odd if she continued to do so, Amy had attended several of Gregory's Survey sessions and later had told him what his trouble was, just where his lack of speaking brilliance lay. "I was thinking about it when Tom spoke at the Club, darling. It isn't that you aren't an interesting speaker, Kitty-pie, but couldn't you use more illustrations?"

She meant jokes.

Tom had a carefully annotated collection of jokes and undoubtedly he was telling the truth when he said the only student who ever went to sleep in one of his classes was later found to be suffering from encephalitis. "Induced by exposure to a colleague of mine whose identity I'm pledged to guard with my life," Tom said when he told the story. His ability to extend and adapt material justified his claim that the bulk of his humorous remarks was original.

Now the thoughts were broken into by two students who were on their way home from the movies. "You know how it is, Doc. You can't study all the time."

"Good show?"

"Hell, no. . . ."

It was useless to try to postpone seeing Tom and Mary. Tonight or tomorrow morning. What difference did it make? You've got to tell them yourself. It wouldn't be fair to let them hear it from someone else. And it's going to be a shock for them. I don't care what Ruby says, it's going to be a shock. It's got to be. Ruby wants to blame Tom; she wants to think him a calculating fiend, anything, just so she can excuse her fair-haired boy from any blame. Sure, that's all there is to Ruby's tirades against Tom. She picked me for a winner and he beat me and she can't take it. When the department budget could stand but one advancement did Tom demand it? No, it was given to him before he knew only one man could be promoted that year. Peebles made that decision. "I'm sorry about it, Kit," he said to me, "but it's logical to give the raise to the married man. I'm sure we'll be allowed more money next year. . . ."

But Tom was a full-fledged professor before Gregory got his assistant-professorship. "Because I'm still a bachelor, Paul?" By then Gregory knew that decisions about advancement had been taken out of Paul's hands. Peebles had resisted longer than most of the department heads but he hadn't been able to do more than cause a slight delay in the trend toward centralization of authority. Tamarack was no longer a university composed of virtually independent colleges which in turn were

159

made up of self-governing departments; the threads of the various schools and departments had been woven into one set of reins.

"I'm touched by Norton's concern for Wilfred Carr's daughter," Paul said after Tom got the professorship. "Too bad Wilfred can't know it. I'm sure he would have wanted to write an ode. Don't misunderstand me, Kit. I approve of our interest in the welfare of the faculty families, if this is what Tom's promotion means. But where's it going to lead us? I'm not saying Tom isn't competent, but I'm tired of the run-around you're getting. I can't do a thing about it. Not a damn thing. Funny, isn't it? I'm head of the department and I can't do a damn thing. Of course you haven't gone out of your way to help me. You don't co-operate the way Tom does. My God, do you ever stop to think about how he gets around? Speeches at the women's club in every leading city in the state, and his picture in the papers. Ruby says he's even been flirting with Mrs. Trumball."

"That's not news, Paul. He's been playing that angle for several years."

"You know nothing on earth would please John Trumball more. Greatest compliment you can pay the man."

"If you think I'm going to make a pass at the old witch . . ."

"Did you say witch? No, I suppose there's a limit. But seriously, Kit, I'm concerned about your future. You don't have to emulate Tom, but you don't need to feel called on to be entirely different. Take a look at what he's been doing. One day we hear Norton say he considers this or that organization worthwhile; next day Tom's chairman of the group. Last week Norton got to talking to me about Tom's out-of-town speaking and I thought it was coming, but did he criticize me for letting Tom take the cuts? No, he complimented me on sending out such a splendid messenger of good will for the university."

"Paul, if you're giving me tips on how to get tenure . . ."

"Never mind, Kit. You hang on. Norton can't fail to see the contribution you're making. He backed down last year, didn't he?"

Gregory started back toward Clayton Place. Paul had been referring to the ruckus raised over Kitner's method of conducting examinations for a couple of his courses. The *Tower City Journal* had got wind of the Kitner system and had given it a big play as an innovation. There'd been nothing startlingly new about Gregory's method. He had allowed students to bring reference books and classroom notes into the examination room and had provided dictionaries and other source material for them. In a statement to the press he'd said he wasn't attempting to equip students for life on desert islands and that he believed they would have access to printed material when they left school. "I'm interested in what they do with facts and opinions," he had said. "I am not particularly interested in training them for *Information Please*." Norton hadn't considered Kitner a messenger of good will for Tamarack; Norton had deplored the shoddy type of cheap publicity a certain inexperienced young teacher had given the university.

"If you call that backing down," Gregory had said to Paul. "He should have made a public apology."

"For George Norton it was backing down; it was turning tail and running. As soon as the paper started publishing those letters from educators all over the country, well, it became a little too hot for George. I liked the way he signed off. Tamarack has always stood for academic freedom, he said, but at the same time any teacher found taking undue advantage of his liberty may soon find himself with more liberty than he desires. Neat. I'm sure it went over with the best people."

"Why didn't he fire me?"

"Because he didn't have a damn thing on you. He couldn't prove that your system failed to teach the students the subjects outlined in the courses. At heart Norton's an educator, Kit. New ideas may startle him, but he can't help coming around after he's had time. Next year . . ."

But the next year had failed to bring Gregory a promotion. Tom had blustered about unfairness and had announced the intention to have a heart-to-heart talk with Peebles. "I'm going to set Paul straight about you," he had said. "You've paid quite enough for that rotten publicity you got last year. If I can convince Paul that you've dropped this experimental . . ."

"It isn't experimental and I have not dropped it."

"If letting them bring books into the examination room . . . ponies and notes . . ."

"The only reason the system isn't used more widely is that it does make the grading arduous."

"Well, Jesus God," Tom had said, "isn't that enough of a reason for you!"

Tom disapproved of Gregory's teaching methods, but he hadn't let that disapproval keep him from giving the head of the department the old what-for. It was barely conceivable that Tom believed Paul Peebles was unappreciative of Kitner. As Paul had said tonight when Ruby had finished her tirade against Dawson, Tom had always displayed a commendable, if blundering, loyalty to his friend. "Whatever you say, Ruby, you'll never make me forget the way Tom Dawson nearly blew my head off about Kit not getting an advance."

And Ruby had sneered and said sure, sure Tom would talk big when he knew he was talking to someone who couldn't do anything.

"Well," Paul had said wearily, "I feel certain that if Tom's had knowledge of this his silence couldn't have stemmed from anything personal against Kit."

Paul's right, Gregory decided when he turned at the walk to the Dawson house. There's nothing personal anywhere.

Pale light from the drawing-room bay indicated that the study was occupied. All right, the sooner I tell them, the sooner it will be over. Gregory found himself smiling when he opened the front door. Ten to one Tom will say this hits him where he lives, he said to himself.

"That you, Kit?" called Mary.

"Yes."

"Come on in here. We're having a nightcap."

"Not for me, thanks," he said as he went into the study. "Ruby gave me a cocktail before dinner."

"Is *that* where you were? Polly didn't know. You really should tell us, Kit. Of course when I found who was calling, I mean I wouldn't have told that Spencer girl, but it might have been something really important. She handed me quite a line about it being urgent. If she calls when you're here what shall I say?"

"It doesn't make any difference." He took the letter from his pocket and handed it to Mary. "It's what you predicted, Tom."

"How do you mean?"

"Meade."

"Oh, God! It's unthinkable, it's unbearable! Kit, you don't mean . . ."

Gregory nodded.

"When that girl called I had a premonition. Mary, give me that thing."

"This is the silliest damn letter I ever read," said Mary. "Do they think you'll take it like a little man and go hang yourself? I never heard of anything so ridiculous. My Lord, they at least had some gossip in connection with Meade."

"My God," groaned Tom, "this hits me where I live."

"Thanks," said Gregory, thinking of the bet he had made with himself.

Mary tossed the letter to Tom. "I should think they'd hate to make it so obvious."

"Kit, I warned you. I told you those Spencers . . ."

"Spencers! Tom, do you actually think the Spencers really had anything to do with this? Don't you see it's just a way of telling Kit he isn't to eat with the Master Race?"

"Mary, I swear sometimes I think you're losing your mind. A man is dismissed on what the administration considers a clear case of *cause,* and you . . . Understand, Kit, I know the charge is unfounded, but I also know you were a damn fool to give them the least shred of evidence. . . ."

"Evidence! This girl chases him for a couple of weeks and then gives her mother a yarn that only Marge Spencer would fall for. I suppose Marge went to Myrtle and sounded off and then Myrtle told George. Myrtle's not a complete fool and neither's George. They know that Spencer kid and all about the terrible time she's had in every school she's gone to. Why, Tom, the president wouldn't believe it, but he'd use it. He wouldn't dare come out and fire Kit for being Jewish, would he? No, that's not in the contract, but if he could get a Jew on a trumped-up cause . . ."

"Listen," said Tom, "for years now you've been trying to put a chip on Kit's shoulder. Keep on trying hard enough and maybe you'll get him to believe it's a cross. That's your ambition, isn't it?"

"I'll be God damned," said Mary.

Tom looked away from her in distaste. "I wish you could find some other way to express yourself. You've got the girls swearing like troopers. . . . Kit, old man, forgive me, but when she talks this way it throws me off my stride."

"That's okay, Tom. I've been thrown off my stride too."

Tom shook his head and sighed. "The devil of it is that the Spencers are such damned important people. I mean since it's a case of their word against yours."

"How do you know that's the case?" asked Mary.

"I can put two and two together, can't I? Unlike you, I do not arrive at five for an answer."

Gregory knocked his pipe against the andirons. He was sorry that Mary had finally seen what he had seen the instant he had taken Trumball's letter from his pocket, that the news had already been broken to Tom. Aside from being sorry that Mary had to learn this, Gregory was sorry to find out that Norton was already reaching beyond the chairman of the department. Norton was discussing English-department problems with Tom even though it would be two years before Paul reached retirement age.

"You are lying, Tom Dawson," said Mary. She was speaking very slowly. "You are a good actor, but I've lived with you long enough to know when you're lying. So's Kit. You can't fool us, Tom. You knew it was going to happen."

"I said I had a premonition. . . ."

"What possible difference can it make?" said Gregory.

Mary was clutching the arms of her chair. "What possible difference? Maybe it doesn't make any difference to you if your best friend connives behind your back, but it makes a lot of difference to me if he happens to be my husband."

Tom's mouth was hanging open. He was shocked. He was not acting, he was really dumbfounded. "Connive! For years I've done everything I could think of to help Kit, and now you . . . Well, it's too much, Mary, too much."

"Norton can think for himself, Mary." Gregory took the letter from the table where Tom had thrown it.

But Mary paid no attention. "Tom, you knew that girl had a crush on Kit. Maybe Ruth didn't say anything to her mother; maybe Marge didn't say anything to Myrtle. . . ."

"Kit, you can't believe this, can you?" Tom looked stricken.

Gregory shook his head. "If you knew anything about it before I did, Tom, you knew you couldn't do anything. It's all right, Tom. She's just upset. A crazy thing like this upsets all of us." He turned to Mary and smiled. "But, Mary, don't you think you might let me be the most upset? After all, my dear . . ."

Gratefully Tom picked up the cue. "I'll say. After all, this hits Kit harder than it does us, but maybe it doesn't hit me where I live!"

"And just where is that?" said Mary. "Tell me. I'd be quite interested to know."

"Go ahead and play truth-and-consequences if you want to," said Gregory. "I'm tired. As Mama always says, there's nothing like a good night's sleep and things will look better in the morning because it's always darkest before dawn. Mama always says think of how much worse it might be." He said good night and went upstairs. How much worse could it be? Well, I could be married to Mary. . . . If she hadn't been quite so ambitious and if I'd been a little less noble . . . Yes, we might be married now. You see, brother, you can always think of something worse.

In his sitting room he looked at the painting Lester Gibbs had given him. It was an abstraction that Lester had called "Comment." The fluid colors revolved around a center that seemed to be an old bone. How very happy Lester was in his bitterness, in his lack of commercial success and even in his lack of critical acclaim. If Lester had been fired from a school he would have turned handsprings to celebrate. When art galleries refused to hang a Gibbs, Lester crowed that it meant he was too good for them, that he was way ahead of his time. That was a genius, Gregory supposed. The ordinary man doesn't know how to rejoice in adversity. If what has happened is good for my soul, my soul and I are so out of contact that I know of no way to reach it. Maybe in this week of grace, this week during which I'm to bring my affairs to an orderly close, I'll find it somewhere, misfiled under intellectual snobbery or romantic conceit.

He turned off the light and went to the bedroom. If he threw a few things into a bag and later on sneaked down the stairs and out into the dark . . . But where would you run? And what would you do when you got there?

9 Among his mother's many philosophical commentaries was the one about there being nothing like friends in time of need. When he started for the campus Monday morning Gregory was thinking that his mother's singularly untroubled life had never permitted her to know the disconcerting state of mind which comes to the person who is the rallying point. Mama had never been the old bone around which swirled moistly hot color. Her industry at friendship may have been very tedious for misanthropes like her son. He hoped that bereaved persons who felt like tearing their hair when Mrs. Kitner came to call were generous enough to remember that Mama always meant well, that her heart was in the right place. God knows I tried to remember that yesterday when they began to swarm.

He had nothing against his friends' hearts, but their vocal abilities grated on his aching nerves. Why was it that schoolteachers weren't content with being great talkers themselves? Invariably they married great talkers. Look at Ted Letting. Obviously Ted adored the sound of his own voice and yet he had married a woman who could talk faster and louder than any female Gregory had ever had the misfortune to encounter. Oh, he liked Kay Letting. Until yesterday he would have said there was no one like Kay. I still say so, but the meaning has shifted.

Was ever a man so badgered by unique friends? During the early part of Sunday afternoon he had tried to join in the activities, but finally he had given up and retired to an obscure corner where he was a lost chord in the antiphonal conducted by Kay and Tom. Kay's choir sang Drastic and Immediate Action: Tom's team, never pausing to practice what it preached, howled for Considered Thought.

In his hour of need a man naturally turns to his church; Sunday morning Gregory had gone to church. It wasn't unusual for him to go, but it was unusual for him to feel that the going was purposeful. He had always admired the minister of the community church that was supported by a large percentage of the Tamarack faculty. The man was an intelligent humanitarian who kept himself informed on what was happening in the world and, if he seemed to lean on the technical language of the historic church, it surely was because he felt that such language solved rather than complicated present-day problems. Gregory had always praised the man for being courageously outspoken in his plea for a society based on the teachings of Jesus, but sometimes he'd wondered if Jesus could have understood the elaborations. And on his way home yesterday he had wondered if his own education had been sufficient. He felt no response to his cry for help and he decided he couldn't benefit from contact with advanced theology.

It isn't that I have any quarrel with postgraduate religion, he said to himself. You'd have to know more than I do about it to get into a quarrel. I seem to have missed the intermediate courses. I've tried to jump from kindergarten to the graduate school. I'm without spiritual resources and I want someone to give them to me quickly and painlessly in a language I can understand. Like Kay Letting, I'm for Drastic and Immediate Action. Perhaps I'm afraid of Considered Thought. But who could devote much thought to religion when the sight of the campus recalled yesterday afternoon's quite nonspiritual discussion?

"We're together on basic tenets," Tom had said. As in all

169

radical movements, yesterday's fight had centered around tactics rather than around objectives. Was that what Lester Gibbs meant when he placed a clean blank bone in the center of his picture? Did he mean that the core of life, being composed of all the surrounding colors, was of necessity a static white, an immutable negation?

When the callers first started to drop in yesterday, Gregory was touched. For perhaps an hour he told himself this was what he'd been seeking in church. The presence of his friends uplifted him to a plane of gratitude he had never explored before. The strong emotion was too exhausting to be maintained indefinitely. He became somewhat ill. The dinner Mary had prepared with special regard for his favorite foods lay more and more heavily on his stomach. He wondered if he were going to throw up; he wondered why his friends didn't know that calls on the bereaved should be brief and formal.

Around four o'clock he endeavored to take his mind off the growing nausea by counting the number of sentences that were completed. A half hour's clocking gave Tom first place with a total of six incontestably finished statements; Kay Letting was second with four and a doubtful fifth—the people on her side of the room may have heard the closing word that Tom's blare had kept Gregory from catching. No one else approached these two contestants during the testing period, if you disqualified all easy gains such as Good-night-no, My-God-how, or Are-you-crazy. Mary, usually right up there among the favorites, didn't even show. As hostess for this unplanned party she was kept busy with ashtrays and drinks, with answering the door, with telling the children again and again that they absolutely had to stay upstairs. To intensify Mary's afternoon the Lettings had brought their two oldest children along, ostensibly to play with the twins. The thumps overhead didn't sound like play, but all four children were healthy and vigorously determined to act out the funny papers.

Although the meeting had been noisier and the language incomparably rougher, Gregory nevertheless had been reminded of an afternoon he had spent in his grandmother's bedroom many years ago. "Now Mother, now Mother," his uncles and aunts and parents had said whenever it was necessary to interrupt the discussion to quiet the rebellious invalid. Getting into the mood of the day, young Gregory had said, "Hush, Grannie. We can't talk if you do." And the old woman had turned on him and said, "Can't the children even keep out of it? Fuss and feathers, Gregory. At least *you* ought to have sense enough to let me die in peace. Wanting to send me way off to some heathen clinic to be pulled apart—at my age! There comes a time, Gregory, when folks should know better than to talk."

Yesterday when it seemed to him that that time had come, he had attempted to put an end to the discussion. Kent had just finished saying things would be very different if Kitner had got tenure way back when he should have got it. "I suppose we've got to admit the Faculty Association knows what it's doing when it refuses to study non-tenure cases," this Byron expert had said. "I admit it's reasonable to give Administration full power to get rid of people who haven't worked out, but Kit's been around long enough to claim special treatment."

"I tell you what tenure would have done for me," Gregory had said then. "It would have given me the right to insist upon being shot instead of hanged." The effort, however, had provided no more than a temporary let-up.

When the wake thinned out and the speakers became tired enough to take turns, Tom was able to enlarge on what he'd been forced to condense earlier. "If I thought there was anything ulterior, I'd tear the school apart. You people know me. Why, I'd go through hell and high water for Kit. And even if he weren't my best friend, if I thought there was the least taint of discrimination in this, why, I'd knock somebody's block off. No, we've got to face it. It's just a rotten coincidence that Kit's Jewish. We've got to be realistic."

"You're the one who isn't being realistic," said Kay.

"Listen, Kay, I know you're sincere, but you just don't understand the situation. It's obvious they think they've got him on a clear case of cause. You don't accuse a man of this sort of thing unless you're darn sure of your grounds."

"You mean you actually believe Kit . . ."

"Where have you been? You know damn well I . . ."

"For someone who knows that, you're certainly . . ."

"If you'd just stop to think about what I've said, Kay. I've been beating my brains out, but I'm damned if I can see a thing we can do."

"There are too many ramifications," said Gregory.

Everyone looked at him in surprise. It had been an hour since the corpse had spoken. "That's my point," said Tom. "As Kit himself says . . ."

"And so we're just to sit by?" asked Ted. "Now wait a minute, Kay. Let me finish. I'm willing to go along with Tom on his conviction that it isn't discrimination."

"Ted Letting!"

"Kay, I didn't say I agree with him. I said I'm willing to go along with him, if only for the sake of the present argument. I just wonder what will happen, though, if we sit by and let

172

what we know to be a faked morals charge go unchallenged. Skip the motive for the present. We agree that the charge is faked."

"Now wait a minute, Ted," said Tom. "I can't let that one go. I agree that Kit is innocent. That's not the same thing as saying the charge is faked."

"Well, then let's keep it very simple," said Ted. "We agree that Kit is not guilty of misconduct with a student. Tom, will you go along with us to the extent of saying that that was what the letter implied? Misconduct with a student?"

"Check. Only I think I'd put it that the letter implies no more than conduct unbecoming a teacher."

"Well, I think we can rule out habitual drunkenness and dope addiction and indecent exposure, but if you want to make it general, all right. Conduct unbecoming a teacher is the charge. Now. Those of us in this room believe Kit's innocent. Right?"

Several persons promptly said, "Right." Several simply nodded. Tom said nothing and he held his head rigid. Undoubtedly he was thinking of Amy. If I weren't here, Gregory thought, he might speak up and say he can't agree to any blanket endorsement of my conduct. I wonder if I'm the only one here who would be tempted to agree with him. I can't make up my mind about a teacher's right to a private life. My private life certainly never injured my teaching ability; Amy and I never made trouble for anyone but ourselves. . . .

"Okay," said Ted, seeming not to notice Tom. "As we all know and as Kent or someone pointed out earlier, our little company union won't study non-tenure cases."

"Are you referring to the Faculty Association?" asked Tom.

"Listen, Tom, if we haven't got a closed shop and a company

173

union here I'll eat it. No national teachers' group has ever been able to get a toehold at Tamarack."

"And why not?" asked Tom. "Because with the F.A. we've got all the organization we need or want."

"You've got an organization too weak to even make a stab at enforcing its decisions," said Kay. "When Wilson was fired and the F.A. recommended that he be reinstated, what happened? Exactly nothing."

"I fail to see where arguing about the F.A.'s going to get us," said Tom. "It isn't as if Kit had tenure and automatically got F.A. investigation."

"That's right, Tom," said Ted. "Let's forget about the Faculty Association. Now this is the second time since I've been at Tama that a man's been canned on a trumped-up sex . . ."

"Look here, Ted, I happen to know for a fact that Meade was as guilty as hell."

"I happen to know he wasn't."

"Why, Ted, long before he was fired we all . . ."

"We did not. A few busybodies said afterwards that they'd been suspecting him, that's all. There was never any evidence . . ."

"I am sorry that I'm not at liberty to tell you about the evidence," said Tom.

For ten minutes the innocence of Meade was furiously defended and denied. Those who had admired Meade's politics said the man's only crime was in being outspoken; those who did not admire Meade's political beliefs, beliefs so out-of-date now that any discussion of them smelled faintly of lavender, said the man was a fool as well as a philanderer.

"Skip Meade," said Ted at last. "I'm sorry I ever mentioned

him. I'm sorry I didn't know how some of you feel, but just in passing I can't help wondering if a half-dozen years from now people who don't know Kit are going to sit around and talk about him the way we've been talking about Meade. We really didn't know Meade, did we? Please, Tom, I've said I'm willing to drop the poor guy. But I'm thinking about *us*. Primarily I'm thinking about myself. If I let this charge against Kit be carried out without a yeep, what's going to happen to *me*, if a student gets ideas about me? Now wait, I know it isn't likely to happen, but for the sake of the argument let's pretend I have sex appeal and that this charge is made against me before I get tenure and . . ."

"Darling! No sex appeal?"

"Kay, I'm serious about this. Any school as large as ours is bound to have a few nuts in the student body. Male as well as female. . . ."

"Bound to have a few nuts in the faculty too, don't you think?" said Kent. "That's a joke, son."

"There's more screening for the faculty," said Ted, ignoring the joke. "Male as well as female, I was saying. I know of a case where . . ."

"For God's sake don't bring perversion into it," said Tom.

"I'm only trying to point out that any one of us might become the target of some obsessed kid. Those of you who have tenure shouldn't feel any too secure—not after the hash the F.A. made of the Wilson case. Sure, you'd get your hearing and your decision and then what? Why, out you'd go, with your moral turpitude intact. I'm not talking about disloyalty charges. That's a rap we can beat elsewhere. I'm talking about this slimy *cause*. If the administration can summarily fire a teacher just on the say-so of a student and if nobody makes a move . . . Can't you see it could lead to a vicious state of affairs? Pretty soon it wouldn't be necessary to locate a disgruntled student. If all they have to do is write a letter saying you're fired for cause, and there's no protest . . ."

Professor Jones cleared his throat. "As one who has tenure and as one whose retirement isn't far off and one not likely to be suspected of any . . . irregularities of the sort we unfortunately are forced to discuss this afternoon . . . There's no secret about my age. I'm in my late fifties. . . ."

"Sixty-three if he's a minute," whispered Mary to Gregory. "Lied about his age when he came here."

". . . nevertheless I agree that our friend Letting, although perhaps he paints too gloomy a prospect, may be somewhat justified. . . ."

Three or four of the younger people began to talk. Everyone always said that once old Jones got started there was no stopping him. Gregory had never yet been present when old Jones had been given a chance to get well under way. Heroically Mrs. Jones tried to restore the focus to her husband, but after a while the elderly couple was frozen out. Unnoticed by anyone but the hostess and the victim of today's session, the Joneses soon departed.

Every time the door bell chimed Gregory had thought the newcomer would be Harriet. He didn't want her to come, but he couldn't help wondering why she hadn't at least telephoned. Grace Lane had phoned. "Well, Kit," she'd said, "a man as handsome as you was bound to get it in the neck some time. If I were you I'd scoot for Hollywood. Why have a relative in pictures if you don't make something of it? I bet Angel Kittyn could get you a job out there."

176

"There's no percentage in our getting sore at each other," said Tom after all but the Lettings had gone.

"I should say not," said Mary. During the afternoon her coldness toward Tom had considerably thawed. Mary had never got on very well with Kay Letting and so naturally when Kay was against Tom, Mary was forced to be for him. "It can't be anything very fancy, but you'll stay for supper, won't you?"

Kay looked at the clock and jumped up. "Is it that late? Ted, round up the kids. . . . Thanks, Mary, but we've got a supper date."

"What a shame," said Mary. "I was counting on your staying."

"But aren't you going to the Goldwaters'?" asked Ted.

After the Lettings had left, Mary said it was lucky for Ted that looks couldn't kill. "Kay could have slaughtered him when he asked if we were going to the Goldwaters'. I wonder why she didn't want us to know."

"If I were going to the Goldwaters' I wouldn't want it published." said Tom. "Why didn't Paul come? Did Ruby say?"

"She said he was writing letters," said Gregory, Writing letters to friends at other schools, about a job for Kitner next year. . . .

"He really should have come," said Mary. "Ruby certainly wasn't any help. Going upstairs to play with the children. They made much more racket while she was with them. Really I can't see why the girls are so wild about her."

"She can whistle like a policeman," said Polly.

"Without any whistle, Mother. Just with her fingers," said Nan.

"Go wash up," said Mary. "As a rule Kay isn't secretive

about their social activities. She must have known we weren't invited. Yes, that explains it."

"Explains what?"

"Why the Goldwaters weren't here."

"Be thankful for small favors," said Tom. "Carl Goldwater would have been the pay-off. Aren't we ever going to eat?"

"It's queer the Goldwaters would invite the Lettings to a party and not include us."

"Nobody said anything about a party."

"Of course it's a party. The Lettings and the Goldwaters aren't chummy enough to just visit back and forth. Anyway they don't owe the Lettings and they do owe us. I had them last year, you know."

"It's all right with me if they never pay you back."

"Me too, Tom. I just think it's funny, that's all."

"All right," said Tom. "Ha, ha. Now how about some food?"

When they had gone to the kitchen Mary said she bet Kay Letting was sorry now. "The way she acted when I offered to take her to my doctor—you'd have thought she was a Catholic. But now that Number Five is obviously on the way . . ."

"That so?" Tom shook his head over the banana he was eating. "I don't know how Ted figures he can do it. It will be at least three more years before he'll get a full professorship, and if he keeps talking the way he was this afternoon he may never . . ."

"Among friends, Tom," said Gregory.

"Sure, but I hope he has sense enough to keep it that way."

Mary put a slice of cheese on a piece of bread. "Do you suppose the Goldwater party was a spur-of-the-moment affair?"

Tom reached for some cheese. "You still worrying about that?"

178

"Just wondering, Tom. Just wondering if maybe it isn't more of a meeting than a party."

"You have any ideas on the subject, Kit?"

Gregory said he knew nothing about the Goldwater soiree.

"Well, they surely would have asked Kit, if it were anything like that, Mary. Anyway I *hope* there's no connection. Anything that bird Goldwater touches turns political. Kit, maybe you're right about him not holding a Party card, but if he doesn't it's just because he thinks it's smarter not to. There's no doubt that he's an out-and-out . . . ."

"So I've been thinking we ought to start something definite before they get a chance," said Mary. "Kit, would you turn the oven on? Tom, if the Faculty Association would sponsor a petition. . . ."

"I don't think much of petitions," said Tom.

"Same here," said Gregory.

"I can't say I blame you, Kit, but that other was different. Student stuff. As a matter of fact I was thinking of something on the order of a petition, a private petition. Really just a dignified letter from the faculty, or from the F.A. officially, asking Administration to give a probationary period in cases of suspected cause where there's no clear evidence or where the evidence seems untrustworthy. Could be worded so no one would object to it. What do you think, Kit? Nothing that would be personally embarrassing, just a sort of generalization about a cooling-off period."

"Nothing would come of it."

"But Goldwater's sure as hell going to do something. If you've got a better suggestion . . ."

"Let's go over and ticktack his windows," said Gregory. He was very tired, but while Tom and Mary were discussing how

179

to word a sort of petition that anyone would be willing to sign but which only a selected few would be permitted to endorse, he looked for the ball of twine Mary kept in the kitchen. Polly and Nan had come from the powder room in time to hear him use a strange term in connection with windows and so until supper was ready he demonstrated the art of ticktacking.

At breakfast this morning Tom had said he wanted to give the matter of a petition a little further consideration. Was it all right with Kit if he waited to discuss the matter with a few other Faculty Association people? "I want to be sure it's the right thing to do, Kit. I got to thinking last night—God, I thought I'd never get to sleep . . . I got to thinking maybe we better wait till we see what Carl's got up his sleeve, if anything. I wouldn't hesitate a minute if it hadn't been for that petition fiasco a while back. . . ."

That petition fiasco was in 1940. Nine hundred students signed a demand that Gregory Kitner's status be raised. "We could have got heaps more names," said one of the girls who gave Gregory the startling news. "I mean everyone we asked to sign it did, but we thought this was enough to give them the idea. Absolutely everyone was willing to sign it." Gregory understood that; he could not remember ever having seen a petition he wasn't willing to sign—if you excepted this one.

The day after the petition committee called on him the Dean of Faculties came to Gregory's office. "I thought I'd drop by," said Trumball, breathing heavily from the climb. "I just wondered if you'd heard about a paper a few of the students have been circulating."

"Three students came to tell me about it yesterday," said

Gregory. "I don't know where they got the idea or the information."

"Misinformation," said Trumball. And then he coughed to blur the contradiction; he was hired to end arguments, not to start them.

"My reading must have been careless," said Gregory. "I didn't notice any misstatement. I believe it said nothing beyond the fact that the undersigned were asking that I be raised from assistant-professorship. It's correct to say I'm an assistant, isn't it? Of course it was optimistic of them to ask for a full professorship rather than an associate, but would you call that misinformation? Lack of realism, perhaps, but . . ."

"I'm not able to discuss semantics with you, Doctor. Not my field, you know. Maybe I used the wrong word. All I meant was that the petition was based on snap judgment that has no background of understanding. One can't generalize about these things, Dr. Kitner. There are so many ramifications."

"I'd be interested to hear about them, Dean Trumball." Trumball was the kind of man whose features you could never quite remember; even when you were with him you were uncertain—maybe it was because of his habit of hiding his nose and mouth behind a handkerchief much of the time. When he and the dean had shaken hands Gregory had thought of the bag of wetwash he had sometimes taken in at the back door when Mary was without household help. He had a feeling he could thrust his hand all the way through Trumball and experience no more than that clammy sensation. "Naturally I've assumed there must be ramifications, but I've never quite understood what they could be, aside from budgetary."

"Dear me, Doctor, I wish I could dismiss budgetary problems as easily as you seem to. In a way the wide publicity about

Tamarack's endowments has been undesirable. Even the faculty seems unable to realize that as yet we haven't received one cent designated for salaries. You may be sure President Norton doesn't overlook the problem when he has the opportunity to speak to men who are planning to leave money to the university, but unfortunately none of them has seemed to respond. It's quite natural for them to be more interested in buildings. You know how it is, Doctor, a man likes to give a lasting, tangible memorial." This was a story the faculty members knew by heart. They were treated to it every time the university received another great sum of money. "In plain words, Dr. Kitner, the more money we receive, the more we are required to watch corners. Would you believe it that not long ago a man who's connected with another school said to me, 'Why, you people at Tamarack have so much money you don't know what to do with it!'"

"No!"

"Actually. Some people are unable to grasp the situation. They think just because Tamarack is the fifth most heavily endowed university in the country . . . they don't stop to examine the strictures of those endowments. Of course you can accept a certain number of additional students without increasing your operating expenses, but over and above that certain number, which I regret to say is very small, the expenses increase tremendously. You yourself know we've had to add to the faculty. And surely you know we've had to do this out of operating funds. There's been no designated bequest to draw upon." Like Norton, Trumball was careful not to stray far from the truth. There had been no bequest designated for salary increases. Neither Norton nor Trumball cared to go into the ramifications which prevented the faculty from benefiting

from several bequests which had not been tied up with desig-
nating strings. "When you think what it costs us to receive a
large amount of money for scholarships, for example. We have
to provide the teachers, the classroom space . . . everything,
for an increasing number of students who are on these new
scholarships."

"Well, the tuition comes in, doesn't it? It doesn't make much
difference to the university where it comes from, does it?"

"But, Doctor, each student costs the school money. It's fantastic the way some people think that just because our tuition
is considerably more than the fees charged by State universities, the student is financing his own education. Well, now, I
don't expect you to be interested in mathematics, Doctor, but I
couldn't help reminding you that the budget isn't an item we
can overlook. Dear, no."

"I recognize the budget as a chief ramification, Dean Trumball, but I believe you used the plural? I would appreciate
knowing what I can do about any other difficulty. If my work
isn't up to par, I'd like to know it."

"Oh, there's never been anything of that sort, Dr. Kitner.
Well, of course there have been times when some of us may
have felt that your methods were a bit too experimental for us.
Not that we wish to stand still, but I'm sure you agree with
me that experimental education is hardly suitable for such a
large university."

"Virtually impossible, I'd say."

Trumball nodded. "We knew you'd come around to that
point of view. Sometimes the young teacher is a bit impractical,
but we believe in academic freedom and so we let our people
work out their own destinies. We've found that almost without
exception the experimentation is dropped after a few years. I

myself deeply envy the men in small schools where it's possible to try out so many of the interesting new experiments, but unfortunately Tamarack's reputation for sound scholarship is far too precious to be risked. If a school like ours went progressive, in a manner of speaking, the very foundations of education would be shaken. I know the word conservative isn't popular with young folk these days, but we oldsters must preserve the educational ideals that have been handed down through the generations." He blew his nose and then examined his handkerchief and appeared to be satisfied with the results. "Yes, I admit we viewed some of your past work with considerable trepidation, but Dr. Peebles assured us that for all your rather unique methods you were getting good results. Most gratifying for Dr. Peebles, I'm sure. He's always been so fond of you. As a matter of fact, that's primarily why I dropped by. I'm worried about Dr. Peebles, you know."

Gregory said nothing. The room seemed to be growing smaller, but as Trumball's vague face came closer its elusive quality increased. Was it morbid to see sinister qualities in the man you'd formerly considered an entirely ineffectual person?

"I imagine you know Dr. Peebles is far from being a well man, though often the closest friends are unaware of progressive deterioration."

"I'm familiar with the case, Dean Trumball. I've had several conferences with his doctor. I don't want to minimize the ailment, but Dr. Peebles has many good years of teaching ahead of him, perhaps not so many as we'd like to think but there's no reason to fear that he won't be able to carry on until time for his retirement." This may have been an overly optimistic interpretation of what Paul's doctor had said, but now was no

184

time to play into those damp hands that were folding and refolding a greyish handkerchief.

"It does my heart good to hear that, Doctor. I hope you'll permit me to tell President Norton. He'll be so happy. . . . Well, this makes my purpose for coming to see you even more important. The fact that Dr. Peebles has more teaching time ahead of him than we'd dared hope makes me all the more eager to see that his final years are spent at the school we all know he loves so dearly."

Now it was coming. Gregory couldn't understand the connection, but he knew it was finally coming. "Was there any possibility, aside from health considerations, that he would be leaving Tamarack?"

Trumball wiped his mouth. "We're all aware of the personality changes that occur in a person who loses his health. We understand why Dr. Peebles is inclined to be more short tempered than he used to be. Dear me, in his position I'm sure I wouldn't be able to carry on with such courage. Arthritis—so painful and crippling . . . We certainly shouldn't like to accept his resignation, Dr. Kitner, but you yourself know we can't perform miracles. We'd do anything in our power to keep Dr. Peebles, but when he expects us to do the impossible and threatens to resign if we don't do it . . . We know his emotional stability has been thrown out of balance by his illness and that in his prime he never would have allowed himself to become excited about something a few students, a few misguided youngsters. . . . Mind, we don't think he had anything to do with originating that petition. We know Dr. Peebles wouldn't resort to subversive tactics. He's always been most outspoken and frank, but unfortunately promotions can't be granted only on the strength of affection between departmental members."

"You misjudge Paul Peebles if you think . . ."

"Please let me finish, Dr. Kitner. I know this is tiresome for you and I do hate to take your time, but we want you to see the picture. A man's well liked by his colleagues and students and his work is satisfactory, and so persons who don't bother to look at the administrative side begin to wonder. If they'd only refrain from jumping to conclusions. Here at Tamarack promotions aren't automatic. We don't operate in accordance with some impersonal slide rule, by which I mean the time factor, Doctor. Length of service isn't the determining factor. Administrative work would be considerably simplified if time were the only criterion. But I don't want to bother you with administrative headaches. After all, that's not your job, is it? But I did think you'd want to know about Dr. Peebles' . . . well, threatening attitude. It may be that he's had time to reconsider by now. Yes, I'm sure by now he's in a more sober frame of mind, but I thought you might want to say a little something to him. As a friend, Dr. Kitner, as a close personal friend who, I'm sure, would hate to see a sick man try to make a place for himself in new surroundings."

"I see. I'm to run interference for you?"

"I've come to you simply as an individual who would hate to see Dr. Peebles spend his last days in . . ."

"Of course the loss of a man of Peebles' repute wouldn't hurt the school? Don't worry, Trumball, he won't leave if I have anything to do with it. It would be quite safe for you to admit you're here as an official rather than an individual. Tamarack couldn't afford to lose Paul and so why not say so? We've lost entirely too many big men."

"Every school has a certain amount of faculty turnover. A healthy situation, in my opinion. Maybe you don't agree with me, but it seems to me that for every what-you-call big man that we've lost we've gained one or two much bigger ones. Particularly in our technology departments we . . ."

"Yes, we'd better stick to those departments when we talk about the new faculty people."

"Speaking officially or unofficially, Doctor, I'm not greatly impressed by Names. I'm interested in Results."

"Well, you've accomplished the result you had in mind when you came here. I'll certainly do what I can to persuade Dr. Peebles to withdraw any threat he may have made."

Trumball smiled and said it didn't matter so much how the various persons went about reaching desired ends. "It's the fact that we arrive at the same place that matters, isn't it?" He said he was happy to have had this informal little chat and as he left he even bestowed a compliment upon the office. "You're very snug up here, Doctor. It must be wonderful to be able to get so far away from the continual buzz of the campus. And so near the lake. It's a shame we can't see it from Hathaway, but of course we can't all have the view, can we? Personally I'll be sorry to see these fine old buildings go. Such charm, don't you think? One almost feels the presence of those who have gone before. . . ." Was it thought of those ghosts that made the dean suddenly cough? After the spasm he spoke of Anderson. "This was Andy's office, you know. My, what an inspiration for you, Doctor. A great teacher and a great soul. Perhaps you never had the opportunity to know him intimately, but many was the time when I'd drop around to have a little chat with him. Yes, to have known Dr. Anderson was to have experienced something very fine."

Had Andy needed so much administrative disciplining? Good for Anderson if he'd forced Trumball to climb the stairs frequently. On his way to Paul's office Gregory wondered if Andy had always given in and if the ramifications had ever made sense to him. . . ."Paul, I gather from what the kids told me yesterday that the front office gave them a run-around about not having a written request." This was a ramification Gregory hadn't stopped to ask Trumball to clarify, a ramification clearly designed only for student consumption.

Paul's hands, so thin that they appeared to be translucent, rasped together. "Twenty-five years, Kit, and suddenly there's a rule I never heard of. It may be there's such a rule somewhere in the archives, but to my knowledge it's never been used before. General practice has been for a department head to make personal requests for promotions he especially wants. For years it's been impossible to get any action without going directly to Trumball and Norton. And now they pull that one about it having to be in writing. Well, far be it from me to try to evade rules. I made Norton get up and give me his desk. I said I wanted him to witness the writing, in case there should be some rule about verification. Oh, I lost my temper and put on quite a display. I'd thought I could make him mad enough to speak the whole truth for once in his life, but I was the only one who got mad. He's smooth, Kit. Why, he humored me—the way a big strong man humors anyone suffering from senility. My God, he was gentle! So what I'd hoped would turn into a good fight was nothing but an exhibition put on by an old fool who never could play politics. But I'll fix him. . . ."

"That's what I came about, Paul." Gregory avoided the blue eyes that the students said made you want to spill your insides to Doc Peebles. "I've been thinking about that petition. It's

188

going to take Norton a while to get over having the students poke their noses into something he considers strictly private. I'd like to let my promotion ride for a while. No use wrecking my future by pushing the request now when Norton's so sore. I don't blame you for going over to put the request into writing, but I do think that's as far as we should go for the time being."

"Are you sure there isn't something you aren't telling me? Look at me, Kit."

Gregory forced himself to laugh, but he couldn't make himself look into those eyes more than briefly. "Paul, there are hundreds of things I'm not telling you, but they are slightly off the present subject. What I'm thinking about now is my great desire to stay at Tamarack, no matter what my status is. Hell, Paul, I like the place and I can get along without more money. I'd just blow it on books, you know, and I don't have much more space left. You press this matter and you might end up in getting me fired."

"Don't be melodramatic."

"Well, maybe not fired, but they could fail to renew my contract. Damned if I can figure out what breed it is, but I want to let the dog lie a while longer. I know you think I should clear out, but I don't want to."

"I certainly do not think you should clear out if you can do something about the intolerable situation."

"But if I don't find it intolerable?"

So that was how Gregory, playing ball in the approved Dawson manner, conspired with Norton to maintain the status quo of the English department. Paul did not resign. He hadn't been taken in, though. The network whose programs originated in the head of Muriel Peterson, Norton's secretary, carried the story of Peebles' next interview with the president. "There's one thing I want understood," said Paul, according to the Peterson story. "I am withdrawing my threat to resign, Norton, but I withdraw it only at Dr. Kitner's direct request."

"I got to thinking about it afterwards," was Muriel's editorial comment. "He kept saying *Dr.* Kitner, but he just called the president plain Norton, as if he didn't have any respect for him at all. Boy, if he didn't have tenure! Personally I'd get him on physical disability. It would be a cinch. Honestly I don't know why the boss keeps these Reds on the faculty, but I guess he just isn't afraid of anything."

A minute or two before the nine-o'clock bell Monday morning, Carl Goldwater stuck his head into Gregory's lecture room. "Come to my office after class," he said. "Very important." Carl spoke with the brusque authority of a commanding officer and for a moment Gregory had a vision of Major Goldwater in his impressively decorated uniform. Carl had done very well in the war and even if the law hadn't forced the university to take him back into the fold afterwards, the school might have been sufficiently dazzled by the Goldwater war record to want him to return, for a while, at least. But people were tired of war heroes by now. The tribute had been paid and the law had been recognized. The time when it would be safe to fail to renew a warrior's contract was nearing. Quite enough to-do had been made over the Congressional Medal. Anyone who gave the matter second thought must have known that Goldwater was serving his last year at Tamarack and anyone who knew Carl very well must have known nothing could please him more than the dream of being fired. Carl would make the most of the failure to renew his contract but naturally he would have preferred a direct and dramatic dismissal. "God," he would say, "if they would just try and get me on disloyalty to country! What I couldn't do to *that* one. Wilson, the old nancy . . . he didn't begin to assign his classes the radical literature *I* shoot at them. . . ."

The handsome face that was usually drawn into an expression of brooding misery had been transformed. Goldwater was beaming this morning. The Major had taken over. He was a born man-eater and now after many starving months he'd found something into which he could sink those fine white teeth. Knowing the something was a part of the Kitner anatomy, Gregory cringed. There were students in the room and there were more students waiting at the door for Dr. Goldwater to remove his hulk, but even had he and Carl been alone Gregory probably couldn't have found the voice to tell his colleague to go straight to hell and stay there. Although Goldwater refrained from saluting, his departure was unmistakably military.

When Gregory started his lecture he leaned heavily on his notes, but after a while he began to notice how normal the class looked. Here and there brightly intent eyes might have fooled a less experienced man, but Gregory knew that the students who were showing breathless interest were those who hoped that classroom avidity would be recalled when grades were being handed out. With the exception of the eager beavers, the class was reacting normally. So the news hasn't got around to the students yet, he told himself. This may be my last chance. By tomorrow they'll be looking at me from another viewpoint; they'll be judging me on the basis of what they've heard outside of class, not on what I'm saying. "Perhaps now is as good a time as any to review the purpose of Survey," he said, though his notes called for no such review. "Survey is one of the required courses generally conceded to be a snap. No other required course is accompanied by such a long list of so-called required reading, but you all know it's possible to get through Survey without cracking a book."

The eager beavers looked shocked. Here and there faces which had been drenched with despair were lifted in hope. "The examination questions are of necessity almost of the true-and-false variety that a lucky guesser can pass. Those who don't want to trust to luck can get by with learning a few phrases they've taken down in class. Recently a former student twitted me about how thoroughly he'd fooled me. He got an A out of Survey even though he hadn't read a single line of any of the assigned books. Unfortunately his pleasant system wasn't working very well at the time he was treating me to his nostalgic memories of his freshman year, but although he wasn't getting A's he was still getting by. He said that by judicious selection of courses he hoped to arrive at his degree without ever having glanced at a textbook. When I asked him why he had come to college he said his reason was purely practical, that a man with a degree can get a better job. The matter of holding that job hadn't as yet entered into his calculations, but of course so skillful a man may be able to hoodwink his employers. As a matter of fact, this student expended more energy in passing Survey than was necessary. He never hired anyone to occupy his seat in the lecture hall nor did he take advantage of the services of those who, for a very small fee, will take the finals. I can provide you with a list of upper classmen who are willing to spare you the bother of writing your own examination paper.

"Sometimes it takes more energy to get an unearned grade than it takes to earn an even better grade, but Survey is a course that can be passed with a minimum of effort. If you are willing to throw four years of your life away, that is your privilege. It does seem odd to hire teachers only for the purpose of playing tricks on them. In general teachers are a rather gullible lot and so much of the sportier aspects of the game are wasted. As my young friend said, it's like taking candy away from a baby, but who gets the candy?

"Each book on the Survey list can supply you with a kind of food that will nourish you for the rest of your lives. The taste for literature is acquired very easily. The student who dips into the Survey books is laying himself open to the formation of an incurable habit. When he has accepted this habit he has proved a willingness to widen his horizons, a willingness to undergo the joys and sorrows of adventure. Through reading we are permitted to live countless lives; we are able to transcend the barriers of time and space, to share the experiences of men and women whose faces we can never see save through the eye of the mind.

"As I said at the beginning of the quarter, it isn't necessary to read the Survey books in chronological order. They were all written by human beings, but if you've a horror of writers who seem to have been deified by the passage of time, start with the contemporary work. After a while you may begin to wonder how much human nature has changed. After a while curiosity will overcome shyness. Why have these books been put on your reading list? To torture you? To bore you to death?

"The student who by some miracle fails to pass Survey but who somewhere along the line begins to grasp the reason why the course is required has taken a step far ahead of the student who contrives to pass without opening a book. Cheating at solitaire isn't very rewarding and after all the most important game each of us plays is a form of solitaire. . . ."

On and on, and still he disregarded the notes which required him to discuss books which had been produced between certain specified dates. Talk about being able to pick up enough in class to save the nuisance of reading the assignment! Today Kitner wasn't giving out anything to be stored for later cramming. No dates, no names, not a single synopsis or quotation. None but the eager beavers hung on to pencils and pens. Tom always said to look out when they stopped taking notes, but Gregory felt that the cessation of stenographic activity could be open to more than one interpretation. There was a chance that the class believed what he was saying today could be remembered without resort to notebook crutches; there was a chance they were too interested in what was being said to risk losing any of it by giving attention to notebooks. Of course I always was an optimist, he thought. Why should they write any of this down? If they appear to be interested it may be only because any change of pace is welcome.

Nevertheless he was happy, so happy that he ran a full minute over the period. During that final period he experienced the teacher's most cherished accolade; not one student lighted a cigarette, not one student made expressive gestures to consult a wrist watch.

When he started for Carl's office Gregory was walking briskly. I'll knock his block off, he was thinking. The fact that Goldwater stood a good four inches higher than he and outweighed him by forty or fifty pounds merely stimulated the resolution to punch the stuffings out of the Major. Smartly he turned into the office Goldwater shared with three other teachers. If each of those four desks had been occupied by its rightful owner and if each of the extra chairs had been filled by a student, the assemblage couldn't have pricked the balloon of Gregory's determination to squelch Goldwater. What a crowd could never have done was accomplished by one small woman who was alone. "Come in," she said. "He'll be back in a minute."

"Oh . . . hello there, Harriet," said Gregory, as if he hadn't quite recognized her for a minute. "Well, in that case I'll go along. I can see him some other . . ."

"He wants you to wait. He'll be right back. Kit, I didn't hear until this morning. I was at my sister's for the weekend. It's the most ridiculous . . ."

"Thanks," he said, and sank into a consciousness of guilt as terrifying as the kind he had experienced when he was thirteen and hadn't had the courage to take his nameless sins down to the rail to be cleansed in the blood of the Lamb.

"If I'd known about the meeting last night I would have taken an earlier train."

He sat on the edge of the desk nearest the door. "I don't know anything about it. I wasn't there."

"I know. Grace said they didn't ask you because they felt they couldn't get anywhere if Tom was there. I suppose they thought they couldn't have you and not have him. There was quite a gang. Not just English."

"Oh," said Gregory. He got out his pipe so that he would have an excuse for not looking at her.

In a moment or two Carl strode into the office and hurried to his desk. The Congressional Medal hadn't got him a private office but it had given him the desk near the window. "Sorry to have kept you waiting," he said as he produced a notebook. "Close the door, Kitner. I had to get my class started. Got them working on a creative piece that should keep them busy the rest of the hour. Remind me to go back to collect the papers. . . . Now I won't take time to give you a complete summary of last night's meeting, but if I can make out Inverly's handwriting. . . . Wouldn't you think a psychologist would do something about his handwriting? God. If I'd known what his scrawl was like I wouldn't have appointed him secretary after the Lettings went home. Kay was acting as secretary, but she got sick. Hell of a time to have morning sickness, I'd say, but I suppose the excitement. . . . Well, here's the approximate setup of the organization."

"Organization?" asked Gregory.

" 'Friends of Gregory Kitner,' " said Goldwater. "See, you're going to be famous. Well, Harriet's to cover Annex. Ted will take the main building. Inverly will organize Psychology and, incidentally, he thinks he can line up a couple of psychiatrists who will testify without fee."

"How's that?"

"When we establish the girl's unreliability, Kitner. You can't do that without psychiatrists and all. Wright will handle Political Science. . . . I see there's a question mark after Drama, but in thinking it over I've decided we want representation there, in case we decide to use the radio. A dramatization on the air might . . ."

"It surely won't have to be carried that far," said Harriet.

"No telling how far we'll have to go. What we have to think of is what may come in the future. That's the only way we can lick them. By being prepared to carry through to the Supreme Court and to use nationwide publicity, we'll have the drop on them. They'll think it's no more than a local flurry, see. What the hell is this? Oh, under Press he's got a note that we can contact a *Journal* man through you. Do you have a friend on the *Journal*?"

"A friend, yes."

"Swell," said Goldwater. "It's a Fascist outfit, but we won't be choosey. I think we can rule out Classical Languages, don't you?" Without waiting for an answer he drew a line in his notebook. "They're perfectly welcome, of course, but I think we'd be wasting time trying to form any cohesive group there." He continued rapidly. After he had finished with the university, he gave what he called the over-all picture. "Kay's going to head up outside support. She'll get Ruby Peebles for co-chairman. I'm going to get through to Mary Dawson as soon as I think of a way to keep Tom out of it. We need Mary for the Woman's Club angle. That's the best place to have the initial rally and of course we'd like to have it rent free and that's where Mary comes in. I'll go to Chicago Friday to interview a couple of lawyers I have in mind. We don't want to take a chance on any local lights who might be hand-in-glove with Norton on the sly. After I've decided which is the man for us, we'll be all set to go. The Fight Fund is already under way and so . . ."

Relighting his pipe Gregory noticed that his hands were trembling. While Goldwater had been talking, many appropriate comments had come into Gregory's mind, but none he felt he could use in Harriet's presence.

"You're down here for something else, Kitner." Goldwater scowled at the notes. "Oh, I remember. You're to get Prentiss to represent the Better Clawsses—nothing like having High Society working for us. You get . . ."

Gregory slid from the desk. "You can stop any time, Carl. I've heard enough."

"Take it easy. If you feel squeamish about approaching Mrs. Prentiss I'll do it myself, but there's no use kidding yourself—she's in it up to her neck, any way you play it. Maybe you don't see that this thing's a hell of a lot bigger than you are. Maybe

197

it's commendable to be shy about having a rumpus raised on your account, but if you're feeling bashful just remember you're no more than a tool in this, a tool we're going to use to pry the veneer from this whole stinking rotten school. Before we're through Tamarack will probably lose its State charter. Norton will be lucky if he can get a job selling shoes and he's not the only one we'll . . ."

"Oh, Carl, I'm sure . . ."

"Harriet, if I were you I'd wait until I had more background. Everyone at the meeting last night had plenty of opportunity to speak up. There was no railroading. We agreed on everything I've told you."

"But I haven't agreed, Carl."

"It doesn't make any difference whether you agree or not, Kitner. Naturally it would be simpler if you were with us. The matter was brought up last night by several who felt you couldn't be depended upon to co-operate. Frankly, I'm among those who have no confidence in your sticking. I'm enough of a realist not to expect you to change your character over-night. Of course right now you're in a highly emotional state. Living in a dream world you weren't prepared to cope with the situation. Besides, I knew you'd run for cover at the mention of Mrs. Prentiss. However, once you've calmed down . . ." Goldwater put the notebook away and got up. "I might as well go back to my class. There's no point in talking to you while you're in this hysterical condition. . . . Harriet, maybe you can do something with him. I understand he's quite susceptible to the female of the species." Smiling, as if the conference had gone exactly as he had anticipated, Carl made a jaunty exit.

Gregory sat on the desk again. "As a Jew," he said, "I have never felt called on to share my gentile friends' obligation to love all Jews. It's quite all right with me if you want to say something anti-Goldwater. In fact I'll be disappointed if you don't."

"I've never liked him," said Harriet, "and right now I hate him, but I think that's beside the point. Kit, you can't submit to this."

"You mean the Friends of Gregory Kitner won't let me? It's more than I can swallow, Harriet. Losing my job was bad enough, but this . . ."

"They won't let Carl run the whole show. He makes a lot of noise, but the others won't let him walk all over them."

"There isn't going to be any show."

"Kit, you can't stop people from doing what they think is right. I know you hate the thought of publicity, but Carl's right when he says principles are at stake. And he's a worker, Kit. He's already found a student who will testify that he heard everything you and that girl said in your office."

"And if I'll just supply the conversation for the kid to swear to? Or maybe Carl will take care of that little item if I stick at the idea of asking a student to perjure himself."

"But this student said . . ."

"I think I know the student Carl means. It's possible Carl browbeat him into saying he'd be willing to lie for a noble cause. He's a good boy, but he did not overhear . . ."

"He said your office door was open."

"I'll bet you he said no such thing. Carl said it. Listen, Harriet, I'm one of these old-fashioned people who believe the ends are colored by the means. If the Faculty Association voted to back a protest I'd be more than willing to be strung up in public, but I'm not joining a guerrilla movement that's based on a pack of lies."

"I certainly wouldn't want anyone to lie and I know the others must feel the same way. If that boy didn't hear anything, he shouldn't testify. There are other ways. From what I hear it shouldn't be hard to prove that the girl is unreliable."

"She's not a girl I admire, but I'm damned if I'm going to be connected with an effort to drag her into court. My God, Harriet, do you think I'm a fiend? Do you think any job could mean so much to me that I'd risk that girl's future?"

"Maybe we could leave that part out. I know I'd rather. They're going to get hold of the men who witnessed that thing at the Town Club last spring and those who resigned because of it. Why, even Grace Lane admits this was all just invented to hide the real reason and you know how quick she is to believe anything against a man. But she called me up at six o'clock this morning and . . ."

"Harriet . . . Grace has known me a long time. I suppose she's come to the conclusion that however I may have conducted myself off-campus, I'm safe enough around the students. There are a lot of people who won't see it that way, though. Haven't you ever heard anything about me to make you see I'm a good target for a morals charge? Norton's no fool. He knows this Spencer charge is flimsy, but he also knows that any morals charge against me will fall on fertile ground."

"Baloney."

"You mean you've never heard anything about me that would make you see why he thinks he has a water-tight case?"

She got up and went to the window. "In this hen roost you hear things about everyone."

"Of course Meade was before your time."

"Don't put yourself in Meade's class. I've heard all about Meade."

"You see what gossip can do? I never knew him very well but I always liked him. Pleasant little guy of average intelligence, maybe a little more than average, but with the bad habit of talking a lot. He got enthusiastic about Russia at a time when it wasn't very smart to be enthusiastic about Russia. He was the kind of person who would become just as talkative later on about eating raw vegetables. Anyone who listened to him for five minutes could tell he didn't know what he was talking about, but Norton didn't listen. All Norton knew was that a teacher named Meade was making a racket, more racket than any of the other faculty Reds were making. So we had Meade for an Example. By firing Meade Norton showed us what could happen to little boys who couldn't keep their mouths shut. After it happened there were people who said they'd always suspected Meade of playing fast and loose with the coeds, but I never heard any such talk before and as a rule the people around here aren't close mouthed about such things. Well, Meade didn't have many intimate friends. Hadn't been here long enough. The friends he did have were too young to be considered trustworthy. It was more comfortable to believe that the administration knew things we hadn't known and pretty soon most of us began to think we'd known those things all along. We hated to think we were really glad to be rid of Meade, but he'd been no help to those of us who considered ourselves liberals. Quite the contrary."

She turned around. "I can't see what any of this has to do with you."

"I was just thinking that people are quick to believe what they want to believe. Not very many people will want to believe that Tamarack would fire a man simply because he's a Jew. It's not going to be hard for them to believe in the moral turpitude of a man whose off-campus activities have been considered unconventional."

"Maybe if you'd made some effort to control your emotions," she said, suddenly lifting her chin and speaking in a voice that shook, "you wouldn't be in this kind of a jam." She snatched her briefcase from Goldwater's desk and, without looking at Gregory again, hurried from the room.

10

When the weather was unpleasant, late afternoon found the path that meandered along the water's edge nearly deserted. Dreading to go home Gregory crouched on the bench he still thought of as Anderson's, although it had been ten years since Andy had sat here and looked out over the unsuccessful lake. Perhaps from the viewpoint of the man who'd had the hole dug, the result was satisfactory. It was said that the lake was Bersbach's personal contribution to Norton's sinus trouble, that he'd had excavation started immediately after he heard that George Norton's doctor was prescribing a dry climate. Lionel Bersbach had made Norton, but after the new president had displayed determined independence the trustee had tried to break him.

Bersbach had been an enormously rich man and his name remained on the leading hotel, the largest factory, the finest subdivision—Tower City was studded with the name of the man who had so thoroughly exploited it. After contriving to get rid of Billy Hathaway, Bersbach had thought to run the university as completely as he had run his factory. "But he picked the wrong man," Anderson had told Gregory. "Once he got in a position of authority Norton wasn't playing stooge. Bersbach was a powerful trustee, but he wasn't the only wealthy man on the board. When he went against Bersbach, Norton went against only one man. The other trustees welcomed a chance to fight Lionel when they could hide behind George's scholarly robes. Toward the end of his life all Bersbach could do was play practical jokes on George. The lake here was one of them. Hell of a looking pond, isn't it?"

The turbulent Tamarack River should have been able to nourish its unnatural child. Geology, Geography and Engineer-

203

ing agreed it could be done beautifully if funds were provided; but Bersbach had turned the lake over to the university without any attached strings beyond the stipulation that it be called Lake Lionel; the puddle had no endowment. One of the major issues in connection with the plan for New Campus was what to do about the lake. Something had to be done or soon the area would revert to its original muck.

Gregory watched the undulation of the space between the path and the comparatively open water. Even the narrow wooden bridges that led to the piers seemed to sway with the wind. Seemed almost to sway in time with the carillon concert that was coming from the Mary Skidmore Leveright chapel. *Humani nihil puto, horresco referens. . . . Fama semper vivat, locum et tenens. . . .* The tune was the child of a marriage between the wedding and funeral marches of all time. Locally it was identified as the Tamarack hymn, officially called "Hail to Thee, My Alma Mater." The glamor of the unofficial *Obscurum* was more than official English could compete with; no student would have soiled his lips with the words printed in the university's handbook. In Latin the song was a chant, an incantation, maybe even a dirty joke. In English it was just another of those tiresome poems about the Lamp of Knowledge in Thy Fair Hand.

Often when Gregory heard the hymn he wondered if Mary's father had been saddened by the popularity of the list of bromides he'd jotted down during an Unavoidable game, but he felt certain that Professor Carr must have been consoled by the belief that students were unable to resist the satisfying feel of Latin when they could have it without effort or credit. *Infra dignitatem, labore honore, Cetera paribus, sacris ludere. . . .*

The carillonneur, attempting to duplicate the effects of the

Glee Club, started the song again. The boys sang it loud, then not quite so loud, and then in an *a capella* whisper. In Latin, of course. Everyone sang it in Latin. Carr's verse had survived as a folk song survives.

Now the music echoed from the opposite shore of the lake. *Obscurum per obscurius, quocunque modo . . . Tempore O mores, jure divino. . . .* Gregory sneezed, remembered he'd forgotten to take his vitamin pill, and started for home.

When he went into the entrance hall Polly and Nan rushed from the study to report what was happening to their favorite radio monsters. "Fine," he said. "Fine." On the mail table was a little pile of letters for him. The top envelope was addressed in a hand he knew well even though he hadn't seen an example of it in some three years. No stamp. She must have sent it around by her chauffeur.

But the girls were saying it wasn't fine, it was terrible. "That's too bad," he said, "but if they don't fix it up today they will tomorrow." No, he couldn't join them for the rest of the program; he had to clean up for dinner.

"That you, Kit?" called Mary from the kitchen. "There's some mail for you on the table."

"I have it, thanks." Was there ever a regular weekday when that table didn't have some mail for him? Even if your friends and family failed you, you weren't forgotten by campaigns and magazines. But of course Amy's letter was what prompted Mary's unusual interest in today's accumulation.

When he reached the third floor he put the letters on his desk and went to the bedroom to undress. After a bath and shave he might feel up to a note from Amy.

In the bathroom mirror he studied the face he was forced to

shave twice daily if he wished to look moderately clean. If it were a stranger's face how old would he guess it to be? His mother, especially since his hair had turned, spoke belligerently about his youthful appearance. "Not a day over thirty," she would say, to introduce her remarks on how young the Kitners kept even though they did grey young and even though they did have those awful dark rings around their eyes. "But I don't know why you couldn't have taken a little after my side. Why, you're fading away to nothing. Before you know it you're going to be as thin as Papa. You remember how your grandfather looked—just a little dried-up stick of tobacco. Gregory, you need to get some fat on your bones so you'll have a reserve in case of sickness. If you hadn't been so thin you'd never gone through such a time with your arm. I don't care what your doctor says, it stands to reason you have to have some reserve. And you'd look younger if you weren't so thin."

For the first time he noticed that the white streaks which Mary had so greatly admired had vanished. You couldn't even tell where they'd been. "Damn if I'm not white," he said in surprise. Here and there were faint powderings, as of coal dust, but the only real clue to what color his hair had been was in his eyebrows. What freak of organic chemistry kept his brows and beard black?

When he combed his hair he decided it must be somewhat thinner. As a young man he had been plagued by the problem of keeping his hair from bushing out; for years he had walked in clouds of scented grease. Now no oil was needed. Well, what age would you guess? Forty? Forty-five?

Perhaps if he wore glasses all of the time, he could hide the under-eye bruises that made so many of the Kitners look either old or dissipated after the age of twenty. The last time he'd seen his cousin Angie he had been shocked to be reminded she had this Kitner characteristic. In pictures Angie could get away with the thirty-two her publicity admitted to; in real life she looked her forty-four.

Studying his beak he couldn't blame Angie for having had hers trimmed. At the time of the operation he had been outraged, maybe just because he and Angie had always been taken for brother and sister. Anyhow he'd resented having Angie turned into a nasal twin of Hedy Lamarr. A solemn promise forced him to keep a post-operation photograph of Angie on his desk, but under that glamorous portrait was the one he liked much better, the one that looked like Angelina Kitner whose real name and real nose had been acceptable enough to Broadway. "But, Gregory," she'd said in defense of the changes, "when I went to Hollywood it was either that or character roles. My God, man, I wasn't ready!"

"You'll find it tough when you *are* ready for character parts," he'd said, but Angie had shrugged the future off. That had been some years ago. In her most recent picture Angel Kittyn had been required to play a fifteen-year-old hoyden at the start of the movie. Remembering exactly what Angie had looked like at the age of fifteen, Gregory had laughed so hard that a woman near him had threatened to call an usher. . . .

Of course what had bothered him and almost all of the other members of the family was the nagging conviction that Angie was ashamed of being Jewish. Her mother was the only one who seemed completely taken in by the talk about professional expediency. Finally Angie had discussed the matter privately with Gregory. "On you it isn't bad," she had said. "Even so, I bet you'd get a lot farther in the world if you'd just have a little of it taken off. When people see you they don't say God, what a handsome man; they say God, what a handsome Jew."

"Thanks for the adjective, but is there anything so very undesirable about being a Jew?" he had asked.

"You haven't been around as much as I have," she'd said. "You don't hear what I hear. I'm with Jews most of the time, darling, and that's where you get the real anti-Semitism. Don't you know the smartest thing a Jew can say these days is how he hates the Jews? Personally I think it's easier to have a little operation. You and I weren't brought up as Jews, Gregory. All we've got are the facial characteristics that are supposed to show the world what we're like inside. Since it looks like the world doesn't approve of what it sees, I say change. If you had a wart on the end of your nose you wouldn't think it was immoral to have it cut off, would you? Well, kid, the so-called Jewish nose isn't à la mode at present and who am I to hold out against fashion?"

He went into the bedroom and put on his glasses, but as they were reading glasses he couldn't get a very accurate idea of what they did for the hollows under his eyes. Good Lord, he thought, suddenly revolted by this womanlike preoccupation, I'm as bad as Angie. Forty-seven's not so elderly. Rather old to be starting all over again, but if I can manage to fill the interim maybe I won't have to start at the bottom. Paul will do his best and Paul's best can't miss being good. The hell of it is the time element.

"Stop thinking about Meade," Paul had said. "That was during the worst of the depression and so he had a double count against him. I'm not saying you won't have to be patient."

Paul didn't know it was more than a matter of patience. Gregory removed the glasses and looked at the portion of his library reflected in the bureau glass. Paul wasn't a collector.

Paul had the sensible attitude that value should be placed on what was in a book, rather than on the binding or the paper or the little marks that could send a collector into ecstasy. Gregory couldn't defend his mania for collecting rare books; it was a disease he had contracted early in life. He liked to think his collection had more than rarity to commend it and that Paul was right when he said the Kitner collection had value far and away beyond the monetary. Oh, Peebles spoke highly of these books; he may even have had some idea of how much money had gone into them. It wasn't likely, though, that Paul would believe that almost every dollar Gregory had in the world was tied up in that collection. Sometimes Tom's eyes would pop over the announcement of a book auction. "Say, Kit, haven't you got a first like this one they list at three hundred? Pretty smart of you to have grabbed onto that one." Tom always assumed that Gregory's purchases involved no more than a couple of dollars. "I bet you could make a damn good thing out of your books if you ever wanted to sell them. Yes, sir, a damn good investment you've got there, Kit."

I'd have to be starving, Gregory assured the reflected library. In his will, drawn as soon as he was able to get to a lawyer after the shattering illness which had taught him a lesson, the library was protected. It was to go to Tamarack University, with the stipulation that it be kept intact. What are you going to do about that will now? asked the mirror. Well, I am not going to let Norton wreck every plan I ever made, he replied. I didn't will the collection to George Norton, did I? It's to go to the university. He pulled his tie into a hard knot.

If it came down to a matter of subsistence he could go to Seyno until Paul's letters bore fruit. What would I do with myself in Seyno? I'm not a creative writer; I'm a research man and I've got to have access to specialized libraries. His mother had never understood this. She was always trying to persuade him to spend all of his vacation time in Seyno. "Why, Gregory, we've got such a nice little library here. It's so quiet, too. And they don't just have novels. Why, they've got every one of your books." Yes, Papa saw to it that the Seyno library received autographed first editions of all Kitner works. The prophet who was without honor in his own home town must also have been without parents. Gregory couldn't walk down a Seyno street without being addressed as Doctor or Professor by men and women he'd gone to school with. Mama and Papa had done their work so thoroughly that it was impossible to console yourself with the hope that the titles were given in humorous sarcasm. My God, but he was respected in Seyno. For his parents' sake he hoped any Seyno publicity about his leaving Tamarack could be handled exclusively by Mama. Mama could say that his writing required his full attention for a while, that his health necessitated a long vacation. . . . I've got to fix it so they'll never know the truth; they mustn't know any of the truth. . . . Fine chance of that if Goldwater is able to carry out even a fraction of his plans. But he's not going to. I'll think of some way. . . .

Amy Prentiss looked the kind of woman who would draw beautifully illegible letters, but no bookkeeper could have beaten the accuracy and evenness of her precise handwriting. The first time Gregory saw Amy's handwriting he had a sinking feeling he must alter some of his notions about the little princess; now, before he opened her letter, he knew it would be the work of two kinds of woman. His guess was that the business woman would be dominant.

"Kit, dear: I can't tell you how upset I am about this impossible charge that links you with that buck-toothed brat of the Spencers. You of all men! Of course I intend to tell George Norton he must retract. I consider it a direct personal insult and a deliberate attempt to defame my character and place me in a position of ridicule. I do not intend to tolerate this. I have not interfered with the running of the university. My own business interests have been so demanding that I simply haven't had the time. And I regret to say that I also had great confidence in George. I see now that this confidence was misplaced. Naturally I do not intend to leave my money to a school whose president has gone out of his way to cast aspersions on me. But I must talk to you before seeing George. Call me at once. Always, Amy."

Gregory folded the letter and put it back into its envelope. I missed it a little when I thought this would be from the department of finance. . . . But I was right a while back when I was suspecting she wanted me to come back. And now's my chance? All I've got to do is let her fasten that gold chain around my neck again and she'll force Norton into letting me keep my job? She might be able to do it. She may even be thinking of making an honest man of me, provided I'll now consent to the terms of the earlier proposals. Amy dear, you're cracking up. What's happened to the woman who considered herself above gossip? Can't you take having to share that gossip with a buck-toothed brat?

After dinner he would write her a thank-you note. Very kind of you . . . appreciate your interest . . . have already made plans. . . .

A scuffling on the stairs warned him that the twins were invading forbidden territory. Mary, convinced that his reason for talking about moving several years ago was motivated by a desire to get away from the children, had ordered the girls never to go to Uncle Kit's apartment without an invitation. The twins got around this easily. When their mother caught them on the third floor they said they had been invited. Gregory would hardly betray such confidence and anyway he didn't mind having the girls around. Sometimes Mary said he was as responsible for her troubles as was that book she'd followed until Polly and Nan were expelled from nursery school for not being good citizens. Now the girls brought home flattering analyses from a progressive school. When Mary had gone to the school to ask why her daughters hadn't learned the simplest fundamentals of reading and counting she'd been told that the school expected to receive some co-operation from the home, that a progressive school was certainly handicapped when someone in the home was subjecting the pupils to reactionary methods. "I wish you hadn't taught them the alphabet," Mary had complained to Gregory. "It seems you've got them all confused."

I might get in touch with Lester Gibbs, thought Gregory now while he was opening the exquisite *Alice* he and the girls were using as a textbook. First I'll try for an advance from the Jennings people. If I can't get one I could still finance a few months of sharing a loft with Les. . . .

In the beginning it had been great fun to live with the Dawsons. The house in Clayton Place had been headquarters for a group of writers and painters and musicians who, although perhaps spending most of their time teaching school or working in stores and offices, were confident that ultimately they would receive recognition for their artistic achievements. The one or two who had managed to turn avocation into vocation no longer lived in Tower City and very few of the others still belonged to the Dawson crowd. The house had ceased to be the kind that casual acquaintances feel free to barge into and Mary's kitchen had stopped being a co-operative cafeteria for Tower City's bohemians. Gregory knew his memories of the old days were burnished by the passage of time and that it was possible that the would-be celebrities hadn't sparkled more brilliantly than the genuine articles which Mary now collected.

In the past four or five years Myrtle Norton's weak heart had forced her to relinquish her grip on the social leadership of the university, and although she served without portfolio Mary Dawson had become Tamarack's hostess. Large bequests designated for speakers' fees had established the university as a favored stop for the circuit riders. The Dawson guest book bristled with names that had impressed Gregory quite a lot before they'd got into that ledger. When students and less-favored teachers enviously told him he was lucky to live where he got to meet so many important people he found himself thinking only of how those encounters dislocated his schedule.

But hadn't the boredom set in before the Important People? You couldn't blame it all onto the women novelists who invariably turned out to be ten to twenty years older than the advance publicity pictures had promised; the celebrated men who were careful not to waste in conversation what might be good enough for the platform couldn't be held entirely responsible for the boredom, either. Living with the Dawsons had stopped being fun when Tom started to take Mary's prediction seriously.

"Some day Tommy's going to be president of the university," she used to say. If Tom asked her to elucidate she would say someone was going to follow Norton and so why couldn't it be Tom? "That's just plain logic," she would say.

How Tom used to laugh! Mary would say she failed to see

anything funny, but it wasn't until Tom stopped laughing that Gregory realized she had been right—the joke had not existed.

That was about the time when Lester Gibbs was hanging around the house a good deal. Like so many of the young men in the Dawson crowd, Lester had probably been in love with Mary. Even the few women who had frequented this salon had granted Mary her prior claim. Tom had never objected to the presence of the love-struck youngsters; indeed Gregory would have said the attentions were more stimulating to Tom than they were to Mary. Tom hadn't objected to Lester on that score. He hadn't liked Lester, but he had tolerated him. You could see that when Tom talked with Les he was making mental notes, that through Lester Tom was taking a speed-up course in Modern Painting. Mrs. John Trumball was an active Friend of Art, and Lester Gibbs provided Tom with tidbits most acceptable to the artistic taste buds of the wife of the Dean of Faculties.

"Les, who would you say is the greatest American painter?" Tom asked the young artist one evening.

Lester smiled. "Well, Tom . . . modesty prevents . . ."

"A hell of a lot more than his so-called modesty is going to prevent that young squirt from ever amounting to a row of pins," said Tom afterward. "Any really big person would know better than make such a statement, even if he did believe he was the greatest. A really big person knows instinctively . . ."

If Tom didn't know it instinctively he knew it strategically. Tom's was a socially acceptable conceit.

A faculty pastime in those days was speculation about who would succeed Norton. Mary entered into these discussions, but she was no Lester Gibbs. Her affectionate confidence in her husband's future wasn't aired outside of the family group. It was when Mary made what struck Gregory as a logical suggestion

214

in connection with the next Tamarack president that he caught a gleam of determination in Tom's eyes. Poor Tom, he had thought, Mary's given him such a build-up at home that he's begun to think maybe there's something in it.

As time progressed Gregory's pity for Tom was overcome by admiration. When you knew what Tom was up to it was fascinating to watch him work. He was the first to propose a candidate; he was the first to groan when the ineligibility of his man was pointed out. "My God," he would say, "is it possible Hendy's that old? I can't believe it. What a damn shame! He would have been so perfect." And in a moment he would be suggesting some other aging professor whose idea of purgatory must surely have been confused with his idea of a college presidency. Tom wailed that he couldn't believe time was slipping by so rapidly; it made him realize he wasn't so damned young any more. Watch it, pal, thought Gregory when Tom said this. Don't let impatience get the better of the strategist.

Gregory followed the campaign with enthusiasm until there was talk about Norton leaving Tamarack to enter national politics. The excitement was confined to Tower City, but it was intense while it lasted. The faculty wasted little time in discussing what sort of president Norton would be for the United States; speculation about a new president for the university was snatched from its idle category. The matter took on an urgency that permitted no horseplay. Overnight one man became the center of campus attention. Paul Peebles was the students' choice, the faculty's choice; it was rumored he was also the trustees' choice. Paul's age, formerly the only thing that had kept him out of serious consideration, was no longer a handicap. If Norton were to leave very soon, Peebles was the one to take his place.

Although even at this time an observant person could have seen that Peebles' health wasn't all that could be desired, he looked more like a tired man than a sick man. There had been no effort to keep his condition a secret; if his friends hadn't said much about knowing he was suffering from an ailment likely to become progressively worse, this reticence couldn't have been attributed to any feeling that there was something shameful about arthritis. At any rate Gregory would have said this was the case.

It was agreed that Paul wasn't eager for the presidency, but everyone knew he would accept it if it were offered to him. In spite of Norton's attempts to stifle all administrative ability on the part of the faculty, Paul was known to have valuable talents in this field. None of Tom's desperate reiterations about Paul's failing health could have diverted the torrent; so strong was the desire to have Peebles at the head of Tamarack that for a while it had seemed as if it must sweep Norton out of office. Norton must have sensed the danger. Less than two weeks after he had announced his willingness to serve his country, he amended the statement; he said that although he would be willing to answer his country's call, his only desire was to stay right where he was. It was doubtful that the country at large was ever much concerned about where George Norton was, but it may have been true that the Norton-for-President campaign died its local death because of support from persons suspected of un-American activities. The united front the faculty presented in behalf of its chief's political career may have had a good deal to do with the failure of that career to survive its birth pangs. Because of the support he received from teachers classified as radicals, Norton was slandered and libeled. In their eagerness to be rid of him the faculty members had only succeeded in attaching him more closely to the university. When it became obvious that he wasn't going to be asked to run, Norton informed the press that he'd decided not to make himself available for any public office whatsoever. "Because of the pressure put to bear upon me by many persons whom I deeply admire, I have given this matter careful consideration and I assure you that my decision has been reached only after many hours of prayer for guidance."

Tom could have saved his breath; he could have retained his poise. Perhaps very few persons noted the hysteria that shook Dawson during the period when it appeared that there would be a change at the university, but hysteria was there. "Of course this is in the strictest confidence," he would say, "but I happen to know that Paul isn't a well man. I hope you won't pass this along. The only reason I'm telling you is that I'd hate for you to get your hopes up too high, but I happen to be pretty close to Paul. I wouldn't want it to get around, but the fact is that he's got progressive arthritis. The prognosis isn't rosy."

"See here, Tom," said Ted Letting, after Tom had given this speech in his presence, "I think you're a little too pessimistic. I was given to understand that Paul can expect at least fifteen more years of active life."

"I wish I could believe that," said Tom. "My God, I wish I could. But let's not talk about it, do you mind? I wouldn't have mentioned it, but I thought it might save Paul some embarrassment. . . ."

After the crisis had been averted, Tom got his bearings again. Time, Paul's arthritis, and Norton's growing favor conspired to restore Tom to sanity. When the talk about who would be the next president reverted to being little more than a parlor game, Dawson discovered rot in every presidential plank put forward.

Gregory wasn't the only one who saw what Tom was doing; now and then someone would drop a word which proved that the attempt to sabotage the Peebles campaign had been re-marked. However, the persons who seemed to know what Tom was up to weren't ones who could interfere with his plans. His maneuvering was neat; in the end there wasn't anyone else to succeed Norton.

As far as Gregory knew, the first time Tom's name was sug-gested was at the Peebles' house. It had always been considered unfair to mention the chances of anyone who was present, but Ruby had no sense of sportsmanship. After Tom had finished saying why Jackson of Princeton would never be available, worse luck, Ruby pointed her cigarette holder and said, "Well, then, it seems to come down to Dawson of Tamarack, doesn't it?"

"My dear Ruby," said Tom, "the presidency of a large uni-versity is hardly a job I'd care to be saddled with."

On the way home Mary asked if he hadn't realized that Ruby was being sarcastic. "I was so embarrassed. Ruby Peebles is the rudest woman in the world. You should have laughed at her. Tom, can't you see that your answer made them all think you didn't consider it such a bad idea?"

"And should I consider it such a bad idea?" asked Tom. Oh, he was sure of himself by then.

Gradually the discussions about the next president had shifted to a subsidiary subject. People stopped talking about who the man would be; they talked about what kind of presi-dent Tom Dawson would make.

"Worse than Norton," said Paul once in a moment of unchar-acteristic animosity. "George Norton can remember what in-tellectual honesty felt like. Tom can't. You can't remember

218

what you've never experienced. I've been forced to see another result of my inexcusable trusting to luck. Think how many times I could have said the word that would have ended Tom's contract here. It didn't take me much more than three years to size him up. Why did I have his contracts renewed? He was adequate, that's why. I'd had so many inadequate teachers. So I let myself be pleased by Tom's adequacy. I let myself be carried away by the romantic notion that it was fine to have Wilfred Carr's son-in-law on the faculty. Wilfred wouldn't have stood for Tom. Wilfred would have seen that where I thought there was nothing one way or another, there was danger, real danger. A man like Tom is a menace to education."

"That's a little strong," Gregory had said. "I'll admit he's no intellectual giant, but I'm sure he means well."

But Paul had shaken his head at this. "That's where you're mistaken. That's where Norton and Tom differ. In his way George Norton really does mean well. I abhor what he's trying to turn the university into, but I can't fail to recognize the sacrificial spirit in which he operates. Tom's different. All his ambition is wrapped up in himself. Thank God I won't be here to see him in a position of power. The only hope, as I see it, is for Norton to have an incapacitating stroke. That would give the school a taste of freedom under Trumball. The faculty could control John if he were ever put in as acting-president. You give our faculty half a chance and it will make quick work of Tom Dawson . . . but I treat myself to dreams."

"It seemed like old times when Amy's chauffeur came around with that letter," said Mary after dinner.

"Amy?" Tom sat up a little straighter.

"Letter of condolence," said Gregory.

"Oh," said Tom. "Decent of her. I always liked Amy." He drummed his fingers on the arms of his chair. "Er . . . Kit . . . I, well, I suppose you've heard something about this thing Goldwater's trying to cook up."

"Yes, but I'm not having any."

"I'm certainly glad you see it that way, Kit. I knew you would, though. It seems they've tried very hard to keep their plots from me, but I have my spies, you know." He chuckled. "You know, Goldwater's such a fool that he's almost funny. What did you say, Mary?"

"Nothing. This handle's hot, that's all."

"You'd be in a devil of a position if they went ahead with this thing, Kit. Now if you're against it I think it would be advisable to . . ."

"I'm going to."

"Going to what?"

"Get out of town. I'll talk to the Jennings people tomorrow about some textbook ideas I have and then I think I'll go to New York for a while."

"Kit!" said Mary. "You can't!"

"I don't see why he can't," said Tom. "Sounds like a pretty sensible idea to me. You wouldn't want him to sit around and roll his thumbs until he gets another job, would you? It's going to take a while for this thing to die down, but with Paul and me working on it . . . I'll bet we can line up something pretty damn good for next year."

"But you can't run out," said Mary. "Don't you see it would look like an admission of guilt?"

"Listen, Mary, you don't know what that Goldwater outfit's up to. I haven't told you about it. Carl's . . ."

"Tom, I know all about it," said Mary. "And without spies.

I probably know a good deal more than you do. In fact I'm on one of the committees. In fact I've promised to get the Woman's Club for the first big rally."

"If you think I'm going to allow my wife to get mixed up in a scheme to turn my best friend into a political football . . ."

"My dear, you have nothing to say about it. If you want to come in with us, all right. If not, all right. It just so happens that I intend to be in there pitching. Don't think you can scare me out by this old talk about politics. We've got Republicans and Democrats and Socialists."

"How about the Commies?"

"I don't know and I don't care. I'm damn tired of this hush-hush for the sake of dear old Siwash. We've kept our mouths shut about hired athletes; we've kept our mouths shut about the quota system; we let people like you talk us out of jeopardizing our morals by trying to do something for Meade; we've let you convince us that the only way to work is through the sacrosanct Faculty Association. Every time we've wanted to make a protest you've talked about throwing the baby out with the bath. You've always said wait till you've cooled off before you do anything. Wait until nothing can be done, you've meant. You had me fooled last night. I thought you really meant to do something through the F.A., but now I know it was just talk to keep us occupied during a cooling-off period. Why, Tom, I've cooled off so often that my temperature's sub all the time." Mary leaned back in her chair. She looked very cool. "You can warn till hell freezes over."

"What oratory," said Tom. "I'm impressed. I'm more than impressed, I'm overwhelmed. I bow to superior intelligence. If you want to go ahead and ruin Kit and me, evidently that is your privilege and who are we to kick? Just don't blame it on me when I lose my job, that's all I ask."

"If you lose your job it will be because you chose the wrong side," said Mary. "I've been thinking about that for quite a while. I'm not speaking morally. I'm speaking from a practical point of view. Did you ever stop to think what might happen if the faculty were to elect the president? It not only *could* happen, Tom, I understand that it *has* happened. You know, no nice trustees or anything. Just a straight election by the faculty. Oh, boy!"

"Pardon me if I show a little surprise. Shall we ask Kit if he's ever heard you speak of wanting me to get into administrative work? Not that I can see that this has a hell of a lot to do with Goldwater."

"A faculty that starts to feel its oats may keep on feeling them," said Mary. "I just thought you might like to think about it, darling. I just thought you might want to start cultivating some more people."

"Thanks for the tip, but it looks as if I can depend on the little helpmeet for that. But would you mind telling us a little of your wonderful plans? What are you oat eaters going to do if Kit leaves town?"

"They talked about that possibility at the meeting. I gather that some of them don't expect much help from him."

"Take a bow, Kit. You'll never get a nicer compliment than that. And what do they propose to do if he runs away, as you term it?"

"He can't stop us and neither can you." She picked up the coffee tray. "You make me tired. Both of you. Why don't you go and live on the moon? Do you think that just because you don't like people like Carl Goldwater, you have a moral right to

222

stay out of anything he's mixed up in? Goldwater's been involved in a lot of peculiar organizations, but for once he's in one that is constructive and absolutely essential. If you two weren't so shortsighted you'd see that what Carl's group is working on is the welfare of teachers everywhere. You ought to be willing to make some personal sacrifice for that, Kit." She turned to Tom then. "Of course if you would rather be with the administration . . . But the time's coming, Tom, when administration and faculty aren't going to be separate."

"Goldwater's to be congratulated," said Tom. "I wonder if the Party ever made a more spectacular conversion."

11 It had been more than a year since Gregory had called at the Jennings building. When he stepped into the reception room he noticed that the furnishings, including a decorative girl at the desk, were new. "Well," he said, "you've done the old place over."

"It's been this way as long as I've been here," said the girl.

"Oh, good morning. My name is Kitner. Would you tell Mr. Harrison I'd like to see him if he has a moment?"

The receptionist's pointed eyelashes rolled back and her black-red lips sucked at the air. For a fantastic moment Gregory thought the startled reaction meant she had heard about him and was frightened. When she recovered enough to tell him that Mr. Harrison was dead, he couldn't help being relieved. "I'm very sorry to hear that," he said. "When did it happen?"

"It's been over a month."

"Please forgive me for not knowing." He waited a decorous minute and then asked if he might see Miss Larson. "If you will tell her I'm here. Kitner. I've had several books published by this house."

"Oh, gee, Miss Larson's too busy. Everything's all balled up since Mr. Harrison . . . before that, if you ask me. But you could see Mr. Jennings. He's got time. Everyone around here works like a dog, except him. If you ask me."

"Perhaps I'd better not. But would you mind asking him if he has a few minutes?"

"That's what I'm here for, brother." She turned to address the mouthpiece of her switchboard. "Nauthor to see you, Mr. Jennings."

"Kitner," said Gregory, but she didn't bother with the name. "He says to come in."

"It didn't sound like that from here."

"Oh, you!" She giggled as she pointed to Mr. Jennings' door. "Just walk in. Oh, wait a sec. What's your name? I got to write it in the book here. Silly, isn't it?"

"Kitner."

"With a C?"

"Why not?"

He tapped on Jennings' door. If the man were determined to send him to hell he could say it directly. . . . "It's been a long time since we met, Mr. Jennings. My name's Kitner."

Jennings had risen. "Glad to see you, Dr. Kitner. Have a chair. Cigar?"

"I prefer a pipe, if you don't mind. . . . I was very sorry to hear about Mr. Harrison. A great loss." Gregory's memory of Harrison was of a worried-looking individual whose conversation centered around the advisability of turning you over to Miss Larson as quickly as possible, but knowing that Harrison had been with the company many years you assumed the loss was great.

Jennings nodded. "Yes, very great loss, but he'd been sick a long time." He lighted a cigar. "I always think it's better to go quickly when your number's up."

Gregory wondered if Harrison had had a choice, but he said he thought so too.

"No use fighting the inevitable," said Jennings and after a contemplative puff or two he turned from the past. "Well, Doctor, what was it you wanted to see me about?"

"I doubt if it's anything you would care to go into, but perhaps Miss Larson . . . I had a letter from Mr. Harrison a couple of months ago. . . ."

"Hung on to the bitter end."

"Poor fellow."

"Yes. Difficult for all concerned. What did he have on his mind?"

"He asked if I would have a textbook ready in the near future. At the time I was rather busy, but now I'd like to talk to someone about several ideas."

"We're always interested in a Kitner textbook, Doctor." Jennings sounded as interested as a man reading an optician's test chart. "The last one had a limited market, of course, but we feel it lends prestige to our list."

"Thank you," said Gregory, belatedly sharing the publisher's regret about the book which lack of selling qualities had forced into prestige caliber. "I'd like to do some intensive work in the next six or eight months." How did you go about lowering the level on which you and this publishing house had operated? All previous discussion of the more sordid aspect had been restricted to letters. The intention had appeared to be that some annoying underling in the company would persist in writing letters about finances and that the recipient of such letters would turn them over to a secretary. The fine relationship between the publisher and the author was thereby saved from contamination. It wasn't going to be easy to ask Jennings for an advance. "I'm not at the university any more, that is, not after this week and so . . ."

"That so? Where are you going?"

"I don't have another job. That's why I want to. . . ."

"That's another kettle of fish. Fed up with teaching?"

"By no means. But I've been fired and I'm not likely to find another place until next year."

Jennings held his cigar out for examination. "Well, well," he said. "I always did say they were a bunch of stinkers over there. Fired, eh? Tell me, Doctor, you ever think of going into the publishing business?"

"Teaching is my field, Mr. Jennings. I've never done anything else." Well, I sold the best suit in the store for ten dollars. . . .

"Textbook publishing. Related, wouldn't you say? I don't mean the business end. That's a highly specialized and quite separate part of the business, but the editorial work isn't much different from teaching. I've always said the ideal man for our type of editorial work is one who has had actual experience in education. Not that I'd say anything against Mr. Harrison. He was a fine conscientious man, but I'm sure he himself would have been the first to agree that teaching experience would have been of inestimable value to him as an editor. Inestimable. For instance, right now when controversial ideas make editorial selection look like a gamble, a man who knows . . ."

Looking past Jennings and out of the large windows that offered a panorama of the city's smokestacks and roofs, Gregory wondered why his advice was being sought. Well, it was likely that Jennings was simply airing his problems in order to avoid a conversation which had given indication of leading to the distressing subject of an advance.

". . . and so from both viewpoints the editor who has been a teacher would seem best equipped to fill the bill. You know our Miss Larson, don't you?"

It had taken Jennings a little longer to reach the brush-off, but like Harrison he had arrived at the happy solution. I'll tell her I won't take a penny less than five hundred. I'll imply that there are other publishers eager to make a deal with Kitner. Of course she'll remind me that the last book flopped.

". . . capable woman. Keeps in fair touch, considering. I

mean she reads. Harrison seemed to have a complex about reading stuff put out by our competitors. Read, I used to say to him. Take a trip. I wanted him to take six months off and tour the country, but he couldn't see it. He thought the company would fold up if he left his desk for a day. All right, I said, if you won't travel to find out what they're thinking about, at least read what the other houses put out. My God, the way he operated was like a bear living on its own fat. . . . Funny, I was sitting here thinking about it when you came in. You'd be surprised how many applications we've had since Harrison's death. Makes me think half the teachers in the country are trying to get out of education. Quite a few from Tama but none I felt would justify the breaking-in period even though I've a natural preference for a local man. Got a kind of sentimental complex about keeping the house a Tower City enterprise, I guess, but I'd just about decided on a Chicago man. Good man. Been in editorial work twenty-five years. Never taught a day in his life, though, and I can't shake off the conviction that a teacher . . . the *right* teacher . . . Well, Doctor, what would you say?"

Gregory said he didn't know enough about the business to have an opinion.

"I'll be frank with you," said Jennings. "Harrison came to us at six, but I know times have changed since then. He was drawing ten when he left, well, died. Right here in his office. Very tough on the women. . . . Man to man, what would you say to eight as a fair compromise?"

It would depend, thought Gregory, on what the Chicago firm had been paying the man, but before he had a chance to say this Jennings conceded that he would go to eight-five. "But that's the absolute top, Doctor. For a start, I mean. Look at it from my side. It's bound to take you a while to get on to the job. Isn't eighty-five fair enough for the first year? Don't get the idea that ten's the top. It isn't. There's no ceiling in this company. Right man will get the right salary. I'm not saying production costs won't have to level off before we can look much higher than ten, but . . ."

Used only to the pussyfooting, roundabout letters which hinted at jobs tentatively available at colleges, Gregory had been slow to realize he was being offered a position. "It isn't the money," he said.

"Then I don't know what it could be, Doctor. Ordinarily I'm not a man to make snap decisions, but the minute you said you were leaving the university . . . well, I got that little go-ahead signal. You know our house. Why, we've published a half-dozen of your books."

"But I know absolutely nothing that your editor should know."

"Come, Doctor, don't be so modest. I admit there are technicalities, but you're forgetting Miss Larson. Why, Miss Larson knows this game backwards and forwards."

"Then why not have her take Mr. Harrison's place?"

"Miss Larson!" A shadow crossed Jennings' face, but it was soon dispelled by the tolerant smile a teacher comes to expect from the more practical workers of the world. "You wouldn't want a *woman* in a job like that, Dr. Kitner. Oh, maybe some women could handle it, but not our Miss Larson. Quiet little soul, why, she'd be the first to . . . No, what we want is a man whose name commands the respect of the educational world."

Gregory sighed. "Then I'm afraid I must tell you why I've been fired. Moral turpitude. The charge is based on a fabrication, but my off-campus reputation isn't lily white and there's no way to disprove the present charge."

Jennings tilted his chair back. "Moral turpitude, eh?" He relighted his cigar and squinted at the smoke he produced. "Well, well. I've had a few dealings with Norton myself. Matter of a chemistry text we wouldn't let go out under our imprint unless it was brought up to date. No trouble about that. Norton wanted it revised, but *he* didn't want to do it. Couldn't, of course. Oh, he had a kid lined up for the job, but he didn't want the kid's name mentioned. Nothing unusual about that procedure, he said. I know that, but I don't like it. The Jennings Company doesn't publish books not written by the people credited with the authorship. Well, Norton said he'd put me out of business. Yes sir, and I thought maybe he could do it. But he couldn't. Maybe he changed his mind and didn't even try, but the fact remains that I sort of got over the idea that George Norton's such a power. I wouldn't be surprised to find I'm not the only one who suspects his bark's worse than his bite." He rolled the cigar around in his fingers. "False teeth, maybe. . . . You don't have to give me an answer this minute. I'll have a contract sent around to your place this afternoon and you think it over."

"I certainly appreciate . . ."

"Don't mention it. Now, look, this may be way off the subject, but it's something I'd like to get into the record. In the Jennings Company it doesn't make a damn bit of difference whether a person's a Jew or a gentile." Jennings leaned over to spit into his wastebasket. "Glad I sent my kids away to college. Place they went may be as bad as Tamarack, but at least I don't have to know so much about it. . . . Not a word now, Doctor. I want you to think it over."

Thoughtfully Gregory went through the reception room. He had no intention of accepting Jennings' dazzling offer, but thinking about it gave him a pleasantly warm feeling. Eight thousand five hundred dollars—as much as the assistant director of athletics got!

"Hey, Mr. Cantor," called the receptionist, "you left your hat on the bench."

When he put his hat on it was with the arrogance of a man who is poor by choice. Think of the tax worries of the rich! Next year Gregory Kitner's tax would be even more negligible than before. But I should have pinned him down about an advance on a textbook, he thought as he got on the bus. A man who can throw talk of big money around that way . . . why, I ought to get seven hundred and fifty out of him.

"In the box, Mac," roared the bus driver. "Put it in the box."

Gregory dropped the change into the fare box.

"Jesus," said the driver, "why bother me for change if you're going to throw it all in?"

"Oh, I beg your pardon," said Gregory.

"Move along. Back in the bus. Let the folks on. Anyone's got a kid they can . . . You don't need to put no money in for the kid, lady. It's on the professor here."

Gregory turned to look into the mirror that hung above the windshield. A former student? Then, deciding that the identification probably meant that he needed a haircut, he obediently shoved his way toward the rear of the bus.

For a while he tried to think he was imagining the difference in today's classes, but it was no use. Even the eager beavers avoided looking at him. When a pair of student eyes did meet his they skittered away as if burnt by the contact. The news had got around. The students acted as if it were against the law to look at Dr. Kitner and indeed as if being in his classes placed them in jeopardy. The few hardy ones who gamely stayed after class to claim papers displayed their uncertainty by either whispering or shouting at him. One of the whisperers asked if he were going to keep his appointments; he snapped that such was his intention. If I live that long, he thought. How long could he endure this sort of thing? Could he last through the week?

At lunch time he went, almost furtively, to the hamburger wagon that parked near the campus. He got sandwiches and cartons of milk to take to Paul's office. Over the grapevine Paul had heard the disconcerting news that Goldwater had telephoned Chicago to retain a lawyer for the Friends of Gregory Kitner. "I assume it means he's afraid of you."

"Not afraid enough to suit me."

"Ted showed me the copy for their letterhead. He was disgusted when I made him take my name from the list of sponsors. I've talked myself blue in the face, Kit, but they won't listen to me. I wouldn't expect Carl to, but I'd thought Ted and some of the others . . . But they think I'm a sick old man who's lost his fight. I don't know. Maybe they're right."

"It's got to be stopped, Paul. What can I do?"

"Well, Kit, the only thing I can think of is for you to go to each one of them and . . ."

"How many are there?"

"They've got around thirty names on the stationery."

"I can see myself going into an effective song-and-dance thirty times. There isn't time, Paul." He imagined what would happen if Carl were allowed to go ahead with his plans: Ladies and gentlemen, tonight the Friends of Gregory Kitner . . .

232

The booming microphone, the crowding faces of friends he had never seen before . . . And after the Woman's Club there would be a courtroom: Is it true the door was open, that you overheard everything said in the office while Miss Spencer was with Dr. Kitner? As a member of the Town Club will you swear that President Norton delegated Dean Trumball to evict Dr. Kitner from the club? As a psychiatrist do you swear that this girl is emotionally unstable? During the years of this man's relationship with Mrs. Philip Prentiss . . . In the name of Democracy, ladies and gentlemen . . . Democracy? In the name of Decency, ladies and gentlemen . . .

Gregory threw his empty milk carton into the wastebasket. "I've got a better idea," he said. "I've got a honey of an idea."

"Don't let Carl Goldwater force you into something you'll regret later on."

"It's a matter of alternatives, isn't it? At the moment I can't think of anything much worse than a nice big rally at the Woman's Club. I've been to Carl's rallies. Remember when he was rallying to keep America out of war? A little later he was using the same props for rallies to get us into it. The boy's an expert at the technique. Any alternative is beginning to look good to me."

As the afternoon progressed, the alternative became almost alluring. The few students who kept their appointments were dull and evasive. The office was stuffy. Gregory told himself he would be happy to leave it forever. When he walked through the campus he noticed that the autumnal coloring had gone drab and dingy. The chapel bells jangled unpleasantly off-key. It will be great to get into new work, he thought when he took the long envelope from the mail table. A job like this falls in your lap and you act as if it's hard to take. What wouldn't

Meade have given for a chance like this? It's practically the same as teaching. Teaching on a really grand scale because you'll be teaching teachers. Snap out of it, man. Don't you know when you're well off?

Ever since a neighbor woman had complained that Polly and Nan were telling her children stories no child should hear, the dining-table conversation at the Dawson house had been designed for little pitchers, and so for some months the neighbors had been deprived of the latest in campus humor and also of the more serious university talk. Tonight, however, the most rigid enforcer of the no-adult-talk rule was the one who broke it. Tom had heard about Goldwater's long-distance call. Tom was worried. "I'm meeting with a few F.A. people tonight," he said. "We want to look into this thing to see if there's anything the Association can do without infringing on the university's rights. We've got to be damn careful not to break down the confidence we've built up for F.A. over the years, the absolute respect the administration's got for us . . . but something's got to be done. I'd hoped Goldwater's gang would have a chance to wake up before he took any definite action, but apparently he was scared of that very thing himself. We've got to do something, but quick."

"Starting next week," said Gregory, "I'm working for the Jennings Publishing Company."

"Fine, but a maniac like Carl's not going to be stopped by the announcement that you're working on a new textbook. It's a nice try, Kit, but I'm afraid it won't do any good."

"But I'm not going to write a new book. I'm going to do editorial work."

"You mean you have a *job!*" said Mary. "You mean that

letter from the Jennings Company . . . I thought it was a contract."

"It was, but not for a book. Do you think I should call the newspapers? Or should the Jennings people announce it?"

"Announce what?"

"Tom, he's taken a job with the Jennings Company. If you'd listen . . ."

"Well, I'll be damned." Tom frowned. He always frowned when events took a turn he hadn't anticipated.

"But, Kit, shouldn't you have thought about it before taking such a drastic step?"

"Now wait, Mary. As I see it this is the best thing in the world." Tom made the statement as if he had advised the drastic step. "That's great, Kit. If I'd had any idea you were willing to leave teaching I could have done something for you. I see Jennings at the club a good bit. Rat of the first water, of course. I certainly wouldn't let him touch anything of mine, but if I'd known you were going to hit him for a job . . . Since you haven't had any previous experience I couldn't have wangled Harrison's job for you, but I bet I could have got you in as assistant to the new man. I suppose he's got you on one of those research editorships. He's slick, all right."

"What happened to Mr. Harrison?" asked Mary.

"He died."

"Was he sick?" asked Polly.

"I didn't know it until today," said Gregory.

"If you two would read the papers," said Tom.

"Was he sick?" asked Nan.

"Now, girls," said Mary. "Of course he was sick or he wouldn't have died."

235

"You don't have to get sick first," said Polly. "You can get run over."

"Or shot," said Nan.

"If you'd talk things over with me before rushing off half-cocked," said Tom. "Did you talk to Jennings or to this new man he's got out from Chicago?" In his determination to keep up with the news Tom was often ahead of it.

"He hasn't got a man out from Chicago."

"I guess it isn't generally known yet, but he's bringing a Chicago man . . ."

"Why, Kit, how wonderful," said Mary. "Tom, if you'd shut up for a minute you might learn something. You dope, Kit's taking Mr. Harrison's place. . . . For a man who rushes off half-cocked he does pretty well, doesn't he?"

"Mary, this continual chatter of yours . . . What the hell are you being so coy about, Kit?"

"Coy? I'm as surprised about it as you are."

"I mailed the letter," said Polly. "I knew about it before Daddy did."

"So did I," said Nan.

"You mean the old skinflint has actually hired you for editor-in-chief?"

"That's what the contract says."

"I'll be God damned," said Tom. But then he began to grin. "Say, this is just between ourselves, but I happen to know that a certain party in Education tried for that job. That's how I happened to hear about this Chicago angle. Smith was telling me Taylor didn't get the job because it was going to a Chicago man who's been in editorial work. . . ."

"Taylor?" said Mary. "As if that old fogy could get a wonderful job like . . ."

236

"Who's an old fogy?" asked Polly.

"Someone you don't know, dear. Eat your dinner."

"I still wish you'd consulted me, boy. I'll bet he's taking advantage of you. I don't know what Harrison was pulling down, but that wasn't any Ford that he drove around town. I'll bet he was getting two or three times what Jennings has got you hooked for. What's he . . ."

"Really, Tom, don't you think we might allow Kit a little financial privacy?"

"What's that? Financial privacy . . . seems to me I remember hearing the phrase when I was a child. I'm just hoping Kit wasn't skinned, that's all."

"Today at school we skinned a cat," said Polly. "A yellow one."

"Polly!"

"It was dead. Peter found it in the alley. Nan didn't get to help."

"I signed up for the next one," said Nan. "Miss Flowers said nobody who worked on this one can be on the committee next time."

"Her name is Powers, Nan, not Flowers. Now we'll say nothing more about dead cats at the table."

"It had yellow eyes," said Polly.

"Polly Dawson . . ."

"But it did, Mother."

"It was a yellow cat, wasn't it?" said Nan. "Jeepers, are you dumb."

"If you two can't behave you can leave the table," said Tom. "Kit, who all knows about this? I suppose we're the last ones to . . ."

"Nan and me knew it first, didn't we, Uncle Kit?"

"Nan and I," said Mary.

"But, Mother, you didn't. It was . . ."

"Quiet!" shouted Tom. "How many times do I have to tell you?"

"I mailed the contract just before dinner," said Gregory. "The girls and I, I mean. I haven't told anyone else."

"Well, this is going to put the quietus on Goldwater. Boy, would I like to see his face when he hears about it." Tom laughed.

"I don't see how you figure this is going to change anything," said Mary.

"You don't? Come down to earth, Mary. Your Friends of Gregory Kitner would have a tough time trying to work up any sympathy for a man who's been kicked upstairs into a job that pays . . . maybe twice what he was getting before?" Tom directed the lift of his voice toward Gregory.

No man whose working years had been spent in teaching school could have any strong prejudices in favor of financial privacy. As far as his own feelings were concerned Gregory wouldn't have minded telling Tom exactly what the Jennings Company proposed to pay, but he couldn't let Tom know that the amount was larger than Professor Dawson's salary. Tom wasn't money mad—no one passionately interested in money would deliberately limit himself to the academic, but at the same time Tom could get very exasperated when he heard reports of the easy profits that lay outside of his chosen sphere. Gregory's nod was designed to comfort Tom, to indicate that although he would be going into a higher bracket he had, like Polly's cat, been skinned.

"This calls for a celebration," said Tom. "Mary, get that bottle of wine we've been saving. Leave it to old Jennings to beat the price down, but if you play your cards right, boy . . . Now I don't pretend to know a hell of a lot about publishing, but . . ."

12 The interstices between Wednesday's classes were stuffed with congratulatory and reproachful speeches. Nobody even pretended to hold Mary's conviction that inasmuch as the Woman's Club had already been scheduled for the first public rally the projected show of the Friends of Gregory Kitner would go on. The news which seemed to be more Tom's than Gregory's had made a lightning round of the faculty; the Friends of Gregory Kitner no longer existed. Gregory became an individual rather than a project. There were those who told him he was a lucky dog and a few who didn't hesitate to say he was a dirty yellow dog. Goldwater, muttering something about a handful of silver, brushed past him in the hall without deigning to give him a second glance. Ted Letting was perhaps the most honest in his reaction. He said an opportunity to do something about a deplorable situation had been aborted, but he made no effort to hide his relief. "I agree with Kay that we can't hope to accomplish anything if we never risk anything," he said, "but, golly, Kit, I don't know how she thinks we could feed the kids and pay the doctor for the new baby if we got into a mess that didn't come out right for us. I guess she's right when she says I'm getting old, but I was getting cold feet. She says I seem to think Norton's a magician, but I'll bet he could have licked us in spite of the teaching shortage. I couldn't help thinking he never would have started this if he hadn't known for sure that he could come out on top, no matter what we did. . . . Put me down as a defeatist, as an ideal junior member of the Faculty Association. I've given up."

At breakfast Tom had asked about the Peebles' reaction; he had allowed Gregory to be the one to tell Paul and Ruby. "Oh, they didn't have much to say," Gregory had replied, hating the memory of how little had been said.

It wasn't that Paul and Ruby hadn't spoken highly of the Jennings Company; it wasn't that they had betrayed lack of confidence in Gregory's ability to handle the new job. "And it means we won't be losing you," Ruby had said, but her enthusiasm had sounded as synthetic as the sort she employed when speaking of literature which couldn't be identified with the Ruby Peebles' School. None of the polite remarks had allowed Gregory to lose the guilty feeling that he had betrayed the Peebles. On the way home, he had treated himself to scathing thoughts about the snobbery of the teaching profession. As if already an alien he had looked upon that small tight world and had told himself it was fenced by complacent conviction of superiority. Did Paul think an honorable man couldn't find a decent life outside of that fence? By magnifying critical thoughts of Paul he had nearly managed to evade the sharp digs of conscience. What was the matter with him? Had he ever signed a pledge never to leave teaching? And even if he'd gone through a ceremony of dedication, couldn't he change his mind?

The slippery glances of his students encouraged defiance. He wanted to yell that it was safe. All right, you can look now —my clothing has been arranged.

He was aimlessly shuffling papers when someone knocked at the office door. He looked at his appointment pad. It was too early for Pug, but perhaps the coach had ordered an early practice. Pug had fumbled a very important one last Saturday and so between now and next Saturday he would have to have special drill in *We'll hoff and we'll poff and we'll blow your team down.* "Come in," he said. Not much longer, he reminded

241

himself. Hired athletes won't be pounding at the door of your next office.

"This hell hole?"

It was one of those fruity voices that make you think of garden-fresh vegetables, in a can, or of tasty chocolate-dipped laxative pills, in an attractive box you'll be proud to show your friends. Springing from his chair, Gregory looked too high. Appropriately the voice came from a tremendous head, but that head was nearer the floor than you would have expected. "How do you do. Won't you come in?"

"Thank you. I'm Grantham, by the way."

"Yes, I know your voice."

The great man gave a slight nod to indicate bored acceptance of fame. What was he doing here, personally conducting a tour through the halls of literature? But Grantham was trailed by no studio audience, no announcer, no sound-effects men; he didn't even carry a script. Knowing the fellow must feel naked, Gregory regretted having to offer such a hard chair.

When he had seen photographs of the famous radio personage Gregory had assumed the pictures to be very old, but Grantham in the flesh was as out-of-date and retouched-looking as his publicity portraits. Except for his regrettable lack of height he was the reincarnation of the type of matinee idol lost in the First World War. "I shall protest," said this walking waxwork. "My God, what a garret. No wonder you're pulling out."

"There's a good view, though," said Gregory. Did I say that or did the walls echo it from a grave? Those were the words Anderson had used when Kitner, who was to take the office over, brashly commented that it wasn't much. That was a little more than ten years ago, ten years ago when, at the age of sixty-five, Anderson was speaking a trace too extravagantly of

242

the joys of retirement. He was going to write, he told Gregory, he was going to reread books he'd never had time to give proper attention to, he was going to do this and that and have a hell of a time for himself; but his voice had quavered when he commended the view from these smudged windows.

Poor old Andy, they used to say, he didn't last long after he retired. A born teacher—he just faded away. It gave them the creeps, they said, the way the old guy kept mooning around the campus as if he had no other place to go. Sometimes when he wasn't in too great a hurry Gregory had stopped to sit with Anderson on that bench near Burnaby. "How goes it in the mines, slaveling?" Anderson would ask. As a rule he kept the conversation on a breezy, humorous level, but once he advised Gregory to get out of teaching. "Get out of it while there's still time, Kitner. Get into something you can hold after you're sixty-five. The doctors and the bosses ought to get together. By God, if they're going to kick you out at sixty-five they ought to do something about these medicos who won't let you die. You know what emeritus means? Out—deservedly out. Now if I could just feel that deservedly part. . . . The hell of it is that I didn't feel that I was through. Maybe that's the way all old men feel, but I wonder if science can prove that a sixty-five-year-old teacher has come to the end of his usefulness. Haven't you ever seen a man who was senile at forty? I don't think much of age as a yardstick for measuring ability. . . ." But why am I thinking about this? Gregory asked himself. I'm not being retired on account of age. He began to slap the papers on his desk in a search for his tobacco pouch.

Grantham had gone to the windows. Tact rather than interest in the view may have taken him there. "The lake wasn't so close when I was in school," he said. "Fellow could make a hell of a splash from here."

"I doubt that. I think he'd just get a face full of mud."

"Not that I'm thinking of jumping just yet." Grantham came back and sat down. "Though I do think I must be out of my mind. After I get over the thrill of having made His Honor crawl . . . Bastard nearly kept me from graduating. After I'd sent my invitations out. I was in a spot, all the relatives and girl friends leaping on trains and sending presents and what not." He got out a gold cigarette case and then worked for a while with a handsome lighter. "Cost a hundred bucks," he said after resorting to Gregory's matches. "Seems I get clipped wherever I turn, but I used the old bean for once in my life. Last week when he came sniffing around I laughed in his damn face. What the hell do you take me for, I said to him. My God, I said, my income tax is more than that. Look, I said, why should I knock myself out for Tamarack? I paid my bills when I was in school, didn't I? Boy, and I never got anything for nothing. You've got to talk a lot louder than that, I told him, if you want me to hear. And he had the crust to say he couldn't see why I'd be interested in the money because if I kept on with the newspaper and radio work I probably wouldn't get to keep much of the Tama dough anyway. You know I think he expected me to say I'd do it for nothing, just as a favor to him, I suppose. I said to him Well, brother, I said, even if I only got to keep ten cents on the dollar I'd screw the university for every damn dime I could get and then some. Did I ask him to make me a proposition? Trying to cash in on my publicity value, that's what he's trying to do. I got it, all right. Norton, I said, you don't fool me one little minute. I don't give a damn what kind of shenanigans you're up to, I said, except when

244

they begin to touch me. And so far, I said, you haven't even begun to touch me." He leaned over to use the ashtray. "Very stiff when he left me. That was last week, see. First part of the week, I mean. A few days later he was singing a different tune. You know, tentative. So I gave it to him and he says to me, Why, Mr. Grantham, he says, you must be joking. Ha, ha, he says, why the head of the department doesn't make any more than that and few of the other salaries come anywhere near the figure." For purposes of dramatization Grantham was doing Norton's speeches in a falsetto that was unjust to a voice nearly as organlike as his own. "Is that so, I said. Well, if I were you, President Norton, I said, I wouldn't go around publishing the fact. . . . I don't know why I'm telling you all of this."

Gregory didn't know either. It was obvious that Grantham hadn't come to crow. Maybe he'd come simply to let off steam. "Our Frannie," Clif Davis had said when speaking of his paper's most valuable asset next to the comic strip that supplied its lifeblood, "is the kind of guy you instinctively hate, but you don't feel right about it. You can't get away from the feeling that the jackass means well." Maybe so. Maybe, meaning well, the jackass had come around to comfort Kitner by reviling Norton. There had to be other pieces before the puzzle could be made into a recognizable picture, though.

"Maybe I ought to see a psychiatrist, Kitner. It can't be the extra money. Maybe I've been harboring a secret yen to lay down the law where it was laid down to me. Revenge motive." The rather pretty face took on so introspective an expression that Gregory felt good manners required him to look elsewhere. "But I'm sunk now, Kitner. What could I do when he met my terms?"

Gregory looked into the hall. Pug Sanderson was standing

there. The boy was probably trying to decide if it were necessary to knock on a door that was open. "Uh, if you're busy, Doc . . ."

"Come in, Pug. Mr. Grantham, this is one of the B2 students, Mr. Sanderson. Pug, Mr. Grantham is taking my work over." When he said this he wondered if the deduction could be correct. Was it possible that the man who for years had provided the English department with lavish ingredients for laughing stock would shortly be a member of that superior group of cooks? I misjudged Carl Goldwater when I thought he was the only one who could give the university a real black eye; Norton can do it every time—there's nobody like him. Come on, Grantham, say I've misunderstood what you've been saying. Tell me you've been hired to give a course in radio at the School of Drama. It just wasn't possible that Francis Grantham had been hired to teach English. The man had difficulty in reading English.

"Is that a fact?" said Pug.

"The football Sanderson?" Grantham stood up and extended a plump hand.

"It sorta depends on Doc here, I guess," said Pug. "I'm not doing so hot in B2, it looks like."

"It doesn't depend on me much longer, Pug. Mr. Grantham is taking over my classes."

Pug let go of Grantham's hand. "Is that a fact?" He seemed to be beginning to get it. You couldn't expect the boy to clutter up his important head with campus chatter. As Hoffman had told Gregory, Pug was almost a mathematical genius, maybe not on paper but certainly on the field, and if practical mathematics wasn't a lot more important than being able to calculate on paper, Hoffman didn't know from up. Reminded that mathe-

246

matics wasn't the subject under scrutiny, Hoffman had said it all added up to the same thing—teachers didn't know a genius when they saw one. "They got to be dead before you birds will give them any credit," the coach had said, and Gregory had answered that Hoffman was doing his share, then. "Because you certainly operate as if you were trying to kill those boys, Hoffman. . . ."

"Maybe I better come around later if you're tied up now, Doc," said Pug.

"You may as well wait until next week for your conference, Pug. Mr. Grantham will be teaching B2 next week." *If I say this often enough I'm going to start believing it. Why, I'd sooner believe that Jefferson was going to take my place . . . much sooner.*

"Is that a fact?"

"It is a trifle fantastic, isn't it?" said Grantham. He had sat down, but he was still stroking the little hand so foolishly entrusted to Pug a few minutes ago.

"Well, gee, I don't have much on my mind," said Pug, "like what would make with a conference and stuff, but Hoffman says I got to stay eligible."

"But absolutely," said Grantham. "Where would the Lionels be without Pug Sanderson? I agree with the coach."

"That's mighty nice of you, Dr. . . ."

"Grantham," said Gregory.

"And no doctor," said Grantham. "Though I'm thinking of asking for an honorary." He laughed to let them see he considered this a joke.

Dutifully Pug laughed, but he didn't look entirely at ease. "You mean you aren't going to have B2 any more, Doc?"

"I'm leaving the university, Pug."

247

The boy seemed astounded. "Is that a fact!" he said. "Why, what do you want to go and do that for?"

"Dr. Kitner is a sensible man," said Grantham. He spoke rapidly and firmly. "Far more sensible than I, I fear. I haven't the slightest hope of ever being able to take his place adequately, but I trust I won't let you and the others down too much, Sanderson."

"Gee, I didn't mean that, Dr. . . . Mr. . . ."

"Grantham."

"Yes, sure, thanks. I only meant that, well, I guess we'd kind of got used to Doc here, and I . . . Say, I know who you are, Mr. Grantham. I used to listen to you when I was a kid. I sure was nuts about those cookies."

"I'm with a different sponsor now," said Grantham, "but I have a . . . well, shall we say, slightly nostalgic interest in Candied Cookies. Maybe you'd like to give the C.C. program a little endorsement some time, you know, just say that part of your training diet was based on Candied Cookies, or something to that effect. You wouldn't have to do anything but read what somebody else would write."

"Gee, I'd like to, Mr. Grantham, but I'm afraid there's some kind of a rule. . . ."

"Oh, I'm sure we wouldn't want to break any rules, Sanderson. But we'll talk about it later. Maybe when you come to see me next week? We don't want to do anything that might jeopardize your position, you may be sure of that. The Lionels need you. . . ."

For three or four minutes there was an animated discussion of what last week's game had done to the chances for the title. Gregory and Grantham agreed that the Lionels still had a very good chance; Pug showed some doubt.

"Listen, boy, if you're worrying about . . . what's this course you're worrying about? B2. Well, I wouldn't let that worry me too much, Sanderson."

"Well, thanks a lot, Mr. Grantham. But I sure hate to see you go, Doc. I mean, well, you were helping me see it, I mean the rules and all, like you said being important . . ." After a few more sentences that tore at Gregory's heart and left his head singularly free of grammatical criticism, Pug went away.

"Sweet Jesus," said Grantham. "He can have straight A, if he wants it. Or do you think that would make him shake my hand again. Perhaps a C would be safer? Well, let's get on with the lesson. After you see that all the football boys are nice and eligible, then what? And what's all this about conferences? Norton never told me anything about conferences. Unpaid tutor stuff, eh? Not me, Kitner. I'm not going to let these kids pick my brain for free."

Did this professional plagiarizer think a brain was a pocket, something liable to be emptied by covetous fingers? "I've always felt that a teacher profits personally as well as professionally from close association with individual students," said Gregory. "All of our classes are so large now that in order to establish any kind of direct contact it's become necessary to set up a system of conferences. The interviews have to be brief, but . . ."

"I'm keeping on with my newspaper and radio work, for God's sake," said Grantham, "to say nothing of various other interests. . . ." He nibbled at a fingernail. "I wish I could work in a angle there between Candied Cookies and Sanderson —I have a piece of the company, see. Nope, conferences are out, as far as I'm concerned. Nothing in the contract about them. I had my lawyer read it and make a summary for me and

I know just what I've let myself in for. I'm not going to let myself be cornered up here by a lot of radio-struck kids hounding me for a job. No. Now what about papers? Norton said you'd have to tell me about that, but I thought I detected a nasty gleam in his eyes when he said it, as if he thought he was getting back at me."

So Gregory explained about papers, about the allowance for readers' fees. "For the past two years I've had to have additional assistance now and then, but in general I've found it possible to get along with one reader. The man I . . ."

"If I can't get an adjustment in that fee, I'll pay it out of my own pocket," said Grantham. "I can take it out of my income tax, can't I? Legitimate business expense. No reading for me."

"But you'll want to keep in touch with the progress your students are making."

"The hell I will. Look, Kitner, they pay me to talk and I talk. Fair enough. Beyond that, no."

"But, Mr. Grantham, when the classes are so large that you can't have recitation . . ."

"The contract says I'm hired as a lecturer. Okay, I'll lecture. Now what about this outline Norton said you'd give me? If you could let me have it today I'll get my secretary busy on it. Fortunately I've saved all my college notebooks. I write shorthand—my mother, poor soul, had the notion that I'd be some rich man's secretary . . . it's been very useful, though. I bet I have a copy of every lecture I ever attended. And I've got a good secretary. When I give her your outline she can start assembling the material. I've a very fine library. I wish you'd come around and see it some time. Autographed copies and all. They're always so pathetically grateful when you give them a plug. . . ."

"I haven't had a chance to check these," said Gregory as he took the file folders from the deepest drawer of his desk. "They were written for my own use and so I'm afraid you'll find them a little spotty."

"That's all right. I'll have the girl transcribe them and then get them back to you. Well, that about covers it, doesn't it? It doesn't seem so bad now that I've talked it over with you. My God, I've made enough speeches in my life not to get stage fright and, popular opinion to the contrary, I do not have to have a microphone in front of my face every time I open my mouth." Grantham smiled engagingly. "Between you and me, I don't feel quite at home without it, but I can manage. I don't think I'll run into any trouble with old Peebles, do you? I understand he's not in very good health these days."

"He gets around."

"Glad to hear it. I always thought a lot of old Peebles. I guess I won't have any trouble there." Grantham looked around the office. "They're going to have to do something about this if they expect me to put in any time in a campus office. I don't know why I should, though. I've got a perfectly good office of my own. But the kids will have to keep out of my way. My God, that's why I gave up the Cookie show. Even after I started with Halls of Literature I couldn't make a move without knocking some damn kid down. Talk about Sinatra. Why, the kids were making my life miserable before Sinatra was out of diapers."

"I think you'll find the university crowd different."

"Boy, you're in a position to be cheerful. Believe me, you have my hearty congratulations for getting out of a job I wasn't smart enough to steer clear of. . . ."

It was too bad, thought Gregory, that Grantham hadn't been apprised of the Jennings connection before he made this call.

His closing remarks wouldn't have had to be quite so hearty. For a while when he and Grantham were standing at the door Gregory wondered if the lengthy farewell were going to include a lifetime supply of Candied Cookies plus browsing privileges in the Grantham library. Grantham was so obviously sorry for him. That's why he spoke slightingly of the students and the job. If he felt the way he claimed to feel, he wouldn't have accepted the offer. And if he continues to borrow from men like Paul, his lectures should be of value. . . . Maybe Jefferson can take on more of the grading.

After he had reassured himself that the prospect for the courses formerly taught by Kitner wasn't too dim, Gregory asked himself if he could think of one student he would willingly turn over to the team of Grantham and Jefferson. I'd be willing to give Ruth Spencer to them, but she's gone. She's the only one. I can't even bear the thought of their having Pug.

He smiled then in recognition of the fact that Pug Sanderson had become one of his favorite students. In this grim world there weren't many persons who would laugh today at a joke you had told yesterday.

Tom was hanging his coat in the closet when Gregory opened the front door. "So *there* you are," said Tom, as if he had been looking high and low. "Have you heard about Grantham?"

"He called on me this afternoon." Gregory went to the mail table. "Scraping the bottom of the barrel, aren't they?"

"I wouldn't say that. Grantham's got a big name, and he's certainly an authority."

"On what? Cookies?"

"Now wait a minute, Kit. I've no desire to get into a fight with you about Grantham's qualifications. It's all right with me if you don't think highly of him, but I think you ought to know that I was consulted."

"Sorry. I thought you disapproved."

"It's the salary that burns me up. I'm not saying I blame the president. He was in a corner, a very tight corner, but I never dreamed that half-pint windbag would take advantage of his alma mater, his own school. To put the squeeze on at a time like this . . . The story's all over the campus. Norton ought to do something about that girl in his office. She tells everything she knows. Everyone's saying he's getting full-professor pay, the lowest, naturally, but all the same it's no less than quite a few of our full professors. . . ."

Gregory could tell that Tom was trying the story on him. Everyone was saying that? Wasn't everyone saying Grantham was going to get as much as a department head? There was no reason to believe that Grantham had lied about the salary. Tom was the one who was lying. Hadn't he just said he'd been consulted? Gregory believed that part. No sane man would admit to having been consulted in the hiring of Francis Grantham unless such had been the case. If I were you that's one I'd get out from under, Tom. That's one I'd let Norton have full credit for. . . . And just when were you consulted, Tom? Was it before I was fired?

"Of course he's on as a lecturer and that means we'll tie a can to him as soon as we can get someone else. But who the hell does he think he is? Bernard Shaw? But don't get me wrong, Kit. I'm not criticizing Norton."

"I know. I get it. It's all my fault."

"Well, when you boil it down I'd like to know who else's it could be. Oh, you can be gay enough about it. You're fixed. Naturally you don't worry about the mess we're left in."

253

"Tom, are you just exercising, or would you like me to throw some of those back?"

"What the hell are you driving at?"

"Okay. Norton began sounding Grantham out before I was fired. It would seem that perhaps this sounding out came a little before Mrs. Spencer appeared with her tale of woe."

"I don't believe any such thing."

"If you're telling the truth, then you weren't consulted at the very beginning. Try to be realistic about your position, Tom. Norton is recognizing you as head of the department, all right, but don't kid yourself that he's paying any more attention to you than he used to pay to Paul."

"He'd hardly expect me to have a part in any plan to fire a friend of mine. Not that I believe any of this cock-and-bull."

"And Grantham's pay will be the same as Paul's. Naturally you had nothing to do with that decision. Tom, for your own sake, soft pedal any comments about Grantham's ability. He's a horse's ass and if you don't know it, I'll bet Norton does. He's worse than a horse's ass, as a teacher he's a crook. But his name will look well in the papers."

"I said we'd get rid of him as soon as we locate a good man, didn't I?"

"The Goldwater crowd has been squelched for the time being, Tom. Don't tell me you're going to get rid of Goldwater. I know you are. I'm sure you've already been consulted about it and I don't suppose you gave the opinion that Carl's just about the best safety device the university can have."

"Come again?"

"Sure, get rid of the crackpots who mess up decent attempts for self-government and there's a good chance you'll get more self-government than you bargained for."

"Listen, Kit, I know you're sore because the F.A. wouldn't help you, but . . ."

"But how's the F.A. taking Grantham? Brother, I bet even Trumball caught his breath when he heard about Grantham's salary. I wouldn't bank too much on Norton if I were you. It strikes me that a situation's been created that may require a little more than he's got. I'd say he's begun to overreach himself. I'd say that when he tries to amend the retirement rule he may find himself up against some real opposition."

"What do you mean—amend the retirement . . ."

"Oh, hasn't he consulted you about that? Strange, he didn't hesitate to let me in on it. But you're still young, Tom. Don't let it throw you."

"I don't believe it."

"Okay. I'd keep my eyes peeled, though, if I were you. Even a company union can turn mean, you know. Might be Norton won't have to amend the rule. Might be he won't be around long enough to care about it."

"Are you having fun with your little pipe dream?"

"Tom, you've always been swell about giving me advice. So now I'm giving you some. You've picked the wrong team. If I were you I'd change over before it's too late, or at least I'd be careful about admitting I was mixing in administrative company."

"Well, thanks. Coming from one who's had such spectacular success, it means even more." Tom paused, perhaps to count ten. Dr. Dawson did not lose his temper. Even when you hit him where he really lived, he did not lose his temper. "You can't get a rise out of me, Kit. I know you're in a hell of a bad mood and I don't blame you. I'm not going to let myself get hot under the collar about anything you say. So let's skip it. The

255

whole thing's giving me ulcers. . . . Where the hell is everybody?"

Gregory started up the stairs but before he reached the landing Mary and the girls stormed into the house.

"Oh, Tom!" said Mary. Then she saw Gregory. "Oh, Kit . . . I have the most ghastly news. Guess who's going to take your place!"

13 Friday breakfast was prolonged by discussion of how to get the Kitner possessions from the campus to Clayton Place. Tom grunted and puffed over his appointment book. "I wish you wouldn't worry about it," said Gregory.

"Tom's going to help you," said Mary.

"Absolutely, old boy. Let's see, I could be at your office at four-thirty. . . ."

"I've got Prose and Poetry from four to six."

"But surely not today, Kit," said Mary.

"Make it five then," said Tom. "That should give you ample time to wind them up."

"I wonder if Grantham will take the Society over," said Mary.

"God forbid." Tom sighed as he put his appointment book away. "I wish I had time for it. Most worthwhile little club, but I don't see how I can take on any more. You might tell them I'll be glad to act in an advisory capacity, Kit, if they can get some other faculty person to attend the meetings. We certainly wouldn't want the group to go out of existence. Fact is I've been trying to work out some way to put it into the curriculum. Norton seems very favorable to the idea. . . . I don't mean to imply that I don't think Grantham's up to it, but he doesn't seem quite the type and anyway I'd rather take a longer view. Rather get someone in there who's going to be around for a while."

"You don't have to worry about Grantham wanting to horn in. He gave me to understand he doesn't intend to become involved in any outside activities."

"Glad he sees it that way. I figured he'd be smart enough to realize his appointment is temporary. Yes, Norton seems very

257

favorable to the idea of converting Prose and Poetry into a credit course. Naturally there will have to be some changes in the setup. You can see that, Kit. If you're going to give them credit, you're going to have to tighten up on the magazine. I'm not saying you haven't done a pretty good job, but I've always felt that with a little sane censorship . . ."

Gregory had organized the Prose and Poetry Society ten years ago. The group put out a quarterly, a mimeographed job, that Tom had found most amusing until one of its stories had been bought by a regular magazine. From then on Tom had spoken encouragingly of the little project and had often said he wished he had time to help with the selection of the material. With commendable pride he later pointed to the established writers who had got their start on the quarterly and generously gave all the credit to his friend Kit. "Kit ought to start collecting agent's fees from those Prose and Poetry kids of his," he would say. "Why, he sends that little quarterly around to the magazines and doesn't even get the postage out of it. . . ."

"I wish you could keep on with the Society," said Mary now. "Since it really hasn't any official connection with the university. . . . I'd be glad to have them meet here."

"Mary, I was just saying that it looks as if it will be having an official connection. Anyway, Kit wouldn't have time. My God, do you think this is a part-time job he's taking at the Jennings Company? Not that I don't agree with you that the Society is going to have a tough time without him."

"It's run itself for years," said Gregory. "I don't even hold voting power."

"That's where I think you've gone a little too far off the track, Kit. Seems to me the batting average would be a whole lot higher if . . . oh, well, you don't want to listen to my ideas.

258

You've got bigger things on your mind. Well, I'll be at your office promptly at five."

"Remember we've got a bridge date with the Trumballs tonight," said Mary. "Try not to be too late for dinner."

"Oh, God." In the privacy of his home Tom made no secret of the fact that he had become very tired of the Trumballs. "The things we have to do. . . . Couldn't we get out of it?"

"I don't see how. They asked us two weeks ago and let us choose the night. . . . More coffee, Kit?"

Gregory looked at his watch. "Only a half cup."

"Oh, I forgot to give you a message. Mother called up after you'd gone out last night. I don't know what she was talking about, but she said to tell you it proved she should have stuck to her guns."

"What guns?" asked Tom.

"I'm sure I don't know. She and Kit are always using double-talk."

Suppose, thought Gregory on his way to the campus, suppose people like Nettie did stick to their individual guns. Suppose she and the others who disapprove of discriminatory restrictions didn't confine themselves to discussions with sympathizers. . . . My God, would I want Nettie to give up her room? And if she had stuck to her guns that's what she would have had to do. And with what result? Why, the River Arms would be tickled to death to get rid of an old woman who had tried to tell them how to run their hotel. They've got a waiting list. I don't know why I should have any feeling of guilt about having advised her to drop her crusade.

And why should I feel guilty about *this*? he asked himself when he was accepting presents from the students. I'm taking

259

nothing under false pretences. By now they've heard all there is to hear and if they want to give me presents, all right.

Oh, students were looking him in the eye today. They were congratulating him about the Jennings job. They said they hated to see him go, but they said it as if they were proud of him. Today, his last day at Tamarack University, his classes permitted no schoolteaching. The day was brimming with gifts, with humorous verses, with cheering and applause. Two graduate students, replete in cap and gown, burst into the three-o'clock with stacks of themes which they demanded he publish in the best calf. He couldn't believe his eyes when he saw that one of these comedians was Jefferson. Jeff whacked him on the back and yelled, "Nice going," and soon was leading a snake dance. The stamping cavalcade was accompanied by a vociferous rendition of *For He's a Jolly Good Fellow*.

Gregory judged that the celebration meant that the students felt he had put one over on Authority and that this gave them marvelous satisfaction. If even the pompous Jefferson could lose his head . . .

It was a drunk man who went blindly into the hall after that three-o'clock, a drunk man who ran into a stiff, noncelebrating figure which suddenly loomed up to block his way.

"Having fun?" asked Goldwater.

Somehow the knowledge that there would be no presents, no singing, no snake dancing when Goldwater left the university provided little consolation. The sight of Goldwater's face, however, was sobering.

No truthful person could say Tom Dawson didn't lift a finger in his friend's behalf. When Gregory came to the office from the Prose and Poetry meeting Tom was busy filling cartons. "I didn't like to go ahead without you," said the perspiring worker, "but it was getting so damned late. I got these cartons at the store. I thought you probably wouldn't think about them. Where the dickens have you been? It's almost six. I had to get Pete to let me in."

"They had a cake. I couldn't very well leave until after they'd cut it."

"What's that you've got? Another present?"

Gregory put the portfolio on top of the bookcase so that Tom wouldn't hurl it into a carton. "They gave me a complete file of the magazine."

"I'm glad one bunch had sense enough not to give you a pen-and-pencil set. My God, it looks like you're going to have to spend the rest of your life under water. . . . Say, those magazines may be worth quite a lot of money by now. First published work of that Youngren fellow, for example. You know I was wondering when you said you'd turned your file over to the library the other day. . . . Seemed too bad for you to feel you had to give it up, but now that they've given you another set. . . . Okay if I keep on just putting everything in the cartons? I don't know why you've kept all this junk. Now that you know you won't be using any of it any more, why don't you . . ."

"There's no use to take the time to sort it now."

"Well, I bet I could move my office in just one of these cartons. I never keep anything unless I'm sure it will be of some value to me in the future."

"Lend me your crystal ball some time."

"I don't see why you have to be so damn touchy," said Tom, but from then on he was extremely thoughtful. How he hurried ahead on the last trip down to the car!

The sight of Tom hurrying was enough to make anyone wonder what was up. As soon as Gregory started down the last flight
of stairs he understood. The Burnaby office door was open and
Miss Chester was standing at the end of the counter near the
key box. So Tom had hurried ahead in order to avoid being a
witness to the turning in of the Kitner keys? Miss Chester
looked as if she too would like to flee the building. All week it
had been evident that Miss Chester was finding her position
difficult. Paul Peebles was her boss and he was making no secret
of his stand on the Kitner case, but the Burnaby secretary
couldn't forget that there was a boss-of-bosses. She was still
speaking to Dr. Kitner, but she wasn't beaming at anyone who
was in the presidential doghouse.

This was the third or fourth time she had acknowledged
Gregory's existence today, but luckily it was late enough now
for her to vary the greeting. "Good evening," she said in a loud
voice. She was holding to the counter as if she might tear it
from its mooring in case of assault.

Gregory nodded. The box in his arms prevented him from
doing anything about the hat that was jammed on the back of
his head. Miss Chester didn't need to fear that she was in for a
scene. He was under no obligation to hand his keys over now.
They were his until midnight, weren't they?

At the stroke of twelve he might take them to Grantham and
say, Here, Grantham, are the keys to those halls of literature
you're always yapping about. Might as well make the embarrassment general. Not that Grantham wasn't already embarrassed. Everyone but the manipulator was ill at ease, and perhaps he had had uncomfortable minutes while Grantham was
holding out. Yes, and there was a chance that Norton was still
uncomfortable about Grantham. Hiring an inexperienced man

who had a poor reputation among scholars was bad enough, but hiring him at an enormous salary was a bad tactical error which indicated that Norton might be slipping. I'd say it's safe to generalize that everyone who has been touched by this wouldn't mind having the clock turned back a couple of weeks. It's conceivable that even Ruth Spencer takes a few minutes out from her plotting; I'll bet she's had lucid moments during which she's seen she was no more than a prop in this tin-whistle opera. That ridiculous and pitiful telegram yesterday . . . poor kid, trying to hang on to the illusion of importance. "Unable to reach you by telephone before leaving," the telegram had said. She gave him her present address, a Florida hotel, but warned him—yes, she was trying to protect her dream—against immediate action. "Am under constant guard but will manage contact later. Meantime all love." He had accepted the telegram as Miss Spencer's sign-off. By telling him she would be the one to manage this later contact she was quitting while her pride was high. When "later" came she could laugh about how utterly hysterical she had been about this really quite amusing old teacher of hers, back in the days when she was still really quite an infant; she could say that she had become really quite bored by it all after a little while and that she'd really been rather cruel to the poor old thing, dropping him that way without any explanation. . . .

"That everything?" asked Tom after Gregory had put the box into the back seat.

Gregory said it was, but at dinner he remembered that a present had been left behind. Tom had been evaluating the loot. "Of course the portfolio from the Society's the biggest thing he got. Quite a few of those kids are making a name for themselves, you know. I'd hazard a guess that ten years from now that collection may be worth several hundred dollars. . . ."

Why couldn't Gregory say, Well, in that case maybe I'd better go back to the campus and get it? I left it on top of the bookcase. What difference did it make to him? If that portfolio meant more to him right now than it could ever mean to anyone who would respect its monetary value, all right, but he didn't have to act as if going back for it were a crime, did he? "You going out?" Mary called from the study when he opened the closet door.

"Yes." Of course when she asked if you were going out she expected you to tell her where and why and for how long and, if money were involved, how much. During the Amy period of his life Gregory had been annoyed by Mary's nosiness, but by reminding himself that no woman this side of sainthood could have leashed her curiosity he had kept himself from banging doors. Tonight, though, he gave the front door a pull that would have provided a crashing finale harmonic to his mood if he had thought to keep his coat tail clear. A cadenza of ripping stitches was all he got for the effort. Let her come to the door to ask if he were having trouble. Trouble, I'll say, no trouble at all. Swinging around he yanked at the coat and with perverse satisfaction heard the tearing of cloth. No trouble. I'll just have to get that new coat you've been pestering me about. And then she would say, Why not, why not . . . now that you're going to be so rich. She'd got that line in several times already. It was plain she was restive under the restraint she had placed upon Tom and that she was willing to share the burden of the Kitner financial privacy. You might as well tell her and be done with it, he said to himself. Mary didn't care for Tom's unskilled bluntness, but unlike Tom she wasn't willing to let the subject drop.

Deciding that he would tell her the first thing in the morning he skidded into a pile of soggy leaves the girls had left at the bottom of the porch steps. And he himself was the one who had called their attention to the irresponsible clearing of the walk. "You've left a regular booby trap there at the foot of the porch steps," he had told them when they were dancing around him and asking what was in the cartons. "Don't expect me to pay you until you finish the job."

"What's a booby trap?" asked Polly.

"A trap for boobies," said Nan. "Uncle Kit's a booby. Uncle Kit's a . . ."

Booby indeed, waving his arms in a futile attempt to grab the railing. Pride, Mr. Editor-in-chief, goeth before . . . but by some miraculous footwork he was able to keep from falling.

Did the bay-window draperies twitch? Had Mary hidden behind them to spy on him? Damn fool, why didn't you wait until they'd gone out? Of course she's spying on you. . . . Ever since it had happened she had been watching him, watching him, the way she watched the girls during the polio season. No matter what the subject was, Mary's eyes hadn't stopped searching his face for symptoms. Now she would be going back to the study to tell Tom that in spite of the new job poor old Kit was still taking the whole thing rather badly.

You bet poor old Kit, with his equilibrium upset by more than a pile of wet leaves, was still taking the whole thing rather badly. I'll never get over taking it badly. Even Paul doesn't understand. Sure, Paul thinks that anyone who would submit so quickly must, in his heart, be glad for an excuse to leave teaching.

The moisture that swept against his face gave him a clue to what Mary was yelling at him when he was trying to slam the door. She was telling him to wear his rubbers, to take an umbrella. How tired I am of her treating me as if I were her child. By golly, if I can't find an apartment, I'll buy me a house. He would buy a little house where he could live alone, without rubbers and umbrellas and an electric contraption called Woodsipyne, the fog machine Mary set going in the bedroom of a disobedient person who threatened the lives of the entire family by risking pneumonia.

Not far ahead of him a woman was carrying an umbrella, but he wouldn't have called this trifle of moisture rain. When the woman neared a street lamp he saw that the umbrella was Paul's, but the woman wasn't Ruby. Ruby's legs weren't bad, but Harriet's were better. Mary, starving herself into the seductiveness of a washboard, didn't know perfection when she saw it. He checked an impulse to quicken his step.

The last time he had seen Harriet she had advised him to exercise emotional control, hadn't she? Then let her walk alone. But where the dickens was she going? She shouldn't be out alone on a night like this. The papers were full of horrible stories about attacks upon lone women. Someone ought to give Harriet Hough a good talking-to. I'd do it myself if she hadn't made that crack about emotional control. . . . She's one of these sentimental women. She'd probably not believe that I'm going back to the campus to get that portfolio—she'd probably think it's some sort of sentimental journey. *One more time* . . .

When they weren't listening to the radio Polly and Nan were playing the old phonograph records Mary had got for them at a church rummage sale. The Dawson collection of records for children was far too valuable to entrust to young demons who had hit each other over the head with *Peter and the Wolf*. Featured on tonight's pre-dinner concert was a singer who kept begging for one more time. Going back and forth between the car and the house Gregory had missed the rest of the words of the maudlin prayer. *One more time, oh, one more time* . . . to enter Burnaby Hall, to climb up to the little office that was Anderson's and then mine and tomorrow Grantham's . . . He knew he would have gone back tonight even if the portfolio hadn't provided an excuse, and he was afraid that Harriet would have understood.

A hundred and ten dollars was a lot of money for a woman's suit. No wonder she had borrowed Paul's umbrella. You wanted out-size shelter for a costume as fine as all that. . . . When the umbrella came into the cones of light the vibrating colors took on a luminous quality. It was a marvelous umbrella. Ruby found it in an art-supply store years ago. It was in a display to demonstrate an indestructible paint. "They had water dribbling down on one side of it and a sun lamp turned on the other side," she had told Gregory. "It was so very beautiful that it made me sick. A work of art being commercialized that way." And so Ruby had bought the umbrella and had given it to her husband for his next birthday. By the time Gregory came to Tower City the umbrella was an established oddity, like Professor Garnet's habit of wearing trouser guards even though he never rode a bicycle. The explanation for these so-called eccentricities was simple. Garnet couldn't endure having cold wind blow up his pant-legs; Peebles carried what looked like a beach umbrella simply because he was in no position to scorn a gift which his wife had admired to the extent of twenty-five dollars.

Now the weird canopy that had proved its value by outlasting dozens of ordinary umbrellas was passing through the Clayton Place gate. Yes, Harriet would use that gate. She wouldn't have sense enough to go around to the main gate where the path was flanked by Quonsets. For the sake of saving little more than two blocks she was risking her life on an unfrequented walk.

Tonight this more heavily wooded section of the campus was a dismal forest and the lamps strung along the path shed vague circles whose rims dripped danger. Gregory had to hurry a little now so that he wouldn't lose sight of Harriet when she went around the next bend. When she started up the steps of Annex he darted into the shadow cast by a fountain which required the passer-by to remember the class of '07, if only for its cemetery taste in drinking fountains. He skulked by the granite crag until a light in her office assured him she was safe. After he got the portfolio he might drop by this way. I happened to notice your light, he would say. . . . But she had on her fine new suit. Would she wear it on this bad night if she didn't have a date? Obviously she was going to meet Teetor somewhere.

If I had a date with her I certainly wouldn't let her go scrambling about in the dark and the wet. I certainly would insist on calling for her at her home. One look at Teetor's silly face showed you that what little intelligence the man had was devoted entirely to himself. He was the kind who would think nothing of having a girl meet him on some corner. And probably keep her waiting. She's come to the campus to get some papers and then she's going to have to stand on some dark corner and wait for that character. Well, if that's what she likes . . .

Lights on the first floor of Burnaby suggested that the janitor was present. Gregory was, then, deprived of using one of his keys for a conscious last time. When had he last unlocked Burnaby's front door? He was forever having to interrupt a night's work at home with a hasty trip to the campus. On the score of absent-mindedness he rated a full professorship. . . . Suppose, on the night I last unlocked this door, a witch had

268

appeared to inform me that it was the last time. . . . **He** wouldn't have been overly surprised. Even though he had rationalized the Town Club incident to the satisfaction of his conscious mind, his subconscious hadn't forgotten that the ice was thin. But his subconscious was as far off the beam as his conscious, at least in one respect. Had that witch predicted that his leaving Tamarack would be tied in with a student, his conscious and his subconscious would have joined in derision. He had never dreamed that the administration could be so ill disposed or even so impractical as to accuse him of any form of dereliction of duty. Gregory Kitner wasn't in Meade's class. Oh no, he was too big for that. He had basked in his pride, in the way he got along with his students, in the friendships he had made and kept over the years of his teaching career. He would have admitted quite readily that there had been blots on the record of his private life, not serious blots, but a slight smearing here and there; but his professional record, the one so much closer to his heart, had been kept spotless. That this could have happened to me . . . *me*!

Was it possible that instead of looking like a mild, middle-aged teacher, he resembled a Shylock whose interest in flesh had nothing to do with debts?

Near the vestibule Pete, surrounded by a battery of buckets, was flourishing a mop. The energetic slapping continued several moments after the door banged shut and then the janitor gave a burlesque start. "Chrise amighty," he said, "you give me a turn . . . Doc."

"Sorry," said Gregory. Until tonight he would have said he entertained none but the kindest of feelings toward Professor Slow Motion, the name each new batch of students invented for Pete, but now he would have enjoyed sticking the janitor's untidy head into one of the scrub buckets. Like Miss Chester, Pete was confronted by a problem. His hesitation before the "Doc" showed his doubt that a fired teacher should be given so exalted a title. Gingerly he tested the no-man's-land between affability and hostility. "I wasn't figgerin' on no one comin' in this-here bad night like it is," he said. "You gonna be around long . . . Doc?" The question was a clever compromise. By asking something that was none of his business, Pete lined himself up with Authority, but by repeating the complimentary title he revealed willingness to accept a parting tip.

"Why?"

"Huh? Oh, I wouldn't wanna go off and leave you to find your way out in the dark."

"I know the way," said Gregory as he stepped around the filthy mop. "Don't worry about me."

Carefully he fitted his feet into the hollows worn in the staircase. There was a time when he walked in the center of the staircase, a time when he tried to save the old steps; but tonight he deliberately climbed the ruts. For the moment he understood Goldwater's desire to blast the whole university to bits.

Fifteen years ago he had doubted that Burnaby would stand another year. Since then the old English building had had its window frames painted twice, a half-dozen rounds had been replaced in the railing of the staircase and several square yards of shingles had been nailed to the roof. During the war Paul Peebles had demanded a whole new roof for Burnaby and for its aging "temporary" annex. Asked if he didn't know there was a war on, Paul subsided until after the war was over. Then of course he was asked if he didn't know now was when we'd got to tighten our belts.

The university had managed to get considerable material

270

for the erection of dormitories. The school was housing its ever-increasing student body, that is, it was providing beds, but as yet nothing had been done about classroom space. Norton's idea seemed to be that once you found places for the students to sleep, everything else would work out in some way. Folding chairs could be brought in; small classes which had been meeting in unnecessarily large rooms could be combined with other small classes or, in the case of nonessential courses, could be dropped. "We recognize no such word as *can't*," said the President when he addressed the faculty at the start of the quarter. "We not only *can* take care of this increased load, we *will!*" He had paused then, as if for cheers, but the applause had been weak. "I am not unaware of our great needs. I share your burden, a burden which, God willing, I dedicate myself to take from you. . . . I'm going to tell you something." He had looked around then as if to make sure no outsiders were present. "I shouldn't tell it yet, but I can't resist. I know the news will bring courage to your hearts. The plan for the new Science Group is so well under way that we may confidently expect to break ground next spring!" That had drawn cheers from certain sections of the faculty, but with the exception of Tom Dawson, who had turned a tentative cheer into a cough, English preserved stolid silence. Paul said afterward that during the speech he'd noticed that a couple of the Classical Arts men were looking his way. "They were laughing at us, Kit. They were thinking now we're beginning to know how it feels. . . . You know what I heard? I heard Norton's thinking of dropping English out of the Commerce requirement, all English but Business Letter Writing. I don't know why he's keeping that in. A good businessman doesn't have to know how to write a letter." What else could you expect from a man who had gone all the way out for the Atomic Age? Norton couldn't turn around without reminding you he was a Man of Science Himself.

What was that sound? Here in the dark of the third floor the explanation that Pete was emptying buckets below was not to be considered. Out in the middle of the weed-filled lake a fabulous creature was practicing George Norton's fat laughter. The sound uncoiled in serpentine revolutions, as if pleasure in the defeat of the enemy traveled sensuously from the smoking nostrils to the tip of the scaly tail. A new twist might be given to the tail that was urged to lash out against those who dared test Tamarack's supremacy. *Lion-EL, give'em HELL!* lacked subtlety. Why not back brawn with psychological cunning? *Give'em the LAUGH, you old Sea-calf!*

LIONEL LEARNS TO LAUGH. . . . Retiring Prof Hears Chuckle. . . . In an exclusive interview Dr. Gregory Kitner told *Tama Topics* that on the eve of his departure from the university he heard our Miraculous Monster . . .

14 The stale-tobacco smell of the office intruded upon his fantasy. Even though he knew he couldn't get them open—he had never remembered to ask Pete for a chisel and hammer with which to undo the crack-sealing of this fall's painting spree—he went to the windows. If he had been able to crane his neck from an open window he still couldn't have seen Harriet's office; it was doubtful that he could have discerned the glow from her light even if the campus hadn't been veiled in mist.

The lake lay like a great black hole bitten into the sky as well as into the earth. Tonight in the winding fog it was easy to believe in the existence of the monster that was supposed to commute between Lake Lionel and the oceans by means of a subterranean passage. You could hear him now as he sucked his reeds.

Peering out into the inclement night Gregory found himself worrying about tomorrow's game. He hoped Pug Sanderson was warmly tucked into bed. When you bent over backwards to be fair to the athletes who, though hired were nonetheless human, you sometimes fell on your face. Pug Sanderson would have to go far to find a more enthusiastic rooter than Dr. Kitner; it was to be hoped that Grantham would be unable to corrupt the innocent who still believed he had to earn his keep scholastically as well as athletically.

But why do I harp on these problems? Perhaps tomorrow, when the keys to this life no longer jingled in his pocket, he would get it through his head that he was out of this particular rat race. Education! Pay your money, or somebody's money, at the business office and pick up your diploma at the other end of the assembly line. It's a pay-as-you-go system and the sooner you pay for it the sooner you'll get your degree. We certainly don't want to detain you—not when we're so crowded. How about a quickie? Four years' credit for the price of two and absolutely no difference in the resulting certificate.

"I'll be glad to be out of it," he said aloud. He had spoken in a tone meant to carry firm conviction, but the words were distorted by this soundbox of an office. The dark became oppressive and frightening. Outside the Lionel was muttering a remark originally made by Francis Grantham. "Why, you damn fool," said Gregory to the monstrous suggestion, "you can no more push me from this window than you can . . ."

Abruptly he turned around to grope for the light.

Save for the nearly empty bookshelves and the cleared desk, the office looked much as it had always looked. On the top shelf of the bookcase were a half-dozen volumes that went with the room. Anderson had said he didn't know anything about them. "Here when I came," he'd said. "You can chuck them in the wastebasket." But Gregory had never bothered to do more than push aside the thick book which dealt with tables of weights and measures, the 1894 compilation of significant statistics, and the four other works which had some way or other found shelf space at the top of the English building. He took the Prose and Poetry portfolio from the bookcase and put it on the desk.

Then he noticed he had neglected to clear the desk spindle. He sat down and began to pull the papers from the spike. As he took the notes off he listlessly tried to remember what they were supposed to remind him to do. The papers written in Miss Chester's admirable hand were easy enough, but his private shorthand was nearly indecipherable. Well, this slip which had nothing but the name Cole on it was simple. I wrote that after the little talk with Jefferson about the Halter College job.

Having jotted down the word which was intended to remind him at least to answer Cole's letter, he'd stuck the paper on the spindle and then forgotten Cole. Where had the letter got to? Was it among the papers he'd taken home this afternoon or had he left some unanswered mail under the pencil tray of the middle drawer?

He opened the drawer and found Cole's letter, along with some others he had meant to answer, in with the supply of stationery that belonged to the university. Under the letterhead he really had no business to be using he started a note. "Dear Dr. Cole: I am turning your letter over to Dr. Peebles in the hope that he may be able to give you some assistance. Inasmuch as I am leaving Tamarack . . ." Without thinking about how pointless it was to spoil the letter and give himself the bother of having to copy it on a fresh sheet of paper, he drew circles, circles within circles, a design that might be said to have some similarity to the one Lester Gibbs used in his "Comment." Gregory Kitner, however, was not commenting; he was wondering. Just why was it that he wasn't writing a different sort of letter to Cole?

Why had he refused to complete that sentence, the sentence in which he had bravely boasted that Norton could no more make him commit suicide than he could make him leave the profession in which he desired to remain? During the past week he had been in no condition for intelligent reasoning, but perhaps he could begin to think more clearly now. If his desire to teach were limited by certain strictures, it looked as if taking the Jennings job could be regarded as a practical move; if it were true that he wasn't willing to accept any but a top job in education, signing the Jennings contract was more than just a quick way to put an end to Goldwater's plot. Evidently I'm so high and mighty that I couldn't consider a position that's open to an inexperienced man who hasn't even got a doctorate. Like Jefferson I apparently scorn a small school that has next to no endowment and no football reputation. For the past four or five years I've complained steadily about the obstacles placed in the way of education by the Tamarack tendency to force one teacher to carry a student load formerly considered too heavy for two, three, and sometimes four teachers. Like Paul, I seem to have assumed that Kitner was available only for the Big Time. Unlike Paul, I was neither patient enough nor optimistic enough to wait and so . . . presto, I'm in another line of work.

Of course it was too late now, but you could speculate on what might have happened. Suppose you'd thought of the opening at Halter? Suppose you'd stopped to think about the many openings, the undesirable type of openings that Paul hadn't taken into consideration. . . . Would Cole, or a man in a position similar to Cole's, be reluctant to hire someone who had been bounced out of a large university on a morals charge? In these times of shortage, how choosey could the president of a small college be? It was possible that Paul's recommendation would have been accepted with alacrity.

But aren't you forgetting something? Something that no talk about moral turpitude or the absence of moral turpitude can hide. Norton believes that the doors of education should be closed to men like me. If Norton means what he says about being willing to keep Stein on, he's not so adamant on the subject as some administrators are. Remember what Baker told you years ago? You didn't like it and so you almost forgot it, didn't you? That girl, Rose Somebody, who complained to you that Baker advised her against majoring in Education . . . Bright girl. I thought she'd be a good teacher and so I went to Baker. "Kit," he said to me, "I advise all of them to keep out of educa tion simply because I can't place them. Don't you know that one of my department's selling points is the placement service? Well, sir, it used to be that I could get jobs for them in the South, but the South's catching up with the North now. . . . If the student isn't religious and has a noncommittal face and name, all right. Maybe this girl you're interested in could get somewhere if she changed her name, but she won't hear to that. I must say I admire her for it but my admiration won't help her. You understand that my personal feelings don't enter into it, don't you, Kit? It's just what experience has taught me. Here at a civilized school we aren't aware of such . . ."

However, like the South, we are catching up. What differ- ence does it make whether I approve of Baker and Norton? I've acted as if I've accepted their vision of the future.

Cole's letter is cordial, but what does cordiality amount to? A person can be very cordial about seeking a Jew's advice and assistance. When he wrote me this letter President Cole wasn't asking me to dinner.

Goldwater and his dramatics about a handful of silver! For the sake of peace and privacy . . . yes, and I admit to a weak- ness for wanting to get away from restricted areas, to the desire to get out of education if the Nortons are going to prevail.

The thought that he might be aiding and abetting Norton and his kind was finally allowed to rise to the surface.

He was crumpling the spoiled letter into a ball when there was a knock at the door. Pete, he supposed, come to whine around for a tip. "All right." He threw the paper into the waste- basket and took his billfold from his pocket.

"I noticed your light when I came around to the lake path," she said.

"Why, Harriet!" Wanting to tell her to stand there at the door so that he might admire the picture she made with all those glittering drops of water clinging to her hair, he told her to come in, come in. He took Paul's umbrella from her and leaned it against the wall. "What in the world were you doing on the lake path?"

"Listening for the Lionel," she said. "It's a perfect night for him."

"It's no night for you to be prowling around." He noticed that a stream was running from the point of the umbrella. "It must be pouring."

"Yes, more than when we came over."

"When *we* came over?"

"I knew you were behind me. You were coming out of the house just as I passed."

"It wasn't very sociable of you to rush on. . . . No, sit in this chair. It's more comfortable."

She took the desk chair. "I didn't rush on. I knew you'd catch up if you wanted to. The fact that you didn't made me hesitate even more . . . to barge in on you this way. But I do want to apologize for what I said . . . what I said in Goldwater's office."

"I don't know why. It was a self-evident truth."

"It wasn't any of my business. Even if it had been, there was no excuse for me to lose my temper. I don't know what got into me."

"Common sense," he said. "It was good advice even though it was a little too late. I'll try to remember it in the future."

"Don't talk that way, Kit. You make me feel like a fool."

"I don't see why."

"Then let's not talk about it. Did I interrupt something? I thought maybe if you'd finished you might want to share an umbrella. I had no idea it was going to rain. I stopped by at the Peebles' on my way over and it began while I was there. It's really coming down now."

He went to the windows to study the weather. "It really is," he said. "I suppose there's no hope of getting a cab, but I was thinking if we could . . . Would you be interested in a cup of coffee? But I suppose you have plans for the evening."

"No."

He returned to the desk. "Since you're wearing your fine new suit I naturally assumed . . ."

"This?" She brushed her fingers on the skirt. "It's sweet of you to know I have a fine new suit, Kit, but this isn't it."

"Well, it's very becoming. I'm sure you wouldn't want to get it wet."

"Paul's umbrella is large," she said. "I had a little trouble getting it up when I left Annex, but once you get the thing hoisted it's quite waterproof. Anyway I like being in the rain. I wouldn't want to take you from whatever you're doing, though."

"I just came to get that portfolio." He pointed to the tooled-leather folder. "A complete file of the Prose and Poetry magazine. The club gave it to me this afternoon and I went off and forgot it. Tom even forgot it. In that collection you'll find the first published work of James Youngren, no less."

"Ouch . . . a very good reason for forgetting."

He laughed. "A lot of people admire the boy. He's getting rich, you know."

"It's a wonderful present in spite of Youngren," she said. "A handsome cover, too. Look, could I carry it when we go down?

I told Pete I'd come to borrow a book and this thing's a regular library. I think he was on the brink of calling the Dean of Women. . . . Haven't you some paper and stickers? You don't want the cover to get spotted."

After she had made extravagant use of the university's supplies, she took the package and went into the hall. The hall was lighted now. Pete was doing what he could to preserve the good name of the English department. Gregory put on his coat and picked up his hat and the umbrella. He pulled the light string and went into the hall. Looking at the keys he had automatically taken from his pocket he said there was no reason to lock the door.

"Go ahead and lock it," she said.

"Why?"

"Oh, I don't know. To keep the ghosts out."

"Or in?"

"Maybe," she said as she started down the stairs.

When they went along Fraternity Row, they were hailed by groups of students. Gregory twirled the umbrella. Once, looking down from his office, he'd watched Paul's whirling greeting and had noticed that in the process the metal tip became a gleaming eye. That's what Lester should have put in the center of his picture; that also is what Lester would call reactionary sentimentalism. Before you go too far in your damnation of Lester Gibbs you might recall that his devotion to what you term negation was aggressive. Are you in a position to criticize a man who gives his life to what he believes a cause more important than self? The thought of Lester's sublimation of self was funny.

"What are you laughing about?" asked Harriet.

"The handle's worn smooth from Paul's flourishes," Gregory said. "It seems to dance by itself."

"What a wonderful life he's had, in spite of his poor health. I should think he'd feel as if he had lived dozens of lives."

Dozens of lives . . . through the generosity of students the teacher's life was limited only by his capacity, only by his ability to absorb experience. . . . The rain beat steadily on the umbrella. Rain on Paul's umbrella was more clamorous than it ever was on ordinary umbrellas. If you wanted to you could say this was because of that lacquer-like finish. Or you could say it was because of the resistant qualities it had borrowed from its owner. . . .

Very sentimental tonight, aren't you, Kitner? But the discovery of unsuspected resources was bound to be somewhat intoxicating. So you thought you could fix me, did you, Norton? You thought you could keep me from even trying. You overestimate yourself, Norton. As Jennings said, the weakness of your bite may be due to false teeth.

Thought of Jennings, however, wasn't welcome. I wish I didn't like the man, Gregory said to himself. I don't want to think about him. Couldn't he see, couldn't everyone see that I haven't been in my right mind?

"Kit, why did you go into teaching?"

"What did you say, Harriet?" Why had he gone into teaching? He had heard no mystical call.

"I asked why you . . ."

"Well, it's pretty far back, you know. I suppose I'd fallen in love with the past. I suppose I thought the closest I could come to living in the past would be in teaching."

"Did you find that it worked out that way?"

"Of course not. I soon learned that knowledge of the past is

281

of no value unless it's used to illustrate the present and to illuminate the future. I learned that a teacher has to act as a selector of the strongest rays and a reflector of the brightest." The umbrella bobbed at a passing student. "That's a bit pompous. I can't claim I ever mapped out such an ambitious program."

"I remember what one of my students said. It was when I first came here. She told me she never could have got through zoology if it hadn't been for what she learned from you in Survey. I thought she was batty. I'd just come from a high school where we'd never left names and dates and paraphrasing long enough to wonder if the required reading might be connected with life. I guess I've got over that kind of kowtowing to the past, but you know, Kit, when you stop placing emphasis on memory work and that sort of thing, the giants of the past seem to shrink. I can't help wondering if we've dropped too many of the old ways."

"You don't need to worry about that as long as they keep you on at Tamarack. . . . Maybe your old heroes are shrinking because you've been dreaming of coming giants. We were making fun of Youngren, but I'll never forget how I felt when I read that kid's first paper for Comp. Any teacher worth his salt discovers a new genius each week, I suppose. There's no optimist like a teacher. Cassandra tears can no more dampen his ardor than raindrops can penetrate this umbrella."

"Then why are you giving it up?"

Giving it up? Had Harriet fallen for the rumor that Kitner was leaving teaching? What a bore to have to keep on with a myth that hadn't been very interesting even at the start. "I thought the reason was fairly clear," he said.

"But it isn't as if you couldn't have got another teaching job."

"Isn't it?"

"Of course not. Twirl the umbrella. That boy's yelling at you."

"Is the entire student body out looking for Paul?"

"Or maybe this Jennings job is just a sort of stop-gap?"

Intelligent girl. That's exactly what it was, a stop-gap no longer necessary. "Well, hardly. It would take at least a year for an inexperienced man to be much more than an overpaid office boy." Jennings isn't going to be very surprised. In fact if he's as smart as I think he is, he's going to be relieved. He'll enjoy his vacation a lot more when he knows that Chicago man is sitting in Harrison's office. Or, if he's still feeling adventurous, he might give Miss Larson the promotion. I'm doing you a favor, Jennings. You didn't like having Harrison die on the premises, did you? Well, how would you like to have a zombie around for an indefinite period? "But where are we going, Harriet? This isn't the best kind of weather for a stroll."

"The Kup's in the next block."

"Fine. Like the more conventional murderer, I am drawn to the scene of the crime."

"Don't talk that way. It isn't funny. And another thing, Kit, you shouldn't have given Pete five dollars. I saw you switch bills after he made that crack. It was pure blackmail."

Of course it was blackmail. Leering at Harriet, the janitor had said they didn't need to hurry, that he wasn't one for shooting off his mouth. "That five dollars was a very small token of my gratitude to Fate. I'm glad I'm not Pete."

"You let people walk all over you," she said. "You've let the Dawsons take advantage of you for years. You let the Jennings Company tie your books up for God knows how long and then you let them buy your name."

283

"The Dawsons have never taken advantage of me. It's the other way around. I've taken advantage of their hospitality for . . ."

"I wasn't finished. You . . ."

"And whoever's been talking to you about my contracts with the Jennings Company is mistaken if he thinks I've never had any say-so." Have I, he wondered. I've always been so pleased to get the books published that any financial return has seemed superfluous. "Well, if they've done me out of anything on my textbooks they certainly made up for it when they offered me that job. Eight thousand five hundred dollars, Harriet." Now that he knew he wasn't going to receive it he had no desire to keep that munificent salary a secret. Years from now he would be bragging about it. Why, once in my life I was offered nearly nine thousand a year as a starting salary for a job I knew absolutely nothing about. This would provide you with more satisfaction than you'd got out of the fortune you lost in Florida real estate. For several hours the small sum Al Sefurth had persuaded you to invest with him had swelled into thousands. You'd enlarged the figure in the repeated tellings until you could no longer remember just how wealthy you had been during those few hours. Too bad Al's first telegram wasn't delivered until after the second one had come through; but even after you'd learned that the original investment had vanished, the delayed telegram had supplied a sort of meditative satisfaction, to say nothing of the conversational pleasure. People got so they didn't bring up the subject of the beatings they'd taken during the depression. They learned that the slightest peep out of them would start me on my experience in Florida real estate. . . .

Harriet was saying she'd had no idea it was that much money.

You could tell she was tremendously impressed. He stifled a desire to tell her about the time he and his pony cleared Deadman's Gully. "Well, it's a big job, you know. And I understand that's considered a starting salary."

"That's wonderful," she said. Why did she sound as if she didn't think it was wonderful? "But, Kit, if you'd been interested in making a lot of money you surely wouldn't have gone into teaching in the first place."

Tenacious, wasn't she? "As I grow older it may be that I become more practical," he said. "One should think about one's old age."

"You have plenty of time for that. It seems to me you would have left Tamarack ages ago if you'd been very practical. When you saw you weren't going to get tenure . . ." She pressed his arm and told him to twirl the umbrella for the two girls who were passing. "I can't help wishing we'd thought of some way to get rid of Goldwater. If he hadn't taken over in such a dictatorial way . . ."

"Let's drop it, Harriet."

"Grace Lane's always told me you won't talk seriously to a woman unless she's a student."

"How perceptive of Grace." The sarcasm he'd intended didn't quite come off. It was disconcerting to have a freak like Grace Lane point to a characteristic you had made a conscientious effort to overcome. "I'd say that's damned unfair, considering all the dull conversations I've sat through with her. . . . Look at the gore falling from the neon. I'd have liked that when I was a kid. I used to sit in the window and pretend the raindrops were warriors slaughtering each other and then draining off in the gutters. You're too young to remember those open ditches. Charlie, the boy next door, and I used to wade in

285

them after the rain. Sometimes we'd find great schools of tadpoles. We pretended they were dragons and killed them as fast
as we could."

"If you'd only see that Norton and Goldwater are no more
dragons than your tadpoles ever were. . . ."

"Look, Harriet, let's pretend it's two weeks ago. Now in the
normal academic world Friday nights are . . ."

"Grace was right."

"And in my dream of a pleasant Friday night there's no Professor Lane. On Friday nights we drop the cares of . . ."

"I've got an eight-o'clock tomorrow morning," she said.
"Don't you know that a beginner, especially a woman instructor,
has six eight-o'clocks a week? For me Friday night is just any
other night."

15

When they entered the smoke-swirling beery atmosphere of the restaurant he was paying homage to the strength of character that had made him resist the impulse to confide in Harriet. What had led him to believe she had any special interest in him? If all that bothered her was the fact that she had to meet an eight-o'clock in the morning . . . She probably wouldn't have come around to Burnaby if Frank Teetor had been at the annex. Maybe Frank had stood her up. That would explain why she's so irritable, not that I care to have it explained. I'll give her a cup of coffee and then take her home right away so she can be bright and shining for that eight-o'clock. "I told you so," he said. "The crazy kids. . . ."

Instead of staying home tonight as a sensible precaution against the exposure they would be subjected to at the game tomorrow, the students were thronging the Kup. His friend Shirley Vernon studied the scene and then said she was afraid they would have to wait a few minutes. "We'll take a table," he said.

"No, there's no hurry," said Harriet. Apparently her chief purpose tonight was to disagree with him. She didn't wait for an opinion from him but went to join the boy and girl who slid over to make room on the substitutes' bench.

A couple of high-school kids, he deduced from their manner of dress and from the way they nudged each other and stared at the umbrella. "Are you superstitious?" he asked.

The two were dressed alike, in blue jeans and plaid work shirts. The one distinguishable, by length of hair and presence of lipstick, as female, looked nervously at Harriet. "He means he'll open it if you aren't superstitious about raising umbrellas indoors," Harriet explained.

The girl giggled. "But isn't it the one who raises it?"

"At least he's protected from the resulting deluge," said Gregory as he moved back to demonstrate. "And when you revolve it the pattern goes into bands. Oh, I beg your pardon, Harriet. More water than I thought."

"Say, that's something, all right," said the boy. "Where'd you get it?"

"It's the property of Dr. Paul Peebles, author of the most comprehensive study ever made of the world's known literature. He is generally conceded the leading authority on American poetry and is also sometimes known as head of the English department of Tamarack University."

"Gosh," said the boy.

"You ought to know these things," said Gregory. "Especially if you've any idea of going to Tama." How young the boy and girl seemed. It was unlikely that Paul and his umbrella would still be around when these youngsters were ready for college.

"How do you think the chances are for tomorrow?" asked the boy. "I mean the Tama game."

Gregory closed the umbrella. This was a sober question not to be turned aside by mysterious allusions to the honkings of a mythical beast. "I think it's going to be very tough," he said. "This team's never played a major game on a muddy field."

"Kit," said Harriet, "I think Professor Johnson is waggling at you."

"Me?" Gregory looked toward the rear of the restaurant. "It's Johnson, all right, but he wouldn't be waggling at me."

"Well, he doesn't even speak to me," said Harriet.

"Is that man a friend of yours?" Gregory asked the high-school couple. "A father or an uncle?"

"Doc, I think Professor Johnson wants you and Miss Hough to come to his booth," said Shirley Vernon.

"But that's quite unfair," said Gregory. "This couple was ahead of us."

"Go right ahead," said the boy. "I mean, we don't even know the guy's name."

"Well, wave at him or do something," said Harriet as she went past the hostess who, apparently feeling that someone should acknowledge Johnson, raised her pencil.

"Let me give you a tip," Gregory said to the boy and girl. "Take a table. Otherwise there's no way for you to get a booth. This young woman here reserves them for her old admirers."

"Doc, you . . ."

"Don't interrupt, Shirley. You know as well as I do that there's not a grain of honor in the Kup system. Now, you two, get a table but don't order. Keep a sharp look-out and pretty soon you'll see someone reaching for his hat. Then you'll have an edge on the favorites Mrs. Vernon is sending in."

"I dig you," said the boy, and he and his girl hurried away.

"Doc, you know we don't cater to the high-school crowd," said Shirley. "Always lying about their age and trying to get beer. Did I ask Johnson to see you?"

"Nevertheless you handled it badly. . . . How's the baby?"

"He'll be ready for your classes before you know it." The young woman winced then. "I'm sorry, Doc. I keep forgetting. Tama won't be the same without you on the faculty."

"Thanks, Shirley, that's good of . . ."

"But I'm sure glad you're going to keep on being around."

"Then see to it you don't give anyone else my priority," he said. It was impossible for him to open his mouth without adding to the falsehood. Before I leave for Kansas or wherever I'll be leaving for, I must get a present for Shirley's baby, to make up for this lie. Not that it was a complete lie. You'd be coming back to Tower City now and then to visit, wouldn't you? Just as Norton couldn't prevent you from leaving your library to the university, he couldn't prevent you from continuing Tower City friendships. Already Gregory saw how delightful it was going to be to visit the Dawsons and the Peebles and the Lettings. He might come through Tower City several times a year, on his way to Seyno. If I go to Halter, it won't be out of the way. . . . And Tom and Mary and Nettie and the girls can come to Seyno just as often as they've come in the past. The thought of leaving the Dawsons made him realize that he was much fonder of them than he'd let himself think. And he had to keep track of Polly and Nan, if only to prove his contention that they would have dimples like Nettie's when they sloughed off their skin-bursting fat.

Where had that Hough woman got to? She had vanished and so he assumed that Johnson had broken his rule about not speaking to her. . . . Fortunately there was no involvement with Harriet that would complicate leaving Tower City. But what an absurd thought! Such a thought had to be based on the assumption that there had ever been a possibility of such involvement. A fallacious assumption. . . . Of course if Harriet would like to go to the theater with me when I happen to be in town, provided she isn't Mrs. Handsome Brute Teetor by then . . . I refuse to subject myself to even a moment of Frank Teetor's company . . . He waved in answer to a call from the large booth, the one tradition gallantly reserved for the use of men only. Robbins, Young . . . he didn't know the other two.

"Plenty of room here, Doc," said Robbins.

"Thanks, but I'm with people somewhere at the back. How's the family, Robbins?"

"We've gained back our birth weight," said Robbins. "You know Dave Young, don't you? This is Art Conroy and that's Jack Wister."

"Hi," said Conroy. Wister belched.

"Wister's a Phi Gam," said Young.

"Naturally," said Gregory.

"Say," said Conroy, "Dave was just telling me you're a brother. I never knew that before."

"He tries to keep it dark," said Young, "on account he wrote *Mother of Men*."

"I'll be damned," said Conroy. "You mean somebody wrote that?"

"Don't mind Conroy, Doc. He's still a little deaf from the recent unpleasantness. But we were talking, Doc. When we saw you come in we got to talking. Any time you want a little rough work done . . . Graduate commandos, you know."

"Thanks. It's an idea."

"If it isn't a private party," said Wister to his beer. "I've got a tropical disease that may be communicable. The medical profession hasn't quite decided if it's safe for me to be at large. So I was thinking . . ."

"That's where we Phi Gams have it over on you Sigs," said Robbins. "We think. We're subtle-like. None of the old-fashioned bang-bang. We're the bacteria boys. Now if Wister started making with the social advances toward certain parties . . ."

A tug at his coat prevented Gregory from hearing the outcome of the argument about whether the situation required Wister to kiss Mrs. Norton. The formerly aloof Professor Johnson, recording secretary of the Faculty Association and generally conceded to be the best-dressed faculty member of Tamarack University, was asking Gregory Kitner of the torn coat to hurry. "We can't stay much longer, Kit. Sitter trouble."

"I'd like to explore the subject more fully at another time," Gregory said to the boys.

"Maybe it wasn't such a bad song," said Conroy, "back in the olden days, that is."

Wister belched. If the boys had recognized Johnson they were not admitting it, unless that belch . . .

"I knew it would be hard for you to break away from those bums," said Johnson as he and Gregory went toward the back of the room. "We certainly aren't getting a very desirable type of student these days. I don't say it's the army experience. I believe in universal military training, all right, but I do say the government's giving college education to a lot of people who are absolutely unsuited . . ." He poked Gregory. "You see what I mean."

The booth they were passing was being vacated by two young men and two young women. One of the women was in an advanced stage of pregnancy. Gregory turned to signal to the high-school couple now crouching at a table near the front.

"Working for the management?" asked Johnson with a touch of the asperity Gregory had been accustomed to receive from him. Then, flaring his nostrils for the benefit of the pregnant woman, the faculty's fashion plate went on to his own booth to announce that the rescue had been achieved.

"We thought you'd never come," said Mrs. Johnson. "How are you, Kit?"

Though she may have bowed in his direction once or twice, this was the first time Mrs. Johnson had ever addressed a remark to Gregory. Were the Johnsons drunk? He said he was fine and as Johnson had taken the place next to Harriet, obeyed Mrs. Johnson's patting hand.

Tom, who had good reason to recognize the symptoms, had always said Bertram Johnson was an opportunist. Mary didn't like Johnson either. She said it was amusing the way the Johnsons had tried to establish a salon, that it was almost pathetic to see how hard they tried to grab off the celebrities. . . . If the Johnsons were opportunists and celebrity grabbers, why were they making a play for Harriet Hough and Gregory Kitner? Harriet had no influence, but it was even more ridiculous to think that this cordiality was inspired by a notion that Gregory Kitner was worth cultivating. He glanced at Harriet, but there was no explanation on her face. She was studying the song titles on the juke-box control.

"I never thought of taking it up professionally," he said when he felt obliged to contribute something to the conversation, "but I've had considerable experience as a sitter."

"Did you see that girl who just left the next booth? My God, when we were in school you didn't see pregnant women all over the place. *We* had to wait. We never expected to have our cake and eat it too." He cleared his throat noisily, in belated deference to Harriet, no doubt. "Now you take those thugs who were talking to you, Kit . . ."

"One of them has a wife and two children in Chicago," said Gregory. It was difficult to keep anger out of your voice, but you had to remember that Johnson wasn't worth anger. "They live with his parents. He can't afford to go see them more than once a month. He's on the waiting list for one of the tin huts. Of course he's hoping that it won't be long before someone flunks out and . . ."

"A sound hope if he's banking on any of my students," said Johnson. "In all of my teaching experience I have never encountered such a sullen, ill-mannered . . ."

"Why talk shop all the time?" said Mrs. Johnson. "Why can't we talk about something pleasant for a change? My goodness, we haven't said a word about Kit's new job. You'd think Bert and I weren't thrilled to tears about it, Kit. My goodness, when Bert told me . . ."

"I tried to catch you on campus as soon as I heard," said Johnson. "You certainly are to be congratulated. I wish I could get out of this racket and into something good like that."

"Amen," said Mrs. Johnson. "Bert's always said the Jennings Company is tops. Haven't you, Bert?"

"Kit doesn't need my say-so, Pet. He knows it. Kit . . . I wouldn't want you to think I was jumping the gun or anything like that, but I have a little manuscript . . ."

Harriet had been playing with a coin she'd taken from her bag. Now she popped the nickel into the box and pressed one of the buttons. "Beat him," she said. "Boy across the way."

Johnson gave her an annoyed glance. "Do you like that sort of thing?"

"It sends me," she said. "Do you have a nickel, Kit? I'll want to play it again."

"As I was saying," said Johnson, "I have this little manuscript . . ."

"Little!" said Mrs. Johnson, or Pet, as Gregory was beginning to think of her. "It weighs about ten pounds. Don't be so modest, Bertie."

Gregory shoved a nickel across to Harriet. "Here."

"Thanks," she said. "It's my favorite. They can't get it all on

294

the card, but it's the 'Texacana Mexicana Wrexicana Jump.' 'TMW Jump,' it says here."

"I'm not familiar with juke-box music," said Pet. "All I listen to on the radio is the symphony. Oh, and the news and Grantham, of course."

"It's exciting about Grantham coming to Tamarack, isn't it?" said Harriet. "I wonder if I can get his autograph."

"I wouldn't want this to go any farther," said Johnson, "but if what I hear about his salary has any basis of truth . . . I'm not saying he hasn't a Name. As a matter of fact I'm not saying I would have been against him at all, at a reasonable salary, but I can't help thinking it wouldn't hurt if the faculty were allowed to talk these things over before decisions are reached."

"Really, Bertie, you sound like that . . . what's his name. You know the one I mean. That Goldstein."

"Goldwater, Pet," said Johnson. "But there's no use talking about Grantham now, I suppose. . . . But I just wanted to give you a little background on that manuscript of mine, Kit. I think I have a new slant on the Romantics and I'd appreciate your opinion."

"I'm no authority on the period," said Gregory. "Why not show it to Jones?"

"Don't you think Jones' approach is dated? Anyway, what I'm after is editorial reaction. I won't pretend I haven't submitted the manuscript a couple of places, but . . ."

"The paper shortage," said Pet. "That was the only reason they wouldn't . . ."

"Kit can make his own decisions, Pet. Kit, if you'll just glance through it. . . ."

As editor at Jennings? "Well, I . . ."

"I don't expect you to pull any punches. If you don't con-

295

sider it publishable . . . okay, we're still friends. I'll bring it around to you next week."

"Well, now that that's settled," said Pet, "maybe you'll let me get a word in edgewise. I've been wanting to invite you to a little party we're having a week from tomorrow night. Both of you."

"I'm so sorry," said Harriet.

"What a shame. I tried to reach you by phone, dear. But you'll come, won't you, Kit?"

"I'm afraid that's the night Harriet and I . . ." What was going on in town? Had the ballet company arrived yet?

"The symphony, you know," said Harriet.

"But why would you go on Saturday?" said Pet. "That's pops."

"I'm way behind in music," said Gregory. "Harriet's going to guide me to musical appreciation in easy steps."

"You mean jumps, don't you?" Mrs. Johnson pushed him to emphasize her joke. "But you must drop around afterwards. Our parties go on forever."

"You do that," said Johnson. "Why, we'll just be getting going by the time the symphony's over."

"Thanks," said Gregory when the Johnsons had finally departed.

"Don't mention it."

"I was about to say the ballet."

"That doesn't start till week after next."

"We might as well take that in too—since we've committed ourselves to the symphony." But what am I saying? I'm not going to be in town.

"I'll go to the symphony with you, but you'll do any dropping in at the Johnsons' on your own. Can't you see it's going to be this way from now on?"

"What way?"

"People drooling all over you. Everyone who has some old thesis stuck away. Maybe I'll hunt mine up. Maybe my friend Kitner-the-editor will bring it out in a beautiful not-too-limited edition."

"That point was demonstrated to me earlier in the day," said Gregory. "In the form of a skit produced by my chief reader, Mr. Jefferson. As usual Jeff's way ahead of me. . . . But here's our girl. May, I'd about decided you girls had gone out on strike. Harriet, would you like a sandwich with your coffee?"

"No."

"Two Kutlet Kakes and two coffees, May." If Harriet had something substantial to eat maybe she would snap out of her bad humor. "You're a very pretty woman," he said when the waitress had gone, "but a scowl doesn't especially become you."

"Gregory," she said, "I can't bear to see you looking so miserable. You've been going around looking as if you'd lost your last friend. You've got circles under your eyes down to your heels."

"That's part of the Kitner trademark," he said. Somewhere in the vicinity of his stomach was a signal. Harriet, though in an out-of-door rather than in a hot-house way, was as beautiful as Amy, but could he fail to see that her chin had a set to it that indicated she might be even more stubborn than Amy? She was as radiant as Sunny Tate, but couldn't he see that the radiance was a screen for intelligence? She was as seductive-looking as Mary Dawson had been fifteen years ago, but was he blind to the firmness of intention that lay in back of that seductive veneer? She'd called him Gregory, the name never used in his Tower City life, the name that inevitably reminded him of family ties. Harriet Hough was a deadly combination of all he had admired in women, and of all he had deplored or perhaps feared. "Our family trademark," he said in a desperate effort to respond to the warning. "In my cousin they call it acting."

But it was no use. This had come upon him slowly. He'd had ample time. Mary had warned him. Tom had warned him. Even Amy. . . . But he'd let it come.

He stared at the initial-scarred table for inspiration. Paper doilies, knives, forks, spoons, water . . . Salt and pepper. No sugar—they were still doling that out only upon request. "Would you care for another nickel?" he asked.

16 Whenever Polly or Nan suspected that unprogressive parents were considering the merits of old-fashioned punishment she would plead for another chance. "But won't you even give me another chance?" was the howl. Well, Gregory had begged Fate for another chance and she had brought it on a tray. The critical situation introduced by Harriet's calling him Gregory was diverted by a tense discussion of whether she was required to eat a sandwich she definitely had not ordered.

And then Gregory's almost too co-operative guardian took the form of table-hopping students. For an hour Harriet and he gave a sort of reception in the booth inherited from the Johnsons. Of course he was happy to see that Paul had been right when he said Dr. Hough was well liked by the student body—not all of the hoppers were Kitner students, though Harriet, during momentary respites pretended to believe him the sole attraction. "I suppose they'll be kissing you next," she had said after two very well-behaved girls stopped by merely to say hello.

Now, back in the rain, back in the dark, they were alone. He looked down the deserted street and saw no one who might be wanting to seek shelter under the umbrella, no one who might be wanting him to spin it . . . but fortunately her apartment wasn't far from the Kup. He wouldn't go in, of course. If she asked him to come in he would remind her of that eight-o'clock she seemed to have forgotten. I'm not a man who is about to make eight thousand five hundred a year. Tomorrow morning, as soon as I've called Jennings, I'll be a man without a job. I prefer to think of it as a teacher tem-

299

porarily without a school connection, but it's about the same in money. . . .

Tomorrow he and Paul would telephone Cole. If Cole weren't interested, well, they would telephone someone else. Wire someone else. Write someone else. If we get together on a practical, unambitious plan we'll turn up something. I'm sure of that. Also I'm sure that it will be years before I'll be making anywhere near eight thousand. If ever. Now just where in this picture do you see a lady who has a penchant for hundred dollar suits?

"I like teaching," she was saying, "but I can't claim to be one who was born to it."

This was fine. She lacked technique. A man of his age was safe around a woman who didn't know that an expert male trapper never discusses herself. "Why did you go into it?"

"Why do lots of people? I couldn't type. I couldn't run any kind of machine. I had to clerk in a store or be somebody's maid or teach school. My parents didn't have college educations and so they thought a diploma was more important than anything else. They thought we'd all get rich if we just graduated from college. So after I graduated I got a job in the local high school. The pay wasn't very good and so the folks thought I should aim for college teaching. I worked on my Ph.D. at nights and summers. It took an awfully long time. I didn't get it until just before we moved to Tower City. The war gave me my chance, you see. Tamarack offered fifty a month more than I was getting at home. So it's been quite different for me, I mean that I went into teaching because it seemed the best way to support my folks. I could go into something else without it killing me."

He should have been prepared for the shift in tactics. She

300

was one of those women who would never let go. "Harriet, I thought we agreed not to discuss it any more."

"All right. Let's talk about something else. Why didn't you get married? I've often wondered."

Because I had the good fortune never to meet up with anyone quite like Harriet Hough. "Would you be interested in the story of my life?"

"A brief résumé will do."

"In the eighth grade . . ."

"Don't bother to go back that far."

"A psychoanalyst would go back farther than that, but if you've no interest in the formative years . . . We find our young hero in college. . . . Sure you don't want to hear about my high-school loves? They were very nice."

"Go on with this college romance."

"There was a college romance, though I hadn't said so, had I?"

"No, you just shied away from it as if you wished you hadn't mentioned college. Was it that bad?"

"Bad? On the contrary. It was charming . . . while it lasted."

"Was she pretty?"

"No, she was beautiful."

That held her for a moment, but only for a moment. "What was her name?"

"Sunny Tate."

"Sunny?"

"Christened Hazel, if you must know everything."

"A name I've never cared for. Go on."

"That's all there is to it. We were engaged. We became disengaged. She married a fraternity brother of mine. She was fond of the pin. A cute little thing, a clover leaf. Are you familiar with it?"

"Oh, I've worn it now and again, though I've never considered it the most attractive of the lot. Why'd she marry this brother?"

"I think because he was a good dancer. I've always been told I lack rhythm and as far as I know he hadn't much else to commend him. I don't recall that she ever mentioned any other asset. He was the one who used to take her around when I couldn't."

"What do you mean, when you couldn't?"

"I was carrying extra courses. I couldn't go to parties all the time. I was trying to hurry things up so we could get married. So I used to get this gigolo to take her around. . . . I paid for all the tickets. I even hired a dress suit for him. Damned if I see how he ever became such a professional dancer. He didn't have enough get-up to find a girl for himself."

"He did all right."

"Yes, he did very well."

"And so your heart was broken and it stayed that way."

"My heart was broken, but the worst part of it was that it didn't stay that way. It was years before I'd admit I'd got over it. Queer way to bolster up ego, but evidently I felt required never to recover."

"You wanted to prove you weren't like her."

"Maybe. But what about you, Dr. Hough? It's not fair to expect me to tell you all about my past if you won't . . ."

"I've always considered it rude to ask an old maid why she never married. Mary Dawson asked me that almost the instant we met. I was twenty-nine. Until she sprang that on me I hadn't realized I was on the shelf. But you can't make me believe you mooned over this Hazel until you met Mrs. Prentiss."

He'd been hoping that by some miracle she would see it wasn't cricket to mention Mrs. Prentiss, but it was futile to expect fair play from Harriet. "I went around some, but there was never anything serious."

"Until you met Mrs. Prentiss. When I came to town they told me it was in its seventh year. That must have been serious. Lane says you and Mrs. Prentiss didn't get married because . . ."

"I don't want to hear Lane's theories. The truth is, as it usually is, very unromantic. Amy refused to leave that mausoleum she calls home and I refused to live there. I catch cold easily."

"You're probably catching your death now. Are your feet wet? Mine are." She sounded very gay. "You can take your shoes off and dry them while I'm fixing your coat."

"My coat?"

"It's torn," she said. "I noticed it when you were paying the bill."

It was a disturbingly domestic scene. Harriet was sitting over there by the lamp and working away at his coat—his protest had been of no avail. He sat with his feet on a hassock and watched the steam curl from the soaked soles of his shoes. She had not got him to take them off. He found some comfort in this minor victory.

As she had predicted, the fireplace wasn't creating such an offensive odor now. "I don't know if you just get used to it," she had said when she lighted the synthetic logs, "or if it **really** goes away after a while. I always open a window just in case it's poison. Would you . . ."

Complaining that he was highly sensitive to drafts, he had raised a window a half-inch. Now he was looking around for something to knock his pipe on. "Don't you women ever . . ."

"On the mantel."

He reached for the ashtray that was heavy enough and large enough. No woman bought an ashtray like this for herself. Had Harriet got it for Teetor?

"What are you going to do with all that money, Gregory?"

"I've been told I need a new coat."

"There's nothing the matter with this coat. When I finish it, it will be as good as . . ."

"The suit you have on looks as good as new to me, and yet I understand you have a new one that cost a hundred and ten dollars."

She put her needle down. "No kidding? Did Mary tell you that? Wonderful. I never dreamed Mary Dawson wouldn't notice that the skirt and jacket don't quite match. Sun faded from the show window. I thought it was a good buy at forty, though." She studied the coat and then took a small pair of scissors from her work basket. "I don't like Mary."

"You just don't understand her."

"It's not her fault if I don't." She snipped at her thread. "She's made it pretty clear I'm not to operate in her territory . . . and she's no piker when it comes to making territorial claims."

"That reminds me. Weren't you going to tell me something about your past? Or don't you have a past?"

"Of course I've got a past. I was really engaged once—not just a fraternity-pin engagement, but we fell out over the housing problem. Like you and Mrs. Prentiss. He was willing for me to keep on working, but he wouldn't live with my parents and there simply wasn't enough money for two establishments. So."

"As simple as that?"

"I wept for weeks. Then he married someone else. I was so furious that I stopped weeping."

"I trust he married an orphan."

"He did better than that. His boss's daughter. Now he's the boss. I saw him last Sunday in church. He's getting bald, but he's still quite good-looking. My sister says she's heard they're having trouble, but of course she may just have said that to make me feel good."

"Did it?"

"Why, of course."

"You mean you think maybe there's a chance you'll get him back?"

"Don't be silly! It was years ago."

"And he's the only one you've ever loved?"

"Heavens, no. I've been in and out of love dozens of times."

"And none of them liked your parents well enough?"

"Dummy, I didn't even get to meet half of them. A girl doesn't, you know."

"I can't understand why you women expect perpetual sympathy. When I think of all the women I've never met . . . Tallulah Bankhead, for example. . . . But even half of dozens leaves us with a sizable number."

"What with my teaching and the graduate work I didn't have a lot of time. So here I am, thirty-three and still a virgin. That's what you were wanting to know, wasn't it?"

"Harriet!"

"It *is* shocking, isn't it? I realize I must be reeking of complexes, but somehow none of my chances seemed very glamorous." With her head bowed over her sewing she looked extremely practical; it was impossible to imagine her in a situation unequal to her emotional control.

He decided this was fortunate—not that he'd thought she would consider him glamorous enough. "Aren't you ever going to finish that damned coat?" he asked.

"It's finished." She got up and put the coat over the back of a chair near the door. Then she turned to him and said, in a most matter-of-fact voice, that she had been warned against him. "Repeatedly, Gregory. Ever since I came to Tower City."

"My dear girl, I assure you . . ."

"Mostly by married women," she said, "though of course Lane . . ."

"Do me a favor. Don't mention Grace Lane for five or six minutes. . . . I presume your advisers have told you I'm old enough to be your father."

"Don't brag. I know how old you are."

"And haven't they told you Frank Teetor's the very one for you?"

She shook her head. "You don't understand women. They don't come in as matchmakers until it's pretty definite that the match is already made." She smiled. "It's a game we play. The career girls say how lucky the married ones are and the married ones tell us we don't know when we're well off."

"Then your girl friends don't think it's a match yet?"

"You mean Frank and me?" She went to the table for a cigarette. Perched on the arm of the chair where she had sat to do the mending, she didn't look quite so practical as she'd looked before. "Frank and I are awfully good friends, though."

"I've noticed."

"He tells me all about the girl he's in love with. It's quite a problem, you know, because she's a student."

Gregory threw a burnt match into the fireplace and then apologized, but Harriet said not to think anything of it, that she was always forgetting the fireplace was a fake. "Once it stops smelling so horrid it almost looks real. Look at those knots."

He had no interest in the gas logs. "I suppose you and Frank, being such chums, discuss *your* problems as well as his."

"Naturally. Frank's complimentary and all, but he does think I'll have trouble getting my problem solved legally."

"Good God!" Gregory kicked the hassock out of his way and started to rise, but then he sank back. "Stay where you are," he said. "Don't come near me. I have to talk to you. I'd hoped to wait, but . . ."

"You don't have to say anything. It's all right."

"It is *not* all right. Unless I break a leg I'll be leaving town. Probably Sunday. Monday at the latest."

"Oh." She reached for the nest of ashtrays near the lamp. "I didn't know."

"Neither did I . . . not until tonight. But I can't go through with that Jennings job. I wish there were some way to make you understand."

"Make me understand?" She sorted out the ashtrays and then studied them before choosing one. "You think I can't understand? Oh, Gregory."

"It's a wonderful job."

"I know."

"I doubt if I'll ever get a chance at anything quite so good.

Not just the money. I'm speaking of the genuine importance of the job."

"Yes, but if it doesn't happen to be your kind of importance . . ."

He nodded, even though she wasn't looking at him. "I haven't talked to Jennings yet. That's why I let that Johnson business ride. I couldn't tell Bertie Johnson when I hadn't told Jennings, could I?"

"Of course not. I didn't mean to force you to tell me. You didn't have to."

"Telling you is different," he said. "It's like telling myself. I didn't see it until now, that's all."

She came slowly to the hassock and pushed it near his chair. Then she sat down. "Do you have any plans?" she asked.

"Yes. Yes, I'm going to teach school. Somewhere. There's an opening in the English department of a little school in Kansas. I think Paul and I'll call up about it tomorrow, after I've talked to Jennings. If the Kansas place isn't interested, well, there are other little places."

"There may be some big places too."

"I'll have that in mind, and Paul will keep me posted. But I'm not going to wait around for perfection. Hell, I might like a small school. For years I've been trying to fit small-school ideas into a mammoth-university schedule. You can't do what I've been trying to do—you just can't do it when you haven't a chance to get acquainted with your students. But that's not important just now. What's important is that I'm not going to be caught in this squeeze play. Jennings is right when he says his business is a branch of education, but it's not my branch. I can't function unless I'm working with students. Back in the old days when sabbaticals weren't just an illusion I got a half-

308

year. I thought I'd do a book during that leave—no classes, no papers, but I didn't accomplish much. Seems I can't knuckle down to any outside writing unless I'm up to my neck in routine. . . . Oh, I got a perverse satisfaction out of the way some people seemed to envy me on account of the Jennings chance. Like a child, I suppose. Norton took my toy away but, look, someone gave me a better one. I tried to think it was a joke on Norton and Company."

"Well, it was."

"No, the joke was on me . . . and Jennings. Of course when Jennings hears I don't want his job even though I don't have anything else lined up . . . well, I imagine he'll be glad enough to be rid of me."

"He should be. Feeling as you do, you wouldn't have been very good." She smiled up at him. "What difference does it make what school you're with? I mean, students are pretty much the same everywhere and you couldn't get into a school that has a much lousier administration, do you think?"

"Not now I don't, but give me time. I used to think I never wanted to have anything to do with administration. I thought that up to a few minutes ago, I guess, but I'm changing my mind about a lot of things tonight. I've an idea I'm going to become very interested in administrative work. I'm feeling as subversive as all hell." He leaned over to touch her face. "I'd be set up about the prospect if it weren't for having to miss our date."

"Well," she said, "there's tomorrow night. And one thing you've got to say for the teaching profession, you usually get a fairly decent weekend. Unless you go a lot farther away than Kansas . . ."

"Harriet, an occasional weekend doesn't fit in with what I have in mind."

"But, Gregory, we've got to be sensible," she said. "Even if we thought it would be all right for me to break my contract without giving notice, it's bound to take you a while. I mean, you can't just go to a town and find a place to live right away."

He put his hands on her shoulders. The idea was to keep her at arm's length, but when he found it wasn't working out that way he hurried back to the sanctuary of his pipe and pouch and matches. "Wait a minute," he said. "You've got to *think* about something like this."

"I've been thinking about it for a long time."

"But, Harriet, have you thought that perhaps your life wouldn't be very smooth if you were married to a Jew?"

"All that bothers me about that is that you could say it, Gregory."

He shook his head. "That's too easy. That's the kind of talk I used to dish out. *I* didn't want to go where I wasn't wanted. Restrictions didn't bother *me*. There was a little card saying *Restricted Clientele* and so did I try to get into that hotel? My God, no. To get me they had to issue an invitation. No Kitner ever went where he wasn't wanted. I didn't stop to remember that I hadn't as yet been ordered off the world; I didn't connect those little signs with gas chambers. All I thought was So you don't want me, okay."

"You'll get over feeling this way."

"Do you want me to? Do you want me to forget how I felt when I met Carl Goldwater in the hall today? My God, when I looked into his eyes I thought I was looking into the eyes of the brother I never had."

"Oh, Gregory . . . not Carl."

"Well, second cousin once removed then. Anyway I felt a kinship I'd never known before."

"That's emotional hooey, Gregory Kitner, and you know it. It's something Norton would say."

"And he's said it strongly enough for me to fall for it, darling."

"All right. *Be* like Carl, but I'm damned if I'm going to be like Mrs. Goldwater." She made a movement of impatience and the space between them dissolved.

It was very late when he was again pushing the umbrella against the rain. Earlier in the evening he hadn't been impressed by the clarity with which he was seeing the way to his future but now, when he knew he should be disturbed about having brought someone else into that uncertain journey, he was singularly optimistic. He laughed aloud at the exorcised specter that had shivered over a watery chuckle.

Emotionally controlled Harriet Hough, who knew exactly how to keep from getting into jams! Poor child, she'd got herself into a permanent jam now. And I'd thought her so practical, he said to himself. Why, she hasn't any practical sense at all.

When he had said he would sell his library in order to buy a house, she had been horrified. She'd acted as if that library were his child, his dearest possession on earth. "Why do you think I've been collecting those books?" he had asked. "So I could have something named for me after I'm gone? The Kitner Collection, and a wreath around my picture? Nuts to that, sweetheart. The library's my bank account, my gilt-edged bonds. Give me time to study the market and I'll bet you I raise twenty thousand on it. And without having to sell what's inside of those books, darling. Remember that. Nobody can ever make me liquidate the ideas those books have given me."

When she had continued to protest he'd pointed to the Prose and Poetry portfolio and said he would leave it with her. "We'll use it as the nucleus for a new library," he'd said. "We can collect as a hobby or even as a part-time business enterprise, but I'm through with collecting as a mania. Those books of mine had come to be a sort of drug. . . ."

Was it illogical to be eager to start upon exile from a world that had never really existed? Goldwater was right and Norton was right—I lived in a dream world; but they were mistaken in assuming I found great satisfaction there. I'd say *they* aren't burdened with much realism. Norton thinks that by dancing his own little set of marionettes he can rule the whole educational theater; Goldwater thinks that by cutting Norton's strings he can transfer life from the manipulator to the dolls. In my dream I thought I could ignore Norton and Goldwater out of existence, just as I thought I could ignore my love for Harriet out of existence.

The rain may have lessened but the increased velocity of the wind was giving the night a character of malevolence. Paul's umbrella bucked and shied. Fearing that it would turn inside out Gregory paused to close it. He grinned after he had put it under his arm. The gesture had reminded him of a small boy who had armed himself with a magic sword before going forth to slay dragons. My dragons aren't exactly the little tadpoles Harriet would like to think, he said to himself, but we'll have a go at them.

Near the Phi Gam house he met a night-hawking student. "Your girl must live an awful long way from the Kup," observed the boy.

Gregory pushed his hat up a little and peered at the boy. "Oh, it's you, Wister. Hell of a night to be taking a tropical disease out for a walk, isn't it?"

"I'd say it's a hell of a night to be carrying an umbrella under your arm," said Wister. "If I ever carried one, which I don't, I'd at least . . ."

Gregory touched the umbrella's worn handle. "Say, this isn't just any umbrella," he said. "This is the Old Man's."

"That's different," said Wister. "Come on, Doc. Nights like this sometimes I don't sleep so good." He took hold of Gregory's free arm. "Come on and I'll walk you home."